D1484530

DEDICATION

I would like to dedicate *Close Remembrance* to my parents, whose help during and after our big move has made all the difference in the world. In general, my husband and I are tremendously grateful to our families for being so wonderfully supportive of our writing. A big shout-out also goes to my nephew, who has made me a very proud aunt.

I must again thank my husband (Dima Zales—a science fiction and fantasy author) for being a phenomenal partner and collaborator in the creation of this work. As with the rest of the series, most of the credit for plot development, scientific elements, and general editing belongs to him.

I would also like to give special thanks to my beta readers and proofreaders, Tanya, Jackie, Erika, Lina, and Kelly. You girls are the best!

And, of course, I would be absolutely nowhere without you, my dear readers. Thank you for every review, for every kind word of encouragement—and, most of all, for buying my books and making my dream of being a writer a reality.

Part I

PROLOGUE

The Krinar walked down the street in Moscow, quietly observing the teeming human masses all around him. As he passed, he could see the fear and curiosity on their faces, feel the hatred emanating from some of the passersby.

Russia was one of the countries that had resisted the most—and where the toll of the Great Panic had been the heaviest. With a largely corrupt government and a population distrustful of all authority, many Russians had taken the Krinar invasion as an excuse to loot at will and hoard whatever supplies they could. Even now, more than five years later, some of the storefronts in Moscow were still bare, their taped-over windows a testament to the tumultuous months that had followed their arrival.

Thankfully, the air in the city was better now, less polluted than the Krinar remembered it being a few years ago. Back then, a heavy smog hung over the city, irritating him to no end. Not that it could hurt him in any way, but still, the K far preferred breathing air that didn't contain too many hydrocarbon particles.

Approaching the Kremlin, the K pulled the hood of his jacket up over his head and tried to look as human as he could, paying careful attention to his movements to make them slower and less graceful. He didn't delude himself that the K satellites weren't watching him at this very moment, but no one in the Centers had any reason to suspect him. He'd made it a point in recent years to travel as much as he could, frequently appearing in major human cities for one reason or another. This way, if anyone cared to profile his behavior, his latest expeditions would not cause any alarm.

Not that anyone would bother profiling him. As far as everyone was concerned, those Krinar who'd helped the Resistance—the Keiths, as they'd been called—were safely in custody, and poor Saur had been blamed for erasing their memories. It couldn't have worked out better if the K had planned it that way himself.

No, he didn't need to conceal his identity from the Krinar eyes in the sky. His goal was to fool the human cameras stationed all around the Kremlin walls—just in case the Russian leaders became alarmed before he had a chance to visit the other major cities.

Smiling, the K pretended to be nothing more than a human tourist as he did a leisurely lap around Red Square, the soles of his shoes grinding into the pavement and releasing tiny capsules that contained the seeds of a new era in human history.

Once he was done, he headed back to the ship he'd left in one of the nearby alleys.

Tomorrow, he would see Mia again.

Saret could hardly wait.

CHAPTER ONE

"Oh my God, Korum, when did you have a chance to do this?"

Mia stared at her surroundings in shock. All the familiar furniture was gone, and Korum's house in Lenkarda—the place she had begun to think of as her home—looked very much like a Krinar dwelling now, complete with floating planks and clutter-free spaces. The only thing that remained from before were the transparent walls and ceiling—a Krinar feature that Korum had allowed from the very beginning.

Her lover grinned, showing the familiar dimple in his left cheek. "I might've snuck away for an hour or so while you were sleeping."

"You went all the way from Florida to here just to change the furnishings?"

He laughed, shaking his head. "No, my sweet, even I'm not that dedicated. I had to take care of a couple of business matters, and I decided to surprise you."

"Well, color me surprised," Mia said, slowly turning in a circle and studying the strange sight that had greeted her upon their arrival back in Lenkarda.

Instead of the ivory couch, there was now a long white board floating a couple of feet off the floor. From what Korum had explained to her once, the Krinar were able to make their furniture float by using a derivation of the same force-field technology that protected their colonies. Mia knew that if she sat down on the board, it would immediately adapt to her body, becoming as comfortable as it could possibly be. A few other floating planks were visible near the walls, with a couple of them occupied by some type of indoor plants with bright pink flowers.

The floor was also different—and unlike anything Mia had seen in any other Krinar houses. She tried to remember what those other floors had been like, but all she could recall was that they were hard and pale, like some type of stone. She hadn't paid them too much attention at the time because Krinar flooring materials didn't seem all that different from something one would find in a human house. However, what was under her feet right now had a very unusual texture and an almost sponge-like consistency. It made Mia feel like she was standing on air.

"What is that?" she asked Korum, pointing down at the strange substance.

"Take off your shoes and see," he suggested, kicking off his own sandals. "It's something new that one of my employees came up with recently—a variation on the intelligent bed technology."

Curious, Mia followed his example, letting her bare feet sink into the cushy flooring. The material seemed to flow around her feet, enveloping them, and then it was as though a thousand tiny fingers were gently rubbing her toes, heels, and arches, releasing all tension. A foot massage . . . only a thousand times better. "Oh, wow," Mia breathed, a huge blissful smile appearing on her face. "Korum, this is amazing!"

"Uh-huh." He was walking around, seemingly enjoying the sensations himself. "I figured this would appeal to you."

Her feet in paradise, Mia watched as he made a slow circle around the room, his tall, muscular body moving with the cat-like grace common to his species. Sometimes she could hardly believe that this gorgeous, complicated man was hers—that he loved her as much as she loved him.

Her happiness was so absolute these days it was almost scary.

"Do you want to see the rest of the house?" He stopped next to her and gave her a warm smile.

"Yes, please!" Mia grinned, as eager as a kid in a candy store.

Three days ago, during one of their evening walks in Florida, she'd mentioned to Korum that it would be nice to see his house as it was before he 'humanized' it for her sake. As thoughtful as the gesture had been at the time, Mia was now used to the Krinar lifestyle and no longer needed the reassurance of familiar surroundings. Instead, she wanted to see how her alien lover had lived before they met. He'd smiled and promised to change the house back promptly—and he'd obviously taken that promise seriously.

"Okay," he said, staring down at her with a slightly mischievous look on his beautiful face. "There's one room that you haven't seen at all yet, and I've been dying to show you . . ."

"Oh?" Mia raised her eyebrows, her heart starting to beat faster and her lower belly tightening in anticipation. His eyes now had a golden undertone, and she guessed that whatever it was he wanted to show her would soon have her screaming in ecstasy in his arms. If there was one thing she could always count on, it was his insatiable desire for her. No matter how often they had sex, it seemed like he always wanted more . . . and so did she.

"Come," he said, taking her hand and leading her toward the wall to their left.

As they approached, the wall did not dissolve as it usually did. Instead, Mia felt herself sinking deeper into the spongy material beneath her feet. Her feet were absorbed first, then her ankles and knees. It was like quicksand, except it was happening right in the house. Giving Korum a startled look, she clutched at his hand. "What—?"

"It's okay." He gave her palm a reassuring squeeze. "Don't worry." The same thing was happening to him too; she could see the floor practically sucking him in.

"Um, Korum, I don't know about this . . ." Mia was now buried up to her waist, and her lower body was feeling decidedly strange—almost weightless.

"Just a few more seconds," he promised, giving her a grin.

"A few more seconds?" Mia was now chest-deep inside the weird material. "Before what?"

"Before this," he said as their descent suddenly accelerated and they fell completely through the floor.

Mia let out a short scream, her grip tightening on Korum's hand. At first there was only darkness and the frightening sensation of nothingness beneath her feet, and then they were suddenly floating in a softly lit circular room with solid peach-tinted walls and ceiling.

As in, literally floating in mid-air.

Gasping, Mia stared at her lover, unable to believe what was happening. "Korum, is this—?"

"A zero-gravity chamber?" He was grinning like a little boy about to show off a new toy. "Yes, indeed."

"You have a zero-gravity chamber in your house?"

"I do," he admitted, obviously pleased with her reaction. Letting go of Mia's hand, he did a slow somersault in the air. "As you can see, it's a lot of fun."

Mia laughed incredulously, then tried to follow his example—but there was no good way for her to control her movements. She had no idea how Korum had managed to somersault so easily. She was moving her arms and legs, but it didn't seem to do much for her. It was like she was floating in water, only without any sensation of wetness.

She couldn't tell which way was up or down; the chamber was windowless, and there was no clear distinction between the walls, floor, and ceiling. It was as though they were in a giant bubble—which probably wasn't all that far from the truth. Mia was no expert on the subject, but she imagined it wasn't easy to create a zero-gravity environment on Earth. There had to be a lot of complex technology surrounding them and negating the gravitational pull of the planet.

"Wow," she said softly, drifting in the air. "Korum, this is amazing . . . Is this something other Krinar have too?"

He had managed to get to one of the walls, and he used it to push off, propelling himself back in her direction. "No—" he reached out to grab her arm as he floated past her, "—it's not something many of us have."

Mia grinned as he pulled her toward him. "Oh yeah? Only you?"

"Perhaps," he murmured, wrapping one arm around her waist and holding her tightly against him. His eyes were turning more golden by the second, and the hardness pressing against her belly left no doubt of his intentions.

Mia's eyes widened. "Here?" she asked, her pulse speeding up from excitement.

"Hmm-mm . . ." He was already bringing her up (or was it down?) to nibble at the sensitive area behind her earlobe.

As always, his touch made her entire body hum in anticipation. Arching her head back, she moaned softly, liquid heat moving through her veins.

"I love you," he whispered in her ear, his large hands stroking down her body, pulling down her dress. It drifted away, but Mia hardly noticed, her eyes glued to the man she loved more than life itself.

She would never tire of hearing those words from him, Mia thought, watching as he pulled away for a second to take off his own clothes. His shirt came off first, then his shorts, and then he was fully naked, revealing a body that was striking in its masculine perfection. The fact that they were floating in the air added an element of surrealism to the entire scene, making Mia feel like she was having an unusual sexy dream.

Reaching out, she ran her hands down his chest, marveling at the smooth texture of his skin and the rock-solid muscle underneath. "I love you too," she murmured, and watched his eyes flare brighter with need.

Bringing her toward him, he turned her so that she was floating perpendicular to him, her lower body at his eye level. Before she could say anything, he was opening her thighs, exposing her delicate folds to his hungry gaze. "So beautiful," he whispered, "so warm and wet . . . I can't wait to taste you—" he followed his words with a slow lick of her most private area, "—to make you come . . ."

Moaning, Mia closed her eyes, the familiar tension starting to coil deep in her belly. Drifting in mid-air seemed to be sharpening all sensations. Without a surface to lie on or anything else touching her body, all she could feel—all she could concentrate on—was the incredible pleasure of his mouth licking and nibbling around her clitoris, and his strong hands stroking up and down her thighs.

Without any warning, a powerful orgasm ripped through her body, originating at her core and spreading outward. Mia cried out, her toes curling from the intensity of the release, and then he was flipping her so that she faced him. Before her pulsations even stopped, his thick cock was already at her opening, entering her in one smooth thrust.

Gasping, Mia opened her eyes and grabbed his shoulders, the shock of his possession reverberating through her body. He paused for a second, then began to move slowly, giving her time to adjust to the fullness inside her. With each careful thrust, the tip of his shaft pressed against the sensitive spot deep within, making her gasp from the sensation.

It seemed to go on forever, those gentle and measured thrusts, each one bringing her closer to the edge but not quite sending her over. Moaning in frustration, Mia dug her nails into his shoulders, needing him to move faster. "Please, Korum . . ." she whispered, knowing that he wanted this sometimes—that he liked to hear her beg for the ultimate pleasure.

"Oh, I will," he murmured, his eyes almost pure gold. "I will definitely please you, my sweet." And holding her tightly with one arm, he reached behind her and rubbed the area where they were joined, gathering the moisture from there. Then, to her surprise, his finger ventured higher, between the smooth globes of her cheeks, and pressed gently against the tiny opening there.

Her breath catching in her throat, Mia stared up at him with a mixture of fear and excitement.

"Shhh, relax . . ." he soothed, his voice like rough velvet. And before she could say anything, he bent his head, taking her mouth in a deep, seductive kiss even as his finger began to push inside.

At first, it seemed to hurt and burn, the unfamiliar intrusion making her squirm against him in a futile effort to ease the discomfort. With his shaft buried all the way inside her, the additional invasion of her body was too much, the sensations strange and unnerving. Once he stopped, however, with his finger only partially inside her, the burning began to recede, leaving an unusual feeling of fullness in its wake.

Lifting his head, Korum stared down at her with a heavy-lidded gaze. "All right?" he asked softly, and Mia nodded uncertainly, unable to decide if she liked the peculiar sensation or not.

"Good," he whispered, beginning to move his hips again while keeping his finger steady. "Just relax . . . Yes, there's a good girl . . ."

Closing her eyes, Mia concentrated on not tensing up, although it was becoming increasingly difficult. The unfamiliar discomfort was somehow adding to the pressure building inside her, each thrust of his cock causing his finger to move ever so slightly, overwhelming her senses. His pace gradually picked up, his hips moving faster and faster . . . and then she was suddenly flying apart, her entire body convulsing from an orgasm so intense it left her weak and panting in its wake.

Korum groaned, grinding against her as her inner muscles rhythmically squeezed his cock, triggering his own climax. She could feel the warm spurts of his seed inside her belly, hear his harsh breathing in her ears as his arm tightened around her waist, holding her securely in place.

When it was all over, he slowly withdrew his finger and kissed her, his lips sweet and tender on hers.

And then they drifted together for a few more minutes, their bodies slick with sweat and wrapped intimately around each other.

* * *

The next morning, Mia woke up and stretched, a big grin breaking out on her face as she remembered what took place yesterday. It seemed that Korum had just begun to introduce her to the various erotic pleasures he had in store for her . . . and she could barely wait to experience it all. Rightly or wrongly, she was now completely addicted to him, to the pleasure she experienced in his arms, and she couldn't imagine ever being with anyone else—especially not with a regular human man.

It was funny: she'd always heard that relationships tended to lose their initial intensity over time, but it seemed like their passion was only getting stronger with each day that passed. Partially, it was the fact that Korum was a phenomenal lover; during his two thousand years, he'd had plenty of time to learn all the erogenous zones on a woman's body. But it was also something more, something indefinable—that unique chemistry between them that had been obvious from the very beginning. Sometimes it scared her, the extent to which she needed him now. The craving went beyond the physical, although she couldn't imagine going even a single day without the mind-blowing pleasure she experienced in his arms. It was as if they were attuned to each other on a cellular level—two halves of a complete whole.

Still smiling, Mia rolled out of bed. Picking up her wristwatch computer, she glanced at it to check the time. To her surprise, it was already eight a.m., which meant that she had only an hour to eat breakfast and get to the lab. Although it was Saturday, it was a workday in Lenkarda, since the Krinar didn't follow the human calendar when it came to weekdays and weekends. Their 'week' was only four days in duration, instead of seven—three days of work, followed by a day of rest. Mia still thought about time in human calendar terms, however, since that's what she was used to.

Korum was already gone, so Mia asked the house to prepare her a smoothie and ran to take a quick shower. Even that was different now after Korum's remodeling efforts. Instead of the shower/jacuzzi combo that she'd gotten used to, the bathroom now had a giant circular stall with the same intelligent technology as everything else in the house. The water came out of everywhere and nowhere, washing and massaging every part of her body, with the water pressure and temperature adjusting to her needs automatically. She didn't have to apply any effort to wash herself, either; instead, lightly scented soaps, shampoos, and some kind of unusual oils were applied to her hair and skin while she simply stood there, letting Krinar technology do all the work.

After the shower was over, Mia stepped out and warm jets of air dried off her body. Her hair was automatically blow-dried too, resulting in smooth, glossy curls that could've been the result of a session at a fancy hair salon. At the same time, her mouth was filled with the taste of something refreshingly clean, as though she had just brushed her teeth.

By the time she was dressed and done with the shower, a strawberry-almond smoothie was already sitting on the kitchen table. Grabbing it on her way out, Mia left the house and headed to work.

Although she had only been gone a week, Mia found that she missed the lab environment. She loved to learn, and the challenge of mastering a difficult subject had never daunted her. Part of her initial reluctance in getting involved with Korum had been due to her fear of losing herself, of becoming nothing more than a glorified pleasure slave. But instead, she seemed to have discovered a way to become a useful part of the Krinar society, to contribute in some small way. By finding her the internship, Korum had done more than simply pad her resume; he'd also demonstrated that he regarded her as a smart and capable person—someone he could not only desire, but respect.

Arriving at the lab, Mia spent most of the day catching up on what she'd missed during her week in Florida. Despite her almost-daily chats with Adam, her project partner, she still felt like she had fallen behind on some of the latest developments. She didn't have a lot of time to get up to speed either, as Adam was planning to leave to visit his own adopted human family that afternoon.

"How did Saret let you do that?" Mia teased. "Leave for an entire week? Korum practically had to strong-arm him to let me go for that length of time, and you're much more useful . . ."

Adam shrugged. "He didn't have much choice in the matter. I told him I'm going, and that's that."

Mia grinned at him, again impressed by the young Krinar. Despite his human upbringing—or maybe because of it—he could more than hold his own with the best of them.

Finally, around four in the afternoon, Adam gave her a bunch of readings and headed out to start his vacation, leaving her alone in the lab. The other apprentices were working on a joint project with the mind lab in Thailand, and they had gone there for a few days to conclude some experiment.

Mia spent the next two hours reading and then went to check on the data that was being generated by the virtual simulation of a young Krinar brain. It appeared that the latest method she and Adam had figured out was indeed a step in the right direction. The knowledge transfer was happening at a faster pace and with fewer unpleasant side effects. Hopefully, they would be able to improve it further by the end of summer—

"How was your vacation in Florida?" a familiar voice behind her asked, and Mia jumped, startled.

Turning around, she took a deep breath, trying to calm her racing pulse. "You scared me," she told Saret, giving him a smile. "I didn't know anyone else was here in the lab."

Her boss ran his fingers through his dark hair. "I'm just finishing up a few things." He looked unusually tense, and Mia thought he seemed tired—a rarity for a Krinar.

"Is everything all right?" she asked tentatively, not wanting to overstep any boundaries. Although she had been working for Saret for a couple of weeks, she felt like she still didn't really know him. He didn't spend a lot of time in the lab, since whatever project he was working on took him all over the world. When he was in the lab, he was usually in his office—although she'd caught him watching her a few times, apparently keeping an eye on the only human he'd ever allowed into his lab.

"Of course," Saret said, his features relaxing into a smile. "Why wouldn't it be? One of my favorite assistants is back."

Feeling slightly awkward, Mia smiled back at him. "Thanks," she said. "It's good to be back. I was just looking at the data, and there's definitely progress—"

"That's good," Saret interrupted. "I look forward to your report soon."

"Of course. I will prepare it tonight—"

"No, no need for that. You can go home early today. It's your first day back, and I know your cheren will be unhappy if I keep you here late."

Surprised, Mia nodded. "Okay, if you're sure . . ." Normally, Saret disliked it when his apprentices didn't put in a full day. He'd even gotten into an argument about that with Korum when Mia had first started the internship. And now it seemed like he actually wanted her to leave . . . Still, she wasn't about to quibble; she had been planning to go home in another hour anyway.

"I'm sure." Saret smiled at her. There was something about that smile that made her uncomfortable, but she couldn't figure out what.

"Okay then, thanks. I'll see you tomorrow," Mia said, walking past him. And as she did, she could've sworn he leaned closer, breathing in—almost as if he was inhaling her scent.

Telling herself that she had an overactive imagination, Mia exited the lab and entered a small aircraft that was sitting next to the lab building. Korum had made it for her for the express purpose of traveling around Lenkarda. Like the wristwatch he'd given her, it was programmed to respond to her verbal commands. Feeling tired after a full day at work, Mia sat down on one of the intelligent seats and ordered the ship to take her home.

* * *

Saret watched Mia leave, his hands nearly shaking with the urge to reach out and touch her.

Having her so close after her long absence had been torturous. The faint sweetness of her scent permeated the lab, and he hadn't been able to stop himself from coming closer, from breathing it in. If she hadn't left then, he would've done something stupid—like bring her toward him for a taste. And he wouldn't have been able to stop with just a taste.

When he tried to analyze his own mind—like every mind expert should—he could come up with a dozen reasons for why he'd become so obsessed with her. First and foremost, she belonged to Korum. Even when they'd been children, Saret had always wanted Korum's toys. His enemy had been inventive even then, altering the designs for popular games and creating something that was better than what anyone else had. Saret had hated Korum for it then, and he hated him now. Of course, he had never let it show. Korum's enemies never fared well. It was far better to be his friend—or, at least, to act like one.

And Mia was the ultimate toy. So small, so delicate, so perfectly human. For the first time, Saret understood why her species kept pets. Having a cute creature to call your own, to stroke and touch at your whim—there was something incredibly appealing in that. Especially when that creature loved you, depended on you ... She would make a very good pet, Saret thought wryly, with that thick mass of hair that looked so soft and touchable.

He was surprised Korum let her spend so much time away from him. Saret had tested him in the beginning, insisting that Mia put in a full day, just to see if that would convince Korum of the ridiculousness of having a human in a Krinar work environment. His nemesis was the last person he would've expected to treat a human girl as an equal. Sure, she was smart—for a human, at least—but she was also young and malleable. It wouldn't take much effort to mold her into whatever he wanted her to be. Whatever she thought she wanted now—none of that really mattered. If she had been *his* charl, he could've easily convinced her to be happy with her role in his life, in his bed. There were so many amusements for a human girl to enjoy: all kinds of virtual and real-life spa treatments, pretty clothes, interesting recordings, fun books ... And instead, Korum had her working nonstop. No wonder she still objected to being a charl. Her cheren simply didn't know how to treat her properly.

Sighing, Saret went back into his office. All the mind analysis in the world didn't change the fact that he wanted her. And soon he would be able to have her. He just needed to be patient for a while longer.

Turning his attention back to his task, Saret brought up a three-dimensional map of Shanghai.

China was next on his list.

CHAPTER TWO

"There's nothing to worry about," Korum said soothingly, placing a white dot on Mia's temple. "They will love you, just like I do."

Mia nervously twisted a strand of hair between her fingers before tucking it behind her ear. "They won't mind that I'm human?"

"They won't," he reassured her. "They know all about you already, and they're very happy that I found someone I care so much about."

After she'd arrived home from work, Korum had surprised her with the news that he wanted her to meet *his* family as well. So now he was about to take her into a virtual reality setting where she would meet his parents. Supposedly, the environment was very lifelike, and she would be able to interact with his parents there as though they were meeting in person.

It was also on Krina.

"Are you sure I shouldn't change?" Mia knew she was

stalling, but she felt ridiculously anxious. "And won't your mom mind that I'm wearing your family necklace?"

"You look beautiful, and the necklace is perfect on you," he said firmly. "My mother will be quite pleased to see it around your neck; she gave it to me explicitly for that purpose—to gift it to the woman I ultimately fall in love with."

Mia took a deep breath, trying to control her rapid heartbeat. "Okay, then I'm ready." At least as ready as she would ever be to meet her extraterrestrial lover's parents—who resided thousands of light years away.

Korum smiled, and the world around her blurred for a second.

Feeling dizzy, Mia closed her eyes, and when she opened them, she was standing inside a large, airy building that vaguely resembled Korum's house in Lenkarda. From the inside, it was fully transparent, and she could see unusual plants outside. Most of the flora was a familiar shade of green, but red, orange, and yellow hues also proliferated. It was strikingly beautiful. The inside of the building had the same 'Zen' feel to it as Arman's house. Everything was a beautiful off-white shade, and the sunlight streaming through the clear ceiling reflected off a gorgeous flower arrangement right in the middle of the room—the only touch of color in an otherwise pristine environment. The flowers seemed to grow right out of an opening in the floor. Along the walls, there were a few familiar-looking floating planks that served as multi-purpose furniture.

"It's lovely," Mia whispered, glancing around the room. "Is this your parents' house?"

Korum nodded, smiling. He looked quite pleased. "It's my childhood home," he explained, reaching out to take her hand and squeezing it lightly.

As usual, his touch made her feel warm inside, and she marveled again at how authentic this virtual reality felt. Somehow, this was even more convincing than the club where he'd taken her once to satisfy her fantasy. All her senses were fully engaged, as though she was physically present here, on a planet in a different galaxy.

Inhaling deeply, Mia realized that the air was a little thinner than what she was used to, as if they were at a high altitude. She actually felt a bit light-headed, and she hoped she would adjust to it soon. The temperature was pleasantly warm, and there seemed to be a faint breeze coming from somewhere, even though they were inside the building. There was also an exotic, but appealing scent in the air. Likely from the flowers, Mia decided. The aroma was almost... fruity. She'd never smelled anything like it before.

As Mia studied their surroundings, one of the walls dissolved, and a Krinar woman walked in. She was tall and slim, with a supermodel's leggy build and shiny dark hair. Her eyes were the same warm amber color as Korum's. It could only be Korum's mother; their resemblance was unmistakable.

At the sight of them standing there, a huge smile lit her face. "My child," she said softly, her eyes shining with love as she looked at her son, "I'm so glad to see you." Like all Ks, her age was impossible to determine; she didn't look a day older than twenty-five.

Letting go of Mia's hand, Korum crossed the room and enveloped his mother in a gentle hug. "Me too, Riani, me too . . ."

Mia watched their reunion, feeling like she was intruding on a private family moment. She couldn't imagine what it must be like for his parents, with their son living so far away. Yes, they could meet in this virtual way, but they still probably missed seeing him in person.

Turning toward Mia, Korum smiled and said, "Come here, darling. Let me introduce you to my mother."

Curving her lips in an answering smile, Mia approached them, noticing the way the K's eyes examined her from head to toe. Her palms began to sweat. What was this gorgeous woman thinking? Was she wondering how her son had ended up with a human?

Pausing a couple of feet away, Mia smiled wider. "Hello," she said, uncertain if she should reach out and brush the K's cheek with her knuckles. She'd learned in the past couple of weeks that it was the customary greeting among Krinar females.

Korum's mother had no such reservations. Raising her hand, she gently touched Mia's cheek and smiled in return. "Hello, my dear. I'm so glad to finally meet you."

"Riani, this is Mia, my charl," Korum said. "Mia, this is Riani, my mother."

"It's such a pleasure to meet you, Riani." Mia was starting to feel more at ease. Despite the woman's luminous beauty and youthful looks, there was something in her manner that was very soothing. Almost motherly, Mia thought with an inner smile.

"Where's Chiaren?" Korum asked, addressing his mother.

"Oh, he'll be here soon," she said, waving her hand. "He was delayed at work. Don't worry—he knows you're here."

Chiaren had to be Korum's father, Mia decided. It was interesting that he called his parents by name, although it made sense too. As long-lived as the Ks were, the lines between generations were probably much less defined than for humans. Although Korum had mentioned once that his parents were much older than he was, she guessed that the difference between two thousand years and a few thousand years was not all that dramatic.

A quiet whoosh interrupted Mia's musings. Turning her head to the side, she saw the wall opening again. A darkly handsome Krinar man walked in, dressed in typical K clothing. Swiftly crossing the room, he raised his hand and touched his palm to Korum's shoulder, greeting his son.

Korum reciprocated the gesture, but he seemed much more reserved than he had been with his mother. "Chiaren," he said quietly. "I'm glad you could make it."

Something in the tone of his voice startled Mia. Was there some tension between father and son?

His father inclined his head. "Of course. I wouldn't miss your visit." Then, turning his attention to Mia, he cocked his head to the side and studied her with an inscrutable expression on his face.

Mia swallowed, needing to moisten her suddenly dry throat. Chiaren's posture, the slightly mocking curl to his lips—it was all very familiar to her. Korum might've gotten his mother's looks, but he'd definitely inherited some personality traits from his father as well. She found the K to be intimidating, with his cool dark gaze and lack of visible emotion. He reminded her of Korum when they'd first met.

"Chiaren, this is Mia," Korum said, stepping toward her and putting a proprietary arm around her back. "She's my charl. Mia, this is my father, Chiaren."

The K smiled, suddenly seeming much more approachable. "How lovely," he said gently. "Such a pretty human girl you've got there. How old are you, Mia? You seem younger than I'd imagined."

"I'm twenty-one," Mia told him, aware that she probably looked like she was in her late teens. It was a common problem for someone of her petite build—a problem that would now never go away.

Chiaren's smile widened. "Twenty-one . . ."

Mia flushed, realizing that he thought her little more than a child. And compared to him, she was. Still, she would've preferred if he hadn't looked quite so amused at her age.

"Mia, dear, tell us a bit about yourself," Riani said, smiling at her with warm encouragement. "Korum mentioned that you're studying the mind. Is that right?"

Mia nodded, turning her attention to Korum's mother. She wasn't certain how she felt about his father yet, but she was definitely growing to like Riani. "I am," she confirmed. "I started working with Saret this summer. Before that, I majored in psychology at one of our universities."

"How are you finding it so far? Your apprenticeship?" asked Chiaren. "I imagine it must be quite different from anything you've done before." He seemed genuinely curious.

"Yes, it is," said Mia. "I'm learning a great deal." Feeling much more in her element, she told them all about her work at the lab, her eyes lighting up as she explained about the imprinting project.

Afterwards, Riani asked about her family, seeming particularly interested in the fact that Mia had a sibling. Marisa's pregnancy appeared to fascinate her, and she listened attentively as Mia detailed the difficulties her sister had gone through before Ellet's arrival. After that, Chiaren wanted to know about Mia's parents and their occupations, and how human contributions to society were typically measured, so Mia spoke for a while about the role of teachers and professors in the American educational system.

Before long, she found herself engaged in an animated discussion with Korum's parents. She learned that they had been together for close to three millennia, and that Riani was almost five hundred years older than her mate. Unlike Korum, who had discovered his passion for technological design early on, both Riani and Chiaren were 'dabblers.' Most Krinar were, in fact. Instead of specializing in a specific subject, they frequently changed their careers and areas of focus, never fully reaching the 'expert' level in any particular field. As a result, while their standing in society was quite respectable, neither one of Korum's parents had come even close to being involved with the Council.

"I'm not sure how we managed to produce such an intelligent and ambitious child," Riani confided, grinning. "It certainly wasn't intentional."

Seeing the puzzled look on Mia's face, Chiaren explained, "When a couple decides to have a child, they usually do so under very controlled conditions. They choose the optimal combination of physical traits and potential intellectual abilities, consulting the top medical experts—"

"Most Krinar are designer babies?" Mia's eyes widened in realization. This explained why all the Krinar she'd met were so good-looking. They had taken control of their own evolution by practicing a form of genetic selection for their children. It made a tremendous amount of sense. Any culture advanced enough to manipulate their own genetic code—as the Krinar had done to get rid of their need for blood—could easily specify which genes they wanted in their offspring. Mia was surprised it hadn't occurred to her earlier.

Chiaren hesitated. "I'm not familiar with that term . . ."

"Yes, exactly," Korum said, giving Mia a smile. "Few parents are willing to play genetic roulette, not when there is a better way."

"But we did," Riani said, looking a bit sheepish. "I got pregnant by accident—one of the few accidents of this kind to occur in the last ten thousand years. We discussed having a child, and we both went off birth control, planning to go to a lab like every other couple we knew. Statistically, the odds of getting pregnant naturally in the first fertile year are something like one in a million. Of course, this was during my musical mastery period, and I got very caught up in vocal expression, to the point that we put off our visit to the lab for a few months. And by the time the medical expert saw me, I was already three weeks pregnant with Korum."

"I'm a throwback, you see," Korum said, laughing. "They had no control over which ancestor's genetic traits I inherited."

Mia grinned at him. "Well, I think it's pretty obvious where you get your coloring from." He could've been Riani's twin brother, instead of her son.

"It's the ambition that puzzles us," Chiaren said, shooting his son an indecipherable look. "It's really come out of nowhere . . ."

Korum's eyes narrowed a bit, and Mia sensed that this was likely the point of contention between father and son. She determined to ask Korum about it later. For now, she was curious about this new tidbit she'd learned about her lover. "So you're not a designer baby, huh?" she teased, smiling at him.

"Nope." Korum grinned. "I'm as natural as they come."

"Well, you came out perfect anyway," Mia said, studying his beautifully masculine features. She couldn't imagine how he could look any better.

To her surprise, Korum shook his head. "No, actually, I didn't. I have a small deformity."

"What?" Mia stared at him in shock. This gorgeous man had a deformity? Where had he hidden it this whole time?

He smiled and pointed at the dimple in his left cheek. "Yeah, right there. See?"

Mia gave him a disbelieving look. "Your dimple? Really?"

He nodded, his eyes sparkling with amusement. "It's considered a deformity among my kind. But I've learned to live with it. Apparently, some women even like it."

Like it? Mia loved it, and she told him so, making him and his parents laugh.

"We should probably get going," Korum said after a while. "It's dinner time, and Mia needs to get some sleep before getting up early for work tomorrow."

"Of course." Riani gave her a warm look of understanding. "I know humans tire more easily . . ."

Mia opened her mouth to protest, but then she changed her mind. It was the truth, even if she wasn't particularly tired right now. Instead she said, "It was very nice to meet you, Riani—and Chiaren. I really enjoyed talking to both of you."

"Same here, dear, same here." Riani gently touched her cheek again. "We hope to see you soon."

Mia smiled and nodded. "Definitely. I look forward to it."

"It was a pleasure meeting you, Mia," Korum's father said, giving her a smile. Then, turning to Korum, he added, "And it was good to see you, my son."

Korum inclined his head. "Until the next time."

And the world blurred around them again, causing

Mia to close her eyes. When she opened them, they were standing back in Korum's house in Lenkarda.

* * *

"I like your parents," Mia told Korum over dinner. "They seem very nice."

"Oh, they are," Korum said, biting into a piece of pomegranate-flavored jicama. "Riani is great. Chiaren too, although we don't always see eye to eye on certain things."

"Why not?"

He shrugged. "I'm not sure. It's always been that way. In some ways, we're too alike, but in others, we're completely different. He's never understood why I spent all my time building up my company instead of just enjoying life and finding myself a mate, the way he did. And he hasn't really forgiven me for leaving Krina and depriving Riani of their only son, even though I frequently visit them in the virtual world."

Mia smiled, seeing shades of her own family in that dynamic. It had been difficult enough for her parents when she'd gone to college in New York; she couldn't imagine how they would've coped if she'd disappeared to another galaxy. She couldn't really blame Korum's father for being upset, particularly if he didn't understand or appreciate his son's ambition.

Still thinking about Korum's family, Mia slowly ate her stew, enjoying the satisfying combination of richly flavored roots and vegetables from Krina. Suddenly, a disturbing thought occurred to her, causing her to put down her utensil and look up at Korum.

"Would you ever want to go back to Krina?" she asked, frowning a little. "You must miss your parents, and it seems so nice there . . ."

He hesitated for a couple of seconds. "Perhaps one day," he finally said, watching her with an unreadable golden gaze. "But probably not for a long while."

Mia felt her chest tighten a little. "What about me?"

"You'll come with me, of course," he said casually, taking a sip of water. "What else?"

She took a deep breath, trying to remain calm. "To another planet? Leaving everything and everybody behind?"

His eyes narrowed slightly. "I didn't say we'd go soon, Mia. Maybe not even within your family's lifetime. But someday, yes, I may need to visit Krina and I would want you with me."

Mia blinked and looked away, her heart squeezing at the reminder of the disparity that now existed between her and the rest of humanity. Thanks to the nanocytes circulating through her body, she would never grow old and die—but she would also far outlive her loved ones. The fact that the Krinar had the means to indefinitely extend human lifespan but chose not to do so bothered her a great deal, making her feel guilty whenever she thought about the issue.

"Mia . . ." Korum reached across the table and took her hand. "Listen to me. I told you I would petition the Elders on your family's behalf, and I have begun the process. But I can't promise you anything. I've never heard of an exception being made for anyone who's not considered a charl."

"But why?" Mia asked in frustration. "Why not share your knowledge, your technology with us? Why do your Elders care so much about this issue?"

Korum sighed, his thumb stroking her palm. "None of us know exactly, but it has something to do with the fact that you're still very imperfect as a species, and the Elders want you to have more time to evolve . . ."

"We're imperfect?" Mia stared at him in disbelief. "What's that supposed to mean? What, you're saying we're defective? Like a part in a car that doesn't function properly?"

"No, not like a part in a car," he explained patiently, his fingers tightening when she tried to jerk her hand away. "Your species is very young, that's all. Your society and your culture are evolving at a rapid pace, and your high birthrate and short lifespan probably have something to do with that. If we were to give you our technology now, if every human could live thousands of years, your planet could become overpopulated very quickly . . . unless we also did something about your birthrate. You see, Mia, it's all or none: we either control everything, or we let you be mostly as you are. There's no good middle ground here, my sweet."

Mia felt her teeth snapping together. "So why not give people that choice?" she asked, angered by the whole thing. "Why not let them choose if they want to live for a long time, or if they'd rather have children? I'm sure many would go for the first option rather than face death and disease—"

"It's not that simple, Mia," Korum said, regarding her evenly. "Overpopulation is not the Elders' only concern, you see. Every generation brings something new to your society, changing it for the better. It was less than two hundred years ago that humans in your country thought nothing of keeping slaves. And now the thought of that is abhorrent to them—because generations have passed and values have changed. Do you think you could've eradicated slavery if the same people who had once owned slaves were still around today? Your society's progress would slow tremendously if we uniformly extended your lifespan—and that's not something the Elders want at this point."

"So we *are* just an experiment," Mia said, unable to keep the bitterness out of her voice. "You just want to see what happens to us, and never mind how many humans suffer in the process—"

"Humans wouldn't be around to suffer if it weren't for the Krinar, my sweet," he interrupted, looking faintly amused at her outburst. "You very conveniently forget that fact."

"Right, you made us, and now you can play God." She could feel the old resentment rising up, making her want to lash out at the unfairness of it all. As much as she loved Korum, sometimes his arrogance made her want to scream.

He grinned, not the least bit fazed by her anger. His fingers eased their grip on her palm, his touch turning soft and caressing again. "I can think of other things I'd rather play," he murmured, his eyes beginning to fill with golden heat.

And as Mia watched in disbelief, he sent the floating table away, removing the barrier between them. Still holding her hand, he pulled her toward him until she had no choice but to straddle his lap.

"You think sex will make it all better?" she asked, annoyed at her body's unavoidable response to his nearness. No matter how mad she was, all he had to do was look at her in a certain way and she was completely lost, turning into a puddle of need.

"Hmm-mm . . ." He was already leaning forward to kiss her neck, his mouth hot and moist on her bare skin. "Sex always makes everything better," he whispered, nibbling on the sensitive junction between her neck and shoulder.

And for the next several hours, Mia found no reason to disagree with that statement.

* * *

After the noise and crowds in Shanghai, the stark landscape of the Siberian tundra was almost soothing. If it hadn't been for the cold, Saret would've probably enjoyed visiting this remote northern region of Russia.

But it was cold. The temperature here, just above the Arctic Circle, was never warm enough for a Krinar, not even on the hottest summer day. Today, though, it was actually below freezing, and Saret made sure every part of his body was covered with thermal clothing before he stepped out of his ship.

The large grey building in front of him was one of the ugliest examples of Soviet-era architecture. Barbed wire and guard towers on every corner marked it as exactly what it was—a maximum security prison for the worst violent offenders in all of Russia. Few people knew this place existed, which is why Saret had chosen it for his experiment.

He openly approached the gate, not worrying about being seen by any cameras or satellites. For this outing, he was wearing a disguise, one of a couple he had developed over the years. It changed not only his appearance, but even the outer layer of his DNA, making it nearly impossible to divine his true identity. The humans knew he was a Krinar, of course, but they didn't know anything else about him.

At his approach, the gate swung open, letting him in. Saret walked briskly to the building, where he was greeted by the warden—a pot-bellied, middle-aged human who stank of alcohol and cigarettes.

Without saying a word, the warden led him to his office and closed the door.

"Well?" Saret asked in Russian as soon as they had privacy. "Do you have the data I requested?"

"Yes," the warden said slowly. "The results are quite . . . unusual."

"Unusual how?"

"It's been six weeks since your last visit," the human said, his hands nervously playing with a pen. "In the past month, we haven't had a single homicide. In the past three weeks, there have been no fights. I've been running this place for twenty years, and I've never seen anything like it."

Saret smiled. "No, I'm sure you haven't. What was the homicide rate before?"

The man opened a folder and took out a sheet of paper, handing it to Saret. "Take a look. There are usually two or three murders a month and about a fight a day. We can't figure it out. It's like all of them had a personality transplant."

Saret's smile widened. If only the human knew the truth. Satisfied, he folded the sheet and put it in the pocket of his thermal pants. "You can expect the final payment by tomorrow," he told the warden and walked out of the room.

He couldn't wait to get back on his ship and out of the cold.

CHAPTER THREE

The following two days passed uneventfully. Mia spent her time working in the lab and enjoying evenings with Korum, deliriously happy despite their occasional arguments. She had no doubt that he loved her—and it made all the difference in the world. One day, she hoped to convince him to see her kind in a different light, to appreciate the fact that humans were more than just an experiment of the Krinar Elders. For now, though, she had to be content with the possibility of an exception being made for her family—something she knew Korum was fighting hard to obtain.

At the lab, the other apprentices were still away, so Mia found herself frequently working alone, surrounded by all the equipment. Saret was in and out, and she would occasionally catch him watching her with an enigmatic expression on his face. Shrugging it off as some weird distrust for his human apprentice, she finished her report and sent it to Saret, hoping that he would give her feedback soon. While waiting, she continued to play around with the simulation, trying different variations of the process and carefully recording the results.

Tuesday was a day off in Lenkarda, and it was also Maria's birthday. The vivacious girl had sent her a holographic message over the weekend, formally inviting her to the party on the beach at two in the afternoon. Mia had gladly accepted.

"So I don't get to come?" Korum was lounging on the bed and watching her get ready for the party. His golden eyes gleamed with amusement, and she knew that he was teasing her.

"Sorry, sweetie," she told him mockingly, twirling in front of the mirror. "No cheren allowed. Charl only."

He grinned. "Such discrimination."

She wore the necklace he'd given her and a light floaty dress with a swimsuit underneath—just in case the party involved any swimming in the ocean.

"Yes, well, you know how that goes," she said, grinning back. "We're too cool for all you Ks."

She loved that she could banter with him now. Somehow, almost imperceptibly, their relationship had assumed a more equal footing. He still liked to be in control—and he could still be incredibly domineering on occasion—but she was beginning to feel like she could stand up to him. The knowledge that he loved her, that her thoughts and opinions mattered to him, was very liberating.

"All right," she said, bending down to give him a chaste kiss on the cheek, "I have to run."

Before she could pull away, however, his arm snaked around her waist, and she found herself flat on her back on the bed, pinned down by his large muscular body.

"Korum!" She wriggled, trying to get away. "I'm

ANNA ZAIRES

running late! You told me yourself it's an insult to be late—"

"One kiss," he cajoled, holding her effortlessly. She could see the familiar signs of arousal on his face and feel his cock hardening against her leg. Her body reacted in predictable fashion, her insides clenching in anticipation and her breathing picking up.

She shook her head. "No, we can't . . ."

"Just one kiss," he promised, lowering his head. His mouth was hot and skillful on hers, his tongue caressing the inside of her lips, and Mia could feel herself melting on the spot, a pleasurable fog engulfing her mind. Before she could completely forget herself, however, he stopped, lifting his head and carefully rolling off her.

"Go," he said, and there was a wicked smile on his face. "I don't want you to be late."

Frustrated, Mia got up and threw a pillow at him. "You're evil," she told him. Now she was extremely turned on, and she wouldn't get a chance to see him for the next few hours. The only thing that made her feel better was the fact that he would suffer equally.

"Just wanted you to hurry back, that's all," he said, grinning, and Mia threw another pillow at him before grabbing Maria's gift and heading out the door.

She managed not to be late, although all twelve of the other charl were already there when she arrived. Maria's invitation message had told her there would be thirteen girls total, including Mia herself.

An unusual musical mix was playing somewhere in the background. The sounds were beautiful, and Mia recognized the melody that Korum sometimes played in the house. However, interspersed with the popular Krinar tune, she could hear the more familiar flute and violin undertones.

The girls were sitting on floating chairs arranged in a circle around a large hovering plank that apparently served as a picnic table. The table was piled high with all manner of delicious-looking fruit and various exotic dishes.

Spotting Mia, Maria gave her an enthusiastic wave. "Hi there, come join us!"

Mia approached, smiling at her. "Happy birthday!" she said, handing Maria a small box wrapped in pretty paper.

"A gift! Oh my dear, you really shouldn't have!" But Maria's face glowed with excitement, and Mia knew she'd done the right thing in asking Korum to help her come up with a present.

As eager as a child, Maria tore apart the wrapper and opened the box, taking out a small oval object. "Oh my God, is that what I think it is?!?"

"Korum made it," Mia explained, pleased by her reaction. Maria obviously knew enough about Krinar technology to understand that she'd just received a fabricator—a device that would enable her to use nanomachines to create all manner of objects from individual atoms. Of course, the computer that Korum had embedded in his palm enabled him to do the same thing without any other devices—and on a much bigger, more complex scale. However, he was one of the very few who could create an entire ship from scratch. Rapid fabrication was a relatively new technology and still fairly expensive, so not all Krinar could afford even a basic fabricator—like the one he had designed for Maria. It was a highly coveted object, Korum had explained.

"Oh my God, a fabricator! Thank you so much!"

Maria was almost beside herself with excitement. "This is so great—I can now make whatever clothes I want!"

"And other things too," Mia said, grinning. The little fabricator wasn't advanced enough to make complex technology, but it could conjure up all manner of simpler objects.

"Clothes," Maria said firmly. "I mainly want clothes."

Everyone around the table laughed at the determined expression on her face, and a red-headed girl yelled out, "And shoes for me!"

"Oh, what am I thinking!" Maria exclaimed amidst all the laughter. "I haven't even introduced you to everyone yet. Everyone—this is Mia, our newest arrival. As you can see, she's unbelievably awesome. Mia, you know Delia already. The lovely lady to her right is Sandra, then Jenny, Jeannette, Rosa, Yun, Lisa, Danielle, Ana, Moira, and Cat."

"Hi," Mia said, smiling and waving to all the girls. The flood of names was a little overwhelming; there was no way she'd remember all of them right away. Normally, she was shy in social situations where she didn't know most of the people, but today she felt comfortable for some reason. Perhaps it was because she already had so much in common with these girls. Few others outside of this little group could even begin to understand what it was like to be in a relationship with someone literally out of this world.

Taking a seat on the empty floating chair, Mia stared around the table with unabashed curiosity. Like her, all these girls were immortal. Did that mean that some of them were older than they looked? For the most part, they appeared young and strikingly beautiful, of various races and nationalities. However, a couple of them were merely pretty, and Mia wondered again why the godlike Krinar were attracted to humans in the first place. Was it the ability to drink their blood? If taking blood was as pleasurable as having it taken, then she could see the appeal.

Turning her attention to Delia, Mia thanked her for letting her know about the party in the first place.

"Of course," Delia said. "I'm glad you could make it. We heard you weren't in Lenkarda for the past week; otherwise, Maria would've sent you the formal invitation earlier."

"Yes, I was in Florida, visiting my family," Mia explained and saw Delia's eyebrows rise in question.

"Korum let you go there?" she asked, and there was a note of disbelief in her voice.

"We went together," said Mia, popping a strawberry into her mouth. The berry was sweet and juicy; the Krinar definitely knew how to get the best fruit.

"Oh," said Delia, "I see . . ." She seemed slightly confused by this turn of events.

"Do you ever go visit your family?" Mia inquired without thinking. "Are they still in Greece?"

Delia smiled, looking unaccountably amused. "No, they're no longer around."

"Oh, I'm so sorry . . ." Mia felt terrible. She'd had no idea this girl was an orphan.

"It's okay," Delia said calmly. "They passed away a long time ago. I now only have bits and pieces of memories about them. We didn't have photographs back then."

Mia began to get an inkling of the situation. "How long ago is a long time?" she asked, unable to contain her curiosity. No photographs? Just how old was Arus's charl?

"Oh, you don't know Delia's story?" said a brown-haired charl sitting to the right of Delia. "Delia, you should tell Mia—"

"I didn't get a chance, Sandra," Delia said, addressing the girl. "I only met Mia once before."

"Our Delia here is a bit older than she seems," Sandra said, an anticipatory grin on her face. "I just love the newbies' reactions when they hear her true age . . ."

Intrigued, Mia stared at the Greek girl. "What *is* your true age, Delia?"

"To the best of my knowledge, I will be two thousand three hundred and twelve this year."

Mia choked on a piece of strawberry she'd been eating. Coughing, she managed to clear her throat enough to wheeze out, "What?"

"Yep, you heard her right," Sandra said, laughing. "Delia is only a bit younger than some of the pyramids—"

And older than Korum. "You've been a charl this whole time?" Mia asked incredulously.

"Ever since I was nineteen," Delia said, looking at her with large brown eyes. "I met Arus on the coast of the Mediterranean, near my village. He was much younger then, barely two hundred years old, but to me, he was the epitome of wisdom and knowledge. I thought he was a god, especially when he showed me some of their miraculous technology. The day he took me to their ship I was convinced he brought me to Mount Olympus . . ."

"Where did you live this whole time? On Krina?" Mia was utterly fascinated. For some reason, she'd thought that Krinar-human liaisons were a fairly recent development. Although now that she thought about it, the existence of the charl/cheren terminology in Krinar language implied that these types of relationships had to have been around for a while.

"Yes," Delia said. "Arus took me to Krina when he left Earth. We lived there until the Krinar came here a few years ago."

Mia looked at her, imagining how shocking and overwhelming it must have been for someone from ancient Greece to end up on another planet. Even for Mia, who knew that the Krinar were not in any way supernatural, a lot of what they could do seemed like magic. What would it be like for someone who had never used a cell phone or a TV, who had no idea what a computer or a plane was?

"How did you cope with that?" Mia wondered. "I can't even picture what it must've been like for you."

Delia lifted her shoulders in a graceful shrug. "I'm not sure, to be honest. I can barely recall those early days at this point—everything is one big blur of images and impressions in my mind. I didn't handle the trip to Krina well, I remember that much. Your cheren—who wasn't even born at the time—has done a lot to make intergalactic travel safer and more comfortable. But back then, it was much more difficult. I was horribly sick during the entire trip because the ship wasn't optimized for humans, and it took me a few days to recover when I got to Krina, even with their medicine."

"Did you want to go?" Mia couldn't help feeling intense pity for a nineteen-year-old who had been taken away from everything she knew and brought to a strange and unfamiliar place.

Delia shrugged again. "I wanted to be with Arus, but I don't think I fully realized what that entailed. Obviously, I don't have any regrets now."

"Are there any charl who are older than you?"

"Yes," Delia said. "There are two of them. One is the charl of the biology expert who developed the process of extending human lifespan. He's almost five thousand years old. And another one is only about five hundred years older than me. She's originally from Africa."

"Wait, did you say he?" This was the first time Mia had heard about a male charl.

"Yes," Sandra said, joining their conversation. "I was surprised too. But some Krinar women—and men—take human men as their charl. It's much rarer, but it does happen. Sumuel—the original charl, as he's known—is actually with a mated couple."

Mia blinked. "Like a threesome?"

"Pretty much," Sandra said with a naughty grin on her face. "It's a somewhat unusual arrangement, but it works for them. The couple's daughter thinks of Sumuel as her third parent."

"The Krinar couple's daughter?"

"Yes, of course," said Delia. "We can't have children with the Krinar. We're not sufficiently compatible, genetically."

Even though Mia had known that, hearing Delia say the words gave her an odd little ache in her stomach. Over the past few days, Mia had been so happy that she hadn't had a chance to dwell on the negative aspects of always being with someone not of her own species. Korum had told her in the very beginning that he couldn't make her pregnant, and she'd had no reason to question that. Besides, she'd had other things on her mind. However, now that Mia was certain of a future with Korum, she realized what that future held—or, rather, what it didn't hold: children.

Mia didn't feel a burning urge to be a mother, at least not right now. Having a child was something she'd always pictured as part of a pleasant, nebulous future. She'd always assumed she would finish college, attend graduate school, and meet a nice man somewhere along the way. They would date for a couple of years, get engaged, have a small family wedding, and start thinking about children after they were married for some time. And instead, she had become an extraterrestrial's charl within a week of meeting him, gained immortality, and lost any chance of a normal human life.

Not that she minded, of course. Being with Korum, loving him, was so much more than she could've ever hoped for. And if somewhere deep inside, a small part of her felt hollow at the loss of her nonexistent son or daughter . . . Well, she could live with that. Perhaps, one day, she could even convince Korum to adopt.

So Mia pasted a smile on her face and turned her attention back to Delia, asking her about her experiences on Krina and what it was like to live for so long.

Over the next hour, Mia got to know both Delia and Sandra, learning about their stories and what the life of a charl was truly like. Unlike Delia, Sandra had only been in Lenkarda for three years. Originally from Italy, she'd met her cheren by accident on the Amalfi coast. For the most part, both Delia and Sandra seemed quite happy with their lives, although Mia got the sense that Arus treated Delia as a real partner, while Sandra's cheren spoiled her rotten, but didn't take her too seriously.

After most of the food at the table was gone, Maria challenged all the girls to a drinking game that seemed similar to truth-or-dare. For the 'dare' portion, they had to drink a full shot of tequila.

"Don't worry," Sandra whispered to Mia, "you won't have a chance to get too drunk—not even if you drink five shots an hour. Our bodies metabolize alcohol really quickly now."

Mia grinned, remembering the last time she'd gotten

wasted. It would've been nice to have all those nanocytes back at that club; it would've saved her quite a bit of embarrassment.

They played for an hour and Mia drank at least six shots, choosing the 'dare' option over answering some very probing questions about her sex life. Other girls had no such compunction, however, and Mia learned all about Moira's preference for black leather pants, Jenny's passion for foot massages, and the fact that Sandra had once had sex in a lifeboat.

Finally, the party came to an end. Feeling mildly buzzed, Mia headed home, eagerly anticipating seeing Korum and finishing what they had started earlier today.

* * *

Saret walked through the slums of Mexico City, dispassionately observing the dregs of humanity all around him. He had already planted the devices in the center of the city, so this excursion served no particular purpose except to satisfy his curiosity—and to reinforce in his mind the rightness of what he was doing.

On the corner, a pair of thugs were threatening a prostitute with a knife. She was reluctantly pulling money out of her bra and simultaneously swearing at them in very colorful Spanish. Saret walked in their direction, purposefully making noise, and the thugs scattered at his approach, leaving the whore alone. She took one look at Saret and ran away too, apparently realizing what he was.

Saret grinned to himself. *Fucking cowards.*

It was already after midnight, and the area was crawling with every kind of lowlife. Drug-related violence in Mexico hadn't gotten any better in recent years, and the country's government actually went so far as to appeal to the Krinar for help with this issue. After some debate, the Council decided against it, not wanting to get involved in human affairs. Saret had privately disagreed with that decision, but he voted the same way as Korum: against the involvement. It was never a good idea to openly oppose his so-called friend. Besides, it made no sense to help humans on such a limited scale. What Saret was doing would be far more effective.

He was heading back to where he left the transport pod when a dozen gang members made the fatal error of crossing his path. Armed with machine guns and high on coke, they apparently felt invincible enough to attack a K—a mistake for which they paid immediately.

The first few bullets managed to hit Saret, but none of the other ones did. Consumed by rage, he was hardly cognizant of his actions, operating solely on instinct—and his instinct was to rip apart and destroy anything that threatened him. By the time Saret regained control of himself, there were body parts all over the alley and the entire street stank of blood and death.

Disgusted with himself—and with the idiots who provoked him—Saret made his way back to the ship.

He was more convinced than ever that his path was a righteous one.

CHAPTER FOUR

The next day, Mia finished running the simulation for the third time and sent the digital results to Saret, hoping that he would get a chance to look at them soon. Without his feedback—or Adam's input—there was really nothing else she could do to move the project forward at this time.

It was only eleven a.m. on Wednesday, and she was already done with what she had set out to do in the lab for the day. Of course, she could always do some mind-related reading or watch some recordings, but that was something she tended to do in her spare time outside of the lab. Lab hours were for doing actual work, and Mia hoped she could find something to occupy herself with until she got the necessary feedback on her current project.

As usual, Saret was gone somewhere, and the other apprentices were in Thailand again. They'd left her alone in the lab—which Mia thought was probably a sign of trust. She doubted Saret would leave just anyone around all the complex lab equipment.

Getting up, she walked over to the common data storage facility—a Krinar device that was light years ahead of any human computer. Mia was just beginning to learn all of its capabilities, so she decided to use the downtime to explore it a little and brush up on some of the other apprentices' projects. The data unit responded to voice commands, which made it easy for Mia to operate it.

The next six hours seemed to fly by. Absorbed in her task, Mia hardly felt the passage of time as she read about the regenerative properties of Krinar brain tissue and the complexity of infant mind development. She took a short break for lunch—requesting a sandwich from the intelligent lab building—and then continued, fascinated by what she was learning. It seemed like the project that took the other apprentices away from the lab was even more interesting than what Mia and Adam were working on. Feeling slightly jealous, Mia decided to ask Saret if she could somehow get involved.

Finally, it was five o'clock. Although Mia typically stayed later in the lab, she decided to make an exception today, since nothing much was going on. Leaving the lab, she headed home.

Arriving at the house, she wasn't surprised to find that Korum wasn't there yet. His schedule was far more grueling than hers, although it helped that he didn't need to sleep more than a couple of hours a night. He actually got a lot of work done at night or early in the morning when Mia was sound asleep.

Making herself comfortable on the long floating plank in the living room, Mia decided to use the time to call

Jessie. They hadn't spoken since before Mia's trip to
Florida, and she really missed hearing her friend's bubbly
voice.

"Call Jessie," Mia told her wristwatch-bracelet device,
and heard the familiar dial tones as the call connected.

"Mia?" Jessie's voice sounded cautious.

"Yep, it's me," Mia said, grinning. She knew that the
call would show up on Jessie's phone as coming from an
unknown number. "How's it going? I haven't talked to
you in over a week!"

"Oh, I'm good," Jessie said, sounding a little
distracted. "How's your family? Did they already meet
Korum?"

"They sure did," Mia said. "Believe it or not, they
loved him. But hey, listen, are you busy right now? I can
call back another time—"

"What? Oh, no, hold on, let me just go into another
room . . ." A short silence, then, "Okay, I'm good now.
Sorry about that. I was just hanging out with Edgar and
Peter. Do you remember Peter?"

"Of course," Mia said. Peter was the guy she'd met at
the club—the one Korum had almost killed for dancing
with her. Mia still shuddered when she remembered that
terrifying night, when she'd thought Korum had found
out about her deception and was going to kill her. In
hindsight, she'd been an idiot; she should've known even
then that he would never harm her. But at the time,
Korum had still been a stranger to her, a member of the
mysterious and dangerous Krinar race that had invaded
Earth five years ago.

"He still asks about you," Jessie said—a bit wistfully,
Mia thought. "Edgar tells me he's really worried—"

"That's nice of him, but there's really no reason to
worry," Mia interrupted, uncomfortable with the

direction the conversation was taking. "Seriously, I'm happier than I've ever been in my life . . ."

Jessie fell silent for a second, and then Mia heard her sigh. "So that's it, huh?" she said softly. "You're in love with the K?"

"I am," Mia said, a big smile breaking out on her face. "And he loves me too. Oh, Jessie, you don't even know how happy he makes me. I could've never imagined it could be like this. It's like a dream come true—"

"Mia . . ." She could hear Jessie sighing again. "I'm happy for you, I really am . . . But, tell me, do you think you'll come back to New York?"

Mia hesitated for a moment. "I think so . . ." She was far less certain now than before. With each day that passed, college and all that it implied seemed less and less important. What use was a degree from a human university if she were to continue living and working in Lenkarda? She learned more in a day at the lab than she could in a month at NYU. Did it really make sense to spend another nine months writing papers and taking tests just for the sake of saying she got her diploma? And, more importantly, would Saret let her return to the lab after such a long absence? Given the rapid pace of research there, coming back after nine months would be almost like starting over.

"You don't sound sure," Jessie said, and there was a sad note in her voice.

"Yeah, I guess I'm not sure," Mia admitted. "Korum is fine with it, but I just don't know if I'll be able to return to my internship if I leave for so long . . ."

"So you like it there? At the K Center, I mean?"

"I do," Mia said. "Jessie, it's so nice here . . . I can't even begin to tell you how awesome some of their inventions are. Korum has a zero-gravity chamber in his house. Can you imagine that? And he's got a floor that massages your feet as you walk on it." Not to mention the fact that Mia was now pretty much immortal—but that was something she was not allowed to talk about outside of Lenkarda.

"Really? A floor that massages your feet?" Jessie sounded jealous now.

"Yep, and a bed that does the same thing to your whole body. All their technology is amazing, Jessie. Believe me when I tell you this: it's not a hardship to be here at all."

"Yeah, sounds like it," Jessie said, and Mia heard the resignation in her voice. "I guess I just miss you, that's all."

"I miss you too," Mia said. "Maybe I'll swing by for a visit in a couple of weeks. Let me talk to Korum about that, and we'll figure something out."

"Oh, that would be so nice!" Jessie sounded much more excited now.

"We'll make it happen," Mia promised, smiling. "I'll let you know when we're coming over. But, anyways, enough about that . . . Tell me about you and Edgar. How are things going on that front?"

And for the next ten minutes, Mia learned all about Jessie's new boyfriend, his latest acting gig, and the stuffed panda he'd won for Jessie at an amusement park. It seemed like the two of them were becoming increasingly close, and Mia was glad he made Jessie so happy. If anyone deserved to have a cute, caring guy, it was her former roommate.

Finally, Jessie had to go to dinner, so Mia said goodbye and went to change before Korum got home. He'd mentioned taking a post-dinner walk on the beach, and Mia wanted to make sure she had her swimsuit ready.

* * *

"So when do you think the Council will finally decide about the Keiths?" Mia asked, taking a bite of sweet pepper stuffed with mushroom-flavored rice. "Are they still doing the investigation?"

Korum nodded, picking up a piece of mushroom with the tong-like utensil the Krinar used in place of forks. "Loris is being difficult, as you'd expect. He's got a couple of Councilors on his side, and he's claiming there's no way Saur could've erased the Keiths' memories. Supposedly, someone from the Fiji lab told him that apprentices don't have access to that kind of equipment."

"Really? So, what, he's still saying that you and Saret are responsible for this?"

"I think he gave up on the idea of framing Saret," Korum said, a mocking smile appearing on his lips. "He's now seeking evidence to come after me."

Mia stared at him, concerned about this development. The black-garbed Krinar she'd seen at the trial didn't seem like someone who could be trifled with—and he truly hated Korum. "Do you think there's any chance he could cause trouble for you?"

"No, don't worry, my sweet," Korum said reassuringly, though his eyes glittered with something that looked like anticipation. "He's just trying to delay the inevitable. He failed as the Protector, and he knows it. Once his son and the rest of those traitors are sentenced, he'll lose all of his standing—and his position on the Council along with it."

"And you don't mind that in the least, right?" Mia asked, regarding him with a wry smile. For better or for worse, her lover tended to be quite ruthless with his opponents—a personality trait that made her glad she was now on his good side.

Korum shrugged. "It was Loris's choice to risk everything for his son. Now he'll pay the price. And if I have fewer people who stand in my way as a result, then all the better."

Mia nodded and concentrated on finishing the rest of her stuffed pepper dish. Despite everything, she couldn't help feeling just a tiny bit sympathetic toward the Protector. After all, the K was only defending his son. She imagined she'd do the same for her child—not that she had to worry about that anymore, she reminded herself. Pushing away the unpleasant thought, Mia looked at Korum instead, studying him covertly as he finished his meal.

Sometimes it was still difficult for her to believe they were so happy together. By Krinar law, she belonged to Korum—a fact that still made her very uncomfortable. As a charl, her legal standing in K society was murky, to say the least. If she didn't love him so much—and if he didn't treat her as well as he did—her life could've easily been miserable.

But she did love him. And he loved her back, with all the intensity in his nature. As a result, he seemed to be trying to suppress his inborn arrogance, knowing that it was important for her to be regarded as an equal. There was still a long way to go, of course—the gap of age and experience was too wide to be bridged easily—but he was definitely making an effort in that direction.

After they were both done with the meal, Korum stood up and offered her his hand. "Up for a walk, my sweet?" he asked, giving her a warm smile.

Mia grinned. "Sure." She loved these after-dinner walks on the beach. They'd done them almost every night when they were in Florida, and she'd learned a great deal about Korum during those quiet times. Taking his hand, she let him lead her outside.

They walked for a couple of minutes in silence, enjoying the soft evening breeze. The sun was just setting behind the trees, and an orange glow lit the sky, reflecting off the water shimmering in the distance.

"You know," Mia said, thinking about their first meeting in New York, "I still don't know your full name. You said I wouldn't be able to pronounce it if you told me, but I've never heard anyone call you anything but Korum."

He grinned. "Our full names are generally only used at birth and at death. Do you still want to hear it?"

"Of course." She imagined something totally unpronounceable. "What is it?"

"Nathrandokorum."

"Oh, that sounds kind of nice," Mia said, surprised. "Why don't you use it more?"

He shrugged. "I don't know. That's just the way it's been with us for a long time. Full names have become nothing more than a formality. I doubt that anyone besides my parents knows that I'm called Nathrandokorum."

Mia smiled, shaking her head. Some parts of the Krinar culture were strange indeed.

They walked some more, and then Mia remembered her recent conversation with her former roommate. "Do you think we might have a chance to visit New York soon?" she asked. "I was talking to Jessie, and it would be really nice to see her . . ."

Korum smiled, looking down at her. "Of course. If you

want, we can go the next time you have a day off. Unless you want to go for longer?"

"No, a day would be perfect. I guess sometimes I still forget that we can just pop on over there whenever we want."

His smile widened. "We definitely can—especially now that most of the Resistance has been captured."

"Where's Leslie?" Mia asked, remembering the girl who had attacked her in Florida. "Is she here, in Lenkarda?"

Korum shook his head. "No, she's in our Arizona Center."

"Is she . . . all right?" Mia was almost afraid to know the answer. The Resistance fighter had teamed up with Saur—the former apprentice from Saret's lab—to try to kill Korum in Florida. Now she was in K custody, about to be 'rehabilitated.' From what Mia understood about the process, the end goal was to change that part of Leslie's personality that made her a danger to society (or to the Krinar, as the matter may be). Rehabilitation—or mind tampering—was the most advanced branch of Krinar neuroscience, and Mia was just starting to learn about it at the lab.

"I assume so," Korum said, his expression cooling. He obviously hadn't forgotten the fact that the girl had pointed a gun at Mia and almost gotten her killed by Saur.

"Could you find out for me, please?" For some reason, Mia felt responsible for what happened to Leslie, even though the girl had attacked *her*. Still, she couldn't help remembering the terror on Leslie's face as she was led away by the K guardians. However misguided the fighter's intentions were, she didn't deserve to be mistreated, and Mia sincerely hoped she didn't get hurt during her rehabilitation.

Korum hesitated, then nodded curtly. "All right, I will." His jaw tightened, however, and Mia could see that he was thinking about the beach incident again. To distract him, she squeezed his hand and gave him a big smile. "Thank you," she said. "I really appreciate it."

"Of course, my darling," he said, his expression visibly softening. "Anything to make you happy—you know that." And bending down, he brushed his lips against her mouth in a brief kiss.

"So what are the guardians, anyway?" Mia asked when they started walking again. "Are they like your police?"

"Something like that," Korum said. "They're a cross between soldiers, police, and one of your intelligence agencies. They enforce our laws, catch criminals, and deal with any kind of threat from humans. Our society is so homogenized at this point that we no longer have war on Krina, the way you do here on Earth. There are still some regional rivalries, of course, and there are always a few crazies who disagree with the way things are done by the government, but we don't have the kind of conflict that would require a standing army."

"So you guys managed to invade our planet without an army?"

Korum laughed. "If you want to think about it that way. Most Krinar males who came to Earth received military-style training because we were expecting some resistance. But no, we didn't need a big army to control Earth; all we needed was our technology."

"Of course." Mia tried to keep the bitterness out of her voice. Loving Korum the way she did made it easy to forget that she was doing the equivalent of sleeping with the enemy—even if the enemy didn't actually intend her planet any harm. It was only during these types of conversations that Mia was unpleasantly reminded of the fact that the Krinar forcefully took over her planet . . . and that the man who loved her did not necessarily have humankind's best interests at heart.

"Trust me, Mia, it was better this way," Korum said, as though reading her mind. "Your government had no choice but to accept the inevitable, and that helped minimize the bloodshed. It would've been far worse if there had been a full-out war between our people."

Mia's mouth tightened, but she nodded, knowing he was right. There was no point in resenting the Krinar's technological superiority; in a way, it did make their invasion as painless as possible. The fact that they invaded at all was a different matter, of course—but Mia didn't have the energy or the inclination to fight that particular battle. Working with the Resistance once was enough.

"Can I ask you something?" Mia said, thinking back to those crazy days when she was spying on Korum. "I don't get one thing about the Keiths' plans. Even if they were successful in getting all the Krinar to leave Earth, wouldn't your people have come back with reinforcements? I know you said they were going to kill *you*, but what about all the others? Are you the only one with the means to go back and forth between Earth and Krina?"

Korum shot her an amused glance. "No, of course not. My company has the most advanced ship designs, but the Krinar have traveled to and from Earth long before I was even born. I think the Keiths were hoping to control the protective field."

"The protective field?"

He nodded. "Up until a dozen years ago, space travel was largely unregulated. Anyone could go anywhere, as long as they had a ship to take them there. Now, however, we have a shield in place to protect Earth from unauthorized travel—the same kind of shield we recently put around Krina."

"There is a shield around Earth?" Mia looked up at him in surprise.

"It's actually a shield around the solar system," Korum explained. "Not like a barrier, but more of a disruptor field. When activated, it messes with our ships' faster-than-light capabilities."

"Why would you want something that can mess with your ships?"

"For security purposes, we want to make sure the Council is informed of—and authorizes—any travel between Earth and Krina. Also, if there happen to be any other intelligent life forms out there, and they use technology comparable to ours, the shields will afford us some protection from them."

Mia gave him an ironic look. "So they can't do to you what you did to us?"

"Exactly." He grinned at her, looking so unrepentant that Mia couldn't help but laugh.

"Okay," she said, returning to her original question, "so what were the Keiths going to do? Use the protective field to keep the rest of the Krinar out?"

"Probably," Korum said, still smiling. "That's what I would've done in their place."

They walked for a few more minutes before they reached the ocean. As usual, this section of the beach was completely deserted. With only five thousand Ks in the Costa Rican settlement, there was plenty of space for everyone and most Krinar tended to keep out of each other's 'territories'—as informal as those were in modern times. Since Korum liked to take evening walks on this particular stretch of sand, the other Ks respectfully stayed clear of it.

"Do you want to go for a swim?" Mia asked, letting go of his hand and kicking off her shoes to test the water temperature with her toe. It was perfect—just cool enough to be refreshing.

Instead of answering, Korum pulled off his shirt, revealing a bronzed, muscular torso. "Absolutely," he said, his eyes turning more golden by the second.

Smiling, Mia took a few steps back and slowly took off her dress, loving the way his gaze was glued to her every move. She could see the erection growing in his shorts, and her nipples hardened in response, her body affected by his desire. The fact that she could do this to him by simply stripping down to her swimsuit was exhilarating—and incredibly flattering.

"Are you teasing me?" he asked, his voice low and dangerously soft.

Her heart pounding with excitement, Mia nodded, watching his eyes narrow at her answer.

"I see," he said thoughtfully. And before she could blink, he was already on her, sweeping her up into his arms and carrying her into the water.

Held securely in his embrace, Mia laughed, reveling in the coolness of the water as they went deeper and deeper. "Is this to be my punishment?" she joked as he paused, waiting for a large wave to pass them by before going further.

"Oh, you want to be punished?" he murmured, looking down at her with a heated gleam in his eyes.

Grinning, Mia shook her head. "No . . ."

"I think you do . . ." he said softly, shifting her in his arms so that he was holding her with only one hand. Before Mia could say anything, his other hand slipped inside her swimming suit and pressed against her sex, unerringly finding her clit and pinching it between his fingers.

She bucked against him, startled by the strong sensation, and he did it again, watching her face closely. "Does it hurt?" he asked, his voice like rough velvet. "Or does it feel good?"

Mia gasped as his fingers increased the pressure. "I don't know . . ."

"Oh, I think you do," he whispered. "I think you know very well . . ." His fingers slipped inside, stretching her open.

"Korum, please . . ." She could feel him curving one of the fingers inside her, rubbing against her G-spot.

"You're wet," he murmured, "so slick I can feel it even in the ocean. It makes me want to fuck you right here and now."

"So do it," Mia breathed, staring up at him. "Fuck me." She was already on the verge of orgasm—all she needed was a tiny push to bring her over the edge.

His eyes flared brighter. "Oh, I will . . ." Within seconds, she was fully naked, the torn remnants of her swimsuit floating around them. His shorts met the same fate, and then he was lowering her to her feet, letting her slide down his body. Looping her arms around his neck, Mia pressed against him. Her breasts felt tender, her nipples sensitized, and she rubbed them against his chest to assuage the ache deep within. His erection nudged at her belly, thick and hot, and her sex pulsed with the need to take him inside.

Leaning forward, she kissed his lips, tasting the salt from the ocean spray and the uniquely delicious essence that was Korum. He groaned, deepening the kiss, and Mia sucked on his tongue, stroking it with her own. At the same time, she reached under the water, wrapping her fingers around his hard shaft. It jumped at her touch, swelling up further, and Korum inhaled sharply, lifting her up and opening her thighs wide. A wave hit them, the water droplets spraying Mia's face, and she closed her eyes, grabbing onto Korum's shoulders with both hands. For a brief second, the tip of his cock brushed against her entrance, and then he pushed inside her in one powerful stroke.

Mia gasped at the invasion, her inner muscles tightening at the feel of him so deep within. Wrapping her legs around his waist, she held him there, reveling in the amazing sensation.

"Fuck," he groaned. "You feel so ... fucking ... good ..." He punctuated each word with a small, shallow thrust, his pelvis grinding against her clitoris, and Mia cried out as a sudden climax ripped through her, causing her sex to spasm around his thickness. He groaned again, and continued thrusting into her, lifting her up and down on his cock with a relentless rhythm that sent her over the edge again, just a few minutes later. This time, he joined her, and she felt the warmth of his release deep inside her belly.

And then they simply floated there, letting the waves rock them back and forth.

CHAPTER FIVE

The next morning, Mia again found herself alone in the lab. Saret was still traveling and hadn't sent her his feedback, so she continued learning about the other projects until her stomach rumbled, reminding her that it was time to eat.

Getting up, she stretched and requested a popular Krinar stew for lunch. The intelligent lab building provided it five minutes later, and Mia sat down to eat at one of the floating table-planks.

For some reason, her thoughts kept turning to the conversation she'd had with Korum yesterday and the Resistance fighter she'd helped capture. Leslie was going to undergo mind manipulation, and Mia couldn't help wondering how much the girl would be changed in the process. She couldn't imagine someone tampering with *her* thoughts, feelings, and memories, and she felt bad that another person would be subjected to something so invasive. Surely there had to be a better way to dissuade

Leslie from her futile fight against the Krinar. Perhaps someone could talk to her, explain that the Krinar didn't have any sinister intentions toward Earth . . . Of course, it was possible that the girl's hatred of the invaders went too deep to allow for rational thinking.

Sighing, Mia finished her meal and went back to the data storage unit. As she was about to pull up the infant mind development project, she paused, remembering a tidbit Adam had mentioned to her at some point. Saur—the K who'd tried to kill Korum—had once been an apprentice in this very lab, and he was supposedly quite good at mind manipulation. If some of his old projects were still stored here, they might help her gain a better understanding of what was going to be done to Leslie.

Suddenly excited, Mia ordered the unit to locate all the data that Saur had added. There was a lot, but she had plenty of time to kill.

Making herself comfortable, Mia dove into the intricacies of the tampered mind.

Five hours later, she got up again, deeply puzzled. She'd just begun to scratch the surface of everything Saur had worked on, but none of it was directly related to memory erasure. There were plenty of notes and recordings on behavioral conditioning and memory implantation—but only brief mentions of intentional memory removal.

If Mia understood it correctly, Saur had never even done memory wipe simulations, much less had any practice with live subjects.

Frowning, Mia stared at the data unit, oddly disturbed by what she'd just learned. Something didn't quite make sense to her. If Saur didn't know how to erase memories, shouldn't Saret have said something about that to the Council? Her boss always knew who was working on which project; he was the one who gave everyone their assignments.

Maybe she was wrong. Maybe there was some other data storage place that she didn't know about where other projects were kept. It was possible: Mia was still new and learning her way around.

It was also possible that Saur simply hadn't bothered inputting some of his projects into the common database. Adam had mentioned once that the dead apprentice was a bit strange—a loner who didn't get along with anyone else. He could've easily had trouble following the lab's protocol.

Still, Mia couldn't shake an uneasy feeling in her stomach, a nagging sense that something wasn't quite right with this picture. She needed to talk to Korum and soon.

Pausing to send Korum a brief holographic message telling him that she'd be home in a few minutes, Mia headed toward one of the exit walls.

And as she was about to walk out, the wall in front of her dissolved, and her boss came into the lab.

"Well, hello there," Saret said, looking down at her with a smile. "You didn't go home yet? I was hoping you'd get a chance to take it easy, with all of us out and about these past couple of days."

Mia smiled back, trying to hide her nervousness. "No, I was just brushing up on some of the other projects here," she said, staying as close to the truth as possible. "The one Aners is working on is really interesting. You know, with the infant mind development?"

"Sure." Saret's smile changed—becoming almost indulgent, Mia thought. "That's a great project for you to get involved with. We can talk about it later, once you and Adam are done with your current task."

"Great!" Mia injected the appropriate amount of enthusiasm into her voice and tried to ignore the way her palms had begun to sweat. "I'm really looking forward to it. Thanks again for giving me this opportunity."

"Of course." Saret's brown eyes gleamed as he took a couple of steps toward her. Pausing less than two feet away, he said, "I'm glad you're having a good time here."

Mia nodded, still maintaining a big smile on her face. Maybe she was being an idiot, but the vibes she was getting from her boss today made her decidedly uncomfortable. All she wanted was to go home and talk to Korum about what she'd learned. Most likely, there was a good explanation for everything, but on the slight chance there wasn't, she didn't want to linger in the lab any longer than necessary. And it was the second time Saret had acted almost . . . weird.

"Okay, then," she said brightly, looking up at his darkly bronzed face. "Please take a look at the report when you get a chance, and I'll head on out for now. Unless you need me?"

Saret smiled again. "I always need you," he said, and there was an unusually soft note in his voice. "But you must have your rest, I understand . . ." And Mia's heartbeat spiked as he leaned even closer, his eyes seemingly glued to her exposed shoulder.

"All right then—" she backed away, "—I'll see you soon." And turning around, she took a step toward the wall leading to the outside.

"Is anything wrong, Mia?" Saret was suddenly in front of her, blocking the way. "You seem worried."

Every hair on Mia's body was standing on end. "Sorry," she said insincerely, forcing a quick laugh. Even to her own ears, it sounded fake. "I'm just thinking about going to New York to see my roommate, that's all."

"Oh, is that right?" Saret cocked his head to the side. "And when are you planning to go?"

"Oh, it won't be for long." Mia cursed herself for blurting out that tidbit and prolonging the conversation. "We'll go on one of the rest days—"

"So why are you so anxious?" Saret asked, a strange look in his eyes. "Is it because you found something you shouldn't have?"

Mia swallowed, a cold chill snaking down her spine. "I'm not sure what you're talking about . . ."

Saret smiled—the same friendly smile that had made Mia like him before. Now she found it frightening instead. "What made you look at Saur's files today?" he inquired casually. "Don't you know it's against the lab protocol to access other apprentices' projects?"

Mia shook her head. She hadn't known, in fact. Staring at Saret, she felt like she was seeing him for the first time. He was Korum's friend. Why was he doing this? Why had he misled everyone about Saur's abilities? And, more importantly, what did he intend to do to keep Mia from telling everyone?

Thinking furiously, she realized that denial would be useless at this point. Somehow Saret knew about Mia's discovery. "Why?" she asked him instead, keeping her voice steady despite the fact that her hands were beginning to shake. "Why didn't you tell the Council Saur couldn't have done it?"

Saret's smile widened. "Because it was convenient to have them think he did," he explained, and there was something triumphant in his gaze. "It wasn't what I originally intended, but it worked out regardless."

Her fear growing by the minute, Mia took a step back.

Her every instinct was screaming for her to get out, *now*. Maybe there was still a good explanation for Saret's actions, but she couldn't take that chance. Casting aside all remnants of politeness, Mia swiftly lifted her wristwatch-bracelet to her face. "Call Kor—"

But she didn't get a chance to complete her request. His hand was suddenly around her wrist, holding it in a steely grip. Strong fingers ripped away the device, crushing it in the process.

"Oh, no," Saret said softly, dragging her toward him until she was pressed flat against his muscular body. "You don't get to call him anymore, you understand?"

Stunned and terrified, Mia stared at the K who'd been her boss and mentor for the past month. His hand was wrapped around her wrist, twisting it in such a way that she couldn't move at all. To her horror, Mia realized that he was hard, his erection pressing threateningly into the softness of her belly.

"What are you doing?" she whispered, hot bile rising in her throat. "Korum will kill you for this, you know that . . ."

Saret's eyes glittered. "Oh, will he, now? He's more than welcome to come find you here. The lab is set up quite nicely for his arrival."

"What?" Surely he wasn't saying—

"I mean, when your cheren arrives, I'll have a little surprise for him," Saret said, giving her a gentle smile. "You see, Mia dear, it's about time you knew the truth about your lover. Come, let's go into my office and we'll talk."

And without giving her a choice in the matter, he pulled her toward the back of the room, his fingers wrapped firmly around her wrist. Upon their approach, one of the walls dissolved, creating an entrance into the space Saret used for private projects.

Her knees weak with fear, Mia stumbled as he tugged her into the opening, the wall sealing shut behind her. Before she could fall, however, Saret caught her, lifting her up in his arms.

"There," he said soothingly, sitting down on one of the floating planks with her held tightly in his lap. "I've got you . . . No need to worry—you'll be all right," he added, apparently feeling the tremors shaking her frame.

"Let go," Mia whispered, pushing at his chest with all her strength. She could feel a hard bulge pressing against her thighs, and her stomach twisted with nausea. Her voice rose hysterically. "Let me go, right now!"

He didn't reply, his eyes darkening as he stared at her. The expression on his face was almost . . . enraptured, Mia realized with horror. For some reason, he wanted her, and there was nothing she could do to stop him if he decided to act on that inclination.

"You said you were going to tell me something about Korum," she said in desperation, her voice shrill with panic. "What don't I know about him?"

Saret blinked, his gaze clearing a little. "Oh, yes," he said, a self-deprecating smile appearing on his lips. "We were going to talk, weren't we? Here, you better have a seat . . ." And lifting her off his lap, he placed her next to him, keeping one hand wrapped firmly around her arm.

Mia immediately tried to scoot back further, but his grip tightened, preventing her from moving from the spot.

"Listen to me, Mia," Saret said, a small frown creasing his forehead, "I know you don't understand why I'm doing this right now and it all seems crazy to you. But, believe me, it's for your own good—for the good of all humanity. What your cheren intends for your people is not pretty, and he needs to be stopped. Do you know what he's trying to get the Elders to agree to?"

Mia shook her head, her stomach churning as his grip softened on her arm, his thumb gently massaging her skin.

"He wants to take your planet from you. Did he tell you that?"

"No," Mia managed to say, her heart pounding so hard she could barely think. Saret was lying to her, of course. He had to be.

"My so-called friend is a power-hungry monster," Saret said, his gaze hardening. "It wasn't enough for him to achieve the highest standing on Krina. Oh no, Mia dear, he had to extend his reign to another planet—to your planet. If it hadn't been for him, we would've never come to Earth. He was the one who convinced the Elders it was necessary to control your planet, to save it for the future generations of Krinar. And now he plans to take it from you completely. Do you understand what I'm saying?"

Mia nodded, wanting to keep him talking. She would listen to his lies for as long as necessary if it would only buy her time. In another few minutes, Korum would realize that she didn't come home as promised. Would he come looking for her then? Walk into whatever trap Saret seemed to be setting? *Please don't let anything happen to him. Please don't let anything happen to him.*

"You see, Mia," Saret continued, "all I want is what's good for your people—what's good for the greatest number of intelligent beings. I want to liberate Earth, free it from the tyranny of Korum and the Council. I want you to have your planet back."

"Why? What does it matter to you?" Was Saret one of the Keiths? And if so, how had he managed to escape detection for so long?

"Why? Because I've always wanted to do something great." Saret's voice was filled with barely suppressed excitement. "All our contributions to society, all this—" he waved a hand toward the lab, "—pales in comparison with liberating billions of intelligent beings, with giving them a better life . . . a peaceful life free from terror. I don't want to be remembered for coming up with yet another way to enhance memories, Mia. I want to be the one to bring peace to Earth."

"Peace to Earth?" That sounded insane to her. "But we're not at war with the Krinar—"

"Oh no, getting rid of the Krinar is just the beginning." Saret laughed. "You see, Mia, I can also give your people a better life. I can make it so you don't have to spend your few short decades fearing war, drive-by shootings, terrorist attacks . . . I can give you what humans have been dreaming about since the beginning of time: a life free of fear and violence. Wouldn't you want that, Mia? Wouldn't you like that for your people?"

"What are you talking about?" Was there such a thing as mental illness among the Ks? Was she stuck here with a madman?

"I know you don't understand now, but you will—I promise you that." Saret's face was almost glowing with fervor. "When your murder rates drop to zero and war is a thing of the past, your world will know that a new era in human history has arrived—and they will thank me for it."

Mia stared at him, unable to comprehend what he was saying for a minute. Then a horrifying and implausible idea occurred to her. "Saret," she said slowly, looking at the K known to be one of the greatest mind experts, "are you talking about some kind of mind manipulation for humans?" *Please let him laugh and tell me it's not true. Please don't let it be true.*

Saret gave her a pleased smile, his hand now caressing her arm, making her skin crawl. "Yes, Mia dear, that's exactly what I'm talking about. I always knew you were bright for your species. You see, over the past few years, I developed and perfected a new technique, a way to monitor certain neural impulses while simultaneously stimulating the pain and pleasure centers of the brain—"

Mia sucked in her breath. "Are you saying—" Her voice broke for a second, and she had to start again. "Are you saying you developed some kind of mind control?"

Now Saret laughed, his brown eyes crinkling with amusement. "No, of course not. Hopefully you've learned enough by now to know that true mind control is impossible. No, my technique allows me to direct certain behaviors—to condition the brain, if you will. Every time someone has a violent thought, for instance, I can make them experience pain. Every time they obey me— pleasure. Imagine: an entire planet full of peaceful humans . . . Wouldn't you want that, Mia?"

What Mia wanted was to throw up. "But how? How can you do something like that on a mass scale?"

Saret grinned, obviously enjoying her reaction. "Well," he said, "that's where Rafor and the rest of the Keiths come in. As you probably know, Rafor was nowhere near as good as your cheren at technological design, but he was decent enough to occupy a high position in his father's company. After Korum put them out of business, poor Rafor was left at loose ends. You see, since he lost his standing, no one else would hire him as a designer, and he was forced to dabble in a variety of subjects that didn't interest him nearly as much as his original chosen field. He even came to me a couple of years ago, asking if he could do an apprenticeship at the lab.

"I declined, of course. He was nowhere near qualified enough to be here. You weren't either, being a human and all, but at least you had the passion for the subject. He didn't even have that." Saret let out a chuckle. "But, in any case, I did offer him a chance to help me out on a private project, to design the nanocytes I needed to implement the plan. He understood immediately what I was trying to do—it aligned well with his own sympathetic views toward humans—and he did an excellent job creating both the nano design and the dispersion mechanism."

Mia listened to him intently, hardly daring to breathe. What he was telling her now was so incredible—and so terrifying—that she could barely process what she was hearing.

"Of course, Rafor failed miserably at the first part of the plan," Saret continued. "He was supposed to get rid of Korum and the rest with the help of the Resistance, but he got caught instead."

Mia swallowed to get rid of the dryness in her throat. "So you erased their memories," she guessed, and Saret nodded, smiling.

"I did. I had no choice. It was the only way to protect myself and the rest of the plan. Plus, it did give the Keiths a chance at the trial."

"So the Protector was right: you were the one all along—"

"He was partially right." Saret's smile was bright and happy. "He thought I erased their memories to help Korum, but nothing could be further from the truth. It hindered your cheren's agenda quite a bit—a nice, if not entirely intentional, side effect of the whole thing."

"Why do you hate him so much? He thinks of you as a

friend—"

The dark-haired K laughed, throwing his head back. "Of course he does—I made sure of that. Only an idiot would want Korum for an enemy. I've seen him destroy those who stand in his way, and I've never made that mistake."

"You're making that mistake now," Mia cautiously pointed out, glancing at where his fingers were still wrapped around her arm. If Korum were here, Saret would already be dead. If there was one thing she'd learned over the past few weeks, it was just how territorial Krinar males tended to be.

"Oh, because I'm touching his precious charl?" Saret said, his eyes gleaming with a mixture of excitement and some other unidentifiable emotion. "Don't worry, Mia dear, you won't be his for long. You'll be free of him soon. Just as soon as he gets here . . ."

Mia's blood turned to ice. "Are you—" She had to stop for a second because she couldn't force the words past the constriction in her throat. "Are you planning to kill him?" she finally managed to say.

"Most likely." Saret smiled at her again—that same friendly smile that made Mia want to scream. "It would probably be easiest. Of course, I could always try to capture him and put him through the same process as Saur. That would be the ultimate prize: having Korum himself in my control—"

"Saur? You mind-controlled Saur?" Mia stared at him in horrified disbelief. Had Saret actually made his former apprentice attack them in Ormond Beach?

"No." Saret looked disappointed at her lack of understanding. "Not mind control. I told you that. Mind conditioning. My technique works very subtly. It doesn't turn people into mindless zombies or whatever it is you're imagining—"

"But you mind-conditioned Saur to want to kill Korum?"

"I did," Saret admitted with a look of pride on his face. "It wasn't easy, believe me. All Krinar have immune system shields that repel nanocytes; it's something that was developed thousands of years ago after someone tried to use medical nanotechnology in warfare. I was only able to penetrate Saur's defenses after dozens of physical injections—and even then, the mind-conditioning only worked because Saur was weaker than most. That's why I wanted the Krinar to leave Earth: because I can't control them effectively. With humans, it's much easier. You're completely unshielded; all I need to do is release the nanocytes into the air in the most populated areas and they'll find their intended targets."

Mia's head was spinning. "So let me get this straight . . . You're trying to get rid of your own kind so that you can mind-control—or, rather, mind-condition— all the humans on Earth?"

"When you say it that way, it does sound crazy, doesn't it?" Saret smiled wryly. "But yes, that is indeed what I'm trying to do. I want to bring peace to your people, Mia. Is that such a bad thing? Think about it for a minute. Wouldn't you want to live in a world where you can walk down the street at night without worrying about getting killed or raped? Where serial killers are the stuff of horror movies, instead of existing in real life? No more school shootings, no more terrorism or war . . . Doesn't that sound like something you'd want?"

Mia stared at him. For a moment, the picture he painted did seem strangely appealing. "Of course," she said. "But what you're talking about is an invasion of our minds. You want to take away our free will—"

"Free will?" Saret raised his eyebrows. "How do you define free will? Your people will be free to live as they please, to be with whomever they want, to do whatever they want . . . They just won't be able to kill or hurt others when the urge strikes them."

"And they will worship you, right?" Mia said, her eyes narrowing. "That's what you ultimately want, isn't it? An entire planet full of puppets who will obey your every command?"

Saret laughed, shaking his head. "Put like that, it does sound awful, doesn't it? But no, Mia dear, that's not how I see it. Your people will worship me, true—but that's because I will be their savior. I will be the one to bring an end to their suffering, to liberate their planet and bring them peace."

"And what are you planning to do with the rest of the Krinar here?" Mia asked, the thought just occurring to her. "Korum foiled your plan with the Resistance, and all your people are still here. Don't you think they would notice if all the humans suddenly became peaceful? If murder rates went to zero overnight?"

"It wouldn't happen overnight," Saret said. "Complete mind conditioning takes many days, if not weeks. But yes, they would ultimately notice, of course—which is why I'll have to get rid of everyone in the Centers and make sure the protective field prevents anyone else from coming here any time soon."

Mia took a deep breath, fighting the urge to throw up. Surely he didn't mean— "Get rid of everyone how?"

He sighed. "By killing them, of course."

All color faded from Mia's face. "Killing all fifty thousand Krinar?" she whispered, unable to comprehend the evil required to do murder on that scale.

Saret shrugged. "The majority of them, yes. Some

might survive, of course, but most will perish."

"Perish how?" Mia could hear the hysterical edge in her own voice. "How can you possibly kill so many?"

"By utilizing that same nano weapon Rafor and the Resistance planned to use as a threat," Saret explained, looking at her calmly. "The design Korum gave us through you was faulty, of course, but it had enough of the right elements that I've been able to hire someone to perfect it. It's almost ready now; my designer is just putting the final touches on it."

"So let me get this clear," Mia said, staring at the psychopath sitting next to her, "you want to murder fifty thousand of your own kind in your quest to bring peace to Earth? And you don't see anything wrong with that?"

"Of course I do." Saret frowned. "Do you think I'll enjoy that part of the plan? I would've gladly sent them back to Krina or tried to control them if I could. But I can't. All I can do is try to make them disappear in as painless of a way as possible. I know it's not exactly consistent with my pacifist agenda. But you see, Mia, the good of the many far outweighs the needs of the few. We should've never come to your planet; it was your cheren's endless ambition that brought us here in the first place. Now we must atone for what we did; we must pay for our sins against your kind—"

"Are you going to kill me, too?" Mia felt her fear fading as a strange numbness started to set in. What he was intending was so horrific she simply couldn't process it fully. "Or are you planning to make me into a puppet? That's why you're telling me this, isn't it? Because you're not worried that I'll tell anyone?"

Saret grinned, releasing her arm and covering her hand with his palm instead. His touch felt scalding on her skin, making her realize how icy her hands had become.

"The thought of you as a puppet is rather appealing, I must say," he said, his eyes darkening again. "And maybe I'll do that eventually . . . But I'd rather not tamper with your mind too much at first. I quite like you as you are right now."

"So what are you going to do with me then?" Mia's tone was almost disinterested. "If you're not going to kill me, that is—"

"I won't kill you," Saret reassured her. "I'm simply going to make sure you don't remember this conversation—or anything else that happened in the past few months. It'll be for the best, you'll see . . . I know you got attached to that monster, and you'd probably miss him if he was gone. But this way, you'll be free from his influence forever. It will be as though he had never been in your life."

Mia stared at him, acidic rage starting to burn in the pit of her stomach. "You're going to kill Korum and erase my memory to make me forget him?"

"No, Mia dear," Saret said, smiling. "I wouldn't be that cruel to you. I will erase your memory first. That way, you won't feel anything when he dies. I don't want to put you through that kind of trauma, you see. Painful memories like that are the hardest to get rid of, and the last thing I'd want is to give you nightmares that linger in your subconscious—"

"You're insane," Mia said, her anger growing by the second. She welcomed the feeling because it helped clear the fog of terror from her brain. "You really think that's a mercy, invading my brain like that? And why do you care about me, anyway? You're about to murder fifty thousand Krinar without a second thought, and I'm just Korum's charl—"

"You know, I've asked myself that same question."

Saret's forehead creased in an introspective frown. "You're just a human girl—a pretty one, to be sure—but nothing all that special, to be honest. I didn't understand at first why Korum was so obsessed with you. But then a funny thing happened, Mia—" he leaned forward, his eyes gleaming darkly, "—I started wanting you myself."

He paused for a second, and then continued, ignoring the look of horrified disgust on her face. "Believe me, it's been hell, seeing you all the time and knowing that I don't have the right to touch you, that *he's* the one taking you to bed every night. But now things will be different. When you wake up, it will be as if he never existed . . . and you will be mine, the way you should've been from the very beginning."

Sickened to her very core, Mia tried to yank her hand away, hot nausea boiling up in her throat. He held her for a second, then let go, watching with a smile as she jumped back like a scalded cat.

"Never," she hissed, backing away toward the wall. "Do you hear me? I don't know what you're imagining here, but I'll never be with you willingly. You might be able to force me, but that's all it will ever be between us, memories or not—"

"Why?" Saret asked, still smiling. "Because you think you're in love with him? What does a twenty-year-old know about love? He seduced you, Mia, that's all. When he's gone from your life, I'll do the same—and you'll love me just as much as you thought you loved him."

Mia laughed, her desperation making her reckless. The thought of forgetting Korum and being forced to share the bed of a would-be mass murderer was so repugnant she thought she'd rather die. Maybe she could goad him into killing her. "Oh, really?" she said contemptuously. "I'm not even the least bit attracted to you, Saret. You're like dog food to me. I wanted Korum from the beginning—from the first moment I saw him. But not you. Never you. Do you understand me?"

As she spoke, she could see the smile fading from Saret's face, his expression hardening. "We'll see about that," he said, getting up and stalking toward her. "Once your memories are gone, you'll be singing a very different tune, believe me."

"No!" Mia screamed as he reached for her. Her nails curved into claws, raked down his arms as he grabbed her. "Get away from me, you sick fuck! No!!!"

Ignoring her yells and struggles, Saret lifted her and carried her out of his office, his arms like iron bands around her body. Walking to the far side of the lab, he placed her on one of the floating planks by the wall. The intelligent surface immediately wrapped itself around her arms and legs, holding her completely immobile while Saret reached into the wall and took out a small white device.

"No!" Mia tried to twist her head as he approached her again. "No! Don't!"

Saret paused for a second, looking down at her. "I'm sorry, Mia," he said softly. "I wish it weren't necessary. If I had only met you first... But this won't hurt, I promise..." And pressing the device to her forehead, he gave her a gentle smile.

That smile was the last thing Mia saw before her world faded into darkness.

Part II

CHAPTER SIX

Korum checked the time again.

Mia should've been home already. Her message had reached him twenty minutes ago, and he'd immediately cut short the testing session with his designers, unable to resist the urge to see her as soon as possible.

While waiting for her, he'd quickly prepared dinner, making her favorite *shari* salad and a mushroom-potato dish from a recipe given to him by Mia's mother. He'd asked Ella Stalis for it before they left Florida, wanting to surprise Mia with it someday. He loved seeing her small face light up with pleasure and excitement when he did things like that. Her happiness meant the world to him these days.

Where was she?

Mildly annoyed, Korum queried his computer to determine her location. The complex device embedded in his palm was completely synced with his neural pathways—so much so that using it was the equivalent of thinking in a certain way. Not all Krinar liked the idea of being so integrated with technology, with many choosing to stick to old-fashioned voice commands and stand-alone devices instead. Korum thought it was idiotic to be so mistrustful, but then again, he had designed the computer himself and understood its limits and capabilities. Many of his kind had no idea how even simple human electronics worked, nor did they have a desire to learn—something he would never understand.

As soon as he sent the mental query, her location came to him with crystal clarity: the lab. She was still at the lab. The tracking devices he'd once embedded in her hands were proving to be quite useful, even now that she was no longer involved with the Resistance.

His lips quirking in a smile, Korum thought about her reaction whenever the topic of his shining her came up. She was like an angry kitten then, all tiny claws and ruffled fur. It made him want to cuddle her and fuck her at the same time—a confusing mix of desires she always evoked in him.

He supposed he should feel bad for shining her. And sometimes, he almost did. She resented the fact that he would now always know her location, not understanding that it gave him a tremendous peace of mind. She was so fragile, so human . . . If he had his way, she would never leave his side; he'd always keep her next to him where he could protect her.

But he knew she wouldn't want that. It was important to her to have her independence, to excel in her chosen field and contribute to society. He understood and respected that, but it still didn't make it any easier on him. When they'd been in New York—before he'd given her the nanocytes that made her less vulnerable—it had been all he could do to let her venture out on her own, especially in a human city where something as stupid as a car accident could easily claim her life. That's why he'd always had a guardian following her then, staying no more than a hundred yards away at any given time. She'd never suspected, of course, nor was Korum ever planning to tell her. But it had been for her own protection; even back then, he hadn't been able to bear the thought of anything happening to her.

Checking the time again, Korum saw that twenty-five minutes had passed. Why was she still at the lab? Had something happened to delay her? If Saret was making her work late again, he'd have a serious talk with him. By now, Mia had proven herself quite useful, and Korum was certain his friend wouldn't terminate her apprenticeship even if she had to work fewer hours.

Sending another mental query, Korum reached out to the communication device he'd made for her—what she called her wristwatch-bracelet. To his surprise and growing disquiet, he couldn't connect to it at all; it was as if there was only emptiness where digital signals should've been.

Something was wrong.

Korum knew it with sudden certainty. Raising his hand, he stared down at his palm, his eyes following the tiny pulses of light playing underneath his skin. It was a way for him to concentrate, to utilize specific mental pathways that were more complex than those required for basic daily tasks.

This particular path was not something he'd used in recent weeks, not since the Resistance was defeated. Mia didn't know about this either, and Korum wasn't planning to tell her. There was no need; he'd stopped using the device to monitor her activities. The only reason why it was still on her is because the process for removing it was fairly complicated—and because he liked the idea of having it there for emergencies.

Keeping his eyes glued to his palm, Korum sent a deep probe, activating the tiny recording device hidden underneath Mia's left earlobe. It would allow him to hear everything in her vicinity and, more importantly, to check on her vital signs.

As soon as the device came on, some of the tension left his muscles. She was okay, her heartbeat strong and her breathing steady.

And yet . . . Korum frowned, listening carefully. Everything was quiet—too quiet. If she was still working, she should've been moving around, talking to whomever had delayed her. Instead, it was as if she was asleep right now.

Asleep . . . or unconscious.

As soon as he thought of the second possibility, he knew he was on the right track. But why would she be unconscious? This didn't make any sense. And was that . . . ? He listened again. Were those someone else's movements he was hearing around her?

His unease morphed into full-blown worry.

Getting up, Korum strode swiftly to the wall and exited the house. Pausing for a few seconds, he sent a mental command to have a transport pod created with all possible speed. While the nanomachines did their job, he reached deep into the recording device's archives. All the recorders he designed worked like that; even when they weren't activated to broadcast in real time, they were still collecting data and storing it internally.

It took a second, and then he was accessing the recorder's memories, scanning through them to find the right spot. He started with the exact moment when Mia sent him her message. Instead of listening to the recording at normal speed, he had his computer create an instant transcript, which he then read in a few seconds.

And as Korum understood what he was reading, every cell in his body filled with volcanic fury.

He couldn't even begin to process the magnitude of the betrayal—nor the sheer evil that was about to be unleashed by a man he'd considered a friend for the past two thousand years. And Mia . . . No, he couldn't think about it. Not now, at least. If they were all to survive, he needed to focus, to control his rage and pain.

Utilizing every ounce of willpower he possessed, Korum reached for the coolly rational side of himself and began to analyze the best way to handle the situation.

* * *

Saret watched impatiently as Korum finally left the house and created the transport pod. Now his nemesis would come looking for Mia, hopefully with minimal—if any—suspicions.

Of course, it would never do to underestimate him. The bastard always had some nasty surprises for those who did. Still, Korum had no reason to think anything sinister was going on, and he would certainly never expect Saret to try to kill him.

It was unfortunate that Mia had come across those files today. Saret had always known that someone could snoop around and figure out that Saur hadn't been quite as knowledgeable about memory erasure as he'd been portrayed to be. Saret should've moved the files, but everyone in the lab knew better than to access other people's work without Saret's explicit permission.

Everyone, except one human girl, as it turned out.

Then again, maybe on some level, Saret had wanted

her to find out. He'd enjoyed explaining his plan to her and watching the emotions on her expressive little face. She hadn't understood fully, of course, still too caught up in Korum's web to think clearly.

It had made him angry, what she'd said about not being attracted to him. She'd been lying, of course, trying to goad him into doing something stupid. He was a Krinar male in his prime; he knew full well that human women desired him. And she would want him too; he had made sure of that.

He would be gentle with her at first, not like Korum had been when they met. Saret had seen some of the recordings from the beginning of their relationship at the trial, and it had made him angry, the way his nemesis had handled her then. Saret would make a better cheren, he was certain of that.

Now where was Korum?

Frowning, Saret looked at the image again. It appeared his enemy was in no hurry. Instead of flying to the lab, Korum was standing next to the ship and leisurely chatting with some Krinar woman Saret had never seen before. He was almost ... flirting with her? *Fucking bastard, already cheating on Mia.*

Well, no matter, Korum would get here soon enough. And when he did, he would be in for a nice little surprise.

Unbeknownst to all, Saret had spent the past several years building a high-tech fortress within the lab. All Krinar buildings were durable, meant to withstand anything from a nuclear blast to a volcanic eruption. His lab, however, went a step further: the walls were weaponized—designed to kill anyone who tried to enter once Saret activated the protection mode. They were also impenetrable by any form of nanotechnology because Saret had installed the same shields that served as the

Centers' defenses.

It hadn't been easy, doing this. Weapons were not something that the general population had easy access to, especially specialized nano-weapons like those embedded in his walls. Saret had been forced to call in a lot of favors and spend a sizable chunk of his personal fortune to get everything set up exactly as he wanted it. It had cost him even more to keep everything a secret.

Now, however, it would all pay off. In another couple of days, the nano-weapon that he planned to use in the Centers would be ready. The dispersion devices with the nanocytes had already been planted in all the key human cities.

All he needed now was patience.

Another ten minutes, and Saret was losing what remained of that patience. What the hell was taking Korum so long? Had Saret underestimated his enemy's attachment to the girl? It looked like the bastard was still flirting with that woman. There he was now, laughing and touching her arm. *What the fuck?* Whatever happened to his obsession with Mia? Had she been just a toy for him all along?

As soon as the thought occurred to Saret, he dismissed it. No, something was up. He was suddenly certain of it.

Was his enemy playing him for a fool? Was he even now being fed a false image? There was no way to tell; the figures Saret was watching looked completely real. But, as Saret knew full well, looks could be deceiving.

He had to face the possibility that Korum had figured out something was going on.

Moving swiftly, Saret armed himself and put on a protective shield that wrapped around his entire body. The lab walls were still his best defense, and he had every intention of confronting his nemesis here, where Saret had the home advantage. He felt no fear, though his pulse spiked in anticipation of the upcoming fight.

Glancing at Mia, Saret made sure that she was still unconscious, lying restrained on the medical float. She might wake up soon, and he was hoping to have all the unpleasantness over with before that happened.

Ignoring the adrenaline rushing through his veins, Saret sat down next to her and stroked her arm, marveling at the smoothness of her pale skin. She looked so pretty, with her dark lashes fanning across her cheeks and that soft mouth slightly parted. What was that human children's story? Sleeping Beauty? Actually, she looked more like Snow White, Saret decided, with her milky complexion and dark hair.

Leaning down, he kissed her lips, brushing them lightly with his tongue. As he'd suspected, she was delicious; just that tiny taste was enough to make him hard. If he had more time, he would've taken her right then and there, unconscious or not.

But he didn't have more time. He needed to stay focused. One way or another, Korum would be here soon.

Getting up, Saret walked over to the image again. By now, he was almost certain it was fake.

Where was Korum?

Saret began to pace, too agitated to sit down again.

When it all began two minutes later, he didn't even notice at first.

A low humming sound was his first warning that something was wrong. The noise seemed to fill the air, gradually increasing in volume until it was almost a roar to his sensitive Krinar hearing.

Then the walls began to melt. Saret had never seen anything like it before: the material designed to withstand a nuclear blast seemed to liquefy from the top down, as if the building was made of wax.

Now Saret tasted fear. Sharp and acidic, it pooled low in his stomach. This wasn't supposed to happen. He was supposed to be safe here, in his carefully constructed fortress . . . but he wasn't. Saret didn't know of any weapon that could do this—that could penetrate the same shields that protected the colonies—but his eyes didn't lie. The walls were literally melting around him.

There was only one thing left to do: retreat and live to fight another day. For a second, Saret considered taking Mia with him, but she would slow him down and he couldn't take that risk. He would have to come back for her.

Casting one last look at the unconscious girl on the float, Saret activated the emergency escape chute and disappeared through the building floor.

CHAPTER SEVEN

"I want him found. By any means necessary. Do you understand me?" Korum was aware that his voice sounded sharp, but he could no longer contain the icy rage coursing through his veins.

Alir, the leader of the guardians, nodded. "We'll bring him to you," he promised, his black eyes cold and expressionless.

"Good," Korum said curtly.

Turning around, he stalked toward the back of the room, where Ellet was sitting beside Mia and running diagnostic tests.

At his approach, the Krinar woman looked up, signs of strain evident on her beautiful face. "She should regain consciousness soon," she said softly. "But, Korum, I'm afraid the damage has been done."

"What are you saying?" He didn't want to believe it, couldn't accept that possibility.

"I'm afraid the scan is showing signs of trauma

consistent with a memory loss. I'm so sorry—"

"No. You must be wrong." His fists clenched so hard his nails entered his skin, drawing blood. "There must be something we can do—"

"I'll look into it," Ellet said, rising from her sitting position. "But this type of erasure tends to be irreversible, I'm afraid."

Korum took a step forward. "I don't want you to look into this, Ellet," he said evenly. "I fucking want you to drop whatever else you're doing and bring her memory back."

Ellet frowned. "You know I'll do my best—"

"Do better than that." Korum knew he wasn't being rational, but he didn't care. He had never felt this way before—so savagely murderous. He wanted to tear Saret apart, to rip him up piece by piece and hear him scream in agony. He wanted to eviscerate the man he'd once regarded as a friend and bathe in his blood, like the ancients used to do with their enemies.

Underneath the swirling rage and bitterness at the betrayal, guilt—heavy and terrible—sat uncomfortably on Korum's shoulders. Mia had been hurt—hurt because of him. Because he'd failed to protect her from the monster in their midst. Because he'd been far too trusting. If it hadn't been for him, she would've never had that internship, would've never been exposed to Saret's sick cravings.

If he hadn't brought her to Lenkarda, she would've never been in harm's way.

How could Korum not have seen it earlier? How could he not have sensed that kind of hatred? His greatest enemy had turned out to be one of his closest friends— and he hadn't known until it was too late.

And now he could see pity on Ellet's face. She knew

how he felt about Mia and could probably guess at his mental state right now. "I will, Korum," she said soothingly. "I promise you, I'll do everything possible to help."

Korum took a deep, calming breath. It wasn't Ellet's fault his friend had turned out to be the worst psychopath in modern Krinar history. "Thanks," he said quietly.

Ellet smiled, looking relieved. "You can take her home now, if you'd like. She'll wake up naturally in a few hours, and it might as well be at your house. The fewer of us she has to deal with at first, the better."

Korum nodded. "Of course." Bending down over Mia's float, he carefully picked her up, cradling her gently against his chest. She was so light, so fragile in his arms. The realization that she could've been killed today was like poison in his veins, burning him from the inside.

Saret would pay for what he did to her—for what he planned to do to them all. Korum would make sure of that.

* * *

Mia let out a small huffing sound and wrinkled her nose, one slim hand coming up to brush a dark curl off her cheek. Her eyes were still closed for now, although it was obvious she was starting to regain consciousness.

Sitting on the edge of the bed, Korum watched her slowly wake up, unable to tear his eyes away. Logically, he knew she wasn't the most beautiful woman he'd ever seen, but it didn't matter. To him, she was perfect. He loved everything about her; each and every part of her delicate little body turned him on. Even now, as she lay there in her pale pink dress, he had to fight the urge to touch her, to bring her closer to him and bury himself deep inside her.

The unsettling mixture of lust and tenderness she evoked in him was unlike anything he'd ever felt before. Like many Krinar, Korum had always regarded sex as a fun recreational activity. Most of his prior relationships had been casual affairs, similar to the fling he'd had with Ellet a few years ago. He liked women and he enjoyed their company outside of the bedroom as well, but he had never wanted to be with one on a permanent basis—had never felt the urge to claim one as his own.

Until Mia.

For some reason, this human girl appealed to his darkest, most primitive instincts. The way he felt about her went beyond sexual desire, beyond a craving for her tender flesh. What he really wanted was to possess her completely, to have her be his in every possible way.

˙It was not an unknown phenomenon among the Krinar. In ancient times, Krinar males needed to hunt and to protect their territory—and they were far more likely to do an effective job if they were strongly attached to their mates. It had been a simple evolutionary adaptation at the time—a male's obsessive fixation on one specific female. Deeper than lust, stronger than love, it was a powerful combination of the two that ensured a man would give up his life to protect his woman and their offspring.

Over the years, as Krinar society became more civilized, that kind of attachment became less important to the species' survival, and the genetic tendency toward it weakened over time. It still happened, of course, but it was a fairly rare occurrence in modern times—which was why Korum hadn't realized what was going on when he first met Mia.

He hadn't understood at first why he was feeling that

way. All he'd known was that he wanted her—and that he had to have her. Even her initial reluctance hadn't been enough to deter him; if anything, her wariness had intrigued him, triggering the predatory instincts he normally managed to suppress.

He had never pursued someone like that before, had never been less than considerate of a woman's wishes, but with Mia, he had been ruthless. He'd gone after her with all the intensity in his nature, disregarding all notions of right and wrong. In less than a week, he'd gotten what he wanted: Mia in his bed, in his apartment—his to take whenever he wanted.

It had taken him far longer to earn her love.

To this day, he couldn't help the anger that stirred in his stomach when he thought about her involvement with the Resistance. Rationally, he knew he couldn't blame her for fighting back, for not trusting him in the beginning. She was a mere child in comparison to him; he should've been more cognizant of her fears, should've patiently seduced her instead of forcing her into the relationship. Perhaps then she wouldn't have believed the fighters' lies, wouldn't have betrayed him the way she did.

But he hadn't been patient. The strength of his emotions had caught him off-guard, blinding him to everything but the need to have her. What had begun as a sexual obsession had quickly become something much deeper, and Korum hadn't known how to cope with that. He'd acted out of hurt and anger, using her against the Resistance as punishment for spying on him, when he should've simply explained everything to her, made her understand his intentions.

The fact that she loved him now was a miracle—one that he was grateful for every day. And if she didn't remember him when she woke up, then he would use that as an opportunity for a new beginning, as a way to make amends for what happened before.

One way or another, Mia would love him again.

The alternative was unthinkable.

Finally, her eyelids fluttered open. She blinked, looking confused, then stared at him in open-mouthed shock.

Gently stroking her arm, Korum smiled. "Hello, my darling," he said, purposefully injecting a soothing note into his voice. What he really wanted was to hug her to him, but that would frighten her if she had indeed lost her memory and he was now a stranger to her.

As it was, he could hear her heartbeat speeding up, feel the sudden tension in her muscles as she realized what he was. Her small pink tongue came out, licking her bottom lip in that unconsciously provocative gesture that always drove him insane. He could see the fear in her eyes ... and it was like a knife to his heart, the pain sharp and slicing.

Yanking her arm away, she scrambled back, toward the other side of the bed. "What am I doing here? Who are you?"

Korum could hear the panic in her voice, and he forced himself to remain still, to not make any movements in her direction.

"I'm Korum," he said instead, looking for any sign of recognition on her face. But there was none. Pushing away his disappointment, he asked, "What's the last thing you remember, my sweet?"

She visibly swallowed, scooting back even further. "I'm in class," she whispered. "I'm taking a test ..."

"What test, my darling? What class are you in?" *Just how much memory had Saret erased?*

94

"My... my Child Psychology class," she answered, her voice shaking slightly.

Korum exhaled in relief. "So it's your Spring Semester." She'd only lost a couple of months, not years as he'd initially feared.

She nodded, still looking terrified. "What do you want from me? Why did you bring me here?" He could hear the rising hysteria in her voice.

Korum sighed. This was going to be difficult. "It's complicated, Mia," he said softly. "Would you like me to explain?"

She nodded again, her blue eyes wide and fearful.

"Then come here, and we'll talk," he said, watching as she tensed further. "I promise you, I won't hurt you in any way... Just sit here, beside me." He patted the bed, needing to have her closer.

She hesitated, and he saw the emotions flitting across her fine-featured face. He could tell the exact moment when she decided she had nothing to lose by accommodating his request. After all, he was a Krinar and thus equally dangerous up close or ten feet away.

Her slim body shaking, she slowly moved back in his direction, watching him warily. When she was close enough, Korum reached out and took her hand, warming her chilled skin between his palms.

She jerked initially, then stilled, her gaze trained on his face.

Korum smiled, some of the tension inside him easing because she allowed his touch. "We're lovers, Mia," he said gently, watching her reaction. "You don't remember me because you lost some of your memory. It's June now, and we're in Lenkarda, our Center in Costa Rica."

CHAPTER EIGHT

Mia stared at the gorgeous Krinar male who was now softly rubbing her hand. What he'd just told her was pure insanity. They were lovers? She'd lost her memory? Out of all the crazy scenarios running through Mia's mind, this hadn't even been on the list of possibilities.

Was he toying with her? If so, why, and what was the real story? Mia tried to control her panic long enough to think, but it was like a part of her brain was filled with fog. Even recent events—spring break, the exams— seemed blurry in her mind, as if they'd happened long ago instead of in the last couple of weeks.

"You don't believe me, do you?" the K asked, his amber-colored eyes watching her with unsettling warmth.

"No, of course not." Her voice was surprisingly calm. All things considered, Mia felt like she was handling this reasonably well. She wasn't crying or screaming, and she was actually carrying on a conversation with an alien who had most likely kidnapped her. An alien who might or might not drink human blood—and who was now stroking her wrist in a way that made her belly tighten with strange excitement.

Why wasn't she more afraid of him? Everything she knew about his kind suggested she should be terrified for her life.

But she wasn't.

She was freaking out because she didn't know where she was or how she'd gotten there—or why she was with a K who claimed to be her lover—but she wasn't truly afraid. If anything, she found his presence oddly comforting, his touch both soothing and electrifying. Had he done something to make her react this way?

"Of course not," he repeated, giving her an understanding smile. "How could you believe something so crazy without proof, right?"

Mia nodded, unable to tear her eyes away from that smile. The dimple in his left cheek fascinated her; it was so boyish, so incongruous with the rest of his appearance.

"All right, my darling." His voice was disconcertingly tender. "Let me show you proof." And still holding her hand, he gestured to the side, where a three-dimensional holographic image suddenly appeared in mid-air.

Mia gasped, startled, and then she saw that the image was of herself and the K beside her. They appeared to be walking on the beach, talking and laughing. The K reached down and picked up the girl in the image, lifting her as effortlessly as if she was made of air. She laughed again, then wound her arms around his neck, kissing him with such passion that Mia's cheeks heated up.

"What is that? Where did you get this video from?" Mia felt herself furiously blushing as the K kissed the girl back, holding her up with one arm and using the other to reach underneath her dress.

"It's just a recording from one of our satellites," the K named Korum explained, watching her with an unusual golden gleam in his eyes. For some reason, Mia could feel herself getting turned on by that look, her heart starting to beat faster and her nipples hardening underneath the thin fabric of her dress. She desperately hoped the K didn't notice; it would be embarrassing—and potentially dangerous—if he knew how much he affected her.

And then she realized what he just said. "Wait, your satellites were spying on us?"

"Our satellites are always recording everything," he explained, those sensuous lips curving into a smile. "But don't worry, my sweet, only our computers get to see it, unless someone places a specific request—the way I did."

Mia's pulse quickened, this time from anxiety. "Are you saying we never have any privacy from you?"

"Of course not," the K said casually. "You don't have much of it from your own government either. You know that, right?"

Mia blinked. She did know that. GPS and cell phones had made it practically impossible for a person to hide, and she knew that various government agencies used all the means at their disposal to track down terrorists and other criminals. As a law-abiding citizen, she'd never thought much about the fact that all her activities—from browsing the Internet to placing a phone call—could be monitored if necessary. She'd just accepted it as a part of life in the twenty-first century. But, for some reason, the idea of Krinar satellites watching her every move was more than a little disturbing.

Frowning, Mia realized she was acting as if the image being shown to her was real. There was absolutely no assurance of that; as advanced as the Krinar were, surely it would be child's play for them to conjure up whatever video they wanted, three-dimensional or not.

"How do I know you didn't make this up?" she said, gesturing toward the image where the couple were now engaged in a full-blown make-out session. Her blush deepening, Mia looked away again.

"You don't, of course," the Krinar said. "I could make this up if I wanted to. I have hundreds of other recordings I could show you, and you'd be smart not to trust any of them."

Mia laughed nervously, surprised by his frankness. "Okay then, how can you prove any of this to me?" She couldn't believe she was even entertaining the idea that this could be real. How could any rational person believe this? Surely she would remember if she'd had sex with a gorgeous alien . . . or even just had sex in general.

The K smiled again. "There are a number of ways," he said. "Let's start with the fact that you understand me right now, even though I'm speaking to you in Krinar."

Mia gaped at him in shock. She had definitely understood what he was saying, even though he'd said the last sentence in a language she was sure she'd never heard before. "Wait, what?" Her words came out in that same language. "You're talking to me in Krinar?"

"Yes, and you're answering me in Krinar too," he said, his smile widening. "And now I'm talking to you in Italian. You still understand me, right?"

Mia nodded, her head spinning from the impossibility of it all.

"That's because you have a tiny implant that acts as a translator," the K explained, this time in English. "I gave it to you as soon as we came here, to Lenkarda. It allows you to speak and understand any known language, both human and Krinar."

"But—" Mia didn't even know where to begin. "How

do I know you didn't just give it to me now? And wait, did I hear you say before that it's June? The last thing I remember is in March. How would I have lost a chunk of my memory? This makes no sense—"

The K sighed and raised his hand, gently tucking a stray curl behind her ear. "I know, Mia," he said softly. "I know this is going to be difficult for you to accept. Let me tell you a little story, and then I'll demonstrate to you that I'm not lying. Okay?"

"Okay," Mia agreed, mesmerized by the warm look on his beautiful face. How could someone that gorgeous be her lover? Maybe this was all just an unusually realistic dream. Could she even now be sound asleep, with her unconscious creating this stunning creature? If he was indeed her lover, then she was the luckiest girl in the world—though she still didn't see how such a thing was possible.

"Good," he said, his golden eyes gleaming. "Then let me tell you about us starting from the beginning . . ."

And for the next twenty minutes, Mia listened in shock as he went through their initial meeting in April and detailed the tumultuous affair that followed as a result. When he began to explain about her involvement with the Resistance, Mia's jaw simply dropped.

"I was spying on you?" Where on Earth had she gotten the courage to do that? Although he was being gentle with her now, Mia had a feeling this particular K could be quite dangerous if provoked. In general, his kind weren't known for their forgiving nature, their violent streak amply demonstrated during the fights of the Great Panic.

"You were," the K confirmed, his jaw tightening a little. "But I was at fault too, because I knew you were doing it and fed you false information."

Mia gave him an incredulous look. "And you're saying

we're lovers? After all that?"

"We're more than lovers, Mia. You're my charl."

"Charl?"

He nodded. "It's our word for what you are to me. The best approximation would be something like human mate."

"Like a wife?" Mia could hear her own voice rising in disbelief.

He smiled. "Not exactly, but you could think of it that way, yes."

Mia stared at him. "But you said I met you in April and it's only June now. When did we have a chance to get married?"

He hesitated for a second. "It doesn't work like that, my darling. There is no formal ceremony in a charl-cheren relationship."

"So then how *does* it work? How is this different from just being boyfriend and girlfriend?" Not that she could even picture this beautiful creature as her boyfriend. But a husband? Her mind boggled at the thought.

"It's different, Mia, because I couldn't give a mere girlfriend what I gave you," he said quietly. "Because by claiming you as my charl, I have brought you fully into our world, with all that it entails."

Mia's heart started beating faster again. "And what does it entail?"

"A much longer lifespan," he said softly. "Freedom from aging and disease. Immortality, as you like to call it."

* * *

Korum could see her eyes widening, skepticism warring with excitement on her face. The curl that he'd just tucked away behind her ear came loose again, refusing to be contained. He loved that rebellious curl; it always lured his fingers to her hair, making him want to touch its soft, thick mass.

In general, he was both surprised and pleased by her reaction thus far. She was naturally cautious, so some wariness was to be expected, but she was far less frightened than he would've expected her to be. She didn't cringe away from his touch, nor did she seem to object to his nearness. Somehow, despite her lack of conscious memories, she must still recognize him on some level, must still trust him not to hurt her.

"You have the ability to make humans immortal?" she asked, a small frown creasing her smooth forehead.

Korum sighed, not wanting to go down that path again. "We do," he said patiently. "But not all humans— only those that become a part of our society. I'm currently trying to get an exception for your parents and sister, though—"

"You know them?" she interrupted. "You've met my family?"

"I do, and I have," Korum confirmed, glad that it was the case. It would've been much worse if she'd lost her memory before their Florida trip. "And that's how you're going to know I'm telling you the truth, my sweet. You're going to speak to Marisa and your parents."

Mia looked startled at the idea, and then her face lit up. By now Korum knew her well enough to understand that he'd just managed to dispel whatever fears she harbored over being separated from her loved ones.

Her strong attachment to her family was one of Mia's main vulnerabilities, and Korum had not hesitated to exploit it in the past—to use it to bind her even closer to him. It had been surprisingly easy to win over both her parents and her sister.· He had carefully researched everything about them before their meeting, and they had reacted exactly as he'd hoped, their initial distrust fading as they saw that Mia was happy and loved. And that made Mia even happier and more attached to *him*. Rightly or wrongly, Korum knew that he would do anything to keep her that way. She might not remember it now, but she had loved him once—and she would again. For now, though, he needed to prove to her that he was neither crazy nor playing a trick on her.

"Here, use this," he said, giving her a new wrist computer he'd made a couple of hours ago. This time, he'd added visual capabilities to it, to make it even easier for her to stay in touch with her family. Showing Mia how to operate the device took another minute, and then she was connecting to her parents' Skype account, her mother's voice and image appearing in the room.

Smiling, Korum walked across the room and sat down in the corner, giving the two women some privacy. He could still hear everything they were discussing, however, and he listened with a great deal of curiosity.

As usual, his little charl seemed very concerned with not causing her parents any worry. Instead of letting on that she lost her memory, Mia kept the conversation light and generic, inquiring about her parents' health and asking how Marisa was doing. Grinning, Korum listened as Ella Stalis blithely chatted about the latest developments in Marisa's pregnancy (three pounds gained!) and how much they'd enjoyed having Mia and Korum in the area.

Though her sister's pregnancy had to have come as a shock to Mia, she gamely oohed-and-aahed at the right moments, acting as if everything was normal. She even managed to laugh and promise to come for a visit again soon, as though she remembered the last trip perfectly. Korum couldn't help admiring her for this; he knew how lost and anxious she must be feeling right now, and he was more than a little impressed with her composure.

Finally, Mia finished her conversation and looked at him. "Do you want this back?" she asked uncertainly, indicating the wrist device he'd given her.

"No, that's yours to keep." Korum got up and walked toward her. "Did this help? Do you believe me now?"

"I don't know," she whispered, and he saw the pain and confusion on her face. "If this is all true, then what happened? How did I manage to lose such an important part of my life? Did I hit my head or something?"

"Or something." Korum tried to push away enraging thoughts about Saret's betrayal. The last thing he wanted was to frighten her right now. Raising his hand, he gave in to the urge to stroke her cheek instead, reveling in the familiar feel of her soft skin underneath his fingers.

She blinked at him, her thick lashes sweeping up and down like dark fans. To his immense satisfaction, she didn't flinch away from his touch. If anything, she seemed to lean toward him, as though she was also craving physical closeness.

Unable to resist any longer, Korum bent his head and kissed her, holding her face gently with his hands. Just a kiss, he promised himself, just one small kiss . . .

At first she was stiff, her mouth closed against the intrusion of his tongue. He could feel her heart beating frantically in her chest, sense her momentary panic, and then her lips softened, parted a bit. Her hands came up, pressing lightly against his chest, as if uncertain whether to push him away or hold him close.

Her response, when it came, was much more tentative

than usual, but it was enough to drive him insane. The taste of her, the smell of her, was intoxicating, like a drug surging through his veins. He deepened the kiss without realizing it, one hand slipping down her back to press her closer to him, his cock so hard he felt like he was about to explode.

It was only her quiet whimper that brought him back to his senses. Lifting his head, Korum looked at Mia, his breathing hard and uneven.

Her pale cheeks were flushed, her lips swollen. He could smell her desire, feel the heat rising from her skin, and he knew that if he reached between her legs now, he would find her wet and slick, her body ready for him. But her mind was a different matter, Korum realized, and the look in her eyes now was that of fear and confusion.

His own body raging with unfulfilled need, Korum fought for control, knowing that he needed it now more than ever. "I'm sorry," he said, forcing himself to let her go. "I wasn't going to do this so soon . . ."

She took a couple of steps back and stared at him, her small chest moving up and down, drawing his attention to the hardness of her nipples underneath her dress. Korum swallowed, remembering their pale pink hue, the way they tasted in his mouth, how they pebbled under his tongue.

No, don't fucking go there now. Lifting his eyes back to her face, Korum said, "I know you're not ready for this yet, my sweet. I won't hurt you, I promise . . ." And he meant it. He would sooner lose a limb than do anything to traumatize her while she was so vulnerable.

She bit her lip, then nodded, crossing her arms around her chest in a defensive gesture that sent a pang of regret through Korum. He hated it sometimes, the all-consuming lust he always experienced in her vicinity. She was so tiny, so delicate, her body unsuited for the hard demands he often placed on it. No matter how careful he tried to be, he knew he wasn't always the most gentle lover, his overwhelming need for her constantly testing his self-control.

"So what happened?" she asked again, still watching him warily. "Why don't I remember you, or my sister getting pregnant, or any of this? How did I lose two months of my life?"

Korum took a deep breath, trying to control the anger still boiling in his veins at the thought of Saret. "Someone I knew and trusted—a man who pretended to be my friend for a long time—did this," he said evenly. "This person wiped out a portion of your memory as a way to get at me . . . and because he also wanted you."

"Really?" Her eyes widened. "Another K?"

"Yes, another Krinar," Korum confirmed before explaining the whole story, starting from Mia's internship and ending with Saret's betrayal. Not wanting to overwhelm her, he downplayed the part about Saret's ultimate intentions for her people, as well as some of the complexities of Council politics. She didn't need to know everything all at once; as it was, he could see that it was already almost too much for her. He wanted to wrap his arms around her and hold her, soothe her distress, but he knew she wouldn't welcome it now—not after the way he'd almost attacked her earlier.

The best thing to do right now was to give her time, he decided. Time and space to think about everything she'd learned.

"I have to go now," Korum said, his heart squeezing painfully at the look of relief on her face. "There are a few things I have to take care of. Why don't you relax, take it easy for now? I'll be back in a couple of hours and we can have lunch. If you get hungry in the meantime, just say what you want out loud and it will be given to you. Unless you're hungry now?"

She shook her head, her dark curls moving around her shoulders. "No, I'm fine, thanks."

"Good. Feel free to explore the house if you wish. I know everything's going to look strange to you now, but it's all fairly intuitive, so it shouldn't be too bad." He smiled, remembering how much Mia enjoyed that aspect of life in Lenkarda. "All the furniture is intelligent, so don't be startled if it conforms to your shape. The house is intelligent too, so feel free to ask it for food or anything you need."

"Okay," she said, giving him a small smile in response. "Thanks."

Pausing for a moment longer, Korum drank in that smile. Then he walked out, leaving her alone to process everything she'd just learned.

CHAPTER NINE

Exiting the house, Korum quickly created a transport pod and headed toward a small round building in the heart of the Center—the gathering place for routine Council meetings. Walking in, he greeted the other Councilors, nodding coolly toward Loris and a couple of his other opponents. While all of them could participate in the meeting virtually, everyone living on Earth had chosen to attend in person today, given the important topic at hand.

Taking a seat on one of the floats, Korum carefully watched the Councilors' faces, seeking to gauge their collective mood. What he'd done to Saret's lab building was bound to have frightened them, shaking their belief in the impenetrability of the Centers' defenses. Some of the Council members failed to comprehend the necessity for technological progress, clinging to what was known and familiar instead of advancing with the times.

"Welcome, Korum," Arus said, turning toward him.

"I'm glad you're able to join us today. Is your Mia all right?"

"She is, thanks," Korum said, appreciating the concern. If anyone understood his feelings for Mia, it was probably Arus, whose devotion to his own charl was widely known. Although they didn't always see eye-to-eye on every issue, Korum respected the ambassador and even liked him to some extent.

Arus inclined his head in response. "Good. I'm glad to hear it. Delia was worried when she heard about what happened."

"Please tell Delia she's more than welcome to stop by," Korum said quietly, aware that the whole Council was watching their exchange. "I'm sure Mia could use a friend right now."

Out of the corner of his eye, Korum could see a smirk on Loris's face. His long-time enemy was clearly enjoying the situation, both the fact that Korum had fallen for a human girl and the entire debacle with Saret. Toxic rage crawled through Korum's veins again, but he didn't let anything show on his face, keeping his expression mildly amused. Let Loris enjoy his discomfort for now; the so-called Protector wasn't going to be on the Council much longer, given his son's now-almost-proven guilt.

"All right then. We have a lot to discuss today." It was Voret, one of the oldest members of the Council. "The guardians reported to us that all of Saret's dispersion devices have been located and neutralized, thanks to Korum warning us about them in time. Apparently, they had been scheduled to go off simultaneously in approximately thirty-two hours from now. We also found the designer who had the nano-weapon. He was in Thailand and has now been arrested. The weapon was already fully functional, and Alir thinks that Saret planned to use it shortly after he succeeded in unleashing the mind-control devices among the human population. Arus, you spoke with the United Nations?"

"Yes. I glossed over the situation when I explained it to them," the ambassador answered. "They already have their hands full dealing with the military leaders who had aided the Resistance, and there is no need to scare them at this point. They just need to be aware that Saret is on the loose, so that their intelligence agencies can keep an eye out for him. I didn't go into any detail beyond informing them that he's a dangerous individual who needs to be apprehended promptly."

"Good," Voret said. "You did the right thing. They already don't trust us, and if they knew about the mind-control devices, they would probably panic again."

"And with good reason this time," Korum said, thinking about Saret's insane plan. "If he managed to get Saur to attack me, imagine what he could've done with human minds."

"Indeed," Voret said, and Korum could see him preparing to approach the topic that was likely of most interest to the Council today. "Now as far as the other events that took place yesterday . . ."

"Yes?" Korum prompted when the other Councilor trailed off. He knew exactly where Voret was headed, but he wanted to hear what he had to say.

Voret gave him an uncomfortable look. "Now, Korum, we all watched the recordings of the events, and some of the things we saw were . . . disturbing, to say the least."

Korum smiled, not the least bit surprised. "Which part disturbed you the most, Voret?" he asked. "Was it the fact that Saret planned to annihilate us all in his quest to mind-fuck the humans? Or that none of us had a clue?"

Voret frowned. "You know I'm referring to the way

you were able to breach the lab's shields. We'll address the Saret situation in greater detail once we have more information from the guardians, but first we need to know if we're safe here, inside our Centers. Did you develop a weapon that can penetrate our force-shields?"

"I did," Korum said, enjoying the expressions of shock and fear on some of the Councilors' faces. "But don't worry—I've also developed better shields. Both are still in experimental mode, which is why no one has heard about this before."

"And you used this weapon yesterday?" Arus asked, raising his eyebrows.

"Yes. I had no choice once I learned how Saret had set up the lab."

"How did you learn that?" It was Voret again.

"By scanning the lab building. Once I knew what Saret intended, it wasn't difficult to figure out that he would have some pretty strong defenses in place. Which he did. I distracted him by feeding him an image of myself from three years ago and used the time to build the weapon based on my experimental designs."

Voret's frown deepened. "And when were you going to tell us about these new designs of yours?"

"When they were ready to be used," Korum said evenly. Voret and the others forgot sometimes that Korum was under no obligation to share anything with the Council. He chose to do so for the good of all Krinar, but he had no intention of seeking the Council's permission and approval on every project.

"Could anyone else gain access to this weapon?" Arus asked, focusing on the more important part of the issue. "Korum, are you certain no one else has these designs?"

"I'm the only one," Korum said, understanding the ambassador's concern. "None of my designers have been involved in this project yet, and no one has access to these files."

"Not even your charl?" It was Loris this time, his voice practically dripping with sarcasm. "Are you sure she can't steal the data and run to her friends in the Resistance?"

Korum gave him a sardonic look. "No, Loris. She can't. Besides, what would the Resistance do with this information without your son? We all know now how useful he was to them . . . and to Saret."

Loris got up slowly, his face darkening with anger. "Those were lies! Nobody would believe them for a minute—"

"Oh really?" Korum said coldly, looking at the black-haired Krinar with contempt. "We all saw the recording—and heard Saret explain Rafor's role in his plans. Your son is as guilty as Saret himself, and he'll be punished accordingly."

Loris's hands clenched into fists, his knuckles turning white. "Saret was *your* friend," he hissed, apparently no longer able to contain himself. "For all we know, you're the one behind it all and are now just waiting for the right moment to use your new weapon on us—"

"Loris, that's enough!" Arus's voice cracked through the air like a whip. At the resulting silence, the ambassador continued in a calmer tone, "We understand your need to protect your son, but, unfortunately, the evidence against him continues to build. Given this new information, we'll need to have another trial session tomorrow. It may be the final session—"

Loris's entire body shook with rage now. "Fuck you, Arus. And fuck all of you. Rafor is not a traitor. That—" he pointed in Korum's direction, "—is the only traitor here, and you are all too fucking blind to see!"

"The only blind person here is you, Loris," Korum

said calmly, watching his enemy unraveling right in front of his eyes. "And tomorrow, when the Council judges the Keiths to be guilty, the entire world will know about your failure."

That appeared to be the last straw. With an enraged roar, Loris launched himself at Korum, leaping across the room with full Krinar speed.

Acting on instinct, Korum turned and twisted his body, reflexively shielding his head and throat. As Loris slammed into him, he met the brunt of the attack with his shoulder, jabbing his elbow into Loris's side as they fell to the floor and rolled toward the middle of the chamber.

With the hard floor scraping his skin, Korum felt his own rage spiking, every cell in his body filling with bloodlust. His fingers curled into claws and raked across Loris's arm, taking out a chunk of muscle and sinew. At the same time, his arm hooked around Loris's neck in one of the more complex *defrebs* moves, baring his throat to Korum's teeth—

"Enough! That's enough!" Strong hands were pulling them apart, dragging them to separate sides of the room. Still rational enough to comprehend what was happening, Korum didn't struggle as Arus and another Krinar held his arms, preventing him from continuing the fight. Loris, however, was completely out of control, twisting and yelling as two other Councilors held him pinned against the wall. Finally, he seemed to run out of steam, panting and glaring at Korum in hatred. His arm was a bloody mess that was just beginning to heal.

"You can unhand me now," Korum said, his own breathing slowly calming as he glanced at the two men still holding him in an iron grip.

"Sorry, Korum," Arus said, his lips curving into a faint smile as he released Korum's arm and took a step back.

"Couldn't let you kill him here."

Voret followed Arus's example, letting go of Korum's other arm.

"That's fine," Korum said, wiping his bloody hand on his shirt. "We'll continue this in the Arena. That's what that was, wasn't it, Loris? A challenge?"

The black-haired Protector stared at him, his chest heaving with fury. "Yes," he ground out between tightly clenched teeth. "You could call it a challenge."

"Good," Korum said, giving him a wide, predatory smile. "A challenge it is, then." He hadn't had a good Arena fight in a while, and he could feel his blood heating up with anticipation.

"Loris, that's not a good idea," Arus said, taking a few steps in the Krinar's direction. Korum was unsurprised by his concern; Loris and the ambassador were usually on good terms, frequently teaming up against Korum and Saret. Korum imagined it must be difficult for Arus now, taking the side of his former opponent against a man he'd considered his ally.

Loris laughed bitterly. "Oh really, Arus? Not a good idea?"

Arus gave him an even look. "He excels at *defrebs*. When was the last time you fought?"

Loris's upper lip curled with derision. "Yeah, fuck you too, Arus. You think I've gone soft? I've had more kills in the Arena than this fucker has had fights."

"Then the challenge has been issued." Voret stepped forward, his voice taking on a formal cadence. "Since the trial is tomorrow, the Arena fight will take place the day after at noon."

And with that, the Council meeting was adjourned.

* * *

Mia sat on the bed, staring blankly at the green forest outside the transparent wall. She was immortal, and she had a K lover—who was something like her husband, but not really.

It was so incredible she could hardly fathom it, her mind twisting and turning in a million different directions.

After the K left, she'd called both Marisa and Jessie, needing additional confirmation of the impossible claims he was making. Both her sister and her friend had been quite happy to hear from her—and both had mentioned Korum in the course of Mia's conversation with them. Marisa had gone on and on about her pregnancy and how much better she was feeling thanks to Korum's involvement of someone called Ellet, and Jessie had asked whether Mia had decided when she and Korum were coming by for a visit.

Still in a state of shock, Mia had managed to give Jessie a vague answer—something along the lines of still needing to talk to Korum—and listened politely as her sister gushed about her newest ultrasound results. To her relief, neither one of them seemed to suspect that anything was wrong, that the Mia they'd spoken to today was far from normal.

She didn't know why she was so hesitant to reveal the truth about her condition to anyone, but she was. She didn't want to make her family and friends worry, yes, but she was also almost . . . embarrassed.

How could this have happened to her? How could her entire family know her alien lover, while he seemed like a stranger to her? How could she have forgotten *making love* to someone so extraordinary? When he'd kissed her, her body had responded in a way Mia had never experienced before—or at least didn't remember experiencing before. It had been almost frightening, the degree to which she'd lost control in his arms. If he had continued kissing her instead of stopping when he did, she could've easily fallen into bed with him—she, who didn't remember going beyond a few kisses with guys before.

The strangeness of her reaction to everything kept throwing her off-balance. He was an extraterrestrial— someone from a different species—yet she was barely freaking out at being told that he was her lover. She even believed him now, after just a few conversations with her family and Jessie. Theoretically, he could still be lying to her; her family could've been threatened or brainwashed to say what they did. Hell, he could've even had them replaced by some kind of robots that looked and sounded like them. It wasn't as if Mia knew what the Ks were truly capable of.

And yet . . . she believed him. Something inside her seemed to recognize him on some level, even if she couldn't consciously remember him. She had been glad when he left her alone, giving her time to digest everything, but now she found herself missing him, craving the comfort of his presence. It made no logical sense, but it was true: a stranger felt more necessary to her than people she'd known her whole life.

Everything he'd told her thus far was one big jumble in her mind. The Resistance, human sympathizers among the Ks, her spying on him—it all sounded more like a movie than anything that could've actually happened to her. Why would she have done something so crazy? How could she have wanted something other than to be with this gorgeous man—alien or not?

Blowing out a frustrated breath, Mia looked down at

her hands, trying to make sense of this insane situation. Why would she have helped the Resistance? She'd never thought there was any point to fighting against the Ks, not after they'd taken control of her planet and basically left humans alone.

Yet she had supposedly fought against the Ks—or at least had tried to help those who did. According to Korum, it hadn't been a very successful effort.

Then again, maybe she was wrong to trust him now. Sure, he'd been kind to her thus far, and her family seemed to like him, but she had no idea what he was really like. What if she was trusting someone who shouldn't be trusted? It's not like she knew what the Ks ultimately wanted from humans. There *were* those rumors about them drinking blood. For all she knew, Korum could've been the one to wipe her memory, making her forget something terrible about him.

Her head was beginning to hurt from all the speculation, so Mia got up and started pacing around the room. Her surroundings were strange and foreign, yet she didn't feel uncomfortable here. She had already explored the rest of the house, marveling at the intelligent floating objects that served as tables, chairs, and couches. They were definitely a major improvement over human furnishings. She also liked the overall house aesthetic, with the transparent walls and ceiling and a clean, Zen-like feel to the entire space.

Could an evil villain live in such a beautiful, peaceful place?

As soon as the thought crossed her mind, Mia laughed out loud, unable to help herself. She was being ridiculous, and she knew it. There was absolutely no reason to build some crazy conspiracy in her mind. So far, Korum had been nothing but nice to her.

In fact, she was very much looking forward to spending more time with him and re-learning everything she had forgotten.

Finally, after what seemed like forever, Mia heard something in the living room. Coming out of the bedroom, she saw that the K—or Korum, as she thought of him now—had just walked in through what appeared to be an opening in one of the walls. As Mia watched, the opening narrowed and solidified, leaving a transparent wall where an entrance used to be.

At the sight of her, his face lit up with what looked like genuine pleasure. "Hello, my sweet." He gave her a wide smile that exposed the dimple in his left cheek. Mia wanted to kiss that dimple. In general, she wanted to kiss and lick him all over, just to see if his smooth golden skin was as delicious as it looked.

Wow, I'm in lust. Mentally shaking her head at the strangeness of it all, she gave him an answering smile. "Hi."

"Sorry it took me so long," he said, walking across the room toward the kitchen area. "The Council meeting was more eventful than I expected. You must be starving by now—"

"I'm all right—" Mia followed him into the kitchen, "—but I could definitely eat. Are you going to order something?" She was beyond curious about how the Krinar fed themselves. It was also encouraging that he was planning to eat, as opposed to doing something scary—like drinking human blood. She really needed to ask him about that at some point; hopefully, the whole thing was nothing more than a weird rumor.

"I was going to cook something," he said, "but

ordering will probably be faster. Here, have a seat for now while the house preps our meal."

Mia gingerly perched on one of the floating planks, making herself comfortable. "You cook?" she asked, studying him in fascination as he sat down across from her.

He smiled. "I do. It's a hobby of mine."

She smiled back, both intrigued and relieved. Her earlier suspicions seemed even sillier now. So far her K lover was about as close to a dream man as one could get, and she couldn't wait to learn more about him. There were so many questions running through her mind she didn't even know where to start.

"Did you get a chance to talk to the rest of your family?" he asked, watching her with a knowing half-smile.

"I spoke to Marisa and Jessie," Mia admitted.

"And? Do you believe me now?"

She shrugged. "I suppose you could've faked those interactions somehow, but I don't know why you would go to those lengths. The most logical conclusion is that you are indeed telling me the truth—even though that still seems crazy to me."

He grinned. "I know, my sweet. Believe me, I realize that."

"So what do we do now?" she asked, unable to look away from that dazzling smile. "Where do we go from here?"

"We get to know each other again," he said, his expression becoming more serious. "And in the meantime, I'll be looking into a way to potentially reverse your memory loss."

Mia's heart jumped with excitement. "Is there a way?"

"Not that I currently know of," he admitted. "But that

doesn't mean it doesn't exist—or that we won't come up with it over time."

"Oh, I see." Mia fought to suppress her disappointment. "In that case, can you please tell me a little bit about yourself? I would really like to know more..."

"Of course, my darling, I would be happy to," he said softly.

And throughout their delicious meal, Mia learned all about her lover's role on the Krinar Council, his passion for technological design, and the fact that he was much older than she could've ever imagined. As they talked, Mia could feel herself falling deeper and deeper under his spell, wanting to give in to the temptation of his smile, his touch, the warmth in his gaze as he looked at her. He was a beautiful and fascinating man, and she couldn't help envying that girl who had been her—the one who'd known him from the beginning, the one he seemed to love.

Memory or not, she could see why she had fallen for him—and she could easily envision history repeating itself.

CHAPTER TEN

Korum watched her animated face over lunch, loving the shy, yet admiring glances she directed his way during their conversation. The attraction between them was as strong as ever, and he had no doubt he would be able to seduce her again. Perhaps even tonight—though she might not be ready for that.

For once, Korum was determined not to pressure Mia into his bed. When they'd first met, the strength of his desire for her had caught him off-guard, causing him to act in ways he would've normally condemned. He didn't want to repeat the same mistakes, no matter how much his cock insisted that she was *his*—that she belonged to him and he had the right to take her, to pleasure her, whenever he chose. Graphic sexual images danced in his head as he watched her enjoying her meal, imagining her soft little mouth nibbling on his flesh instead of the piece of fruit she was consuming.

It didn't help that he was still on an adrenaline high

after Loris's attack. Fighting often boosted his already strong libido, the increased aggression translating into a primitive urge to fuck. It was always that way with Krinar men—and human ones too, as far as he knew. Violence and sex had been intertwined since the beginning of time, both appealing to the same male drive to dominate and conquer.

But no matter how much his body demanded it, Korum didn't want to push her. She seemed to be responding so well to the entire situation, looking at him with curiosity and desire instead of fear. If he could just be patient, she would come to him herself, lured by the same need that crawled under his skin.

So, as the lunch went on, Korum kept a tight leash on himself, not even touching Mia in case his good intentions flew out the window. He told her more about the nanocytes in her body and showed her some of the capabilities of Krinar technology, creating a silver cup using nanos and then dissolving it the same way. He also explained about her internship and how she had already begun to contribute to the Krinar society, enjoying the way her eyes lit up with excitement at the thought.

Toward the end, as they were finishing dessert—a platter of freshly cut mango with pistachio sauce—Korum noticed that Mia seemed a little nervous, as though there was something on her mind. Unable to resist any longer, he reached across the table and took her hand, massaging her palm lightly with his thumb.

"Is there something you'd like to ask me, my sweet?" he said, smiling, watching as a pretty blush crept across her cheeks.

"Um, maybe . . ." The color on her face intensified. "Okay, you're probably going to laugh at me, but I just have to know . . ." She swallowed. "Is there any truth to the rumors that you guys drink blood?"

At her innocently provocative question, Korum almost groaned, his cock instantly hardening to the point of pain. She didn't know, of course, that human blood and sexual pleasure were inseparable in the mind of a modern Krinar—and that bringing up the topic like that was the equivalent of asking a Krinar to fuck you. Even the most amazing sex paled in comparison to the ecstasy of the combined act of blood-drinking and intercourse.

"There is some truth to them," Korum said carefully, glad that she couldn't see his raging hard-on. "It was once necessary for our survival, but it's not any longer." And trying to suppress his overwhelming need to take her, he went through the complicated story of Krinar evolution and the seeding of the human race.

"So now you drink blood for pleasure?" Mia asked, staring at him with a shocked, yet intrigued expression on her face.

"Yes." Korum hoped she would drop the topic before he completely lost it.

She didn't. Instead, she looked at him, her cheeks flushed and her eyes bright with curiosity and something more. "Did you—" she stopped to moisten her lips, "— did you ever take my blood?"

Korum thought he might literally explode. Something of what he was feeling must've shown on his face because she gulped nervously and pulled her hand out of his grasp. *Smart girl.*

There was a moment of awkward silence, and then she asked hesitantly, "Why do your eyes do that? Turn more golden, I mean . . . Is that a Krinar thing?"

Korum took a deep, calming breath. When he was reasonably certain he wasn't going to pounce on her, he replied, "No, it's just a weird genetic quirk. It's most common among people from my region of Krina. My mother has it too, and so did my grandfather."

"Your grandfather?"

Korum nodded. "He was killed in a fight when my mother was about my age."

"What about your grandmother and your other grandparents?"

"My grandmother from my mother's side died in a freak accident when she was exploring one of the asteroids in a neighboring solar system. Some even thought it was a suicide, since my grandfather was killed only a few years before that. As for my father's parents, they dissolved their union shortly after my father's birth—one of the very few couples to do so after having children. Apparently my grandmother wanted out, but my grandfather didn't—and he ended up getting into an Arena challenge with the man she took as her lover. My grandfather didn't survive, and my grandmother took her own life shortly after that, apparently too sick with guilt to go on living. It was not a happy story."

Her eyes filled with sympathy. "Oh, I'm sorry—"

"It's all right, my sweet. It happened before I was even born. It's unfortunate, but death is a tragedy that happens to everyone at one point or another. Humans might view us as immortal because we don't age, but we are still living beings—and we can still be killed, no matter how advanced our technology is or how fast we heal. That's why the Elders are so revered in our society: because it's nearly impossible to live that long without meeting with one deadly accident or another."

"You've mentioned these Elders before." Mia was clearly fascinated. "Who are they? Do they rule Krina?"

"No." Korum shook his head. "They don't rule in the sense of being involved in politics or anything like that.

That's what the Council is for: to deal with ongoing matters. The Elders provide guidance and set direction for our species as a whole."

"Oh, I see." She looked thoughtful for a second. "So how old are they?"

"I believe the youngest is just over a million Earth years," Korum said, smiling at the look of wonder on her face. "And the oldest is somewhere around ten million."

She stared at him. "Wow . . ."

"Wow indeed," Korum agreed, enjoying her reaction.

When the lunch was finally over, they took a long walk on the beach and talked some more. Korum held her hand as they leisurely strolled on the sand, reveling in the feel of her small fingers squeezing his palm so trustingly.

He had been worried initially that her memory loss would set them back months, that she would be frightened of him again. But instead, it seemed as if a part of her still knew him—maybe even still loved him. Her calm acceptance of the situation was both surprising and encouraging, particularly since there was no guarantee they would ever be able to reverse the damage Saret had caused.

After the Council meeting, Korum had visited Ellet, hoping that the human biology expert had made some progress toward finding a fix. While the human brain was not her specialty, Korum had hoped she might've been able to learn of some research being done in that direction. To his tremendous disappointment, Ellet hadn't come across anything, despite reaching out to dozens of Krinar scientists on both planets. She had also spoken to all the mind experts at the other Centers. As far as she knew, there was no way to undo a memory wipe of the kind that Saret had used.

"So what made you decide to come to Earth?" Mia asked as they stopped to sit down on a pair of large rocks. In front of them, a small estuary flowed into the ocean, serving as an obstacle to further passage but creating a very scenic view. "I know you told me how you planted life here and basically created humans, but why come here and live alongside us? From what you've said, Krina sounds like a very nice place to live. Why bother leaving it?"

"Our sun is an older star," Korum explained, repeating what he'd once told her. "It will die in about a hundred million years. At that point, we'll need another place to live—and Earth appeals to us for obvious reasons."

She frowned, wrinkling her forehead in a way he found very endearing. "But that's so far away . . . Why would you come now? Why not wait another ninety million years or so?"

Korum sighed, recalling their last discussion on this topic. "Because your species was becoming very destructive to the environment, my sweet. We wanted to make sure that we had a habitable planet for when we needed it." That was the official story, at least. The full explanation was more complicated and not something he was ready to share with Mia quite yet.

Her frown deepened. She obviously didn't like hearing that—but then his charl tended to get defensive when he criticized her kind. He couldn't really blame her for that; she was as loyal to her people as he was to his.

"So when your star begins to die, all the Krinar will come to Earth?" she asked, her eyes narrowing slightly.

"Most likely," Korum said. He actually hoped that wouldn't be the case, but he couldn't tell her that yet.

"Then what would happen to us? To the humans, I mean? Do you really intend to live with us side by side? Wouldn't the planet be too crowded then?"

Korum hesitated for a moment. She was asking all the right questions, and he didn't want to lie to her—but he couldn't tell her the truth yet either. The last thing they needed was for some rumors to spread and cause the humans to panic again.

"Not necessarily," he hedged. "Besides, that's not something we'll have to worry about for a very long time."

She looked at him, obviously trying to decide how much he could be trusted. Korum could practically see the wheels turning in her head. He loved that about her: her unabashed curiosity about everything, the logical way her mind processed information. She was young and naive, but she was also very intelligent, and he had no doubt that one day she would leave her own mark on society.

For now, though, Korum needed to distract her from this particular line of questions. Smiling, he reached over and brushed her hair away from her face. "So what do you think of Lenkarda so far? Are you starting to feel more comfortable, or is it still very strange to you?"

She gave him a small smile. "I don't know, honestly. It's not as strange as it should be. I don't *remember* anything here, but it's like I know it on some level. And it's the same thing with you—"

"I'm as familiar to you as the furniture?" Korum teased, watching as her smile widened into a full-blown grin.

"You are . . ." She laughed ruefully. "I don't understand how any of this works, but you're not nearly as scary as you should be. None of this is, for some reason."

Korum felt his chest expanding to fill with something very much like happiness. "That's good, my sweet," he said, stroking the softness of her cheek. "You shouldn't be scared of me. I would never hurt you. You're my everything; you're my entire world. I would sooner die than hurt you. Believe me, there's no reason to be afraid . . ."

As he spoke, he could see her smile fading and a strangely vulnerable expression appearing on her face instead. "Do you—" she swallowed, her slim throat moving, "—do you love me?"

"I do," Korum answered without hesitation. "More than anyone I've ever loved in my life."

"But why?" She seemed genuinely confused. "I'm just an ordinary human, and you're—" She stopped, her cheeks turning pink again.

"I'm what?" Korum prompted, wanting to see more of that pretty blush. He wasn't sure why he found it so appealing, but it never failed to arouse him. Then again, she turned him on simply by breathing, so it wasn't all that surprising he found her flushed cheeks irresistible.

The color in her face deepened. "You're a gorgeous K who's been around since the dawn of time," she said quietly. "What could you possibly see in me?"

Korum smiled, shaking his head. His little darling had never understood her appeal, never realized how tempting she was to the male of both species. Everything about her, from the soft, thick curls on her head to the creaminess of her skin, seemed to be made for a man's touch. She might not be classically beautiful, but in her own delicate way, she was quite striking, with those large blue eyes and dark hair.

In hindsight, Korum should've known better than to

let her work in such close proximity with another unattached male. He couldn't really blame Saret for wanting her, for craving something that he himself was so obsessed with. He wanted to tear his former friend apart for what he'd done, but he understood—at least partially—why Saret had done it. If the roles had been reversed, and Mia had been someone else's charl, Korum didn't know how far he would've gone to get her for his own, how many taboos he would've broken in his quest to possess her.

Of course, her physical appeal was only a part of it now. Reaching over, Korum took her hand again. "I see in you the woman I love," he said, not even trying to hide the depth of his emotions. "I see a beautiful, smart girl who's sweet and brave and has the courage of her convictions. I see someone who'll do anything for those she loves, who'll go to any lengths to protect those dear to her. I see someone I can't live without, someone who brightens every moment of my existence and makes me happier than I've ever been in my life."

Mia inhaled, her eyes filling with moisture. "Oh Korum . . ." Her slender fingers twitched in his grasp. "Korum, I don't even know what to say—"

"You don't have to say anything," he interrupted, ignoring the pain of her inadvertent rejection. "I know I'm still a stranger to you. I don't expect you to feel the same way about me now as you did before. Not yet, at least . . ."

She nodded, and a single tear rolled down her face. "I hate this," she confessed, her voice breaking for a second. "I hate that such a big part of my life disappeared, that I lost everything that brought us to this point. I need you, but I don't know you, and it's driving me crazy. I loved you too, didn't I? Even though all that stuff happened between us, we were still in love, right?"

"Yes," Korum said, his hand tightening around her palm. "Yes, we were very much in love, my darling." And unable to resist any longer, he gently wrapped one arm around her back, bringing her closer to him. She buried her face against his shoulder, and he could feel the wetness from her tears on his bare skin. The sweet scent of her hair teased his nostrils, her nearness making his cock harden again.

Don't be such an animal. She needs comfort now, Korum told himself. And ignoring the lust raging through his body, he let Mia cry, knowing she needed this emotional release.

After a minute, she pulled away, looking up at him through tear-spiked lashes. "I'm sorry," she whispered, "I didn't mean to cry all over you . . ."

Korum smiled, wiping away the wetness on her cheeks with his knuckles. "You can cry all over me any time you want." Her tears were as precious to him as her smiles. He hated to see her sad, but liked the feel of her slender body in his arms, enjoyed being the one to soothe her, to make her pain go away.

Even if, more often than not, he had been the cause of that pain.

* * *

They spent the rest of the day together on the beach, with Korum patiently explaining everything Mia had once known and forgotten about the Krinar. He told her about blood addiction and xenos, the Celebration of Forty-Seven and the importance of 'standing' in Krinar society. She listened attentively, asking questions, and Korum gladly answered them, knowing how much she needed to catch up on.

"So do you have the concept of money? How does your economy work?" Her eyes were bright and curious as they continued their discussion over dinner.

"Yes, we definitely have the concept of money." Korum paused to take a bite of his peanut-flavored soba noodles. "We work and get paid for the contributions we make to our society. The greater the contribution, the greater the pay, regardless of the field. However, wealth is not as important to us as it is to humans. Our economy is neither purely capitalist nor government-run; it's kind of a blend of the two. For the most part, everyone has their basic needs met. There's no such thing as homelessness or hunger on Krina. Even the laziest Krinar lives quite well by human standards. But, to have anything beyond food, shelter, and daily necessities, you have to do something productive with your life—you have to contribute to society in some way."

She was looking very interested, so Korum continued his explanation. "Financial rewards are only a part of the reason why people work, though. The main motivation is the need to be respected, to be recognized for our achievements. Few Krinar want to go through life having others look down upon them. You see, for us, having a low standing is almost like being an outcast. Someone who's never done anything useful in his life will ultimately find himself treated with contempt by others. Having a high standing is much more important than being wealthy—although the two usually go hand-in-hand."

"So wealthy Krinar have a high standing, and vice versa?" Mia asked.

"No, not necessarily. One could be wealthy through inheritance or family, but that doesn't mean that person will have a high standing. Rafor, Loris's son, is a prime example of that. His father gave him all the wealth he could possibly need, but he couldn't give him a good standing. That can only be earned—or lost—through one's own efforts."

Mia looked puzzled. "Wait, how do you lose standing through your own efforts?"

"There are a number of ways," Korum said. "Committing a crime is an obvious one. So is doing something dishonorable, like cheating on your mate. It's also possible to lose standing by failing at something important. For instance, Loris took that risk by assuming the role of the Protector for his son and the Keiths. Once they are judged guilty, his standing will be much lower and he'll no longer be on the Council. That's why he challenged me to the Arena today—because he has very little to lose at this point."

Her eyes widened with surprise. "What do you mean, he challenged you?"

Korum hesitated. Perhaps he shouldn't have mentioned it to Mia just yet, but it was too late now. "Remember I told you about the Arena earlier today?" he asked.

"You said it was a way to resolve irreconcilable differences . . ." A small frown appeared on her face.

"Yes," Korum confirmed, "it is. And that's what Loris and I have: an irreconcilable difference of opinion. I think his son is a traitorous lowlife, and he disagrees."

"So he challenged you to a fight? But I thought you said those were dangerous—"

"They are." Korum smiled in anticipation, familiar excitement zinging through his veins. He needed this sometimes: the danger, the adrenaline, the raw physical challenge of subduing an opponent. As much as he enjoyed fighting during defrebs matches, he was always aware that it was just a game, that everyone would walk away with nothing more than a few scrapes and bruises. There was no such guarantee in the Arena, which is what made it so thrilling.

"So you could be killed?" Mia's eyes were beginning to glisten with moisture, and Korum realized that she found the idea more than a little disturbing. He definitely shouldn't have brought this up yet.

"There is a small chance," he said carefully, not wanting to upset her further. "Although killing is technically illegal, it's usually forgiven if it happens in the heat of an Arena battle. But you don't need to worry, my sweet. I can take care of myself."

She didn't seem convinced. "You said he hates you." Her voice quivered a little. "Wouldn't he *try* to kill you?"

"He can certainly try," Korum said, "but I'm not going to let him. You have nothing to worry about—"

"He's not a good fighter?"

"He is," Korum admitted. "Or at least he used to be. I don't know his skill level these days."

"Don't do it," she said, reaching over to grab his hand. "Please, Korum, don't do this fight—"

"Mia . . ." He sighed, covering her hand with his own. "Listen to me, darling, once a challenge has been issued, it cannot be undone. I can't walk away from this fight, and neither can Loris. We're both committed, do you understand that?"

"No," she said stubbornly, "I don't. I don't want you to risk your life like that—"

"It's not as big of a risk as you think," Korum said. "When he attacked me today, it took me all of ten seconds to get to his throat. If that had been an Arena fight, he would've been declared a loser at that point." It was equally likely that Loris would've been dead, but Korum didn't want to tell Mia that. Human women and violence generally didn't mix well—especially when the woman in question was a sheltered young girl.

"So when is the fight supposed to be?" She still looked upset.

Korum sighed. He really should've kept quiet about this. "The day after tomorrow," he said. "At noon."

CHAPTER ELEVEN

Mia stood in the circular room that functioned as a shower stall, letting water jets pummel every inch of her body. Under normal circumstances, she would've loved the novelty of showering in an alien dwelling. Like everything else in the house, the shower was intelligent, adjusting automatically to her needs. All Mia had to do was stand there and let the amazing technology wash, scrub, condition, and massage her. It was wonderfully relaxing—or would've been, if she could just turn her brain off and not think about what Korum had told her at dinner.

He'd been dismissive of the danger of the upcoming fight, but Mia couldn't be so blasé. When he'd mentioned Loris's challenge, her blood had run cold, gruesome images of dismembered bodies flooding her mind. What if something happened to Korum? He wasn't truly immortal; he could be killed, just like his grandfather.

The thought of Korum dying was unbearable,

unimaginable. It didn't matter that Mia had only known him—or remembered knowing him—for a day.

This day had been the best one of her conscious life.

Spending time with Korum had been incredible. She had never had that kind of connection with anyone else before, had never felt so magically alive in another man's presence. It went beyond sexual desire, beyond simple physical need. It was as though every part of her longed to be with him, to soak in his essence. She wanted him with a desperation that made no sense, with a passion that was almost frightening in its intensity.

Somewhere in the back of her mind, Mia knew she was acting irrationally, completely unlike herself. A normal person in this type of situation would ask Korum to take her home, back to New York or Florida, where she could come to terms with the memory loss and gradually re-enter her normal life—such as it was these days. She shouldn't want to cling to an extraterrestrial, shouldn't be so calm about living in his house, separated from everyone and everything she could recall.

And yet she didn't want to ask him, didn't want to think about leaving him even for a moment. Mia had no doubt her psychology classmates would've had a field day analyzing her strange reactions, from the ease with which she'd accepted the impossible to her unhealthy dependence on a man she'd known for only a short period of time. But she didn't care; all she knew was that she needed Korum—and that he seemed to need her too.

Had her former boss—Saret—known it would be like this? Had he realized that erasing a part of her memory didn't destroy whatever it was that bound her and Korum together? Somehow Mia doubted it. If what Korum had told her about Saret's intentions was true, the mind expert would've been unpleasantly surprised by her continued attachment to Korum and lack of interest toward him.

After the shower was over, Mia stepped out of the circular stall, letting the water drip off her onto the strange sponge-like substance on the floor that kept massaging her feet. Korum had explained that all she needed to do was stand there and let the technology take care of her bathroom routine, so Mia was taking him at his word.

Sure enough, warm jets of air quickly dried off her body, while a small tornado seemed to engulf the area around her head, blowing around each strand of her hair and filling her mouth with a taste of something refreshingly clean. By the time it was done, Mia was dry from head to toe, her curls defined and shaped to perfection, as if she'd just emerged from a fancy hair salon. Her mouth also felt like she'd just brushed her teeth.

Nice.

All that was left was to put on some clothes. Pulling on a thick, fluffy robe that Korum had thoughtfully given her earlier, Mia looked at the mirror that made up one of the walls, noting the sparkle in her eyes and the flush that colored her cheeks. Her heart pounded in anticipation, and her stomach felt like it was hosting an entire colony of butterflies.

If there was even a small chance that she might lose Korum in two days, then every moment they had together was precious. And as nervous as the idea made her, Mia wanted to know her lover fully—to experience again that which she had forgotten.

She wanted Korum to take her to bed.

* * *

Korum sat on the edge of the bed, waiting for Mia to finish her shower. He'd showered already, using his fist to take the edge off the lust that had ridden him hard all day.

Spending so much time with her, touching her, smelling her—it had almost driven him insane. Under normal circumstances, they would've had sex a couple of times on the beach, or when they'd gotten home before dinner. And instead, he'd had to content himself with a few light touches and caresses that had only added to his hunger, making his skin prickle and his cock swell with need. If he hadn't masturbated in the shower, she would've been in serious danger of getting jumped this evening. As it was, Korum was still feeling quite edgy, and he was hoping to work off some of his excess energy by going for a defrebs session early in the morning—or at night, as humans thought of the hours between three and four a.m.

It was already past eleven in the evening, which was Mia's normal bed time. Korum wasn't the least bit tired himself, but he wanted to tuck her in and hold her until she fell asleep—even if doing so would torture him further. It was important to start getting her accustomed to him, to get her to feel comfortable with his touch . . . because Korum didn't know how much longer he could go without having her.

To distract himself, he looked down at his palm, sending out a mental query to check on the progress of the search for Saret. The guardians had found traces of Saret's presence in Germany, but then his trail had gone cold again. However he was moving around, he was managing to do so out of sight of Krinar satellites and other spying devices—a feat that Korum reluctantly admired, even though the thought of Saret on the loose made him see red.

"What are you doing?" Mia's softly spoken question jerked him out of his absorption with the search.

Looking up, Korum smiled at the sight of her standing there, her small feet bare and the robe wrapped all over her slender body. Her hands were twisting together in a gesture that betrayed her nervousness. "I'm just checking up on a couple of things," he replied. "How was your shower? Did you like it?"

She moistened her lips, drawing his attention to her mouth. "It was awesome," she said. "Like everything else here."

"Good," Korum said, watching her closely. Was she afraid to be near a bed with him? Gentling his tone, he said, "Come, let's go to sleep, my sweet. You've had a long day. You must be so tired."

She nodded uncertainly and approached him, her movements imbued with an unconscious sensuality that was as much a part of her as those beautiful curls. Korum shifted and raised his knee slightly, seeking to hide the erection tenting his pants again.

When she was a foot away, she stopped, and he could hear her rapid heartbeat. A warm, feminine scent reached his nostrils, sending more blood rushing toward his groin.

She was not afraid, Korum realized. She was turned on.

Hardly daring to breathe, he reached out and took her hand, bringing her closer until she was sitting on the bed next to him. At his action, he could hear her heartbeat spiking, a mixture of apprehension and excitement written on her face.

"Mia," he asked softly, "are you sure?"

She nodded, her soft mouth trembling. "Yes," she whispered. "I'm sure . . ."

His body reacted to her words with painful intensity, his cock hardening further and his balls drawing up against his body. But when he leaned over to kiss her, he kept his lips gentle, tender—as her first time should be.

She'd come to him that other first time too, but she'd done it as a challenge, as a way to assert her independence and spite him in some small way. He hadn't cared then, glad to just have her there, in his apartment, in his bed. And in his rush to take her, he'd hurt her, tearing through her virginity with all the care of a rutting animal.

This was his chance to make up for it. She was a virgin again—in mind, if not in body. And Korum was determined to make sure that there would be no pain for her this night, only pleasure.

He kissed her softly, with just his lips at first, stroking her hair and back with soothing motions. She tasted fresh and sweet, her scent familiar and enticing. Her small hands came up, curved around the back of his neck, her fingers reaching into his hair, sending shivers of pleasure down his spine. Not wanting to deepen the kiss, Korum moved his lips to her cheek, then the underside of her jaw, tasting the sensitive skin there.

She moaned, arching her head back, exposing more of her pale throat to his mouth, and Korum kissed her there too, fighting the urge to take her blood at the same time. He would do it, but not today, not for this first time.

Carefully, so as not to startle her, he pulled at her robe, opening it as he continued kissing her, his mouth moving to her collarbone and then below.

Her body was beautiful, slim and curved in all the right places, her skin smooth and inviting to the touch. Korum slowly ran his hand over her breasts and her flat belly, marveling at the delicacy of her frame. His palm could almost cover her entire ribcage, his skin strikingly dark against the pale perfection of hers.

He could see the pulse beating rapidly in the side of her neck, hear her elevated breathing, and he knew she was as anxious as she was aroused. Raising his head, Korum caught her staring at him, her face flushed and her lips slightly parted.

"I love you, Mia," he murmured, reaching up to move that stray curl off her face. "You know that, right?"

She nodded shyly, still watching him with her huge blue eyes. Those eyes made him want to slay dragons for her, rip apart anyone who dared try to hurt her.

"Don't be afraid, my darling," he said, sliding one arm under her knees and another around her back. Lifting her up, he placed her carefully in the middle of the bed. "I'll make it good for you, I promise . . ." And moving back for a second, Korum removed his shirt and shorts, letting his erection spring free.

Before she had a chance to do more than give him one apprehensive glance, Korum climbed on top of her, nuzzling her neck and shoulder again until she let out a quiet moan. Then he slowly began to make his way down her body, ignoring his cock's insistent throbbing. There would be times when he would take her hard and fast, but this wasn't going to be one of them. Tonight was all about her.

Cupping the round globe of her breast, he delighted in its firmness, in the way her nipple hardened against his palm. Her breasts weren't large, but they were perfectly shaped, just right for her slight frame. Bending his head, he tasted her nipple, laving it with his tongue, then sucking on it with a firm pull.

She moaned again, arching toward him, and he

repeated the treatment on the other breast, enjoying the way her nipples looked afterwards: all pink and shiny.

Her stomach was next, and he kissed the soft skin there, tonguing her belly button and feeling her abdominal muscles tensing as his mouth continued moving lower. Her legs were closed, so Korum pulled her thighs apart, ignoring the hitch in her breathing as he gazed upon her moist folds and the dark triangle of curls above. Like the rest of Mia, her pussy was small and delicate, sweeter than anything he'd ever tasted.

Lowering his head, Korum breathed in her intoxicating scent and then gently licked the area around her clitoris, teasing her, letting her arousal slowly build. As he continued, he could hear her gasping every time his tongue approached her sensitive nub, feel the way her hips kept rising off the bed toward his mouth. He knew she was very close to the edge, but he wasn't ready to let her go over. Not yet at least.

Moving his hand, he used his index finger to slowly penetrate her, sliding it inside her slick channel, carefully stretching her, readying her for him. She was so tiny inside she even felt tight around his finger, and Korum suppressed a tortured groan as his cock twitched against the sheets in painful arousal.

She cried out as his finger slid deeper, rubbing against that spot that always drove her insane, and then Korum could feel her convulsing, her inner walls pulsing around his finger as she found her release.

Unable to wait any longer, he crawled back up her body, keeping her thighs open with his knee. Holding himself up with one elbow, he used his other hand to direct himself to her small opening, letting the head of his cock slide inside, and then pausing to let her adjust to his size.

At his entry, she inhaled sharply and grasped his shoulders, gazing up at him. His entire body straining from the rigid control he was exerting over himself, Korum began to push in further, keeping the penetration gradual and slow to avoid hurting her. As his cock went deeper, sweat beaded up all over his body and his breathing became harsher, more erratic. She was warm, wet, and tight—and Korum thought he might literally explode on the spot.

Using all his willpower, he paused when he was all the way in, letting her get used to the feel of him deep inside her body. "Are you okay?" he managed to ask in a rough whisper, looking down at her.

She licked her lips. "Yes."

"Good," Korum breathed. He wasn't sure he could've stopped if she'd said otherwise. He was seconds away from orgasm, his balls drawn tightly against his body and his spine prickling with the familiar pre-release tension.

But he didn't want to come yet, not until he'd had a chance to pleasure her one more time. Using his right hand, Korum reached between their bodies, finding the place where they joined and lightly stimulating her clitoris with his fingers. At the same time, he began to move inside her, partially withdrawing and then pushing back in.

She moaned again, her fingers tightening around his shoulders and her sharp nails digging into his skin. He could feel the heat rising off her body, hear her breathing changing, and he knew she was almost there. Finally letting go of his restraint, he began to thrust with increasing speed, climbing the peak higher and higher, every muscle in his body shaking from the intensity of the sensations. Suddenly, she cried out, her inner muscles clamping down on his cock, and he exploded with a roar, his seed shooting out in several powerful spurts.

When it was over, Korum rolled off Mia onto his back and pulled her on top of him, so that she lay partially draped over his chest. They were both breathing hard, their bodies limp and covered with sweat.

Korum knew he should say something, but he couldn't seem to gather his thoughts. There was sex—and then there was what he experienced with Mia. He'd never imagined that he could want a woman so much, that he could get so much pleasure out of the simple act of fucking.

It wasn't as if he was inexperienced. Far from it. In his centuries of existence, he'd engaged in sexual acts of every type and every flavor. There was no stigma associated with promiscuous behavior in Krinar society, and unattached individuals were encouraged to experiment to their hearts' content.

Yet Korum could not remember ever feeling the kind of bone-deep satisfaction he experienced with Mia. He'd always wondered how mated individuals—or those who had a charl—remained faithful throughout their lives. The idea of not having variety had seemed strange and unnatural to him. Since meeting Mia, however, he couldn't imagine wanting to be with another woman. She was all he wanted, all the time, every time.

His breathing finally calming, Korum looked down at the curly head lying on his chest. Feeling content, he stroked her hair, grinning when he heard a quiet yawn.

"Want to take a quick rinse and then go to sleep?" he murmured, still smiling as she looked up.

She gave him a deliciously sleepy look, then yawned again. "Sure, that would be nice . . ."

Laughing softly, Korum wrapped his arms around her and got up, carrying her toward the shower. Still holding her, he stepped inside and sent a quick mental command to the water controls. Two minutes later they were clean and dry, and Korum carried her back to bed, enjoying the trusting way she clung to him the entire time.

Placing her back on the bed, he lay down beside her and pulled her into his embrace, curving his body around her from the back. Utterly relaxed, he closed his eyes and let her even breathing lull him into sleep as well.

CHAPTER TWELVE

Slowly waking up the next morning, Mia stretched and smiled, remembering last night. The entire experience had been amazing, like something she could've only dreamed of. Was sex always like this? Or was it just sex with Korum?

After that first time, he'd taken her again at some point in the night, waking her up by sliding into her. Somehow she had already been wet, and she'd orgasmed within minutes—something she would've expected to be difficult, given how satisfied she'd felt after the previous time.

But she was apparently as insatiable as her alien lover.

Grinning like a Cheshire Cat, Mia got up, put on a peach-colored sundress, and did her morning bathroom routine. Korum was already gone, so she asked the house for some yummy breakfast and then curled up on one of the floating planks that functioned as a couch. "Some reading material, please," she requested, and laughed as a razor-thin tablet-like device floated toward her from one of the walls.

Yesterday, when Korum told her about her role at the mind lab, he'd mentioned that she used to keep work-related documents and recordings on this tablet. Mia was intensely curious about it, trying to imagine how she'd functioned in a Krinar work environment given her unfamiliarity about their technology and science. From what Korum had explained, a lot of the knowledge had been transferred to her via the same process that was used to teach Krinar children, and she was secretly hoping that she'd retained some of it despite the memory wipe. She certainly felt more comfortable in Lenkarda than could be expected, and she was pretty sure she knew things about the brain that were far beyond what she'd learned in college.

Using a verbal command to open one of the files, Mia made herself comfortable and began the process of re-learning everything she had partially or completely forgotten.

* * *

"The Council has reached a decision."

Arus's words carried throughout the large arena-like room where the public portion of the trial took place. Almost every Krinar on Earth—and many residents of Krina—were there virtually or in person.

Korum leaned forward, waiting to hear the words that would seal the fate of the traitors. In front of him, he could see Loris standing straight, garbed all in black. The Protector's fists were tightly clenched, knuckles almost white, as he braced himself to hear his son's sentence.

"Rafor, Kian, Leris, Poren, Saod, Kula, and Reana,"

Arus said clearly, "the Council finds you guilty of conspiring with the human Resistance movement to attack the Centers and endanger the lives of fifty thousand of your fellow citizens. You are also found guilty of breaking the non-interference mandate by sharing Krinar technology with the said Resistance movement. Additionally, Rafor, the Council judges you guilty of aiding and abetting the dangerous individual known as Saret in his plan to commit mass murder and illegally manipulate human minds."

The Protector visibly paled, and the Keiths looked like they were punched in the stomach. A murmur ran through the crowd, then died down as the spectators fell silent to hear the rest.

"The sentence for the above crimes is complete rehabilitation."

Korum leaned back, listening to the uproar in the audience. In that moment, he felt uncharacteristic pity for Loris, who had just lost his only son. Whatever their differences had been in the past, it wasn't Loris's fault Rafor had turned out to be a failure and a criminal. Korum couldn't blame Loris for wanting to defend his child, no matter how undeserving that child was.

However, Korum had no regrets about the role he'd played in their conviction. Rafor and his friends got exactly what they deserved: an almost complete erasure of their personalities. They were too dangerous to be subjected to partial rehabilitation, their actions too heinous to be forgiven. If there was one thing Korum despised, it was someone who tried to hurt his own people for the sake of greed and power—the way these traitors had.

The brief flicker of sympathy he felt for Loris died down as the Protector turned and gave Korum a hate-filled glare. Loris's face was colorless underneath the bronzed tone of his skin, and his eyes glittered with something resembling madness. It was the look of someone who had nothing left to lose, and Korum recognized that his opponent would do everything in his power to leave him lying in pieces tomorrow. Of course, Korum had no intention of letting that happen. He didn't want to kill Loris, but he would do what was necessary to defend himself.

After the uproar in the crowd died down, the Keiths were taken away, and Korum got up, heading toward the exit. What he wanted now was Mia, but he couldn't go home yet.

He needed to reach out to the Elders again to move the project forward—and to check on his petition about Mia's parents.

* * *

"You have a visitor, Mia."

Startled by the unfamiliar female voice, Mia looked up from her reading material. Through the transparent wall, she could see a young human woman standing outside. Blowing out a relieved breath, Mia realized that the voice she'd just heard had to be Korum's intelligent house letting her know about the guest.

"Of course," Mia said, as though she talked to alien technology all the time. "Can you please let her inside?"

"Yes, Mia." And the wall in front of the visitor dissolved, creating an entrance.

Getting up from the floating plank, Mia smiled at the dark-haired girl who gracefully stepped through the opening.

"Hi," Mia said, knowing she was probably greeting

someone she'd already met before.

"Hello, Mia," the girl said, giving her a gentle smile. "I know you don't remember me, but I'm Delia. We've met a couple of times before. I'm also a charl here in Lenkarda."

"It's nice to meet you again, Delia." Mia was glad that her guest seemed to know about her condition. "I apologize in advance about my lack of recognition—"

"It's not your fault," Delia interrupted, her large brown eyes soft with concern. "How can you even apologize for something like that? I came by to see if you were all right after what happened. It must be so devastating, to wake up not knowing where you are or how you got there . . ."

Mia studied the girl, noting her quiet, yet luminous beauty and the maturity that belied her apparent youth. "Thanks, Delia," she said. "I'm actually surprisingly okay. I don't know why, but I seem to be dealing with everything quite well."

"And Korum?"

Mia gave her a questioning look. "What about Korum?"

"Is he—" Delia hesitated a little. "Is he being kind to you?"

"Of course." Mia frowned. "Why wouldn't he be? He's my . . . cheren, right?"

Delia gave her a radiant smile. "Of course. I was just heading to the waterfalls, where you and I first met. Would you be interested in coming with me? It's a really beautiful spot. I don't know if Korum showed it to you yet—"

"He hasn't," Mia admitted. "And I would love to join you." She was curious about this girl—this other charl— and she was hoping to find out more about Lenkarda and her former life there.

"Great," Delia said, still smiling. "Then let's go."

The walk to the waterfalls took a little over twenty minutes. As they made their way through the forest, Mia asked Delia about her story, wanting to find out how she'd become a charl. Then she listened in shock and fascination as the Greek girl told her about meeting Arus on the shores of the Mediterranean almost twenty-three centuries ago and how her life had unfolded since.

"When I first arrived on Krina, humans were treated very differently than they are today," Delia explained. "Two thousand years ago, many Krinar thought we were little better than primates, with our lack of technology and primitive social mores. A few, like Arus, recognized that we were not all that different from them, but most refused to think of us as an equally intelligent species. That attitude still persists today to a certain extent, although the rapid pace of progress here in the past couple of centuries has impressed many on Krina."

"They thought we were like monkeys?" Mia frowned, not liking that at all.

Delia nodded. "Something like that. I can't really blame them; after all, they were the ones to create us and make us into what we are today."

"How did they do that?" Mia asked, having wondered about that for a while. "I mean, a Krinar can almost pass for a human, and vice versa. Appearance-wise, it's like they're a different human race, rather than a separate species. I know they guided our evolution, but it's still kind of crazy ..."

"It's actually not all that crazy," Delia said. "They tinkered with our genes for millions of years, suppressing those traits that would've made us look different from them. They allowed certain subtle variations—like eye, skin, and hair color—but they ensured we would be very similar to them otherwise. It was something their Elders wanted, I believe."

Mia looked away, pondering that for a while as they continued walking through the forest. "So what do you think they want with us now?" she asked once they reached their destination.

"The Krinar?" Delia sat down on a grassy patch near the water and turned toward Mia.

"Their Elders," Mia clarified, sitting down next to her.

"Who knows?" Delia shrugged. "Even the Council doesn't fully know the motivations of the Elders. They're something like gods to them, although the Krinar don't have religion in the traditional sense."

"I see." Mia considered everything she'd learned so far. "So how do the Krinar think of us now? Korum said I worked in one of their labs. Surely they wouldn't let me do that if they thought that I was just an unusually smart monkey. Not to mention, they marry us . . ."

"Marry us?" Delia looked surprised. "What do you mean?"

"Isn't that what being a charl is? Like being married to one of them, only without the official ceremony?" That was the impression Mia had gotten yesterday from her conversation with Korum.

Delia regarded her with a thoughtful brown gaze. "I guess you could think of it that way," she said slowly. "Particularly if you apply the definition of marriage as it used to be in the past."

"In the past?"

"Yes," Delia said. "Before your time. When a wife lawfully belonged to her husband."

"What do you mean, belonged?"

"By Krinar law, a charl belongs to her cheren, Mia. We don't really have any rights here. Korum didn't tell you that?"

Mia shook her head, feeling an unpleasant tightness in her chest. "Are you saying we're their . . . slaves?"

Delia smiled. "No. The Krinar don't believe in slavery, especially not as it was practiced during my time. Most charl are very well treated and loved by their cheren. They truly do regard them as their human mates. But it's not exactly the type of equal relationship a modern girl like you would be accustomed to."

Mia stared at her. "How so?"

"Well, for instance, a Krinar doesn't need your permission to make you his charl. Arus asked me, but many cheren don't."

"Did Korum ask *me*?" Mia waited for the answer with bated breath.

"I don't know," Delia said regretfully. "I've never been privy to the particulars of your relationship. However, from what I know about Korum—and from the fact that you helped the Resistance before—I would guess that he wasn't quite as considerate of your feelings as he should've been."

Mia frowned. "What do you mean, what you know about Korum?"

Delia looked at her, as though weighing whether to proceed further. "Your cheren is a very powerful, very ambitious man," she finally said. "Many on the Council think he has the ear of the Elders. He's also known to be quite autocratic and ruthless with his opponents. That's why I was initially worried about you—because I didn't think Korum would be a particularly caring cheren. But I think I was wrong. From what I could tell, you seemed happy with him before. The last time we met, at Maria's birthday, you were practically glowing. And even now, when most women would be feeling lost and intimidated, it looks like you're doing well—and Korum has to be the one responsible for that."

Mia studied the other girl, wondering if there was something else Delia was not telling her. "You don't like my cheren, do you?"

"I don't know him personally," Delia said carefully. "I just know that Arus and he have clashed in the past over a number of different issues. But I'm glad he's good to you. When I first saw you, you seemed so young and vulnerable . . . and I couldn't help but worry about you. Now I see that you're stronger than I originally thought. You might even be a good influence on Korum. Arus thinks your cheren truly loves you—which is something we would've never expected from him."

"I see." Mia drew in a deep breath and looked away, trying to process what she'd just learned. Perhaps her silly thought about Korum as a villain wasn't as far-fetched as it seemed. Not for the first time, she wished she could remember the past couple of months, so she could better understand this complex relationship she was in. What exactly was Korum to her? What did it mean to be his charl? And which was the real Korum? The tender lover of last night, or the ruthless Councilor Delia had described?

Perhaps he was both. Mia considered that for a minute. Yes, she could definitely see how that could be the case. After all, Korum himself had told her about how he had used her in the past to crush the Resistance. Yet he seemed to truly love her now—and Mia couldn't help the warm feeling that spread through her at the thought.

Turning back toward the Greek girl, Mia looked at

her. "Delia," she said quietly, bringing up a topic that had been worrying her since yesterday, "do you know what happens in an Arena fight?"

"Yes." Delia gave her a sympathetic look. "You know about Loris's challenge?"

"Korum told me about it yesterday," Mia said. "Have you ever seen one of these fights? Are they common?"

"They're not as common as they used to be a long time ago, but they still happen with some regularity. There are usually a couple of fights a year, sometimes more."

"And how dangerous are they?"

Delia hesitated for a second. "Arena fighting is the number one cause of death for the Krinar," she finally said. "Followed by various accidents."

Mia felt like she'd been punched in the stomach. "Does someone always die during a fight?"

"No, not always. Sometimes the winner can control himself enough to stop in time. Generally, though, Krinar men don't have the best control over their instincts during the heat of battle." The Greek charl didn't seem particularly bothered by that.

Mia swallowed. "I see."

"But to answer your earlier question, I do think Krinar attitudes toward humans are changing," Delia said, coming back to their previous discussion. "Two thousand years ago, the idea of a human working in a Krinar lab would've been unthinkable. They've come a long way since then, and I see things improving more and more every day. The fact that they're living here on Earth, among us, is a game changer in many ways. They see now that we truly *are* their sister species, that we have the potential to achieve as much as they did."

"They no longer think we're just smart monkeys?"

Mia said, only half-jokingly.

Delia smiled. "Some still do, I'm sure. But it's no longer the consensus view. And the more relationships like yours and mine there are, the more accepted humans will become in the Krinar society." She paused for a second. "So you see, Mia, you don't have to be fighting the Krinar to help your people. You just have to get one of them to fall in love with you."

* * *

Five thousand miles away, Saret got up and smiled at the human girl lying curled in a little naked ball in his bed. She was petite, no more than five feet tall, and her dark brown hair fell in soft waves around her narrow face. Other than her brown eyes, she looked very much like Mia. He'd found her in Paris yesterday.

She stared at him, and he could see the fear and hatred on her small face. It was unfortunate that she'd been engaged when he met her, with her wedding planned for next month. She had been understandably resistant to his attentions, and he didn't have the time to seduce her properly.

It had been wrong to take her, of course. Saret knew that. At this point, however, it didn't matter. Everyone already thought him a monster, and stealing one human was a harmless prank in the grand scheme of things. He had bitten her during sex, so he knew she'd found pleasure with him too. She wasn't Mia, but he had still enjoyed fucking her, pretending that the slim body in his arms was the one he truly wanted.

Saret knew he had no hope of eluding the guardians for much longer; it was only a matter of time before he would be captured. Now that he had gotten a chance to think, he realized how Korum had known what to expect. It was very simple, really. His enemy must've been monitoring his charl even more thoroughly than he had admitted to Saret. In hindsight, Saret should've expected something like that; it was his own fault he'd underestimated Korum's obsession with Mia.

No, Saret knew he wouldn't be able to hide for much longer. He'd been utilizing various disguises, but he could sense the guardians getting closer. Yesterday, he had taken a risk and connected to the Krinar network. He'd tried to hide his identity, but he was sure Korum would eventually find his traces in cyberspace. Still, Saret had needed to know what was happening in Lenkarda and whether the Council had found out about his plan.

What he'd learned had made him both angry and excited at the same time. Angry—because his carefully planted nano dispersion devices had already been discovered and neutralized. And excited—because he finally knew how to get rid of Korum once and for all.

His enemy's upcoming fight would be his last.

Saret would make sure of that.

CHAPTER THIRTEEN

The first thing Korum saw when he entered the house was Mia, curled up on the long float and absorbed in whatever she was reading on her tablet.

At his entry, she looked up and smiled, her face bright with excitement. "Hi," she said. "How was your day?"

Korum felt a surge of tenderness, even as his body reacted predictably to her nearness. "Hello, my sweet," he said, stepping toward her and bending down to give her a brief kiss. He had been thinking about her all day today, reliving every moment of the previous night in his mind. He couldn't wait to re-introduce her to the pleasures of lovemaking, to taste her delicious body over and over again.

He wanted to take it slow again, but the second his lips touched hers, her slender arms came up, looping around his neck, and all his good intentions evaporated in an instant. Her mouth was soft and sweet as he deepened the kiss, her scent warm and feminine. He could hear her breathing speeding up, smell her desire, feel her body arching up toward him . . . and his blood almost boiled in his veins.

Without a conscious thought, his hands went to her dress, and the fragile fabric ripped underneath his fingers, exposing the delicate flesh underneath. She gasped, and he could feel her nails digging into the back of his neck as he sucked at the tender spot near her shoulder. Her heart rate spiked, and she moaned as his hand went to her thighs, pushing between them to get to her tight opening.

She was hot and slick around his fingers, and Korum used the last vestiges of his self-control to bring her to orgasm by rhythmically pressing his thumb against her clit. As soon as she convulsed with a soft cry, he knew he could not hold out any longer. Tearing off his own clothes, he grabbed her legs and pulled her toward him until only her upper body was lying on the float. Then he pushed inside her in one powerful thrust.

She cried out, her body tensing, and Korum groaned as her inner muscles squeezed his shaft, preventing him from going deeper. Her eyes snapped open, focusing on him, and Korum held her gaze, knowing that she could see the dark craving written on his face. His cock throbbed inside her snug channel, and it wasn't enough. The animal inside him needed to possess her on a level that went beyond the sexual, to imprint himself on her mind as well as body.

"You're all mine," he whispered harshly, hardly realizing what he was saying. "Do you understand me?"

She just stared at him, her face flushed and her lips slightly parted, and Korum could feel his temperature rising. A wave of pure possessiveness swept through his body. His buttocks tightened as he pushed deeper into her, holding her thighs wide open to aid in his penetration. She gasped, her face contorting with a mix of pain and pleasure, and he could hear her breath catching in her throat.

Leaning forward, he let go of her legs and slid one arm under her upper back, bringing her closer. His other hand found its way to her hair, holding her head partially arched back, her slender neck exposed. "Say it, Mia," he commanded, driven by a primitive need to claim her. "Say you're mine."

"I'm..." She seemed to have trouble saying the words, her blue eyes clouded with some unknown emotion, and the urge to dominate her grew stronger. Bending his head, he took her mouth in a savage kiss, his hand slipping down to her folds and his thumb pressing hard on her clitoris. Her inner walls tightened around his cock like a fist, and she moaned into his mouth.

"You're mine," he repeated, drawing back for a second, and she nodded, staring up at him, her lips swollen and shiny.

"Say it."

"I'm yours." Her whisper was barely audible, but it satisfied his craving for now.

Leaning down, he kissed her again, more gently this time, even as he began thrusting with a smooth, steady tempo. His balls drew up against his body as pure, unadulterated pleasure coursed through his veins, all courtesy of the small girl in his arms. Closing his eyes, Korum let the sensations wash over him, reveling in her taste, in the feel of her soft skin under his fingers... in the tight clasp of her body around his cock.

And just when the pleasure became too intense, he felt her convulse around him with a soft cry, sending him over the edge.

* * *

A few hours later, Korum woke up to the familiar feel of Mia lying pressed against his side. Her breathing was quiet and even, and he knew she was deeply asleep, worn out by his sexual demands. He'd managed to abstain from drinking her blood this time, since he'd indulged fairly recently, but he hadn't been able to stop himself from taking her a couple more times throughout the night. Sometimes he wondered if it was normal, the way he craved her all the time. He'd always had a strong sexual drive, but he'd never felt the urge to have one woman over and over again. With Mia, he simply couldn't get enough, and he wasn't sure he liked being so dependent on one tiny human girl.

In general, his obsession with her bothered him on multiple levels. As happy as she made him, the depth of his feelings for her was unsettling. If he ever lost her . . . Korum couldn't bear to even think of that possibility, his chest squeezing in agony at the idea.

Slowly disengaging from her, Korum got up, trying to be as quiet as possible to avoid waking her up. She needed far more sleep than a Krinar, and he always made sure she got enough rest. Even with the nanocytes in her body, she was still far too fragile and vulnerable for his peace of mind. If he had his way, she would never go anywhere alone, always staying safely by his side.

But Korum knew she would hate it if he restricted her independence too much. As it was, she resented the few safety measures he'd implemented. She viewed the tracking devices as a way to control her, as an invasion of her privacy, not understanding how important her safety and well-being were to him.

It was already five in the morning—a late start to the day for Korum. Normally, he would already be working at this time, but he hadn't gone to sleep until three hours ago, staying up late to satisfy his hunger for Mia. He needed her even more than usual, feeling edgy and restless in anticipation of the upcoming fight.

He wasn't afraid. In fact, the prospect of danger excited him. It had always been this way; in his youth, he'd even provoked a couple of fights just to feel that rush of adrenaline. As he got older, however, he'd learned to suppress that part of his nature, to use sports as an outlet for excess energy. As a result, he hadn't been in a real fight—with the exception of Saur's attack in Florida—for a solid eighty years.

He did worry about having Mia at the Arena, though. The venue would be crowded, with almost every Krinar on Earth attending the event in person. Those on Krina would watch virtually. The idea of having her out in public after everything that happened made him uneasy, even though he knew there was little real danger. The fight was to be in Lenkarda, while Saret was somewhere out in the human world.

Still, Korum would've kept her away if it weren't for the fact that doing so would be the equivalent of insulting her in public. Arena fights were considered to be one of the most important and interesting parts of Krinar life, and everyone—charl included—was expected to be there. Deliberately excluding Mia would make it seem like Korum was punishing her for something—which couldn't be further from the truth.

Thinking about it further, Korum decided to have two guardians watching Mia at all times. He would also arrange to have her sitting next to Delia, just in case his charl needed reassurance from an older, more experienced friend. That way, he wouldn't have to worry about her during the fight—and thus be able to fully concentrate on his opponent. Even a moment of inattention in the Arena could be deadly.

In the meantime, he had a few hours before the main event. The best thing to do at this point was to catch up with his designers and make sure that they were working on the prototype of the shielding technology he'd recently developed. Voret and the rest of the Council were understandably worried about utilizing the old shields now, so that project had to take priority.

Casting one last look at his sleeping charl, Korum left the house.

CHAPTER FOURTEEN

Mia waited for Delia to pick her up, her foot tapping nervously on the floor. She was almost sick with anxiety in anticipation of the fight, and she was glad the other charl was going to be with her during the event.

To distract herself, Mia took a deep breath and looked down at the gleaming material of her white dress. Korum had left it for her this morning, and she'd figured she was supposed to wear it to the event. Unlike the usual light and flowing Krinar clothing, her outfit today was made of some stiff, relatively thick cloth and fit her body closely. It had a subtle shine to it, as did her sandals today. Korum had also given her a beautiful necklace to put around her neck. If Mia didn't know better, she would've thought she was getting dressed up for her own wedding.

She hadn't seen Korum this morning, although he'd called and promised to meet her in the Arena before the fight officially began. When they'd spoken, she could hear a note of barely suppressed excitement in his voice, and she knew he was looking forward to this barbaric ritual.

It still struck her as odd that she felt so attuned to him after just a couple of days. She could sense his moods, discern his emotions. She could even predict some of his reactions. When he'd come home last night, she'd known exactly what would happen when she wrapped her arms around his neck and transformed an innocent kiss into something more. As much as she had enjoyed their first night together, it had been obvious to her that Korum was holding himself back, that he was trying to make allowances for her 'inexperience.' And, while she had appreciated his restraint, it somehow wasn't enough. Last night, she hadn't wanted sweet and gentle; she'd wanted him wild and out-of-control, his true nature fully revealed.

His possessiveness both scared and thrilled her. If she didn't want him so much, she would've been frightened by his passion, by his insistence on her giving him every part of herself. It made her wonder what would happen if she ever tried to leave him. Would he let her go, or would he stop her from going home? Could he stop her? If Delia were to be believed, humans had very few rights inside Krinar settlements—an idea that bothered Mia quite a bit.

Of course, none of that mattered right now, in light of the upcoming fight. Looking impatiently at her wristwatch-bracelet device, Mia saw that it was already twenty minutes before noon. *Where was Delia?* The wait was heightening Mia's anxiety.

Two minutes later, she finally saw a small transport pod landing outside, next to the house. Delia came out of the aircraft and waved to her. Relieved, Mia smiled, glad to see the other girl. Arus's charl was wearing a dress that was similar to Mia's, and she looked stunning, her dark hair smooth and threaded with some strange-looking jewelry.

Quickly exiting the house, Mia approached the Greek girl. "Thanks for picking me up," she said as she got closer.

"Of course," Delia said. "I would've done it even if Korum hadn't asked. You must be so frightened right now."

"I'm beyond frightened," Mia admitted. "I feel like I could puke when I think about it."

Delia smiled. "I can see that. Here, come inside, and we'll head over there."

"Has Arus ever been in one of these fights?" Mia asked, following her into the aircraft and taking a seat on one of the floating chairs inside.

"A few times," Delia replied, giving her an understanding look. "And every time I thought I'd have a heart attack. Believe me, I know exactly what you're going through."

"It was probably worse for you," Mia said. "At least I've only known Korum for a couple of days." Although it might as well have been a couple of years, given the nearly paralyzing fear she was feeling at the thought of losing him.

Taking a deep breath, Mia tried to calm herself by studying her surroundings. After all, she had never been in an alien aircraft before—or, at least, didn't remember the experience. To her surprise, she could see that the inside of the pod resembled the interior of Korum's house to a large degree, with light colors, transparent walls, and floating seats. There was no obvious 'technology,' as she was used to seeing it in the human world. Instead, everything seemed to work effortlessly, almost like magic.

As the aircraft took off, Mia could see the green forest through the transparent floor. In the distance, the blue waters of the Pacific Ocean sparkled in the bright sun. It was a beautiful day, and, under any other circumstances, Mia would've greatly enjoyed the ride. As it was, she couldn't stop thinking about what was to come.

Another question occurred to her, and she looked up, meeting Delia's gaze. "How long do these fights tend to last?" Mia asked, her imagination conjuring up a horrifying day-long bloody ordeal.

"Anywhere from a few minutes to a couple of hours," the Greek girl said. "It really depends on how evenly the opponents are matched. There's also a short ceremony before, and a longer one after, during which the winner celebrates."

"Celebrates how?"

Delia smiled, and there was a mischievous twinkle in her brown eyes. "Well, an unattached male will often choose one or more unattached females, and they will couple in a *shatela*—a tent-like structure in the middle of the Arena. Attached men will usually do the same with their mate."

Sex in public? Was Delia serious? Mia could feel furious color flooding her face. "And those with charl?"

Delia laughed. "That depends. Arus is very considerate when it comes to my human sensibilities, and he would usually just kiss me in the Arena and wait until we got home to celebrate properly. Others have been known to treat their charl just like Krinar women in this situation."

"So you're saying that if Korum wins, he might want to have sex in front of everyone?"

"Perhaps," Delia said, grinning. "Nobody will really see you, though, since you'll be inside the shatela. They might only hear you."

"Oh great. That makes it so much better," Mia muttered. She remembered what Korum had told her about the Celebration of Forty-Seven, and how she had been glad that, as a human, she wouldn't be expected to participate in the exhibitionist spectacle. But now it seemed like there was no getting away from it—unless Korum 'respected her human sensibilities.' Just one more thing for her to worry about during the fight.

Before she had a chance to think about this further, the transport pod landed quietly in a wooded area.

"We're here," Delia said, getting up.

Mia got up as well and followed her out of the aircraft. It looked like they were in the middle of the forest. "Where is here?"

Delia turned toward her, and Mia was shocked to see an excited gleam in her eyes. "The Arena," she said and gestured toward a tree-covered hill in front of them.

Mia raised her eyebrows but didn't say anything as they walked toward the elevation. She could hear a dull roar in the distance, like a massive waterfall of some kind. Was the Arena near a river? Carefully stepping forward, she concentrated on avoiding bugs or whatever else could be crawling in a Costa Rican jungle. Her thin-soled sandals were not exactly hiking-friendly, and Mia sincerely hoped she wouldn't get stung or bitten before they got to the fight. If she recalled correctly, tarantulas were one of the hazards of this part of the world—although she was now supposedly immune to such dangers, with the nanocytes circulating throughout her body and quickly repairing any cellular damage.

As they got further up the hill, Mia realized that the sound she was hearing was the muted buzz of a crowd. Somewhere nearby, thousands of Ks were gathered to watch the fight. Apparently eager to join them, Delia ran up the rest of the hill, moving with almost Krinar-like grace herself. "Here it is," she said, turning toward Mia and pointing straight ahead.

Her heart pounding and her palms sweating, Mia hurried to catch up with the other charl. When she reached the top of the hill, she stopped dead in her tracks. The green valley below was a spectacle unlike any other she had ever seen in her life. Thousands—no, tens of thousands—of Krinar were gathered below. Tall and golden-skinned, the aliens were dressed in blindingly white clothing that shimmered in the sunlight. While the majority mingled on the ground, a number of them occupied floating seats that were arranged in circles around a large clearing. It was like a round football field, only with the spectators floating in the air instead of sitting in the bleachers—or like a high-tech version of an ancient Roman amphitheater. The latter was probably a better comparison, Mia thought, given what was about to take place.

"Mia! There you are!"

Turning to her right, Mia saw Korum approaching them. Unlike everybody else, he was dressed in his usual clothes—a light-colored shirt and pair of shorts. Coming closer, he pulled her to him for a quick hug and kissed her forehead. "How are you, my sweet?" he asked, looking down at her with a warm smile.

Mia could feel her heart beating faster at his nearness. "I'm good. Are you ready for the fight?"

"Of course." He stroked her cheek with his fingers, then turned toward Delia. "Thanks for bringing Mia here," he said, giving the other girl a smile. His left arm was still wrapped around Mia, holding her pressed tightly against his side.

"It was my pleasure," Delia said, giving Korum a regal nod. "I'll let you two catch up. Mia, when you're done, please come join me. We're sitting over there." She pointed toward a row of floating seats that were closest to the clearing.

"I'll bring her there in a minute," Korum promised, looking faintly amused at the other girl's imperious manner.

As soon as Delia disappeared into the crowd, he bent his head and brought Mia up for a more thorough kiss, one of his large hands cupping her skull and the other holding her lower body pressed against his. She could feel the hardness of his erection pushing against her belly, the strength of his arms surrounding her, and heat flooded her body, culminating in the sensitive area between her legs. His lips and tongue teased and caressed her mouth, pleasuring her, consuming her, until she forgot all about the crowds around them, caught up in a sensual daze.

When he finally let her come up for air, she was desperately clinging to him, heedless of their public location.

"Fuck," he cursed in a rough whisper, lifting his head and staring down at her with bright golden eyes, "I can't wait for this fight to be over. You drive me insane sometimes, you know that?"

Mia licked her lips, tasting him there. She was so aroused she could barely stand it, her hips moving involuntarily, trying to rub against him. Yet something nagged at the back of her mind, breaking through the fog of desire clouding her brain.

She pushed at his chest, trying to put some distance between them so she could think. "Delia said . . ." Mia hesitated, not knowing how to phrase it. "Delia said the victor celebrates by, um . . ."

"By fucking?" Korum asked, his eyes still filled with a golden glow. "Is that what she told you?"

Mia nodded, her cheeks burning.

Korum took a small step back, but still held her close. "It's true," he said, his voice low and husky. "If I win, I would be expected to celebrate that way. Would it be a problem?"

Mia stared up at him. "You mean . . . You'd want to do it in public?"

"It's not exactly public, my sweet," he said, one corner of his mouth tilting up. "We'd be in a shatela—a structure specifically designed for that purpose. But yes, I would very much like to fuck you after the fight. Your sweet body would be my reward."

* * *

Korum could see her pupils expanding, making her blue eyes look darker. Her breathing was uneven, and her cheeks were a pretty pink color. She was turned on, almost as much as he was right now. If this was already after the fight, he was sure she wouldn't protest if he brought her to a shatela, stripped off that tight dress, and plunged his cock between her thighs. He liked the idea of claiming her in front of everyone; it appealed to something primeval deep within him.

"Korum, I—"

"Shhh," he said, lifting his finger to her lips in a gesture he'd seen humans make. "Don't worry about it now. I won't force you to do anything you don't want to do."

And Korum meant it. He had not set out to prove anything when he kissed Mia, but her reaction clearly demonstrated her susceptibility to him. Despite the memory loss, she was as strongly attracted to him as before—a realization that filled him with bone-deep masculine satisfaction. He would never force her, but he also likely wouldn't have to. He suspected his little charl was more adventurous than she thought herself to be.

She was still watching him warily, so he bent his head and kissed her delicious mouth again. Just a brief kiss this time, no more than a brush of his lips against her own. His body screamed for him to do more, to take her now, but there was no time. He had to go get ready for the fight.

But even a small kiss was enough to distract her right now. Her eyes looked soft again, hazy with desire. Korum had to force himself to look away in order to regain control.

"Come," he said hoarsely, "let's get you to your seat. I have to go now, but I want to make sure you're settled with Delia before I leave."

"Of course." She seemed anxious again, some of the color leaving her face. "Is it starting at noon sharp?"

"Yes," Korum said, taking her hand and starting to lead her through the crowd. "We tend to be punctual, so we have exactly ten minutes before the ceremony begins."

They walked toward the front row, where Delia and Arus were already in place. Only one float next to Delia remained empty, and Korum led Mia there. As they approached, the crowd parted, letting them through. His acquaintances gave him polite nods as they passed, while others stared at him and his charl with unabashed curiosity. This didn't bother Korum one bit. As a Council member with a certain reputation, he was used to this type of attention. Mia was a figure of interest as well, given rumors of her involvement with the Resistance. The Krinar did not consider staring rude; on the contrary, it was a sign of respect to look at someone directly.

"Oh, good," Delia said as they got to her seat. "I was worried you wouldn't make it before the start of the fight."

"No worries, we're here," Mia said, blushing a little. Korum suppressed a smile, knowing she was embarrassed about their public make-out session. His little darling was still such an innocent; he enjoyed her shyness almost as much as he liked curing her of it.

Arus gave Korum a level look. "We'll take good care of Mia, I promise. You don't need to worry about her right now."

"Thanks," Korum said, glad that the other Councilor understood his unspoken concern. Even knowing that it was safe, he still felt uncomfortable leaving Mia alone in public. What happened with Saret had left an indelible impression in his mind, and he knew he would have to work hard to overcome his fear of losing her.

All around them, other Krinar settled in their floats, clearing out of the aisles and emptying the Arena field. Less than five minutes remained before the start of the ceremony, and Korum still had to prepare, mentally and physically, for what was to come.

"I have to go," he said reluctantly, watching Mia's eyes fill with moisture at his words.

"Be careful," she whispered, looking up at him. "Please, Korum, be careful." And wrapping her arms around his waist, she gave him a fierce hug, holding him for several long seconds.

Touched, Korum hugged her back and then gently stepped out of her embrace. "I love you," he said, giving her one last smile.

"And I love you," Mia whispered as he started to walk away.

Korum stopped in his tracks, hardly daring to believe his ears. Turning his head, he saw that her eyes were glistening with unshed tears. He wanted to grab her, to ask her if she really meant it, but there was no time. Instead, he gave her the biggest smile he could and continued on toward a small structure on the far side of the Arena.

The ceremony was about to begin.

* * *

Mia sat down on her floating seat, feeling like a vise was squeezing her heart. Despite all of Korum's reassurances, she knew there was a very real chance that she was seeing him for the last time.

The thought was so agonizing that Mia couldn't breathe for a moment.

"Mia? Listen to me, Mia. He's going to be fine, okay?" It was Delia, her voice calm and soothing.

Mia blinked, focusing on the other charl with effort. "I know," she said with a confidence she didn't feel. "Of course, I know that."

The Krinar male who was with Delia gave her a reassuring smile too. "She's right, Mia," he said in a deep, quiet voice. "Your cheren is very good at this. He's never lost a fight yet. I'm Arus, by the way. We've never met in person before."

"Oh, hi," Mia said, automatically offering her hand for a handshake. "It's nice to meet you."

Arus's smile got wider. "No handshake allowed, I'm afraid," he said gently. "I wouldn't want to end up on that field facing Korum next."

"Oh, right." Mia withdrew her hand, mildly embarrassed. "I'm sorry; I forgot. Korum did tell me a little bit about your customs yesterday."

"You have nothing to be sorry about," Delia said. "I'm very impressed by how quickly you're re-learning everything. It took me a long time to get as comfortable as you seem to be right now."

"Yeah, I don't know why that is," Mia admitted. "Maybe I'm remembering things on a subconscious level."

"You also seem to have strong feelings for Korum already," Arus observed, his dark eyes filled with speculation as he looked at Mia. "More than could be expected in this situation. I wonder why. I'm not a mind expert, but this seems fairly unusual."

"Really?" Mia frowned in puzzlement. "I thought maybe a memory erasure procedure doesn't get rid of memories completely—"

"It's supposed to," Arus said. "If it's a standard memory wipe, then you should be as you were a few months ago: with zero knowledge of our world or Korum. The fact that you're adjusting so quickly is . . . interesting, to say the least."

Mia looked at him, wondering what it all meant. Ever since she woke up in Lenkarda, her feelings and reactions have been strange. Was it possible that Saret had screwed up and didn't succeed in erasing her memories fully after all?

A loud chime-like sound startled Mia out of her speculations.

The pre-fight ceremony was beginning.

A tall Krinar male dressed in an unusual blue outfit stepped out of one of the small structures on the edges of the Arena and walked toward the middle of the field.

"That's Voret," Delia whispered, leaning toward Mia for a second. "He's one of the oldest Council members."

Mia nodded, her eyes glued to what was happening

below.

"Residents of Earth and those watching us on Krina right now," Voret said, his deep voice filling the entire amphitheater, "welcome to the ancient rite of the Arena Challenge. As all of you know, the fight today is between two of our esteemed Council members: Loris and Korum. The cause of this Challenge, like all others, is a disagreement that can only be settled in blood."

Voret raised his arm and blue light seemed to flow from his fingertips, becoming a giant three-dimensional image floating in mid-air. It showed a strange forest, with green, yellow, red, and orange plants. "For generations, we have gathered in the Arena to witness the resolution of such a disagreement. It all began after the Great War, when we nearly tore each other apart after the demise of the *lonar*—our source of life-giving blood. Violence was a way of life then—and it would still be today if not for the Arena Challenge."

The floating image began to change, as though a camera was zooming in on a particular portion of that alien forest. Mia stared in fascination as the image showed a Krinar male, dressed in some brown-colored scraps of material, leaping through the trees with a speed that would make Tarzan jealous. Below him, small humanoid creatures were scurrying on the ground, their bodies covered with light blond hair and nothing else. These had to be the lonar, Mia realized, seeing the predatory look on the Krinar male's face as he stalked them from above. He wasn't as beautiful as the modern Ks; his features were rougher, less symmetric, though he still had the typical K coloring of dark hair and golden skin.

"We have evolved as hunters. Predators." Voret's voice echoed throughout the Arena. "We need violence. We crave it. For a peaceful society to function, we need an outlet—a way to resolve disagreements that would otherwise lead to conflict and war. The Arena is that outlet."

The Krinar in the image leapt from the trees above, jumping down on the ground in front of the hapless lonar. They screamed in fear, their cries oddly monkey-like, and turned to run, but it was too late. One of them—a female—was already caught in the K's steely embrace, and he was slicing his sharp teeth over her neck. Bright red blood trickled down her neck and chest, its color startling against the primate's light-colored fur.

"The extinction of the lonar nearly destroyed us. The fact that we survived is a testament to the heroic efforts of those scientists who came up with a blood substitute in the middle of war and chaos."

The image changed now, no longer showing the forest or the Krinar feeding on the helpless female. Instead, three strong-featured male Ks were displayed, their harsh faces more similar to the ancient hunter's than to the gorgeous Krinar surrounding Mia.

"In the Arena, we honor all those who came before us—and all those who will come after. With this rite of violence, we honor peace—and the laws that make it possible."

Now the floating image was showing the same colorful forest as before—only this time it was populated by the pale oblong structures that served as modern Krinar dwellings. A couple was strolling through the woods, a K male and female, wearing the light-colored clothing Mia was used to seeing. They looked beautiful and happy, walking together while holding hands. The image lingered for a few seconds, then winked out of existence, leaving only Voret standing in the middle of the Arena.

He remained quiet for a second, and then his voice

boomed again. "Now it is time for the fighters to join me. Loris and Korum, please enter the Arena."

Mia held her breath as the two Ks emerged, Korum from a structure to the right of Mia and Loris from a structure to the left. Instead of the usual Krinar attire—or the formal white clothing of the spectators—they each wore a pair of calf-length pants that were the color of fresh blood. Their feet and chests were bare, except for swirls of red paint that decorated their arms and torsos.

Swallowing to moisten her dry throat, Mia stared at her lover in fascination. He looked gorgeous—and utterly savage. Sitting in the front row, she could see the yellow-gold color of his eyes, light and striking against the bronze hue of his skin. His semi-nakedness only accentuated the power of his body; his muscles flexed and rippled as he walked, his posture graceful and threatening at the same time.

The other Krinar was an inch or two taller, with a slightly bulkier build. The expression on his hawk-like features was dark and full of hatred.

The two fighters approached the blue-clad figure in the middle of the Arena, pausing respectfully a couple of feet away. Voret turned toward Loris and addressed him, "Loris, you have chosen to challenge Korum today. Is that true?"

"Yes," the Krinar said, his eyes glittering with the same dark anticipation Mia could see on Korum's face.

Voret nodded, apparently satisfied. Turning to Korum, he asked, "Do you accept Loris's challenge?"

"I do," Korum replied.

"Then let the fight begin."

CHAPTER FIFTEEN

Korum watched as Voret lifted his arms—a signal to begin. At the same time, the float that was underneath Voret's feet activated, lifting the Councilor into the air high above the Arena. It was the only way the Mediator—a role filled by Voret today—could stay safe during the fight.

His eyes glued to his opponent, Korum slowly began circling Loris, looking for the best opportunity to strike. He could feel his heart beating harder, the blood circulating faster through his veins. His mind was clear and razor-sharp, focused entirely on his enemy. It was always that way for him in the Arena; the adrenaline boosted Korum's concentration, enhanced his reflexes. Somewhere in the back of his mind, he was aware that Mia was watching him right now. He could feel her gaze on his skin, and it gave him even more of a rush than the upcoming fight itself.

Loris responded by moving in a slow circle as well, his dark eyes burning with hatred. Korum gave him a taunting smile, wanting to enrage him further. It was one of the most basic principles of defrebs: the fighter who keeps a cool head wins. When Loris had attacked him in the Council meeting chamber, it had been laughably easy for Korum to subdue him—partially because the Protector had been completely out of control.

A smile: such a simple thing, but it worked. Loris's jaw tightened, the muscle near his ear twitching. And then he struck, his right arm lashing out, his fingers hooked into a deadly weapon.

Korum avoided Loris's strike with ease, his body twisting at the last moment. At the same time, his foot kicked out, hitting Loris's knee with so much force that Korum could hear the other man's joint snapping in half.

Loris screamed in pain, stumbling back, and Korum leapt on top of him, using the momentum from his jump to bring the Protector to the ground. Up-close combat was dangerous, but less so now that his opponent was partially—albeit temporarily—crippled. His fist smashed into Loris face, once, then again and again, each movement lightning-fast. At the same time, Korum's knee slammed into Loris's side, bruising his internal organs.

This was not going to be a long fight.

In fact, subduing the Protector was so easy that Korum should be able to avoid killing him altogether.

* * *

Two rows away from Mia, Saret waited for the perfect moment to strike, all of his attention focused on the combatants. It was risky to be so close to the stage, but it maximized his odds of success—and put him within grabbing distance of Mia, if the opportunity presented itself.

Of course, when he'd chosen this location, he didn't know Korum's charl would be so heavily guarded. Not only was she sitting next to Arus, but there were also at least two guardians watching her. Saret had spotted them earlier. They tried to blend with the crowd, but their sharp gazes betrayed their true purpose: they were there to protect Mia.

Saret wondered if Korum suspected anything, or if he was just being paranoid about his charl's safety. Either way, it looked like Mia was out of Saret's reach for now—at least while Korum was alive. Once his enemy was out of the way, however, it would be a different matter. Unless another influential Krinar took Mia as his charl, she would be brought to Krina, where Saret would be able to claim her under his other identity.

Saret's interest in different identities had started several centuries ago, long before he had begun developing his plans for humans. He had been put in charge of rehabilitating a criminal who was a master of disguises, pretending to be three people at once, complete with different physical appearances, legal documents, and established lives. Saret had been so fascinated that he'd spent countless hours learning all about the man's craft. The criminal had been more than happy to tell him everything he knew in exchange for a milder version of rehabilitation than the one he'd been sentenced to.

Saret's second identity had started off as a joke, as a way to see if he could get away with something like that in their technologically advanced society. And, to his surprise, he'd discovered that he could; all it took was the right tools, knowledge of several government databases, and a couple of centuries to create a convincing new persona.

Saret—the mind expert—was now considered a criminal. Juron, however, was a law-abiding citizen of Krina who was currently doing some individual space exploration in the Krinar solar system. It would be Juron who claimed Mia as his charl next.

All Saret needed was to kill Korum right now, and at least that part of his plan would be successful. Then he could try to bring peace to Earth again.

His current disguise was yet another identity he had started to develop here on Earth. It was not as airtight as that of Juron, but it was good enough to get him past all the security and into Lenkarda for the fight. No one suspected right now that the man sitting so close to the stage was the most wanted Krinar in the universe.

Saret glanced at Mia again, then looked away. It wouldn't do to stare at her openly, even though many others were doing the same thing. She was oblivious to everything, all of her attention focused on the fight. Saret cursed under his breath. It seemed like his little experiment had backfired in a major way, and she was growing attached to that bastard again.

That was really unfortunate. Now she would be more than a little upset when he died.

Slowly raising his hand, Saret aimed at the stage and waited for the perfect moment. When Korum jumped at Loris, Saret knew the time had come.

Taking a deep breath, he activated the weapon.

* * *

Korum raised his fist to deliver another blow, and in that moment his arm froze.

A wave of pain traveled down his body, starting at the back of his neck. His limbs felt uncontrollably heavy, his muscles shaking with the effort of holding himself up. *A basic stun weapon.* Korum knew it with sudden certainty. The guardians' scanners were designed to catch anything dangerous, but this kind of stunner used an older, simpler technology—one that was much more difficult to detect from a distance.

Reflexively clutching the back of his neck, Korum felt himself sliding off Loris's body. His back hit the ground, leaving him lying there helpless, unable to move for a few precious seconds. To the spectators, it would look like Loris had delivered him a hidden blow of some kind; the stunner possibility would not occur to anyone right away.

Despite the danger—or maybe because of it— Korum's mind operated with crystal clarity, analyzing the situation in an instant. There was only one person motivated enough to risk doing something like that.

Saret. He was here at the fight.

The hit had been to the back of Korum's neck. He knew what a basic stunner felt like, had experienced its sting before. Just like a human gun, it was a weapon that had to be aimed from a specific location.

A location that could be triangulated.

Ignoring the pain and weakness racking his body, Korum sent a mental query to his internal computer . . . and then he knew.

His enemy was only steps away from Mia.

Fear, sharp and gut-wrenching, slithered through Korum's veins, followed by a rage so intense his entire body shook with it.

He couldn't save himself right now, but he'd be damned if he failed to protect Mia again.

Closing his eyes, Korum focused on connecting to the guardians' private communication network.

* * *

Mia stifled a scream as she saw Korum jerk convulsively and then slide off Loris's body. Up until now, he had seemed invincible, utterly in control of the situation. She had even begun to relax, some of her fear ebbing as she'd witnessed her lover's effortless display of skill in the Arena.

Until everything changed in an instant.

What happened? She could see Korum clutching the back of his neck as if something bit him there. He seemed dazed, weakened by something.

What the fuck happened?

She could see Loris rising to his feet. He was already moving better, his Krinar body recovering from the injuries Korum had inflicted on him.

And Korum was still lying there, like he couldn't move. Even his eyes were closed, preventing him from seeing his opponent.

"No!" Mia heard her own scream echoing through the Arena. Delia grabbed her arm, keeping her from jumping from her seat as Loris attacked Korum's prone body.

She could see the glee on the other K's face as he struck again and again, could smell the metallic odor of blood that turned their painted bodies a brighter red.

It was Korum's blood.

"No!" Another agonized scream tore from her throat. Now there was a sickening sound of fist connecting with flesh, over and over again. "No, stop!" Mia wrenched her arm out of Delia's hold and jumped to her feet.

"Mia, don't! You can't interfere—" The Greek girl tried to grab her again, but Mia shook her off like a fly, desperate to get into the arena.

She managed to take two steps before a steely arm

went around her waist, pressing her against a hard male body. Mia clawed at that imprisoning arm, heedless of all but the slaughter happening in front of her eyes. "Stop the fight! It's a setup! Can't you see? He can't fight! It's a setup!" The arm only tightened further. "Let me go! Let me fucking go!"

Mia was vaguely aware that she was screaming like a banshee, yelling out anything that came to mind, but it didn't matter. Arus was holding her now, and she was furiously fighting him, trying to twist out of his grasp. It was impossible to win against a Krinar, but it didn't matter.

Mia was past any semblance of rationality.

* * *

Korum could feel the blows from Loris's fist, his body shuddering in agony as the Protector's claw-like fingers gouged out chunks of his flesh.

Emboldened by Korum's apparent weakness, his enemy was taking his time torturing him before inflicting the killing blow. The pain was shocking, nauseating, but Korum fought the darkness that threatened to pull him under, knowing that all would then be lost. He was vaguely aware that his kidneys and spleen were damaged, that his ribs were crushed and his left collarbone broken, but it didn't matter because he could feel the effect of the stun shot starting to wear off.

In the background, he could hear Mia screaming and crying, the pain in her voice ripping at his heart. With each second that passed, the debilitating weakness that rendered him so helpless was dissipating, his body beginning to function with a semblance of normality.

He needed to survive a little longer. Just a little more,

and he might stand a chance, instead of lying there like a piece of meat.

For now, though, he was still far too weak. To fight back at this point would be deadly. Loris was playing with him, putting on a show, trying to regain his standing through this display of his fighting prowess—but at any sign of renewed resistance from Korum, he would go straight for Korum's throat.

So Korum let the blows rain down on him, not even groaning when Loris kicked him over and over again. He ignored the pain of bones breaking and tendons ripping apart, concentrating only on remaining conscious.

And when Loris finally reached for his throat, Korum gathered every bit of strength in his damaged and torn body . . . and let his rage boil over.

His left arm—the only limb that remained semi-functional—hooked around Loris's throat with a deadly grip, pulling the Protector close. And before his opponent could react, Korum's teeth were sinking deep into his flesh, biting through his spinal column and severing the connection to the brain.

Blood spurted everywhere: in Korum's eyes, his hair, his mouth . . . He was covered with blood, the taste and smell of it consuming him, adding to the black fury surging through his veins. He was no longer thinking or reasoning; he was bloodlust incarnate, craving more and more. His teeth sank into Loris's throat again, ripping at it, tearing it apart, until there was nothing left.

CHAPTER SIXTEEN

Saret watched in shock and furious disbelief as Loris's severed head rolled down the field. The Councilor's dark eyes were open and unseeing, his mouth slack and covered with blood.

All around him, the crowd was going wild. People were on their floats, in the aisles, screaming and stomping their feet. Korum's name was being chanted over and over again, making Saret feel sick to his stomach.

He had to get out of there. Now, before it was too late. He could analyze his failure later; all that mattered at this point was getting away.

Rising from his seat, he joined the screaming spectators in the aisle. Out of the corner of his eye, he could see Mia struggling against Arus, trying to get to her lover. Saret desperately wished he could grab her and take her with him, but she was too well-protected here. He would have to come back for her again.

Pushing through the crowds, Saret slowly made his way toward the exit, doing his best not to draw undue attention to himself. He was almost there when he felt a sudden zapping sensation through his entire body.

Stunned and helpless, he collapsed on the floor, barely cognizant of the guardians surrounding him.

* * *

Korum didn't know how long he remained in that mindless state of rage. It could've been minutes or hours. By the time he came back to his senses, Loris's head was lying several meters away from his body, his eyes vacant and his neck looking like it had been savaged by a wild animal.

Dead. His opponent was dead.

Korum's own body was in agony, and he could feel the darkness trying to overtake him again. Only the knowledge that there was still something he needed to do kept him from the sweetness of oblivion.

His greatest enemy was not the one lying on the field; he was the one hiding among the spectators—and Mia was still in danger.

Groaning in pain, Korum managed to get up on his hands and knees, his muscles shaking from the effort. He was dimly aware that the crowd was cheering for him, that Voret was formally announcing him as the winner.

None of that mattered to him now. All he cared about was Mia, and getting to her before Saret did. Korum's body was healing, but not fast enough, and he cursed himself as his shattered femur refused to hold his weight, his leg collapsing beneath him as he tried to get to his feet.

"We got him. It's all right; she's safe." Strong hands were suddenly holding him up, helping him get to his feet. It was Alir—the leader of the guardians.

Korum's head spun, and his stomach churned with

nausea as his damaged body protested the new vertical position. "Where is he?" he managed to say, his voice hoarse and ragged.

"There." Alir pointed near the exit with his left hand while providing support for Korum with his right.

Korum squinted in that direction, the sun blinding him for a moment. When his vision cleared, he saw an unfamiliar Krinar being collared by three guardians. The man's features were completely different from Saret's, his eyes larger and his chin more prominent.

"He's got a very good disguise," Alir said, understanding Korum's unspoken question. "Even the outer layer of DNA is different, which is how we didn't detect his presence before. But the shooter's coordinates you sent us matched this man's location perfectly, and an internal DNA sample showed that it is indeed Saret."

Intense relief mixed with bitter regret, leaving Korum conflicted about this turn of events. He had wanted to be the one to catch Saret, to punish him for what he'd done to Mia. But instead, his former friend was now in the hands of the Krinar law keepers. No matter how badly Korum wanted to kill him, Saret would now live to stand trial.

"Korum!" Mia's voice reached his ears, jerking him out of his dark thoughts. Looking up, he saw her slight figure running down the field, her dark hair flying behind her. The happiness that filled him at the sight was so acute that he forgot all about Saret and his betrayal, focusing only on the girl he loved.

Then she was next to him, and he could see that she was pale and shaking, her dress torn in one spot. Her beautiful face was wet with tears. One pale arm lifted toward him, her hand trembling as though she wasn't certain if she could touch him. "You're alive," she whispered, and he could hear the disbelieving note in her voice. "Oh my God, Korum, you're alive . . ."

And Korum realized exactly what she was seeing. He was covered with blood, both his own and that of Loris. He could taste its metallic tang on his tongue, smell it surrounding him, and he knew it was all over his hair, his face, his mouth.

Fuck. He must look like something out of a nightmare, especially with the rapidly healing parts of his body where Loris had torn out chunks of his flesh.

Remembering her reaction to Saur's remains on the beach, Korum mentally cursed himself for letting Mia see him like this. He had been hoping to avoid killing Loris partially for this reason—because he didn't want his little human traumatized by seeing her lover brutally kill someone. This should've been an easy fight, one during which Korum could've restrained himself, kept from giving in to the primitive instincts of his species. If it hadn't been for Saret's interference, Korum could've easily subdued his opponent, defeating him but graciously letting him live. And instead, he had been utterly savage, like a cornered animal.

His legs were already feeling better, so Korum shrugged off Alir's support and carefully reached for Mia, bringing her toward him. He knew there was a chance he might repulse her now, but he needed her. Needed to feel her softness, to inhale her clean, sweet scent.

To his surprise, she wrapped her arms around him, holding him so tightly that it hurt his half-healed ribs. She was shaking, her slender body trembling in his embrace.

"It's all right, my sweet," he murmured, some of his tension draining as he realized she was not afraid to touch him. "It's going to be all right . . ."

"I thought—" With her face buried against his

shoulder, Mia's voice was barely audible. Her hands were icy on the bare skin of his back. "I thought he killed you . . . Oh God, Korum, I thought you were dead—"

"No," he soothed, reveling in her apparent concern for him. "No, my darling, he didn't. It's over now—"

A sob broke out of her throat. "He hurt you. I saw him hurting you, again and again. Korum, he was killing you—"

"It's okay, I'm all right," Korum whispered, his heart aching at the horror in her voice. "Everything's going to be fine. I'm sorry you had to see that. It wasn't supposed to be like that, believe me . . ."

She drew in a shuddering breath and pulled back to look up at him. Her eyes were reddened, her lashes dark and spiky from tears. "What happened? I saw you fall and then it was like you couldn't fight anymore. Did Loris cheat somehow? Did he do something to you?"

"It wasn't Loris," Korum explained, trying to keep the fury out of his voice. "It was Saret. He was in the audience, just a few seats away from you. He shot me with a stunner—a weapon similar to a stun gun—so I couldn't move for a bit."

She gasped. "He tried to kill you? Is that what the commotion over there was about? I wasn't paying attention—"

"Yes," Korum said. "I sent the guardians after him as soon as I realized what was happening."

"You sent the guardians? How?"

"Remember I told you I have an embedded computer?" Korum asked.

Mia nodded, staring at him. She still looked pale, even though the tremors wracking her frame were beginning to subside.

"I was able to use it to contact the guardians."

She blinked, and he could see that she wasn't absorbing what he was saying, her mind still consumed by what had just happened.

Alir stepped in front of him, making Korum aware of his presence again. "The victory ceremony is about to start," the guardian said quietly. "Are you able to participate?"

Korum considered it for a moment, holding Mia against his side, then gave Alir a short nod. "I should be fine." He was still in pain, but it was a healing kind of pain. His body was repairing itself from the inside, the cells regenerating themselves. In another few minutes, he would be almost back to normal.

Of course, given everything that happened, a regular ceremony with a public claiming of his charl was out of the question. Even though his recovering body was beginning to stir at her nearness, Korum was fully cognizant of his current appearance. He was dirty, sweaty, and covered in blood—not exactly appealing to a human girl. She had also just been through a major shock, and the last thing she needed was to deal with unwanted sexual advances from a man she probably now saw as a savage killer.

Alir inclined his head in a gesture of respect and walked off the field, his tall, broad frame moving with a warrior's gait. Korum had played defrebs with the man several times in the last couple of years, and he'd lost more than once. The guardians were excellent fighters, their profession requiring them to stay in top shape, and Korum was glad that he'd never had to face one of them in the Arena.

"All you have to do is stay with me right now," Korum told Mia when Alir was further away. "Under the circumstances, the post-fight ceremony will be brief."

"Because you're hurt?" she asked, and he could hear the strain in her voice.

"No, I'll be fine. But you're not ready for anything like a victory celebration right now," Korum said softly. "What we need is to go home."

* * *

As the ceremony began, Mia tried to focus on the event, but her mind kept flashing back to the gruesome images of the fight.

Flash. Korum lying on the ground, unable to move.

Flash. Blood spraying everywhere. That terrible gloating expression on Loris's face.

Flash. Korum striking back with the speed of a cobra. The sudden terror on the other Krinar's face.

Flash. More blood.

Flash. Loris's head torn off his body.

No, stop it! Mia wanted to scream, but they were in public, and she couldn't do it, couldn't embarrass Korum like that. He was holding her hand now, and they were on a large float in the middle of the Arena. The same Krinar who had led the beginning of the ceremony was speaking again, saying something else about the history of Arena fighting, but his words were sliding past Mia's ears. There was a sense of unreality to the proceedings; Mia kept feeling like she was inside a dream—or, more aptly, a nightmare.

Only Korum's touch felt real. She wanted to crawl into his embrace and never come out. When he had held her earlier, she'd felt some of her terror ebbing away, but now she felt cold again, her teeth chattering despite the heat of the bright Costa Rican sun.

He was alive. Mia still couldn't believe it. It had to be a

miracle of some kind. How could anybody survive those kinds of injuries? She had known the Krinar healed quickly, but Korum had been almost literally torn apart. There had been so much blood. *Oh God, the blood.*

Mia swallowed hard, trying to contain her nausea. If she never saw the color red again, it would be too soon. No wonder the Krinar preferred light colors in their daily lives; they probably needed the contrast after the violent spectacle of the Arena.

Korum had almost died today. Her alien lover—so strong, so seemingly invincible—had been nearly brought down by treachery. For a few dark moments, Mia had been sure that he *was* dead—and she had wanted to die too. It had felt like her heart was being torn open, each blow to Korum's body smashing something deep within her soul. She had never experienced such agony before, and she never wanted to feel it again.

She was dimly aware that Voret had stopped speaking, that he was addressing Korum now, asking him about a celebration. She saw Korum starting to shake his head, and something came over her. Acting purely on instinct, she leaned closer to Korum and whispered in his ear, "I want you. Please, Korum, I want you."

He turned his head to look at her, his expression incredulous, and she squeezed his hand, wordlessly telling him that it was okay, that he could celebrate in the way of his people.

Rightly or wrongly, she needed him now, and she didn't care about anything else.

Mia could see his pupils expanding, his irises turning a brighter shade of gold. With the blood and dirt covering him, he looked like a savage, like one of those ancient hunters Voret had shown at the beginning of the ceremony. She wanted him so much she ached with it, her body needing to affirm life in the most basic way possible.

He hesitated for a second, staring at her, and then he raised his hand, curving his large palm around her right cheek. "Mia . . ."

"Please, Korum." She held his gaze, knowing that he could see the sincerity of her intentions on her face. She needed to feel his touch on her skin, needed him to make her forget the horror of the past hour.

His eyes glittering, he leaned forward and said softly, "You don't know what you're asking, my sweet. I can't be . . . gentle right now."

Mia swallowed, her inner muscles clenching at his words. "I don't want you to be."

He looked at her for another few seconds, and she could see the pulse beating in the side of his muscular neck. Then, as though unable to help himself, he bent his head and kissed her, his arms wrapping around her and pulling her onto his lap.

In the background, Mia could hear the crowd roaring, the spectators cheering and stomping their feet, but it didn't bother her. All she could concentrate on was the heat of his mouth consuming hers, the pressure of his erection against her buttocks, the feel of his strong hands rubbing up and down her back. There was a faint metallic taste that should've repelled her, but instead it turned her on even more. The man kissing her right now was a predator, a killer—and she wanted him exactly as he was, no holds barred.

Lifting his head, he stared down at her for a second, his breathing heavy and his skin flushed underneath the streaks of grime and blood. All around them, the crowd was going wild, chanting their names. Mia had a sudden thought that that's what rock stars must feel like, surrounded by their screaming fans.

As though in response to that, a strange music began to play, with notes so deep that Mia could feel the vibrations deep in her bones. The rhythm was uneven, almost jerky. It should've sounded discordant, unpleasant, but instead, it added to the pulsing heat between her legs, making her skin feel tighter and her heart beat faster.

Korum was reacting to it too, his cock hardening even more, pushing into the softness of her bottom. Still holding her, he stood up and began walking toward a tent-like structure in the center of the Arena, carrying her like a prize of war.

Mia clung to him, feeling almost intoxicated. Her head was spinning, and everything seemed surreal, as though it was happening in a dream. The psychology student in her recognized that it was her brain's response to trauma, that she wasn't thinking clearly, but it didn't matter. She was dying with need, and Korum was the cure for what ailed her.

They got to the tent, and he placed her on her feet, keeping her pressed against his body. Instead of them going inside, the tent appeared to move and flow around them, mostly covering them from the view of the crowd. Mia was vaguely aware of the thinness of the walls, of the fact that thousands of curious Krinar eyes were watching the structure right now, but she wasn't fully processing that information. They had some kind of privacy, and that was good enough for her.

As soon as the tent walls stopped moving, Korum took a step back, releasing her from his embrace. "Take off the dress." His voice was unusually rough, and she could see the tension in his powerful shoulders. With his eyes a bright yellow, he looked wild, more animal than man. "Take it off, Mia."

She obeyed, shimmying out of the dress, her excitement mixed with a tiny dollop of fear. He hadn't even touched her, and she could see that he was already close to losing control.

Before her dress even hit the ground, he was already on her, one of his hands delving between her thighs and another grabbing her hair. His mouth descended on hers even as his finger pushed inside, into her small opening. He was rough, almost frantic, and Mia realized that he hadn't been lying before, about not being able to be gentle. She was wet, but her muscles still tensed involuntarily, her body resisting the aggressive penetration.

Suddenly, he withdrew his finger and used the hand holding her hair to push her down, onto her knees. Tiny rocks and gravel dug into the soft skin of her kneecaps. "Suck it," he said harshly, tearing open the front of his pants. "I want your mouth right now."

His erection sprang free, brushing against her cheek. Mia opened her mouth, letting him inside, and he groaned as her lips closed around the head of his cock. He tasted salty, the tip already coated with pre-cum. She swirled her tongue around his shaft, mimicking what she'd once seen done in porn. He let out a sound that sounded like a growl, and his hands fisted tighter in her hair, holding her head steady as he began to move his hips, fucking her mouth with his cock.

Mia focused on taking small breaths, trying not to choke as most of his length pushed into her mouth, pressing against the back of her throat. He thrust again and again, and then he was coming with a harsh groan, his seed shooting out in warm, salty spurts. When he was done, he slowly withdrew from her, his cock still semi-hard.

Swallowing, Mia licked her lips and stared up at him, strangely aroused by what had just occurred. Pleasuring him like this turned her on, almost as if he had been touching her too.

He held her gaze, and she could see that his eyes remained bright, his hunger as strong as ever. His sex was stirring again, hardening in front of her face. One orgasm had just taken the edge off, she realized as he pulled her up onto her feet.

When he touched her again, he was gentler, his desire more controlled. His hands and mouth traveled down her body, caressing and worshipping every inch of her skin. Mia closed her eyes, quiet moans escaping her throat as pleasurable tension began to gather low in her belly. Then he was kneeling in front of her, his face at the level of her hips, his hands cupping the smooth curves of her buttocks. Bringing her toward him with one hand, he used the other to penetrate her with one finger, being much more careful this time. At the same time, his mouth delved into the soft curls at the apex of her thighs, his tongue reaching between her folds to stroke her clit.

Mia jerked from the startling lash of sensations, her entire body tensing as his finger rubbed against the sensitive spot deep inside. She could feel the growing pressure, and her knees began shaking, her legs suddenly too weak to support her weight. If it hadn't been for his finger inside her and his hand on her ass, she would've collapsed, falling down on the ground beside him.

"Come for me," he whispered, his hot breath washing over her sex, and she did, his words sending her over the edge, providing that elusive something she didn't even know she needed. Everything inside her tightened and released, the pleasure so sharp it felt like an explosion along her nerve endings.

When the pulsations stopped, he withdrew his finger and tugged her down again. This time, they were both kneeling on the hard ground. Looking at her, he lifted his hand and slowly licked his finger—the one that had just been inside her. "I love your taste," he murmured, his eyes filled with such hunger that her mouth went dry. "It makes me want to fuck you again and again, just to have it on my tongue."

Mia drew in a shaky breath, her sex clenching with need.

Before she could say anything, he lay down on the ground, lifting her up and placing her astride his thighs. His cock was completely hard again, standing up straight from his body. "Ride me, Mia," he said, watching her with a half-lidded gaze.

"Yes," she whispered, "I will." And grasping his thick length with her right hand, Mia guided him to her opening, her eyes closing as the broad head began to push inside. She lowered herself slowly, teasing them both, and was rewarded with a low groan that escaped from his throat.

When he was all the way inside, she opened her eyes, meeting his burning gaze. With his face streaked with grime and blood, he looked dangerous—cruel even. She was almost literally riding a tiger—a predator who could tear her apart in the blink of an eye. Instead of scaring her, the thrill of it only added to the desire coursing through her veins.

As she began to move, she kept her eyes trained on him, watching as tiny beads of sweat appeared on his forehead and a muscle pulsed in his jaw from his apparent effort to restrain himself. His hands tightened on her hips, his fingers digging into her soft flesh, and then he was lifting her up and down on his cock, going deeper and deeper with every stroke.

The tension inside her spiraled again, and Mia threw back her head, her mouth open in a soundless scream. A powerful orgasm rippled through her body even as Korum kept thrusting faster and faster, seeking his own release. When he came, the grinding motions of his pelvis intensified her aftershocks, leaving her completely wrung out. Breathing hard, Mia collapsed against his chest, her muscles like limp noodles and her mind emptied of any thoughts.

She was so relaxed she didn't even react when he pulled her higher, bringing her neck closer to his mouth. It was only when she felt a strange slicing pain that Mia realized what was happening . . . and her world dissolved into an ecstatic frenzy of blood and sex.

Part III

CHAPTER SEVENTEEN

Korum woke up to the unfamiliar feel of hard ground underneath his back. Before he even opened his eyes, he remembered everything that had occurred earlier—including Mia's voluntary participation in the celebration.

He could feel her slight weight on his arm, hear her quiet breathing, and he knew she was deeply asleep, worn out from the double ordeal of the fight and the celebration. Moving carefully, Korum freed his arm, gently lowering her head to the ground. Then he stood up and created fresh clothes for both of them. A pair of shorts for himself and a robe for Mia—just enough to afford them some coverage in case any spectators remained in the Arena.

He was thirsty and hungry, but otherwise he felt great, his body practically thrumming with energy. The scientists said there was no physiological need for lonar or human blood, given the genetic fix, but many on Krina thought that some kind of a psychological need remained.

Korum wasn't certain if he believed that, but he did know that he rarely felt as satisfied as those times when he indulged himself with Mia.

Holding the robe, he crouched next to her and studied her for a few seconds, enjoying the sight of her naked body. He rarely got a chance to watch her like this; usually his need for her was so intense he couldn't look at her bare flesh without fucking her immediately afterwards. Even now, after last night's sexual marathon, he could feel the warm stirrings of desire—although it was nothing compared to his usual craving.

She was lying on her back, one slim arm extended over her head and the other bent across her ribcage. Fascinated by her breasts, Korum reached out and stroked one pale mound, smiling when the nipple hardened at his touch. Her skin was as soft as anything he had ever felt, its silky texture a constant lure for his fingers.

Wrapping her in a fluffy robe, he lifted her up. She didn't even stir, her sleep so deep it bordered on unconsciousness. It was always like that after he took her blood: her human body needed to recuperate from the excess of sensations.

And so did his, albeit to a lesser extent. Korum could see how others had gotten addicted to their charl; Mia's blood was a powerful temptation for him, its effect more potent than that of any drug. He used to think blood addicts were weak, but now Korum wondered if there was really that much difference between physical and emotional addiction. He certainly couldn't imagine needing Mia more than he already did.

Carrying her out of the shatela, Korum walked toward the grassy area where he'd left his transport pod. He hadn't bothered disassembling it earlier, so it was now waiting for them.

Looking around, he saw that the Arena was completely empty. It was also early morning, the sun just beginning to come up. Grinning, Korum realized that he must've been in the shatela much longer than usual. It was his first time celebrating with a human, and it was by far the best experience he'd had.

They reached the transport pod, and Korum sent a quick mental command to have them taken home. A minute later, they were walking into his house, with Mia still asleep in his arms.

As soon as they were inside, Korum headed straight for the cleansing room—the bathroom, in human terms. He was still covered in dirt, dried blood, and sweat, and some of the grime had rubbed off on Mia, leaving her pale skin marred with dark streaks.

Another mental command from him, and the water came on, warm jets softly massaging their bodies and rinsing away all traces of yesterday's activities. Korum enjoyed the sensation; it was both energizing and soothing at the same time. A few minutes later, both he and Mia were clean and dry, and he carried her to bed, knowing she needed to get more sleep. She was so exhausted she hadn't even woken up during the cleansing.

Laying her on the bed, Korum let the intelligent material flow around her and then covered her with a soft sheet, knowing that she liked the feel of blankets. Kissing her forehead, he took one last look at the girl he loved and headed out to start his day.

* * *

"He refuses to talk to us," Alir told Korum as they walked toward the other side of the guardians' building. "He says he will only talk to you."

"Will he now?" Korum said, not bothering to hide the sarcasm in his voice. "And what gives him the impression he's in a position to make demands?"

Alir shrugged. "I don't know. But he seems convinced that you will be interested in hearing what he has to say. He says it has to do with Mia."

Korum's hands clenched into fists at the mention of his charl. The fact that Saret dared bring up her name—

"The report for the Elders is ready," Alir said, changing the topic. "Would you like to review it?"

"Yes," Korum said. "Send it to me. I'll run it by the Council."

Alir nodded. "Will do."

They had reached their destination, and Alir stopped before going in. "Do you want me there?"

"No." Korum was certain of that. "I want to speak to him alone."

"Then he's all yours." Turning around, Alir walked back, leaving Korum on his own.

Korum waited until the leader of the guardians was gone, and then he took a step forward, toward the wall that shielded his enemy from his view. The wall dissolved, forming an entrance, and he stepped inside.

Saret was sitting on a float, a crime-collar around his throat. Korum smiled at the sight. He remembered having an argument with Saret about the collars a few hundred years ago, with his former friend trying to convince him that the collars were demeaning and unnecessary. Korum had disagreed, believing that the shame of the crime-collar was part of the deterrent for would-be criminals.

It was good to see Saret wearing one now, particularly in light of his views about it.

"I see you're out of your disguise now," Korum

observed, studying his enemy's familiar features. "Miscalculated a bit, did you?"

Saret gave him a cold smile. "Apparently. I underestimated how much Loris hated you. If I had known he would try to prolong the process of killing you, I would've shot you twice."

"Live and learn," Korum said. "Isn't that what humans say?"

"Indeed." Saret's eyes gleamed with something dark.

Korum gave him a mocking look and sat down on another float, stretching out his legs in a gesture of disrespect. "You wanted to talk to me," he said coolly. "So talk."

"All right," Saret said. "I will. How is Mia doing, by the way? She seemed a bit upset yesterday."

Korum felt a surge of anger, but kept his expression calm, amused. "She was. But she's happy now, as I'm sure you can imagine."

"Of course she is," Saret said. "And adjusting so well to life here, isn't she? It's almost as if she didn't lose her memory fully, wouldn't you say? It's like she still knows you on some level, maybe even loves you. And she's so accepting of everything. Nothing fazes her for long. Amazing, isn't it?"

Korum froze for a second, a chill running down his spine. The only way Saret could know that would be—

"Yes," Saret said. "I see you're on the right track. I miscalculated again, you see. Mia was supposed to end up with me, not you."

"What did you do to her?" Korum said quietly, the fine hair on the back of his neck rising.

Saret laughed. "Nothing too awful, believe me. I merely made sure she would be receptive. She's still herself . . . mostly."

"What did you do?" Without even realizing what he was doing, Korum found himself out of his seat, his hand wrapped around Saret's throat.

Saret made a choking sound, his hand tugging at Korum's fingers, and Korum forced himself to release him, taking a step back. He was shaking with rage, and he knew he would kill Saret if he didn't put some distance between them.

"It's called softening," Saret said, rubbing his throat. His voice was raspy from Korum partially crushing his trachea. "It's a new procedure I developed specifically for humans. A softened mind doesn't feel fear as sharply. It's also more open to new impressions, new ideas." Saret paused dramatically. "New attachments. In fact, such a mind seeks something—or, rather, someone—to attach to."

Korum stared at Saret, ice spreading through his veins.

"And that someone can be anyone, you see. It should've been me—but instead, it was you."

You're lying. Korum wanted to scream, to deny what he just heard, but he couldn't. It made too much sense. The girl he met in New York wouldn't have accepted everything with such ease, wouldn't have invited him into her bed after knowing him for just a day. She would've been frightened and mistrustful, and he would've had to earn her trust and affection all over again. And instead, she seemed to love him with hardly any effort on his part.

Except she didn't. Not really. Her feelings for him weren't real. None of it was real. Her behavior, her apparent attachment to him—it was all a result of Saret's procedure.

"Does she still have her memories?" Korum buried the agony deep inside, where it couldn't cloud his thinking. "Or did you erase them anyway?"

Saret grinned, visibly delighted by the question. "No, the memories are gone. It just seems like they're there because she's absorbing everything like a sponge, learning at an incredible rate. Pretty soon, she'll be more acclimated to our world than she was before—if she's not already."

"Can you undo it?" Korum knew it was futile, but he had to ask.

"What, the softening or the memory loss?"

"Both. Either."

Saret's grin widened. "I can't. And even if I could, I wouldn't. You might have her now, but you'll never truly have her. You'll never know if anything she feels for you is genuine—or if she would've felt the same about any other man who spent time with her upon her awakening."

Korum looked at the man he'd once considered a friend. Memories of their childhood, happy and carefree, flashed through his mind, leaving the bitter taste of regret in their wake. "Why?" he asked quietly.

"Why do I hate you?" Saret lifted his eyebrows. "Or why did I do all of this?"

Korum just continued looking at him.

"The answer is the same to both," Saret said, his grin fading. "I was tired of always being in your shadow. No matter how much I achieved, how high I climbed, I was always just Korum's buddy. Korum the inventor, Korum the designer, Korum who brought us here to Earth. Your ambition knew no bounds—and neither did my hatred of you."

"Yet you supported me," Korum said, the pain of the betrayal somehow distant, not fully reaching him yet. "You were always on my side on the Council. You helped me get us here, to Earth."

"I did," Saret agreed. "Because I knew it was foolish to

do anything else. Even the Elders dance to your tune these days, don't they?"

Korum didn't justify that with a response. Instead, he gave Saret a look of contempt. "So all your grandiose plans for humans, your supposed desire for world peace, it was all out of petty jealousy?"

"No," Saret said, his eyes narrowing. "I saw a way to shape history, and I took a chance. What could be a greater achievement than peace for an entire planet? Do you think any of your gadgets could compare to that?"

"An achievement that would've involved the deaths of fifty thousand Krinar."

"Yes," Saret said, and he had the gall to look regretful for a moment. "That would've been unfortunate. Unavoidable, but unfortunate."

"Unfortunate?" Korum could hardly believe his ears. "What is wrong with you, Saret? How did you get to be this way?"

Now Saret was beginning to look angry. "What is wrong with *me*? You ask me that while you're standing there, with Loris's blood still fresh on your hands? You think something is wrong with me because I wanted to better the lives of billions by killing a few thousand? How many Krinar have you killed in the Arena, Korum? Twenty, thirty? And what about humans? You think I don't know that you enjoy killing, just like the rest of our fucked-up race?"

Korum stared at him, trying to understand this man he'd known his whole life. "You're wrong," he said quietly. "I don't enjoy killing. I didn't want to kill Loris yesterday—and I wouldn't have if you hadn't interfered. I like the fights themselves, not the end result of them. And that's how our fucked-up race is, as you should know, since you're the mind expert here. We love danger and violence—we crave it—but we don't have to be murderers."

"And yet we are," Saret said. "You can fool yourself all you want, but that's what we ultimately are. We came to Earth and thousands of humans died during the Great Panic as a result. And what you want to do now will result in more deaths. She won't forgive you for that, you know."

"Won't your procedure take care of that?" Korum said, his mouth curving into a bitter smile. "Isn't she going to love me now no matter what?"

Saret shook his head. "No. With enough provocation, her love will turn to hate. You just wait and see."

CHAPTER EIGHTEEN

Mia woke up with a scream, her heart racing and her skin covered with cold sweat.

In her dream, Korum's body had been a mangled, mutilated corpse, swimming in a river of blood. She had tried to save him from that river, to pull him ashore, but it had been futile. The current had been too strong, tearing him out of her hands and carrying him away, down to the waterfalls, where the water was as dark as dried blood.

Sitting up straight, Mia tried to get her breathing under control. It was just a bad dream. Korum had won the fight. He was safe.

Safe—and fully recovered, if yesterday's celebration was anything to go by.

Remembering just how recovered he had been, Mia immediately felt much better. Her lover's stamina was literally out of this world. The pleasure he had given her had been incredible, almost more than she could stand. She'd never felt such ecstasy as when he'd bitten her; she never could've imagined that such sensations even existed.

Smiling, she climbed out of bed and headed toward the shower. The fight was over, Saret had been captured, and there was nothing else to fear.

She and Korum were safe at last.

Humming to herself, Mia let the cleaning technology do its thing while she stood there thinking about her lover—and how essential he had become to her again.

When she was clean and dry, she went to the kitchen and had the house prepare some breakfast for her. According to the information on her tablet, her lab partner Adam was supposed to return from his week-long vacation today—which meant that Mia could start relearning everything she had forgotten about her apprenticeship.

The lab wouldn't be open, given the recent events, but she was hoping there would be some way for her to continue learning about the mind. The subject fascinated her now more than ever.

* * *

Korum walked aimlessly down the ocean shore, letting the roar of the pounding surf drown out the cacophony in his head. For the first time in his life, he felt lost. Lost and hopeless . . . and angry.

His anger was directed mostly at himself, though a healthy portion of it was reserved for Saret. Korum hadn't let himself think about his friend's betrayal before, too focused on Mia and her memory loss. Then the fight had consumed his attention. Now, however, there was nothing to distract him from the fact that a man he'd regarded as a friend had turned out to be his greatest enemy.

Korum knew he wasn't universally liked. It was a state of affairs that had never bothered him before. He was respected and feared, but there were only a few individuals he'd ever considered his friends. Most of them remained on Krina, busy with their lives and careers there. Saret had been the only one to accompany him to Earth.

Even as a child, Korum had always been self-sufficient. He had discovered his interest in design early on, and that passion had consumed his life—until Mia. Now he had two passions: his work and the human girl who was his charl. He wasn't a loner, but he rarely needed the company of others. Unlike most, Korum was just as happy by himself—or now spending time with Mia—as he was surrounded by people.

Saret's betrayal proved to be agonizing on multiple levels. Korum had trusted Saret; he'd confided in him for centuries, sharing his goals and dreams. They'd played together as children, discussed their sexual conquests as teenage boys, and often worked toward a common goal as members of the Council. When had Saret begun to hate him? Or had it always been that way and Korum had just been too blind to see it? Could any of his friends be trusted, or were all of them like Saret, just waiting to strike when his back was turned?

These thoughts were both painful and disturbing. Self-doubt was not in Korum's nature, but he couldn't help wondering whether he had brought this upon himself. He knew he could be harsh and arrogant at times—even ruthless when it came to achieving his goals. Had he done something to make Saret hate him to such extent? Or was it simply jealousy, as Saret himself had intimated?

Reaching the estuary where he'd sat with Mia on the rocks before, Korum stripped off his clothes and waded into the surf, letting the water cool him down. He'd always found the ocean therapeutic. The power of the waves appealed to him, and he especially liked it when the current was strong, as it was right now with high tide. It picked him up, carrying him out to deeper water, and Korum let it, floating along until the shore was a few miles away. Then he began to swim back, the tug of the current providing enough resistance to make it a challenge. The mindless exertion of swimming helped clear his mind, and he felt a tiny bit better when he finally emerged from the water.

Sitting down on the rocks, he let the sun shine down on his bare skin, warming him up again. The worst thing about Saret's betrayal wasn't what it did to Korum: it was the consequences for Mia. She had not only lost her memories, but her freedom of thought as well. Whatever she felt for Korum now was involuntary, a byproduct of this 'softening' Saret had done to her. His sweet, beautiful girl was not the same person she'd once been; her mind had been tampered with in the most unforgivable way.

She had been afraid of that, Korum remembered. When she'd first arrived in Lenkarda, she had been hesitant about the language implant, afraid of having alien technology in her brain. Korum had been amused at the time, but it turned out she'd been right to fear. Saret had been dangerous all along.

And Korum had failed to protect her. The thought gnawed at him, eating him from the inside. He, who had never failed at anything before, had been unable to protect the person who meant the most to him. Could Mia ever forgive him for that? And if she could, how would he know whether her feelings were real? If Saret were to be believed, she would now accept most things with equanimity, her reactions different from what they would've been before.

Getting up, Korum pulled on his clothes and began walking home. It would be a lengthy walk, but he was in no rush. Mia was there, and, for the first time ever, he was less than eager to see her.

He would have to tell her what he learned today. She would want to know, would want to make her own decisions about what to do next.

And if she chose to leave him, he would have to let her go.

Even if it killed him to do so.

* * *

Mia exited the house and walked to the transport pod that was waiting for her. She'd messaged Adam from her wristwatch-bracelet device, and the K had agreed to meet with her, sending his little aircraft to pick her up and take her to the lab.

Getting in, Mia settled on one of the floating seats, feeling it adjusting around her. She was getting so used to K technology that she didn't even have to think about how to use anything—it was all starting to seem perfectly natural to her.

She was curious to meet her former partner and dive back into that part of her life in Lenkarda. She had found a few recordings where Adam was explaining something, and she had been impressed with not only his intelligence, but also his ability to take complex subjects and put them in simple, easy-to-understand terms.

Two minutes later, she landed in a clearing in front of a mid-sized building that looked like it had been through something extraordinary. The walls were partially gone, as though something had melted them from the top down, but the interior looked perfectly intact.

Adam was standing there, waiting for her. As Mia emerged from the pod, he smiled—a bright and genuine smile that lit up his handsome face. He had what Mia was coming to think of as typical K coloring: dark hair and eyes and that beautifully bronzed skin.

"Well, howdy there, partner," he said, his eyes crinkling attractively at the corners. "I heard our boss turned out to be Doctor Evil and practiced some of his craft on you."

Mia grinned, immediately liking this Krinar. "Yep, you heard right. You leave for a week and that's what happens."

"So you don't remember me now?" he asked, his expression becoming more serious. "How much did he wipe out?"

"When I woke up here a couple of days ago, my latest memories were from March," Mia explained, watching as the K's jaw tightened.

"That fucking bastard," Adam said, anger seeping into his voice. "I'm sorry, Mia. I wish I'd been here—"

Mia waved her hand dismissively. "Don't be silly. Nobody suspected anything; he was too good. He even managed to sneak into the fight yesterday and almost kill Korum."

"Yeah, I heard about that too," Adam said. "I watched the recording of the fight this morning."

"Oh, right." Mia tried not to blush. If Adam had seen the fight, then he might've also watched the celebration afterwards.

"Do you want to go inside?" Adam asked, motioning toward the ruined building. "I think we can extract a lot of the files and data. I spoke with the other apprentices, and they're fine with it."

"Sure," Mia said quickly, grateful for the change of subject.

Walking up to the building, they climbed through a ragged opening in one of the walls. The usual wall-dissolving mechanism appeared to be malfunctioning—which was hardly surprising, considering the condition of the building.

"What's going to happen to the lab?" Mia asked when they were inside. "What's the normal protocol for something like this?"

Adam shrugged. "There is no normal protocol. This lab is Saret's, so technically we're now trespassing on his property. Although I think the government might own it now, given Saret's crimes. I'm not really sure how these things work. My best guess is that most of the information will be transferred to the labs in the other Centers—and maybe some other mind expert will want to open a new lab here in Lenkarda."

"What about you? Why don't they have you take over the lab?"

"Me?" Adam raised his eyebrows. "I'm too young and inexperienced as far as they're concerned."

"You are?" Mia looked at him in surprise. He looked to be a man in his prime, outwardly similar to Korum. "How old are you?"

"Oh, that's right, I almost forgot that you don't remember." Adam smiled. "I'm twenty-eight, only a few years older than you. I am also a fairly recent arrival in the Centers. I grew up in a human family, you see."

"You did?" Mia's eyes went wide. "How?"

"I was adopted as an infant," Adam said. "Now why don't we start going through some of Saret's files and see if there's anything useful there? Maybe we can shed some light on your condition."

Mia was dying to ask more questions about Adam's origins, but he didn't seem to be in a mood to talk about it, so she focused on the task at hand instead. Adam showed her how to operate some of the lab equipment, and they began digging through mountains of information, searching for anything memory-related.

Six hours later, Mia got up and rubbed her neck, her brain feeling like it would explode from everything she'd learned today. Adam was still as focused as ever, going through file after file with no trace of tiredness.

Hearing Mia's movements, he looked up from the image he was studying and gave her a warm smile. "You should go home, Mia. It's getting late. I'll work here some more, and then I'll leave as well."

Mia hesitated. "Are you sure?" She was mentally exhausted and starving, but she felt bad leaving Adam on his own.

"Of course," Adam said. "Now go. This is plenty for today."

* * *

Korum paced in the living room, too wound up to sit still. When he had gotten home an hour earlier and found the house empty, his immediate thought had been that something had happened to Mia—that Saret had found a way to get to her after all.

Of course, that wasn't the case. A quick check had revealed her location, and then it had been easy to access the satellite images and see her talking to Adam outside Saret's lab several hours earlier. Still, those few seconds before Korum had been assured of her safety had chilled him to the bone.

Now he was fighting an urge to go to the lab and bring

Mia home. He wanted to hold her and feel the warmth of her body in his arms, maybe for the last time. Once he told her the truth about her condition, she would be more than justified in wanting to leave him. As terrible as her memory loss had been, the other procedure was far more invasive, altering her brain in a way that she would likely find unforgivable. Now she would never know if the way she felt about Korum—or about anything in general—was real or if it was a result of what Saret had done.

A dark temptation gnawed at Korum. What if he didn't tell her? What if she continued in blissful ignorance, happy with her life as it was? Other than Saret and Korum, no one else knew the truth. He could keep her, and she would love him—and he would be the only one to know it wasn't real love.

A couple of months earlier, Korum wouldn't have hesitated. He had wanted her, and he'd simply taken her, disregarding her wishes. If he had been faced with this dilemma then, it would've been an easy decision to make: keep her and all else be damned. But he couldn't do that anymore, couldn't treat her like a child or a pet, as she'd once accused him of doing. He wanted her to stay, but it had to be of her own free will—even if that free will had been somewhat tampered with.

No, he had to tell her, and he had to do it soon.

Finally, Korum saw a pod landing outside. Mia came out, and the aircraft took off, heading back to wherever it came from.

Despite his black mood, Korum couldn't help smiling as she entered the house. She was dressed in a cream-colored dress that left most of her back bare, and her dark hair was pinned up in a thick, messy knot. The hairstyle was surprisingly sexy, exposing her delicate nape and drawing his attention to the elegant column of her throat.

"Honey, I'm home," she said, grinning from ear to ear.

Unable to help himself, Korum laughed and picked her up, bringing her up for a thorough kiss.

When he lowered her back to her feet, her smile was almost blinding. She looked at him as though he was her entire world—and Korum's heart felt like it would shatter into a million pieces.

"How was your day, my sweet?" he asked, his hands still holding her waist.

"It was great," she said, still grinning. "I met Adam again. He's very nice. I like him a lot."

Korum felt a surge of jealousy, but he tamped down on it, refusing to give in to the emotion. Mia had always liked her partner, but, as far as Korum knew, her feelings were entirely platonic. Besides, the young K already had a human he was obsessed with; Korum had found that out during a background check he'd done on Adam shortly after Mia started working with him.

"We did a lot of digging through Saret's files," Mia continued, her eyes shining with excitement. "Adam thinks we might learn something useful about my condition this way."

At that moment, her stomach rumbled and her cheeks turned pink in response, making Korum smile. "I'm guessing someone's hungry," he teased.

"Busted," she said, laughing.

Smiling, Korum let her go and headed to the kitchen. A few minutes later, they were sitting down to a meal of grilled vegetable sandwiches with miso-avocado dip.

Mia quickly devoured everything on her plate, and so did he, his appetite strong after his swim earlier today.

For dessert, Korum had the house make them a kiwi-mango pie with a crust made of ground macadamia nuts—and tea for Mia.

As they were enjoying the treat, Korum reached across the table and took her hand, stroking the middle of her palm with his thumb. "Mia," he said quietly, "there's something I have to tell you."

She froze for a second, apparently reacting to the serious note in his voice. "What is it?"

"I spoke to Saret today," Korum said, his fingers tightening around her palm. "He didn't just wipe out your recent memories. He also did something to make you . . . more accepting of things."

* * *

Mia stared at her lover, unable to believe what she was hearing. "What? What does that mean?"

"He called it 'softening'," Korum said, and the expression on his face was grim. "It was apparently a way to make you more amenable to his advances. If he didn't lie about it, you don't experience fear as strongly as you did before . . . and you're also more open to new impressions."

Mia frowned. "I don't understand. How would this have helped Saret?"

"Because you're not only more open to new impressions—which explains why you're acclimating so well—but you're also prone to new attachments." Korum's mouth was tight with anger.

"New attachments?" And then it dawned her. "He thought I would fall in love with him? That's insane!" She laughed, inviting him to share the joke.

Korum didn't respond, and her amusement faded.

"Wait a second," she said slowly. "Are you saying what I think you're saying?"

"I'm sorry, Mia. I really wish it wasn't true."

Automatically shaking her head, Mia pulled her hand out of his grasp and rose to her feet. "But that's ridiculous," she said. "Are you saying that I'm not myself? That everything I think and feel is a product of some madman's procedure? That what I feel for *you* isn't real?"

Korum got up as well. "It's all my fault," he said, his voice heavy with guilt. "I should've been there. I should've protected you from him—"

"No." Mia refused to believe this. "How do you know he wasn't lying? Wouldn't it make sense for him to lie?"

"It would," Korum said. "It would make all the sense in the world. And that's why I want to have you seen by the mind lab in Arizona. We'll go there tomorrow."

"But you don't think he's lying."

"No." Korum gave her a pained look. "I don't."

"Why not?" Mia whispered, her voice starting to shake.

"Because you haven't been fully yourself, my sweet," he said gently. "The differences are subtle, but they're there. You've noticed it too, haven't you?"

Mia sucked in her breath. She had. Of course she had. She'd wondered at how well she was adjusting to her new world, to living in an alien colony with a lover she'd just met. A lover who was now as necessary to her as food and air.

"Couldn't there be a different explanation for this?" Mia knew she was clutching at straws, but the alternative was too much to process. "What if my memories aren't really gone? What if they're still there, suppressed somewhere deep inside? That would explain everything:

why I feel so comfortable here, why I'm learning so fast, why I fell in love with you—"

Korum closed his eyes for a moment. When he opened them, his gaze was bleak. "You didn't, Mia. You didn't fall in love with me. You barely know me."

"But if I still remember you on some level—"

He drew in a deep breath. "You don't, my sweet. Ellet ran tests on you before you woke up, and there were signs of damage consistent with a memory loss. I really wish it were otherwise, believe me."

Mia blinked, swallowing hard to contain the growing knot in her throat. He thought she was damaged. Defective. Incapable of real emotions. "So what now?"

"It's your decision," Korum said, his voice oddly flat. "You can either stay with me or return to your old life."

"Return to my old life?" She could barely say the words. "You . . . Y-you want me to go?"

"What? No!" He looked startled at the idea. "Of course I don't want you to go. You're my entire life now, don't you understand that?"

Mia almost shuddered with relief. He still wanted her, despite the damage from the procedure.

"You are my entire life as well," she told him. "I know you think the way I feel is the result of what Saret did, but I don't believe it. I loved you before, despite everything that happened between us, and I fell in love with you again in these past couple of days. You may not think it's real, but I know my own mind. Yes, I noticed I'm not reacting to things as I would've expected, but so what? Isn't it a good thing that I'm learning so fast? That I'm becoming as comfortable in Lenkarda as I was once in New York? Even if it is a result of Saret's procedure, it doesn't change the fact that that's how I am now—that that's the way I think and feel. It doesn't make my emotions any less strong . . . or any less real."

As she spoke, the little grooves of tension bracketing his mouth began to dissipate. "Are you sure, Mia?" he asked, his eyes filling with familiar golden heat. "Is this what you really want?"

"To be with you? Yes!" Mia had never been more certain of anything in her life. The thought of leaving him, of going back home and never seeing him again, was unbearable. When she'd thought he was dead, she had wanted to die too. Life without Korum was not worth living.

"Then you will be with me." His voice was rough, his hands hurried as they reached for her and pulled her into his arms.

His mouth was ravenous, like he wanted to consume her, and Mia responded in kind, her hunger matching his. She ached for his touch, his embrace. The shocking ecstasy of their post-Arena lovemaking had left her wrung out, drained, and yet she already wanted more. More of Korum, more of the magic.

His hands were frantic on her body, ripping off the dress, leaving it lying in shreds on the floor. His clothes met the same fate. Before she could blink, she found herself pressed against the wall, her thighs spread wide as he lifted her up, rubbing his erection against her bare sex.

"Fuck," he growled. His expression was that of a man in pain, his breathing harsh and uneven. "I have to be inside you, Mia. Now."

"Yes," she whispered, holding his blazing gaze. "Yes . . . please . . ."

As though she had given him permission, he plunged into her, his shaft unbearably thick and long, stretching her, filling her to the brim. Mia cried out, the pleasure-pain of his possession as intense as it was startling. With the way he was holding her, she was completely open to him, unable to control the depth of his penetration in any way. He was in so deep she could feel him nudging against her cervix, her channel tightening in a futile effort to keep him out.

He paused for a brief second, letting her catch her breath, and then he began hammering into her, his thrusts pressing her into the wall. Mia moaned, her body overwhelmed by the sensations. There was no slow build, no gradual transition from discomfort to pleasure; instead, the orgasm hit her suddenly, her inner muscles spasming around his cock with no warning.

He groaned, his pace picking up further, and she climaxed again with a scream, unable to control her body's helpless response. Her skin was too hot, and she was panting, gasping for breath, but he was relentless, driving her toward her third peak mere minutes after her second.

And just when Mia thought she couldn't take anymore, he came with a savage roar, his head thrown back and his cock pulsing deep inside her.

* * *

The next morning, Korum waited impatiently as Haron—the mind expert in the Arizona Center—carefully examined Mia.

She was lying on a float, her eyes closed and her expression relaxed. She had been lightly sedated to allow for a more thorough examination of her brain. Haron was brushing her hair back, exposing more of her forehead to attach his equipment there.

Korum had given the other male permission to touch her in this instance, but he still felt like ripping him apart for it. He had been equally angry to learn of Arus restraining her during the fight, even though he knew it had been for Mia's own protection. The territorial instinct was primitive—and completely irrational given the circumstances—but Korum couldn't help it. When it came to Mia, he was no more evolved than an amoeba.

By the time the examination was over, Korum was in a dark mood. "Well," he demanded as soon as Haron put away his equipment.

The mind expert lifted his broad shoulders in a shrug. "I don't know," he said, giving Korum a puzzled look. "Her brain is healthy, but it does show signs of recent memory erasure. There's also something else, something that I've never seen before."

"The softening procedure," Korum said. "Do you think it could be that?" He had told Haron about Saret's claims, and the mind expert had been very intrigued.

"It could be," Haron said. "I honestly haven't come across anything like this before. If Saret says he invented the procedure, then that would make sense." He sounded admiring, making Korum want to do something violent to him again.

"Can you fix it?" Korum already knew the answer but he had to ask.

Haron shook his head. "I don't think so, not without chancing some real damage to her brain in the process. Whenever we come up with something new here, we do extensive testing in a simulated environment first, before experimenting with live subjects. I could try, of course, if you want—"

"No." Korum could never take that kind of risk with Mia. "Forget it."

As their ship headed back to Lenkarda, Korum held Mia on his lap. She was awake but a little groggy, and she seemed content to just sit there, with her head resting on his shoulder. He stroked her hair, enjoying the feel of soft curls under his fingers.

Their conversation yesterday had gone very differently than he'd feared. Mia had been shocked and disbelieving at what Saret had done, but what had upset her the most was the idea of leaving him. And Korum had been glad. He had been so fucking glad and relieved that she wanted to stay. He honestly didn't know what he would've done if she'd said she wanted to go home. He wanted to think that he would've let her . . . but, deep inside, he knew otherwise. He couldn't bear the thought of being apart from her for a day; how would he have survived a lifetime without her?

He wouldn't have. It was that simple. He would've tried if that had been what she wanted, but the odds of failure would've been high. Korum had no illusions about himself. Altruism was not in his nature. He would've suffered for a while—out of guilt for letting her get hurt, out of desire to make up for past wrongs—but he would've eventually come for her.

She stirred in his arms, interrupting his musings. Raising her head, she gave him a sleepy smile. "Where are we going now?"

"Home, my darling," Korum answered, the remainder of his black mood fading as he gazed upon her beautiful face. As much as he wanted to reverse Saret's procedure and undo any damage done to this exquisite creature, he was happy to have her no matter what. Even if she didn't truly love him now, he hoped she would develop genuine feelings for him over time.

And Korum would make sure her love didn't turn to

hate when she learned the truth about his plans.

CHAPTER NINETEEN

The next month flew by. Korum found himself busier than usual, with his designers finalizing the new shields for the Centers and the Council trying to decide Saret's fate.

After several meetings, it was determined that a trial like that of the Keiths would not work in this instance. With Saret having been a long-term member of the Council, nobody was completely impartial and emotions were running high. Korum wasn't the only one who had considered Saret a friend. The mind expert had been generally liked, with his seemingly laid-back personality and friendly manner. The magnitude of his attempted crime was beyond belief, and even complete rehabilitation seemed too mild of a punishment for what he had intended. Finally, the Council reached out to the Elders for guidance—an initiative on which Korum took the lead, since he had other things to discuss with the Elders as well.

Between that and his regular work, Korum barely

found time to sleep—because he also wanted to spend as much time with his charl as possible. Mia's attachment to him seemed to be growing every day, and Korum no longer doubted the strength of her feelings. As she'd said, whatever Saret had done to her, that was the way she was now—and they both had to accept it.

On the plus side, Korum kept getting surprised by how well Mia was adjusting to everything . . . and how independent she was becoming.

Prior to her memory loss, she had been hesitant to wander around Lenkarda on her own, wary of his people and intimidated by some of their technology. Other than going to the lab and to a few scenic places he'd shown her, Mia had usually stayed home with him. Her free time had also been more limited, given the rigid schedule Saret had set for his apprentices. Now, however, since she and Adam were largely learning on their own, Korum discovered that his charl appeared to have a thirst for adventure—and indulged it at every opportunity.

One day she went swimming in the ocean near the estuary, on a day when the current was relatively weak. Nonetheless, Korum—who had gotten into the habit of checking on her location every hour—felt his blood freeze in his veins when he saw that she was a good quarter-mile away from shore. He'd immediately gone straight there, only to find her swimming leisurely, clearly enjoying herself. By the time she came out of the water, he'd managed to calm himself enough to have a rational discussion about the dangers of this particular spot, and she had agreed to be more careful going forward—but Korum still felt shaken by the incident for several days after that.

Her other excursions were less dangerous. She developed a fondness for hiking and recording images of the local wildlife with her wristwatch-bracelet device. Howler monkeys, iguanas, even some large insects—she would record them all and send the images as photographs and videos to her family, to share more with them about her new home.

She also grew closer to Delia, frequently meeting her for morning walks on the beach. Korum encouraged the friendship, glad that Mia was building other relationships in Lenkarda. Maria came by sometimes as well, and Korum had made it a point to invite her and Arman to dinner a couple of times.

Their main disagreement revolved around Mia's status as a charl. "Don't you understand how that makes me feel, knowing that legally I belong to you just because I'm human and you said so?" she told him once. "Don't you see how barbaric that is?"

Korum didn't view it that way at all. Yes, she was his—his to protect, his to love and cherish. Taking a charl was a serious lifelong commitment. Under Krinar law, Korum was responsible for Mia's actions. If she ever broke the mandate, for instance, he would be the one to answer for it to the Elders. Mia would never again be a regular human, not with the nanocytes in her system; even if she left him, Korum would always have to watch over her, to make sure she didn't reveal any non-public information about the Krinar. A charl was neither a slave nor a pet, and most cheren thought of them as their human mates—something that Mia couldn't seem to grasp.

"How could I be your mate when I don't have any rights here?" she said, and her stubbornness made Korum want to bend her over his knee and spank her pretty little behind. "I never agreed to be your mate—or your charl— in the first place, did I? And besides, we can't even have children together . . ."

Korum couldn't argue with that last point, and the charl issue remained unresolved, hanging over their heads and occasionally popping up during some more heated conversations—although those were becoming increasingly rare as their relationship evolved.

Seeing that Mia was becoming comfortable with Krinar technology, Korum gave her a fabricator of her own—a more advanced version of what he had made for Maria's birthday. It was powerful enough to create anything Mia needed in the course of the day, including a transport pod.

Her happiness at this gift had been off the charts.

"Thank you! Oh my God, Korum, thank you so much! This is awesome!" She almost smothered him with kisses, her eyes shining and her entire body vibrating with excitement. For the next several hours, she played with the fabricator nonstop, creating and un-creating one thing after another, while Korum basked in her joy.

Shortly after that, Mia decided to go to New York—in an aircraft she created herself. Korum gave her the design for that; it was a more complicated machine than the transport pod that was used around the Center. She made the ship while he watched with a smile, proud of how much she had learned already.

They went to New York together, since Korum was reluctant to have her so far away on her own. He knew it was illogical; after all, she had lived in the human city for years before they met with no harm coming to her at all, and both Saret and the Resistance had been eliminated as a threat. Still, he couldn't shake his irrational fear for her safety. It was either go with her or forbid her to go at all, and Korum knew she would not take well to the latter option.

On the morning of their trip, Mia used the fabricator to make them human clothes.

"Hmm, let's see," she said, grinning wickedly. "How about a pink T-shirt for you?"

"Sure." Korum stifled a laugh at her crestfallen expression. "I'd love a pink T-shirt." His people didn't associate colors with gender, and he personally liked all pastel shades. He knew she'd been hoping he would bristle at what she viewed as a feminine outfit, but he couldn't care less—as long as she didn't make him wear a skirt. He would draw the line at a skirt.

"Fine," she grumbled, "you're no fun." But she created a pink T-shirt anyway, which Korum put on without any hesitation. Thankfully, the jeans she handed him were of the regular dark blue variety.

"You know," she said thoughtfully, studying him after they were both dressed, "pink actually looks hot on you."

Korum laughed. "Why, thank you, my sweet. I'm flattered." She looked very sexy herself, dressed in a pair of well-fitting jeans, high-heeled ankle boots, and a silvery tank top that showed off her newly toned arms and shoulders. With the nanocytes in her body, Mia had significantly more endurance when it came to physical activity, and her recent interest in hiking and swimming had done wonders for her slim body. Korum had always found her irresistible, but now he could barely keep his eyes—and hands—off her.

"You told Jessie we'll be landing on her roof?" he asked as they entered the ship.

"Yep. She knows we're coming and even got permission from the building manager."

In order to save time, they had decided to go directly

to Jessie, instead of flying to one of the designated Krinar landing areas. The idea behind these areas was to minimize disruption to the human population in the big cities. Even today, the sight of Krinar aircraft frequently resulted in car accidents. Apparently, frightened human drivers tended to be distracted drivers. As a Council member, Korum could get away with not following this landing guideline, but he still tried to be circumspect in large cities like New York.

Jessie greeted them on the roof when they landed. She was standing there with a young human male who could only be Edgar, her new boyfriend. Korum recalled seeing him once before, at the nightclub where Korum found Mia dancing with another man. That particular incident wasn't one of Korum's favorite memories.

Nevertheless, he smiled at Jessie and Edgar, determined to play nice. He knew Mia's former roommate was concerned about her. She had been a witness to the rocky start of Korum's relationship with Mia, and he still wasn't her favorite person—something Korum planned to remedy today.

Mia smiled too, and he could see that she was genuinely happy to see her friend. She was also nervous, judging by the tight clasp of her fingers around his palm. For some reason, she still hadn't told her friends or family about her memory loss. When Korum had confronted her about it, she'd given him some vague answer about not wanting to worry anyone and he'd had to be content with that.

"Mia!" Jessie flew at her as soon as they stepped out of the ship, and the two girls hugged, laughing and squealing.

Korum grinned at their exuberant reunion, then stepped forward, offering his hand to Edgar in a human greeting gesture. "Hello. I don't think we formally met."

"No, we haven't," Edgar said dryly, accepting his handshake. "The last time I saw you, your hand was wrapped around my friend Peter's throat. I'm guessing that wasn't a great time for introductions."

"Indeed," Korum said, his eyes narrowing a bit. This human dared to remind him of that day? Peter had been lucky Korum had been able to control himself as well as he had. Every time Korum thought of that boy kissing Mia, he saw red. *Play nice*, he reminded himself, and rearranged his features into a more friendly expression. "So you're an actor," he said, steering the conversation toward a topic the human would be sure to enjoy.

"I am." Edgar took the bait. "I'm on that newest show on CBS. It's called *The Vortex*. Maybe you've heard of it?"

"I've seen all the episodes," Korum said. "I'm actually a big fan. I couldn't believe what happened with Eva last week—I never would've expected her sister to turn up like that."

Edgar's eyes lit up. "Oh no way! You watch the show? Is it popular among the Ks?"

It was popular among one particular K who needed to watch it as preparation for this trip. "Sure," Korum said. "We like entertainment as much as humans."

Mia had finished hugging Jessie and came up to Edgar as well. "Hi, Edgar," she said. "It's great to see you again."

Korum concealed a smile. Little liar. She didn't remember the guy at all, but she was putting on a good show. Edgar wasn't the only actor here today.

"Hi, Korum." It was Jessie. There was a familiar look of distrust on her pretty face, and Korum inwardly sighed. Out of everybody, this particular friend of Mia's would be most difficult to win over. He could see it in the stubborn tilt of her chin as she looked at him. She resented him for taking Mia away from her—and for his initial high-handed tactics.

It was a good thing Korum was always up for a challenge. "Hello, Jessie." He gave the human girl a warm smile.

They went inside, to the apartment Jessie had shared with Mia. Korum knew that a number of NYU students lived in the building due to its proximity to campus and reasonable (for New York) rent, but Korum had always thought the place was unfit for habitation. The paint in the hallways was peeling, and he could smell the rot in the old, musty walls. When he'd first met Mia, he couldn't wait to get her out of there and into his comfortable penthouse.

Jessie had prepared a veggie platter, beer, and some chips for them to snack on, and the four of them sat down in the living room. Later on, Korum planned to take them all out for a restaurant meal, but for now, this was as good of a spot to hang out as any.

Korum purposefully sat down next to their hostess. Mia sat on her other side, and Edgar made himself comfortable on a beanbag chair across from Korum. A couple of beers later, any hint of initial awkwardness had dissipated and conversation flowed freely. For a couple of young humans, Mia's friends were actually quite interesting, and Korum found himself unexpectedly having a good time. Jessie and Edgar had great chemistry together, joking around and teasing each other, and he could see Mia's initial tension draining away as nobody seemed to suspect anything about her lack of memory.

When everybody was sufficiently relaxed, Korum began his charm campaign against Jessie. He started off by inquiring about her summer, and then listened attentively as she told him all about her internship with a large pharmaceutical company. Korum already knew this, since he'd done his research prior to coming to New York. However, he also knew that people liked to talk about themselves, so he kept asking Jessie questions. In the meantime, Edgar was showing Mia posters of his latest show on the other side of the room.

"Is this company your first choice for full-time employment?" Korum asked Jessie, and she nodded, a hopeful look on her face.

"It's the first choice of everyone who's not going straight into medical school," she explained. "Since I want to do research first, this would be the perfect place to do it. It's super-competitive, of course. They hire ten times as many interns as they need full-time research assistants for next year, so even having an internship there doesn't guarantee an offer."

And just like that, Korum knew what he had to do. "You shouldn't worry," he said gently. "I'll put in a good word for you with the management."

"You would?" Jessie looked at him in astonishment. "You know Biogem's management?"

"I do," Korum said. It wasn't much of a lie, since he would know them soon.

"Oh, wow. You don't have to do that, Korum," she protested faintly, but Korum could see that her heart wasn't in it. She wanted this very badly, and he was handing it to her on a silver platter.

"I want to," he said firmly. "You're obviously deserving of this opportunity, and I know Mia would want you to have it."

Jessie smiled uncertainly. "Well, in that case, thank you. I would appreciate any help in that direction."

And Operation Jessie was complete.

When the beer and snacks were no longer enough, they went out for an early dinner. Korum took them to a new French restaurant that was getting rave reviews—and that was known for serving traditional meat-based dishes at astronomical prices. He stuck to his usual plant-based diet, but Mia and her friends each ordered something from the animal kingdom. Korum didn't mind if they indulged once in a while. The Krinar had been mainly concerned with the environmental impact of human dietary habits, and occasional meat-eating wasn't nearly as disastrous for the planet as what humans in developed countries had been doing before.

After dinner, they went out for drinks. Knowing that the girls wanted some privacy, Korum unobtrusively maneuvered himself and Edgar toward the far end of the bar, letting Mia and Jessie be on their own next to the window. He still kept an eye on them, just to make sure they weren't bothered by anyone, but otherwise, he focused most of his attention on Edgar.

"Do you play any sports?" he asked Edgar when their beers arrived. It was one of the many things the Krinar had in common with humans: games that required physical ability and skill.

The actor nodded. "I played soccer in college, and I still do that occasionally for fun. I also recently took up boxing, to get in shape for my next role."

"Oh, really?" Korum said. "Do tell me about it."

* * *

Mia smiled to herself when she saw Korum and Edgar on the other end of the bar. She knew exactly what he was doing and why: her lover wanted her and Jessie to have some girl time.

"Wow, Mia," Jessie said after the bartender handed them their cocktails. "I have to say, I'm beginning to see why you fell for him. He's so much nicer than I initially thought."

Mia grinned. "Yeah, he's great." She had no idea how Korum had been when they met, but she had some suspicions based on what he'd told her—and what she'd observed from his interactions with others over the past month. The love of her life was definitely not someone she would ever want for an enemy.

"You seem different too," Jessie said. "Stronger, more confident . . . and even more beautiful. Whatever he's doing for you seems to be working."

"He makes me happy," Mia told her. "Oh, Jessie, he makes me so unbelievably happy. I never thought I could be in love like that. It's like a fairytale come true."

"Complete with an extraterrestrial Prince Charming?"

Mia laughed. "Sure." Korum was not exactly Prince Charming, but she didn't plan on telling Jessie that. She liked the new friendly dynamic between her lover and her friends, and she had no intention of upsetting it.

No, she knew that Korum was far from perfect. She loved him, but she was not blind to his flaws. He was possessive to the extreme, paranoid about her safety—and manipulative when he needed to be. She hadn't missed the way he had deliberately spent time with Jessie, softening her up. It had worked too; her former roommate seemed to have a much better opinion of him now.

"It doesn't bother you that he's so much older?" Jessie asked, her dark eyes gleaming with curiosity. "Edgar is twenty-six, and he jokes that I'm the younger woman. I can't even imagine dating someone Korum's age . . ."

"He's not that old for a Krinar, believe it or not," Mia

said, smiling. "There are some who are much, much older. But, yes, sometimes the age gap is a challenge. There are definitely times when I feel like he's amused by me. He never makes me feel stupid or anything like that, but I know he thinks I'm very young."

"He doesn't treat you like a kid?"

"No." Mia shook her head. "He doesn't. He's ridiculously overprotective, but that's as far as that goes."

Jessie regarded her thoughtfully. "Do you think this is a long-term thing for you?" she asked, a small frown marring the smoothness of her forehead. "I mean, marriage and the whole enchilada? How would that even work with a K if they don't age like we do?"

Mia took a big gulp of her cocktail and coughed when it went down her windpipe. "Um, I'm not sure we're at that point yet," she said when she finally caught her breath. Korum had impressed on her that nobody outside of Lenkarda was supposed to know about her lengthened lifespan. It had something to do with a mandate set by their Elders. Mia hated the restriction, but she knew better than to break these rules. As Korum had explained, humans who knew too much would get their memories wiped—and Mia would never want to subject any of her friends or family to that process.

"But eventually?" Jessie persisted. "Have you thought about that? If you guys stay together, what happens when you get older? And what about kids?"

Mia shrugged. "We'll cross that bridge when we get to it." She didn't want to think about children right now. It was the one thing guaranteed to spoil her good mood. The DNA differences between humans and Krinar were too great to allow for biological offspring—a fact that made sense but was still agonizing to dwell on.

"Anyways," Mia said, wanting to change the subject,

"how about you and Edgar? How serious are you two getting?"

Jessie's smile was as bright as the sun. "I met his parents last week," she confided. "And next week, I'm taking him to meet mine."

"Wow . . . Jessie, that is big!" As far as Mia knew, this was the first time her friend was going to have a guy meet her family. Although Jessie's parents had been in America for a long time, they still retained some of the traditional Chinese customs and attitudes. Bringing home a boyfriend was a serious matter, and the boyfriend in question had to be ready to answer some very probing questions about his career and future life plans.

"Yeah," Jessie said wryly. "I warned Edgar that he's going to get grilled, but he's cool with that."

Suddenly, Mia felt a light touch on her bare arm. "May I buy you ladies a drink?" an unfamiliar male voice asked, and Mia turned her head to see an attractive dark-haired man who looked to be in his late twenties.

"We're here with our boyfriends," Jessie said quickly, an anxious note in her voice.

"Okay, no problem," the guy said, and disappeared into the crowd.

Mia looked at Jessie, eyebrows raised. Her friend had just been uncharacteristically rude, and she couldn't figure out why. And then she saw where Jessie was looking.

Korum was staring in their direction, his jaw tightly clenched and his eyes a bright golden yellow. Mia smiled and waved to him, wanting to diffuse the tension. She knew he didn't like any man touching her, but the guy had been harmless.

"He's not going to flip out again, is he?" Jessie sounded scared.

ANNA ZAIRES

"What? No, of course not," Mia said automatically, and then she remembered Korum telling her something about an incident at a nightclub in the early days of their relationship. He'd said that she and Jessie had gone out on their own, and some guy had kissed her. Based on Jessie's reaction, Mia guessed that Korum had downplayed his own response to that.

"Uh-huh," Jessie said doubtfully.

"He won't," Mia said with confidence, looking directly at Korum. She knew perfectly well that he could hear her.

He stared back at her. His eyes still had those dangerous golden flecks in them, but one corner of his mouth tilted up, a ghost of a smile stealing across his face. Mia continued looking at him, her own eyes narrowed, and the smile became a full-blown grin, transforming his features from merely gorgeous to out-of-this-world sexy. Then he turned away and continued speaking to Edgar, as though nothing had happened.

"Holy shit," Jessie breathed, her eyes huge. "You did it! Mia, you fucking did it . . ."

"Did what?"

"You tamed a K."

CHAPTER TWENTY

Another two weeks passed after the New York trip. Mia found herself loving her new life ... and contemplating not going back to finish her last year of school.

Lenkarda was as close to paradise as she could imagine. Summer was the wet season in that region of Costa Rica, which meant sunny mornings and tropical rain showers in the afternoon. As a result of all that rain, everything turned lush and green, with the waterfalls and rivers full to bursting. Mia often spent her mornings exploring the woods nearby, taking pictures of the local wildlife, and the second half of the day working in the lab with Adam.

Haron, the mind expert from Arizona, had agreed to take over Saret's lab as a temporary solution to keep the place open. Too much important research had been going on there to simply shut it down. Mia had first met the K during their brief trip to Arizona and she wasn't sure she liked him that much. She got the feeling he regarded her as something of a medical curiosity, due to her condition.

Nevertheless, he didn't mind if she continued working in the lab, and he mostly left her and Adam alone—which suited Mia just fine. With each day that passed, Mia became more and more entrenched in life in Lenkarda. Her friendship with Delia continued to develop, and the two girls often went swimming and snorkeling together—something that eased the minds of both of their cheren. "At least Delia can call for help if anything happens and vice versa," Korum said one evening while they were lying in bed. "And she knows which areas to avoid."

Korum's overprotectiveness drove Mia insane. When she complained about it to Delia, the older girl laughed. "Oh, just get used to it. Arus is the exact same way, believe me. You'd think after centuries together he'd realize I'm capable of taking care of myself, but no. If he had his way, I'd never leave the house without him."

"How do you cope with that?" Mia asked, studying her hands. She knew about the tracking devices there, and she *really* hated them. When she'd found out about the shining—after questioning Korum as to how he always seemed to know her exact location—she had been furious and insisted that Korum remove the devices. He refused, explaining that he needed to know that she was safe. They ended up having a long argument that culminated in Korum taking her to bed. The devices were still there for now, but Mia had every intention of removing them at the first opportunity.

Delia shrugged her slim shoulders. "I don't know," she said. "I know that Arus loves me and that he's afraid of losing me. I'm as necessary to his existence as he is to mine—and I try to make allowances for that. Over time, both of us have learned the value of compromise, and you and Korum will too."

Having Delia for a friend was like having a mentor and a girlfriend all wrapped up in one graceful package. At times, she was as wise and mysterious as a sphinx, but, other times, she was just like any other young woman Mia's age, acting as playful as a teenager. This unusual personality mix was relatively common among the Krinar, Mia discovered. They lived for a long time, but they never felt *old*. Their bodies were as healthy at ten thousand years of age as they were at twenty, and everybody around them shared their longevity, so they rarely experienced the types of losses that an unusually long-lived human would.

"You know, you don't fit the stereotype of a brooding immortal at all," Mia told Korum once, after a particularly fun play session in their zero-gravity chamber. "Shouldn't you be all moody and hating life instead of enjoying it so much?"

Korum grinned in response, white teeth flashing. "How could I hate life when I have you?" he said, lifting her and twirling her around the room.

When he finally put her down, Mia had been breathless with laughter.

"Life is to be enjoyed, my sweet," he said, still holding on to her, the expression on his face unexpectedly serious. "That's why I love you so much. I *enjoy* you, Mia—you enhance every moment of my existence. Your smile, your laugh—even your stubbornness—make me happier than I've ever been before. Even when we're not together, the thought of you makes me feel content, because I know that you're here, that when I come home, I can hold you, feel you—" his eyes gleamed brighter, "—fuck you."

Mia stared at him, her nipples hardening as her skin prickled with arousal.

"Yes," he said, his voice low and husky, "let's not

forget about that last part. I very much enjoy fucking you. I love the way you moan when I'm deep inside you, the flush on your cheeks when you're turned on . . . I love the way you smell, the way you taste. I want to eat you like dessert . . ." He reached between her legs, his fingers parting her folds, stroking her there, spreading the moisture around her opening. "Your pussy is sweeter than any fruit," he whispered, sinking to his knees and lifting the bottom of her dress, "more delicious than chocolate . . ."

And Mia nearly climaxed right then and there at the first touch of his tongue. Moaning, she buried her fingers in his hair, holding on to him as his skilled mouth brought her to a peak, pleasuring her until she shattered into a million pieces.

* * *

"Say that again," Korum demanded, staring at Ellet.

"I think I found someone who can reverse Saret's procedure and undo Mia's memory loss," Ellet repeated, crossing her long legs. They were sitting in Ellet's lab, where Korum had brought Mia after rescuing her from Saret's clutches.

"Who?"

"An up-and-coming apprentice at the Baranil lab. Apparently she has just developed a way to undo almost any mind procedure. It's all very hush-hush, which is why we didn't know about this earlier. You can imagine the implications of something like that. Everyone who's undergone any kind of rehabilitation would want this."

"The Baranil lab," Korum said, staring at Ellet. "On Krina."

"Yes."

"I see." Korum got up and started to pace.

"Do you even need it anymore?" Ellet asked, staring at him with her large dark eyes. "Mia seems quite happy as is . . . and so do you." There was a slightly wistful note in her voice.

Korum glanced at her sharply. Though they had been lovers, he'd never had any deeper feelings for Ellet—and he had been sure she didn't have any for him either.

As though to answer his unspoken question, Ellet smiled. "I'm happy for you," she said softly. "I really am. What you and I had has been over for a long time. I just never thought a human girl would be the one to make you feel this way."

Korum sighed, running his hand through his hair. "Me neither, Ellet. Believe me, it's quite a shock to me as well."

"Oh, I believe you," Ellet said, still smiling. She was beautiful—objectively, Korum recognized that—but her looks now left him cold. Every woman he saw these days was measured against Mia and found wanting—another side effect of his obsession with his charl.

"Can you please connect me with this apprentice?" Korum asked, returning to the subject at hand. "I'd like to speak to her."

Leaving Ellet, Korum headed toward his own laboratory, where his designers worked. Although they could all work remotely, meeting only in virtual environments, something about physical proximity tended to foster the creative process, resulting in improved team cohesiveness and more innovative project outcomes.

Entering the large cream-colored building, Korum greeted Rezav, one of his lead designers, and went into his office, a private space where he usually did his best work. This past week had been a quiet one, with his employees relaxing after last month's rush to finalize the designs for the new shields. Normally, this would've been the perfect time for Korum to work on his own designs—but the past couple of weeks had been far from normal.

Making sure that nobody could enter his office, Korum attached a virtual reality node to his temple and closed his eyes. When he opened them, he was standing next to a large river, surrounded by the familiar green, red, and gold tones of Krina vegetation.

The sun was bright, even hotter than at the equator on Earth. Korum could feel its rays on the bare skin of his arms, and he basked in the pleasant sensation. Drawing in a deep breath, he let his lungs fill with pure, clean air and the heady aroma of blooming plants.

"Quite different from Earth, isn't it?" a deep voice said to his right, and Korum turned his head to see Lahur standing there, less than five feet away. He hadn't heard the Elder's approach—but then no one could move quite like Lahur. The ancient Krinar was the ultimate predator, his speed and strength as legendary as the man himself.

"Yes," Korum said simply. "Quite different." If there was one thing he had learned during his recent interactions with the Elders, it was the importance of saying as little as possible. Lahur—the oldest of them all—liked silence and seemed to have contempt for those who spoke unnecessarily.

The fact that Lahur was speaking to Korum at all was incredible. Korum was no stranger to the Elders, having appealed to them numerous times for various Council matters. However, all of his prior communications had been done through the official channels, and the Elders almost never met with the Councilors in person—either virtually or in the real world. So when Korum had reached out to the Elders on Mia's behalf several weeks ago, he had never expected to have his request taken seriously, much less to be granted a virtual meeting.

A virtual meeting that had somehow turned into an entire series of interviews in the weeks to come.

Lahur stared at him, his eyes dark and unfathomable. Like Korum, he had been conceived naturally, not in a lab, and his asymmetrical features were closer to those of the ancients than to the modern Krinar.

"We have considered your request," the Elder said, his unblinking gaze trained on Korum.

Korum didn't say anything, only inclined his head slightly. Patience was the key here. Patience and respect.

"You wish your charl's family to be brought into our society. To have them share her extended lifespan."

Korum kept silent, holding Lahur's gaze with his own.

"We will not grant you your request."

Korum fought to hide his disappointment. "Why?" he asked calmly. "It's just a few humans. What harm would it do to bring them to Lenkarda and have them share fully in my charl's life?"

Lahur's eyes darkened, turning pitch black. "You argue for them?"

"No," Korum said evenly, ignoring the way his pulse had picked up. "I argue for her—for Mia."

Lahur stared at him. "Why? Why is one of these creatures so important to you?"

"Because she is," Korum said. "Because she means everything to me." He knew he had just done the equivalent of exposing his throat to Lahur, but he didn't care. It was no secret that Mia was his weakness, and trying to hide it from a ten-million-year-old Elder was as pointless as beating one's head against a wall.

To Korum's shock, a faint smile touched Lahur's lips, softening the harsh lines of his face. "Very well," the Elder said. "You have convinced me—and I'll give you one chance to convince the others. Bring the humans here and let them speak on their own behalf." He paused for a second, letting the full impact of his words hit Korum. "I would like to meet this Mia of yours."

CHAPTER TWENTY-ONE

"What's wrong?" Mia asked after the second time Korum fell silent, as though absorbed in his thoughts.

They were eating a late dinner on the beach—a romantic outing Korum had suggested the day before. Mia had expected something over the top . . . and it was. All around them, hundreds of tiny lights floated in the air, looking like a cross between stars and fireflies. The sun had already gone down, and these lights, along with the new crescent-shaped moon, were the only sources of illumination.

For their meal, Korum had prepared dozens of little dishes, mostly of the finger-food variety. They ranged from tiny sandwiches made with a delicious artichoke paste to some exotic fruits Mia had never tasted before. It was a spread fit for a king. Mia had been greatly enjoying everything—until she noticed Korum's oddly distracted manner.

"What makes you think something is wrong?" he asked, his lips curving in a sensual smile, but Mia wasn't fooled. There was definitely something on his mind.

"Don't you think I can tell by now when you're worried about something?" Mia cocked her head to the side, staring at her lover. He could still be a mystery to her at times, but she was getting to know him better with each day that passed.

He looked at her, his gaze almost ... calculating. "You're right, my sweet," he said finally. "There is something I need to talk to you about."

Mia swallowed. The last time Korum had needed to talk to her about something, she'd found out that her mind had been tampered with. What could it be this time?

"It's nothing bad," Korum said, seemingly understanding her concern. "In fact, it's all good news."

"What is it?" Mia couldn't shake an uneasy feeling.

"We found someone on Krina who can reverse Saret's procedure," Korum said, watching her closely. "She can undo everything he's done to you—including the memory wipe."

"Oh my God . . ." Mia didn't even know what to say. "But, Korum, that's awesome!"

He smiled. "It is. And there's something else."

"What?"

"Do you remember my petition to the Elders about your family?"

Mia almost stopped breathing. "About making them immortal like me?"

"Yes."

"Of course I remember," Mia said, her heart beginning to pound in her chest with a wild mixture of hope and apprehension.

"There's a chance they might grant it."

This time, Mia couldn't contain an excited scream.

Jumping to her feet and laughing, she launched herself at Korum, who got up just in time. "Thank you! Oh my God, Korum, thank you!"

"Hold on, my darling," he said, gently pulling her away. "It's not that simple. It requires something you might not want to do."

Mia stared at him, some of her excitement fading. "What?"

"We would have to go to Krina and take your family with us."

* * *

That night, Mia couldn't sleep. She kept waking up every hour, her mind buzzing with a million different questions and concerns. As Korum had explained, the trip to Krina would serve two purposes: to undo Saret's procedure and to present Mia's case in front of the Elders. "They want to meet you," he had said, shocking Mia into silence.

A large warm body pressed against her back, startling her out of her musings. "You're awake again," Korum murmured, pulling her into his arms. "Why aren't you sleeping, my darling?"

"Why do the Elders want this?" Mia couldn't stop thinking about it. "Why do they want to see us? I thought they were like your gods or something. What could they want with me and my family?"

Korum sighed, and she felt the movement of his chest. "They're not gods. They're Krinar, like me—only much, much older. As to why they want to see you, I don't know. They have taken an unusual interest in my petition, meeting with me several times and asking a lot of questions about you and your parents."

"And they didn't say they would grant your request,

right?" Mia turned in his arms, so that she would be facing him.

"No," Korum said, the faint glow of moonlight from the transparent ceiling reflecting in his eyes, "they didn't. However, Lahur said he would give us one more chance—and he implied he would be on our side."

"Lahur is the oldest?"

"Yes. He's the one who's lived for over ten million years."

Mia shivered, goosebumps appearing on her arms.

"Cold?" Korum drew her closer, pulling a blanket over them.

"No, not really." His naked body was like a furnace, generating so much heat that she was never cold when she slept next to him. The temperature in Korum's house was always comfortable too—cooler at night, warmer during the day. It was tailored specifically to meet their needs. When Mia had lived in Florida, she'd always hated air-conditioning; the cold air was too startling after the heat outside, and usually cranked up too high for her taste. In Lenkarda, intelligent structures kept the inside of the buildings at a perfect temperature, creating micro-zones of climate around each person.

"We don't have to go, you know." Korum gently stroked her back. "We can stay here. You've adapted to everything so well. If the memory loss doesn't bother you, then nothing has to change—"

"No," Mia said, burrowing against his chest. "If it was only that, then we could consider staying. But my parents, my sister . . . If there's even a chance they can live a longer life, we have to do this. I could never live with myself otherwise."

"I know, my darling," Korum said softly. "I know that."

"Couldn't we meet with the Elders virtually?" Mia drew back to look at his face. "That's how you met with them, right?"

"Yes," Korum said. "But they don't consider that a real meeting. When Lahur said he wanted to meet you, he meant in person, in real life."

"Old-fashioned, is he?" Mia said wryly.

Korum laughed. "That's the understatement of the century."

Mia fell silent, thinking about the upcoming trip again. "Do you think we'll be back soon?" she asked after a few seconds.

"I don't know," Korum said. "It depends on what the Elders want."

*   *   *

The next day Korum watched as Mia rang the doorbell at her parents' house. He knew she was worried about this part: telling her family about Krinar life extension capabilities and convincing them to go to Krina.

She was wearing human clothes today, a pair of shorts and a T-shirt. As much as Korum liked seeing her in dresses, he had to admit that the shorts looked good on her, showing off her shapely legs. Maybe he should have her dress like this more frequently.

Mia's mother opened the door with a huge smile on her softly rounded face. "Mia! Korum! Oh, I'm so glad you two came by!" She embraced Mia first, and then Korum found himself enveloped in a perfumed hug.

Smiling, he brushed a light kiss on Ella Stalis's cheek and stepped into the house, following the two women inside. Mocha, the tiny dog Mia had called a Chihuahua, ran out of one of the rooms, barking happily and trying to jump at Korum. He bent down and petted the little animal, which immediately rolled onto its back and presented its belly—apparently to be rubbed as well.

"Wow, Korum, she loves you," Mia said wonderingly. "I can't believe she acts that way with you. She's normally so shy with strangers . . ." And to prove her point, Mia extended her hand to the dog, which instantly turned over and ran away.

Korum grinned. It seemed like small, cute creatures had a thing for him.

Mia's parents had a lovely place—the epitome of what he thought of as American human. It had a comfortable, lived-in vibe, with overstuffed couches showing minor signs of wear and family photographs everywhere. Korum particularly enjoyed seeing those of Mia as a child. She had been a pretty toddler, with her long curls and big blue eyes. For a second, those photos made him ache to hold a daughter of his own, with Mia's features—a strange and impossible urge he'd never felt before.

Mia's father walked into the living room just as they sat down on the couch. Mia jumped to her feet. "Dad!"

"Oh, Mia, honey, I'm so glad to see you!" Dan Stalis embraced his daughter, kissing her cheek.

Korum got to his feet as well and extended his hand in a human greeting. "Hello, Dan."

"Korum, it's good to see you as well," Mia's father said, shaking his hand. He was more reserved than he had been with Mia, and Korum knew her father was still partially on the fence about their relationship. Korum couldn't blame him; if he had been in the human's shoes, he wouldn't have been nearly as accepting of someone taking his daughter away.

"Where's Marisa?" Mia asked when everybody sat down again. "Is she coming?"

"Yes, she should be here in a few minutes," her mother replied, still beaming with happiness at having her daughter home. Mia was glowing as well. Watching them, Korum was more convinced than ever that he had done the right thing in reaching out to the Elders. His charl would've been miserable if she'd had to watch her parents aging and withering away, knowing all the while that Korum had it in his power to prevent that from happening.

"Can I offer you some tea? Maybe some fruit?" Ella asked, addressing Korum. "Are you two hungry? I made a delicious beet salad yesterday—"

"I'm all right, thank you," Korum said, softening his answer with a smile. "We ate just before we came here."

"I'll take some tea," Mia said. "But don't worry, mom—I'll get it myself." Getting up, she walked toward the kitchen, leaving Korum by himself with the two older humans.

Ella and Dan Stalis were watching him strangely, almost expectantly, and Korum had a sudden flash of intuition. They thought he and Mia were getting engaged—and likely expected him to ask them for permission, in the old-fashioned human way.

Korum felt an unexpected flicker of regret for letting them down. That wasn't why he and Mia had come today at all, nor had the idea ever occurred to him before. As far as he knew, no Krinar had ever married a human; it just wasn't done that way. By claiming Mia as his charl, Korum had already made a commitment to her—even if she didn't necessarily view it the same way.

To his relief, the doorbell rang again, diffusing the awkward moment. Both humans got up and hurried to the door, letting their older daughter and her husband in. Mia came out of the kitchen as well, a broad smile on her face.

Korum stood up to greet them as they walked into the door. He kissed Marisa on the cheek and shook Connor's hand, genuinely glad to see the young couple. Mia's sister was just beginning to show, her trim figure rounding out with the baby, and she looked radiantly happy.

At the light brush of his lips against her cheek, Marisa blushed, her fair skin as sensitive as Mia's. Korum suppressed a smile. He knew human women found him attractive, and he rather liked having that effect on them. It was better than having them cringe in fear, as they sometimes did because of what he was.

Connor didn't seem to mind his wife's reaction, smiling as calmly as before. Korum couldn't understand his placidity. If Mia had blushed at the touch of another man, that man's lifespan would've been numbered in minutes. Humans were definitely more laid back about such matters; some males were as possessive as the Krinar when it came to their women, but the majority were not.

Mia greeted them next, and then everybody walked back to the couch area.

"All right, baby sis," Marisa said, taking a seat on the sofa. Her husband pulled up a chair next to her. "Tell us what's going on."

Mia took a deep breath and Korum squeezed her hand for encouragement. "I'm immortal," she said baldly. "I can now live as long as Korum—and if you come with us to Krina, you might be able to also."

For a moment, there was complete silence in the room. Then everybody started speaking at once. In the cacophony of voices, it was impossible to hear any specific question. Only Dan Stalis was quiet, leaning against a table and observing the proceedings with an expression of mild curiosity on his face.

"You're not surprised," Korum said, looking at Mia's father.

"No," Dan said. "I'm not."

"Why not?" Korum asked.

"Because it makes all the sense in the world," Dan Stalis replied. "How else could you and Mia be together? She has never talked about a future with you, yet she never seems upset when we bring it up. How could that be when she loves you and wants to be with you? And besides, you cured my migraines with nothing more than a small capsule. It's not that big of a stretch to think your people could cure other things, like cancer or heart disease." He paused for a second. "Maybe even aging."

Korum smiled, involuntarily impressed by the human.

"Dan, you never said anything to me." Ella's tone was bewildered. "In all the times we discussed Mia, you never once voiced these suspicions to me!" Her voice rose at the end, her eyes narrowing as she stared at her husband.

"It was never anything more than a guess," Dan said soothingly. "Ella, sweetheart, I didn't want to get your hopes up in case I was wrong."

"So are you now a K?" Marisa was looking at her sister with a shocked expression on her face. "Do you drink blood too?"

"Wait," said Connor, "can we go back to the part where we can all be immortal if we go to Krina?"

Mia opened her mouth to reply, and Korum squeezed her hand again. "Let me try to explain, my sweet," he said, "and then we'll answer any other questions your family might have."

Everybody fell silent, staring at him, and he continued, "We do have the means of curing cancer—and aging and any other maladies that may plague humans. The way that's done is by the insertion of nanocytes—nanomachines that mimic the functions of cells in a human body. They clean up any and all ongoing cellular damage and allow for rapid healing of injuries. That's all they do; there's no transformation from one species to another.

"Mia has these nanocytes in her body. I gave them to her a couple of months ago. And you're right, Dan. That's the only way we would be able to be together longer term."

Korum paused and surveyed the room. "The reason why Mia didn't tell you about this earlier—and why you've never heard of this before—is something called the non-interference mandate. It's set by our Elders. We're not allowed to do anything that would significantly alter the course of natural human progress. That's why we don't share our technology or science with you: because doing so is forbidden. The only exceptions to that rule are humans we call charl: those like Mia, with whom we enter into serious relationships."

"But why?" Connor asked, frowning. "Why have that mandate in the first place?"

"I don't know," Korum admitted. "There are many theories, the most popular of which is that the Elders are still conducting their experiment in regard to your evolution. They were there to see the beginning of your species, and they want to see how you turn out with minimal interference from us—"

"What do you mean, in the beginning? Just how old are these Elders of yours?" Dan interrupted, looking at Korum.

"Old," Mia answered for him. "Very old. Like ten million years old."

Mia's father visibly paled. "Ten *million* years old?"

"Yes," Mia said. "When Korum said they were there for the beginning of the human race, he wasn't kidding. Two of the Elders were actually in charge of overseeing our evolution way back when. Right?" She looked up at Korum.

"Yes, exactly," he confirmed.

"So if there's this mandate in place, why are you telling us about this stuff now?" Mia's mother asked, looking confused. "And what was that you said before, about going to Krina?"

"I petitioned the Elders on your behalf," Korum explained. "To have you undergo the same procedure as Mia. They didn't exactly agree to it, but they made a very unusual request: to see Mia and your family in person."

"The Elders want to see *us*?" Ella Stalis looked like she was about to faint.

"Yes," Korum said. "They want to see you and Mia in person."

"Why?" It was Dan again.

"I don't know," Korum said honestly. "I wish I could tell you."

"So let me get this straight . . . They want us to come to Krina, but they don't guarantee that they will give us these nanocytes?" Connor asked, his frown deepening. "They're asking us to leave our lives behind on the remote chance that this might happen?"

"Yes." Korum didn't bother to sugarcoat the situation.

"What would happen if you disobeyed these Elders?" Marisa asked, her slender hands twisting together. "If you broke the non-interference mandate?"

"It depends," Korum said. "If it's just a minor infraction, it results in a loss of standing—that's something like our reputation—and there are frequently financial and other penalties. If it's something more serious, then it's treated as a criminal offense on par with murder."

"Oh," Marisa said faintly.

"So let me get this straight," Dan Stalis said. "You're giving us the possibility of having an infinitely long lifespan, but only if we go with you to another planet."

"Yes."

"And what would happen if we refuse?" Connor asked, a stubborn look on his face. "What if we don't want to uproot our entire lives to fly off into space?"

Korum shrugged. Truth be told, he wasn't certain what would happen if any of Mia's family decided against accepting the Elders' invitation. In the normal course of events, if humans found out something they shouldn't have, they would have a portion of their memories erased. But this was different, and he didn't know what guidelines applied in this case.

"No, Connor, you can't refuse," Mia said, glowering at her brother-in-law. "Don't you understand? If the Elders grant our request, you and Marisa—and your baby— would be able to live for thousands of years. How could you refuse something like that? And, mom, dad, you guys will be young again. Wouldn't that be awesome?" She cast a pleading glance around the room. "Please, don't make me watch you all die because you're scared. Korum is offering you a shot at immortality. How could you turn that down?"

CHAPTER TWENTY-TWO

The next two weeks passed in a flurry of preparations for the departure. Mia's parents, Marisa, and Connor each requested a leave of absence from their jobs and put their finances in order. Of them all, Connor seemed the most hesitant, though Marisa convinced him that they had to go—if only for their baby's sake. After many discussions, it was decided that if the Elders didn't grant them immortality, then they would come back to their regular lives—after first signing an agreement not to reveal any confidential information about the Ks. If the petition succeeded, however, then Lenkarda would be their new home, just as it was for Mia.

To alleviate any concerns about her sister traveling during pregnancy, Mia spoke to Ellet and had her examine Marisa one last time. "She's perfectly healthy," Ellet reassured them, "and routine space travel shouldn't pose any issues. Now if she went off exploring new galaxies, I would be worried, but a simple trip between

Krina and Earth—that's the safest thing there is these days."

Mia called Jessie and spoke to her, explaining that she would be away for a while and won't be coming back for the school year. Jessie wasn't the least bit surprised, though she did cry when Mia said she didn't know how soon she would return. Since Mia couldn't tell Jessie the real reasons for the trip, she had to let her think it was Korum's business taking them away.

"Can Jessie come too?" Mia asked Korum after that heart-breaking conversation. "I know you said family only, but she's like family to me—"

"No, my sweet," Korum said regretfully. "The Elders even balked at Connor coming along. I had to work very hard to convince them that a brother-in-law is the equivalent of a real sibling. If Connor's parents had been alive, I don't think it could've worked—that would've been too many humans to get an exception for."

Mia swallowed. She hadn't realized how close she'd come to losing her sister, who would've likely chosen to stay behind with her husband. It was the first time Connor's lack of family was in any way a plus. Mia had always felt sorry for her brother-in-law because his mother, a single parent, had passed away from breast cancer seven years ago . . . but now that fact may have enabled Mia's family to stay together.

Adam prepared a bunch of notes and recordings for her to take to the mind lab on Krina. "Don't forget to give it to that apprentice," he told Mia. "It's got everything I could find in Saret's files about memory loss and softening. It's not much—he must've destroyed most of the data before—but it might help them figure out your condition."

"Thanks, Adam." Mia smiled at the K. "It was

awesome having you for a partner."

Adam grinned, white teeth flashing. "Right back at you, partner. Ping me when you guys land and settle in; I'd love to hear how your meeting with the Elders goes."

"Of course," Mia said. She knew Adam had a very good reason for wanting to know the outcome of Korum's petition: his entire adopted family was human— as was the mysterious girlfriend he never talked about.

* * *

"Saret is going to be on the ship with us," Korum told Mia as they walked on the beach the evening before their departure. "The Council wants him back on Krina so the Elders can try him themselves."

Mia's stomach twisted with remembered fear. She still had occasional nightmares from the Arena fight— horrifying dreams in which Korum didn't emerge as the victor. Saret had come far too close to killing her lover, and she could never forget the agony of those moments when she'd thought she lost Korum.

As though reading her mind, Korum said, "There's nothing to worry about, my sweet. He'll be locked up the entire trip."

"Which will only be a couple of weeks, right?" Mia asked.

"Yes," Korum confirmed. "Getting sufficiently far away from Earth is what's going to take the longest. This is a very crowded solar system and we have to make sure nothing interferes with our ship's warp capabilities."

Mia laughed, forgetting all about Saret for the moment. "Warp capabilities? Like the warp drive in our science fiction—the thing that lets you go faster than the speed of light?"

"Yes," Korum said. "Very similar to that. It bends space-time, allowing us to travel from one point in the universe to another almost instantaneously."

"How does it do that?" Mia asked in fascination. Physics had never been her strongest subject, but even she knew that weird things happened near the speed of light—and that faster-than-light travel had been considered impossible until the Ks arrived.

Korum smiled, apparently pleased by her interest. "I can't explain fully without going into some complicated math, but I can give you a rough idea," he said. "Essentially, our ships create a huge energy bubble that causes a contraction in the space-time in front of it and an expansion in the space-time behind it. That's what propels us from one place to another—the push-and-pull of space-time itself. We don't need to reach the speed of light at any point; we bypass it altogether."

"Wouldn't something like that require a lot of energy? What do you use for fuel?"

"Well, the energy bubble around the ship uses a combination of positive and negative energy," Korum said. "Negative energy is something that your scientists are just now beginning to explore. And yes, you're absolutely right: warping space-time requires a tremendous amount of energy. Fortunately, we have it in abundance. We also use antimatter as a fuel source; that's what powers our ship when we're not in warp mode."

Mia's eyes widened. "Antimatter?"

"It's the most powerful energy source there is," Korum explained.

Mia fell silent, thinking about the magnitude of what she was about to do. Tomorrow, she would leave Earth for an as-yet-undetermined length of time, with a lover who wasn't even human. She was entrusting the fate of her entire family into his hands.

It should've been a scary thought, but somehow it wasn't. Instead she was almost giddy with excitement. How many people got a chance like that? To see a different planet, to go to Krina—the origin of all life? And meeting the Krinar Elders . . . She still couldn't wrap her mind around that one. She, a regular human girl, would see the actual creators of mankind.

It was enough to make anybody's head spin.

* * *

The next morning they went to Florida to pick up Mia's family, flying in a larger transport pod Korum had created specifically for that purpose. Everyone was already gathered at Mia's parents' house, with their bags packed and ready. Even though Korum had explained that they didn't need most of their things, the humans insisted on bringing their own clothing and other items they saw as necessities.

This time, Korum landed the pod on the street in front of the Stalis house. Mia had explained that her parents already told all their neighbors about the upcoming trip (though not the reason for it), and nobody would be too shocked to see an alien aircraft landing in their quiet neighborhood.

Emerging from the pod, Korum and Mia walked to the door and rang the doorbell. All around them, people were slowly coming out of their houses, driven by curiosity about their neighbors' extraterrestrial connection. Korum could hear their whispers, giggles, and gasps of excitement and fear. An older couple a few houses away were on the phone with their children, complaining that the 'K evil' had come to Ormond Beach. They likely thought he couldn't hear them, not realizing how acute Krinar senses were.

None of this bothered Korum. In the past, he'd tried to be considerate, to make sure that his presence in the small town didn't draw too much attention to his charl's family. Now, however, it didn't matter. If the Elders agreed to their request, Mia's relatives would never be able to return to their regular lives.

Marisa opened the door to let them in. "Hi guys," she exclaimed brightly. "Come on in! We're almost ready."

"Awesome!" Mia had a huge grin on her face as they entered the house. "Are you excited? I know I am—"

"Oh my God, am I excited? Are you kidding me? I haven't slept for two nights . . ."

Korum smiled and followed the two sisters as they continued chattering all the way to the kitchen. Mia's parents and Connor were already gathered there, eating their breakfast.

"Korum!" Ella exclaimed, her eyes lighting up. "Will you join us? I made some potato pancakes with fresh berry jam."

"Sure," Korum said, sitting down at the table. "I'd love some pancakes." Mia and he ate about an hour ago, but he was curious to try the dish Mia had said was her mother's specialty.

In that moment, Mia came up behind his chair and kissed his cheek, her hair tickling the back of his neck. "Already hungry?" she teased, her hands gently kneading his shoulders. Her easy display of affection made him want to hug her. He hadn't known how much he needed that from her until she started touching him like that in the past few weeks. Before, he had almost always been the one to initiate physical contact, both of the sexual and more casual variety.

Of course, whenever she was this close to him, he got hard, but the discomfort was a small price to pay. Korum shifted in his seat, raising his knee slightly in case any of his human companions happened to glance under the table.

"Mia, honey, how about you?" her mother asked. "Do you want some pancakes too?"

"I'd love some, mom, thanks." Mia let go of Korum's shoulders and sat down in the chair next to him. Korum reached over and took her hand, craving more of her touch.

"Ooh, so lovey-dovey," Connor said, chewing on a pancake. "Look at those two, Marisa."

"Shut up, Connor," his wife said, walking over to put the water to boil. "It's not like they're an old married couple like us." But there was a big smile on her face as she said it, and Korum knew she was joking. From what he had seen, Marisa and her husband were very affectionate with each other.

Korum didn't mind Connor's teasing; he loved Mia and had no intention of hiding his feelings from her family. Let them see how much he cared for her. After all, they were trusting him enough to leave their entire lives behind.

He hoped the Elders wouldn't deny them the nanocytes. He hated the thought of disappointing Mia's family—and Mia herself. Somehow, almost imperceptibly, Korum had grown to care about these people. In the past two weeks, he'd had a lot of interactions with each of Mia's relatives, answering their questions about Krina and what to expect during the trip—and he'd found that he genuinely liked them. He saw shades of Mia in both her parents and her sister, and frequently found Connor's company amusing. If someone had told Korum a few months ago that he would feel this way about a bunch of humans, he would've laughed in their face. But ever since he met Mia, his predictable life had gone down the drain.

Ella Stalis brought out the pancakes and served everyone. Tasting his portion, Korum immediately complimented her cooking, loving the combination of sweet jam with the savory potato. She glowed, obviously pleased. In that moment, Korum could see the beauty she must've been in her youth—and would likely be again after the procedure.

Finally, all the food had been eaten and dishes put away. Korum helped clean up, loading everything into the dishwasher. Human appliances had always interested him for some reason; they were so primitive and graceless, yet they managed to do their job for the most part.

At that moment, the tiny dog ran out of one of the rooms, barking and jumping at Korum again. Before he had a chance to do anything, Marisa grabbed it off the floor. "Mocha!" she chastised the animal. Turning to Korum, she gave him an apologetic smile. "Sorry about that. We kept her in the bedroom so she's not in the way while we're packing, but she got out somehow—"

"That's okay; I don't mind," Korum assured her. Then a sudden thought occurred to him. "What are you going to do with the dog when you leave?"

Marisa stared at him. "She's coming with us, of course."

Korum blinked slowly. "I see."

"That's not a problem, is it?" Marisa asked anxiously. "I know my parents would die without her—"

"No, it's not a problem," Korum said. Unexpected, but not a problem. He should've known they would want to bring the furry creature; humans often had unnatural attachments to their pets. He would have to make some last-minute adjustments to the ship's layout to accommodate the dog's presence, but it wouldn't be anything major.

Twenty minutes later, everybody was ready to go. Korum brought five large suitcases outside and loaded them onto the aircraft, ignoring the curious stares from the neighbors.

"Be careful, they're heavy," Dan Stalis admonished him, and Korum suppressed a smile. Mia's father clearly didn't understand the full extent of the differences between Krinar and human bodies. The suitcases were no heavier to him than Ella's little purse was to her. Still, his concern was rather touching.

When they were all inside the aircraft, Mia made sure they were comfortably seated on floats. Her mother held the dog on her lap, clutching it with a desperation that betrayed her nervousness.

"Goodbye, Ormond Beach. Goodbye, Earth," Mia's sister whispered as the aircraft took off, carrying them upward, beyond Earth's atmosphere, where the big ship awaited them for their interplanetary journey.

CHAPTER TWENTY-THREE

As their ship ascended, Mia watched the shrinking buildings and landmarks below. The pod's transparent walls and floor allowed for an amazing 360-degree view. Within seconds, their aircraft was above the clouds and blinding sunlight streamed in, causing Mia to squint until Korum did something that minimized the glare.

"Wow," Marisa breathed, echoing Mia's own feelings. "This is so not like traveling by airplane . . ."

"We're moving much faster than your planes," Korum explained. "In another few minutes, we'll be reaching our destination right outside of Earth's atmosphere."

Mia reached over and squeezed his hand. Her heart was pounding with excitement and trepidation, and she could only imagine how the others must be feeling. Her dad was looking a little pale, and her mom was holding Mocha so tightly that the little dog was squirming. Even Connor was uncharacteristically quiet, a look of awe on his face.

"It'll be all right, my sweet," Korum said, leaning over to kiss her temple. "Everything will be fine."

"I know," Mia said quietly. "It's just incredible, that's all."

He smiled, showing that sexy dimple in his left cheek. It made him look even more gorgeous than usual, and Mia desperately wished they were alone right now, instead of surrounded by her family.

As though reading her mind, Korum whispered to her, "Later," and Mia felt her cheeks heating up. His smile changed, became more suggestive, and she pinched his arm in response.

He lifted his eyebrows questioningly, and Mia gave him a frown. "Not in front of my parents," she mouthed, and his smile turned into a full-blown grin.

Determined not to let him make her blush, Mia looked down, watching with barely controlled excitement as they got further and further away from Earth. When she was little, she had dreamed of being an astronaut, of going to the stars and exploring distant galaxies. Like most kids, she had grown out of that, eventually choosing a more suitable profession. Now, however, she was being given a chance to live that long-ago childhood dream, and it was beyond amazing.

Soon, they were so far away that she could see Earth in its entirety—a beautiful blue planet that looked far too small to be home to billions of people. Looking at it, Mia couldn't help but realize just how vulnerable the entire human race was, tied as they were to this one place that looked so defenseless in the vastness of space.

"What are you thinking about?" Korum asked, reaching over to stroke her knee.

"I was thinking I understand now why the Krinar want to diversify," Mia said, "why you don't want to bet your survival on any one planet. It looks so fragile like this . . ."

"Yes, it does, doesn't it?" Korum's hand tightened on her knee. When she looked up at him, he was looking at her with a strange expression on his face. Before she could ask him about it, though, she heard her mom gasp.

"Oh wow, Korum!" Ella Stalis exclaimed. "Is that your ship?"

Mia looked up. They were approaching something that looked like a large bullet. Dark-colored, it was surprisingly plain-looking, completely unlike any starship she had ever seen in science fiction movies.

"That's it?" she asked, trying to keep the disappointment out of her voice. Krinar transport pods looked more advanced and futuristic than this ship that could supposedly go faster than the speed of light.

"That's it." Korum smiled. "It's not quite how your people imagined it, is it?"

"No, it's not," Connor said, speaking for the first time since their transport pod took off. "How did all those thousands of Krinar fit into that? It looks kind of small . . ."

"Oh, this is not the ship that brought us here," Korum explained. "You're right; that one is much bigger. This ship is something that I made specifically for our journey. There are only about seventy of us who are going to Krina this time; there was no need to use the bigger ship for so few people."

"You can do that?" Mia's dad asked, staring at Korum in disbelief. "Just like that, you can create a ship that can go to a different galaxy?"

"Korum can do it," Mia said, understanding her dad's confusion. "Not every Krinar can. He is the one who came up with this design. Right?" She looked at Korum.

"Yes," her lover confirmed. "This particular design is mine. We had ships with faster-than-light capabilities before, of course, but these are the latest generation. They're safer and easier to operate."

"I see," Dan said, looking at Korum with a mixture of shock and respect. The same emotions were reflected on Ella's face. Apparently Mia's parents had not understood the extent of Korum's technological prowess until this moment.

As the pod approached the ship, Mia could see one of the ship's sides dissolving to let them in. Since all Krinar houses had similar entrance technology, she barely blinked at the sight. Her family, however, found it very impressive.

"How exactly does this intelligent stuff work?" Marisa asked. "Do the walls actually think for themselves?"

"No," Korum said. "This is not artificial intelligence in the true sense of the word. It's not self-aware in any way. When I say 'intelligent technology,' what I really mean is that it's an object that's able to carry out its specific function in a way that mimics the capabilities of an intelligent being. So, for instance, my house can make meals, maintain temperature that's just right for our bodies, keep out unwanted visitors, and clean itself. It performs those tasks as well as a human or a Krinar would—but you can't really carry on a conversation with it."

"That's so cool," Connor said. "Do you guys have robots that you *can* talk to?"

Korum smiled indulgently. "Yeah, those were popular a few thousand years ago and then kind of went out of style. Now they're mainly used to entertain small children, although some adults like them too."

Before Connor could ask any more questions, their

pod touched the floor of the ship, landing softly. Marisa clapped. "Bravo! That had to be the smoothest ride ever."

Korum laughed, rising from his seat. "We're here," he said. "Until we reach our destination, this will be your new home."

When they disembarked, Korum gave them a tour of the ship. Despite its unassuming outer layer, the inside of the spacecraft was as beautifully decorated as any Krinar house. Light colors, floating furnishings, exotic plants— the ship had everything Mia had gotten used to in Lenkarda, and she immediately felt at home there.

Mia's parents were beyond impressed. "Korum, this is so gorgeous," her mom kept saying. "And the view! Dear God, the view!"

The view was truly stunning. The outer walls of the ship were see-through from the inside, just like in most Krinar buildings, and there were plenty of areas where one could observe space in all its glory. Without the interference from the atmosphere, everything was sharper, clearer, the stars looking brighter than anything Mia had ever seen on the ground.

Korum had prepared special quarters for Mia's family, closely replicating the interior of her parents' house. "I hope this works for you," he told them. "If not, I can change it to anything else you prefer."

"Oh, no, this is perfect," Mia's dad said, walking over to sit down on a big overstuffed couch. "All that floating stuff is a bit intimidating, to be honest with you."

"Good, I'm glad you like it." Korum smiled, and Mia wanted to kiss him for his thoughtfulness. "I'll have a special area made for Mocha as well, to make sure she can run around and use the bathroom there."

The few Ks they met during the tour were pleasant to Mia's family, having been already apprised of their presence by Korum. They all stared, of course, but Mia was already used to that. Two of the female crew members seemed particularly intrigued by the little dog that Mia's mom insisted on carrying around with her.

"That is so cute!" One of them exclaimed, reaching over to pet Mocha. "Oh, I've never seen one of these up close!"

The dog tolerated the attention, but Mia could see she wasn't happy about it. It seemed Korum was the only K Mocha truly liked.

After the tour, Mia's family decided to rest. Her sister was particularly tired, worn out by all the excitement. "It's nap time," Connor said, smiling at his wife, and she nodded, stifling a yawn.

Mia and Korum were finally on their own.

* * *

"Looks like it's just us," Mia said, smiling at Korum. They had just gotten to their own private quarters, complete with a large circular bed similar to the one in Korum's house.

"Indeed." His eyes were starting to gleam with the familiar golden light.

Holding his gaze, Mia slowly and deliberately hooked her thumbs under the straps holding up her sundress and pushed them down over her shoulders. "Oops," she whispered. "I can't seem to take this off. I might need your help . . ."

Korum's nostrils flared, and she could see the tension invading his muscles. "Come here," he growled.

Mia shook her head. "No. You come here." She knew

exactly what she wanted, and it did not involve Korum taking over this time.

His eyes narrowed. He looked dangerous now, like a wild predator who couldn't be controlled, and her heart started beating faster from the thrill of what she was trying to do. "Come," she repeated, crooking her finger at him.

He came. Or, rather, he practically leapt across the room. In a second, he was next to her, his muscular body large and intimidating, pressing her against the wall. "You need help with this dress, do you?" His fingers tugged at the flimsy straps, the thin material nearly coming apart in his strong hands.

"Yes," Mia breathed, looking up at him. "I do. Be gentle, though. And after you take it off me, I want you to undress for *me*."

His eyes turned almost yellow. "Is that right?"

"That's right," Mia said. "And then I want you to lie down on the bed." Her heart was pounding so hard it felt like it was about to explode, and her body was melting with need. She wanted him badly . . . but on her own terms.

For a second, she thought he wouldn't comply, but then he took a step back. "All right," he said, his voice unusually rough. "Turn around."

Mia suppressed a triumphant smile and did as he asked. The dress she was wearing was human-style, with a zipper in the back, and his fingers felt hot on her bare skin as he unzipped it all the way. As soon as he was done, Mia stepped to the side and let the dress drop to the floor. Underneath, she was wearing a tiny blue thong— something she'd put on this morning specifically with Korum in mind.

He sucked in his breath. "Mia . . . You little tease . . ."

She lifted her brows. "You don't like?" She did a little twirl, pretending not to see the explosive heat in his gaze as he stared at her.

A muscle pulsed in his jaw. "Are you torturing me?"

"I don't know," Mia purred. "Am I?" Turning her back to him, she bent over and slowly pushed down the thong, the way she'd seen it done in movies. Then she stepped out of it. When she turned toward him again, he looked almost feral, his eyes glittering and his hands clenched into fists.

"Your turn," Mia said, watching him in fascination. Would he lose control and take her now? She loved it when she could get him into that state, completely mindless with need for her. His savage passion didn't frighten her; instead, it made her want him even more.

He took a deep breath, then another, and she saw his hands slowly unclenching. Then, still staring at her with a burning gaze, he pulled his T-shirt over his head and unzipped his jeans, pushing them down his hips. He wasn't wearing any underwear, and he was already fully aroused, his erection aggressively jutting out.

Mia's mouth went dry at the sight. Her lover was male perfection personified. Every muscle on his powerful body was clearly defined, the smoothness of his golden skin marred in only a few places by a smattering of dark hair. She wanted to jump on him and lick him all over.

"Lie down on the bed," she managed to say, her voice thick with desire.

He did as she asked, but she could see that his self-control wouldn't last long. Suddenly, an idea came to her. "My fabricator, please," she said out loud, knowing the intelligent ship would understand what she wanted. Sure enough, a few seconds later, one of the walls dissolved and Korum's gift floated out directly into Mia's hands.

"What are you doing?" Korum asked, watching her warily from the bed, and she gave him a wicked grin.

"You'll see."

Holding the fabricator in her hand, she told the gadget, "Handcuffs with a key, please," and then waited while the nanomachines did their job.

Korum sat up, staring at her with an unreadable expression on his face. "And what do you think you're doing with those?"

Mia put down the fabricator and picked up the handcuffs. "Putting them on you, of course."

"Oh really?"

"Yes, really," Mia said firmly, climbing onto the bed next to Korum. "Now give me your wrists."

He hesitated for a second, then extended his hands, the lust on his face now tempered with amusement. "You think those will hold me?"

"Probably not," Mia admitted, putting the handcuffs on him. Each of his wrists was as thick as both of hers combined, his forearms bulging with muscle. "But that's not the point, is it?"

"What *is* the point, my sweet?" he asked softly, watching her with a heavy-lidded gaze. "Are you trying to prove something?"

Instead of answering, Mia gave him a light push, getting him to lie flat on his back with his handcuffed arms raised over his head. Then she climbed on top of him, straddling his stomach until his erection was only a couple of inches from her opening. Leaning down, she braced herself on his chest and whispered in his ear, "The point is that you're mine, and I get to do whatever I want with you."

He drew in a sharp breath and his hips arched, trying to bring his cock closer to her entrance. "And does that include letting me get inside your tight little pussy?" His voice sounded hoarse, strained with need.

"Oh yes." Mia moved down until his shaft was between her nether lips, her clitoris rubbing against its side. The skin covering his cock was soft, almost delicate, and she closed her eyes, savoring the feel of it against her sex.

"Mia . . ." he groaned, bucking underneath her. "Put it in. Now."

Deciding not to torture him—or herself—any longer, Mia wrapped her hand around his length and guided him into her. Biting her lip at the stretching sensation, she slowly lowered herself until his cock was almost all the way in. She paused, getting used to his thickness, and then let him in deeper, not stopping until he was in all the way.

He groaned again, his arm muscles flexing with the effort to keep from reaching for her right then and there, and his cock jerked inside her. Mia knew he was dying to take control, to make them both come, and she wondered at his unusual restraint.

She didn't have to wonder long. Before she could move again, she found herself flipped over onto her back, his large body pressing her into the mattress. His eyes were wild, his gaze unfocused. He had managed to tear apart the metal links holding the cuffs together, and his hands were on her thighs, holding them wide open for his thrusts.

Crying out, Mia wrapped her arms around his neck, barely able to hold on as he hammered into her, driven solely by the primitive instinct to mate. Her body slid back and forth on the mattress with each movement of his powerful hips, and the intelligent bed softened around them, became more like a pillow in texture, protecting her from any injuries.

Her first orgasm hit her like a freight train, and Mia screamed, bucking in his arms, but he was merciless, utterly relentless. The second one, mere moments later, made her literally see stars, yet he continued fucking her, ferocious in his need.

It was too much. Mia felt like she would break apart, like she would shatter from the intensity of the sensations. Her body was no longer her own, her mind was no longer her own. There was only heat and sweat and his body, over her, in her, surrounding her. They were melded together, fused by the white-hot ecstasy of their joining.

By the time he shuddered over her, Mia was incoherent, her voice hoarse from her screams and her body shaking from the unending swells of pleasure. And just when she thought it was over, she felt his teeth slicing across the vein in her neck . . . and sending her spiraling even higher.

CHAPTER TWENTY-FOUR

If anyone had told Mia an intergalactic voyage would be as easy as going on a cruise, she would've laughed out loud. Yet it was indeed the case. They spent almost a week flying away from Earth at sub-light speeds—so as not to cause any disturbances with the warping of space-time—and then they activated the warp drive, landing within a few days flight to Krina. All of this was done so smoothly that Mia didn't feel anything. It wasn't until Korum told her they were in a different galaxy that she knew the ship had made the jump.

"Are we going to see the Elders right away?" Mia asked as they were lying in bed the evening before their arrival. Since they were both less busy with other matters, she and Korum had spent a lot of time with each other during the trip. Mia was taking a break from learning about the mind, and Korum didn't have any urgent Council issues to worry about. Mia slept late, hung out with her family in the mornings, and spent the majority of her day with Korum—an activity that invariably culminated in several hours of sexual bliss.

"No," Korum said. "We'll go see the mind expert first, to restore your memory." And to undo the softening—but that part went unsaid. Mia knew they were both anticipating and slightly dreading the reversal of the procedure, unsure of just how much—if anything—would change between them as a result.

Staring at the transparent wall in their bedroom, Mia could see unfamiliar stars and constellations in the sky. They were already in the Krinar solar system, a strange and beautiful place with ten planets circling a star that was roughly 1.2 times the size of Earth's sun. Krina was the fourth planet in terms of distance from its sun, and it was strikingly similar to Earth in its size, mass, and geochemical composition. "That's why Earth is so important to us," Korum explained. "It's closer to Krina than anything else we've come across in all the years we've been exploring the universe."

The main difference between the two planets lay in its moons. Earth had only one, while Krina had a grand total of three—one about the size of Earth's and two smaller ones. "We get some spectacular tides," Korum told her. "They're more like small tsunamis. Earth is better in that sense; in most places, you can live right next to the ocean and not have to worry about anything more than an occasional hurricane. On Krina, the ocean is more dangerous, and we don't have any settlements within twenty miles of the shore."

To Mia's surprise, she learned that when Korum referred to the ocean on Krina, he meant The Ocean—as in, one huge body of water. Unlike Earth, where the original supercontinent of Pangaea had broken apart into several continents, Krina had one giant landmass that served as home to all the Krinar. Tinara, Korum had called it.

That fact also explained something that had puzzled Mia before: the relative lack of variety in Krinar appearance. Her lover's people all tended to be dark-haired with bronzed skin, and, while there were variations in coloring, there were significantly fewer differences among Ks than between humans of different races. The Krinar were more homogeneous—which made sense if they had all evolved together on this supercontinent.

"So why does your cousin Leeta have red hair?" Mia asked. She'd met the beautiful Krinar woman a couple of times since her memory loss. "Is there a gene for that in the K population?"

Korum shook his head. "No, not really. Some of us have hair with a slightly auburn tint to it, but nothing like the shade Leeta is wearing now. She has altered the structure of her hair molecules since coming to Earth, probably because she likes that look."

"And there are no blond, blue-eyed Krinar?"

"No," Korum said. "No Krinar with hair as curly as yours either. With your curls and blue eyes, you'll really stand out on Krina."

"Oh great," Mia muttered. "I'll be stared at even more."

Korum smiled. "Yes, you will be. But that's not a bad thing."

Mia shrugged. She knew the Krinar didn't regard staring as rude, but she was still uncomfortable with that specific cultural difference. "So when are we meeting your family?" she asked, switching gears. "Are they going to be there to greet us when we arrive?"

"No. I told them we'll visit them right after you regain your memory. You've already met my parents once before, and you'll probably feel better if you remember that original meeting."

Mia yawned and turned over, pressing her back against Korum's chest and letting him spoon her from behind. He hugged her, pulling her closer. "Go to sleep, my sweet," he murmured in her ear, and Mia drifted off, feeling warm and safe in his embrace.

* * *

"Oh my God, is that it? Is that Krina?" Marisa rose from her seat, pointing at the planet that was growing in size before their eyes. Mia was staring at it too, her heart beating like a drum from anticipation and excitement.

"Yes," Korum confirmed, smiling at them. "That is indeed Krina."

They were all sitting around a floating table, having breakfast. It was their last meal on the ship before their arrival. Connor was unusually quiet again, and Mia could see that her parents were just picking at their food, apparently too nervous to eat normally.

They were sitting in one of the rooms that had a wall facing the outside of the ship—a wall made of the same transparent material as the Krinar houses. Korum had chosen it on purpose, to let them watch as they approached Krina for the first time.

Their ship was moving with incredible speed, and soon the planet was visible in greater detail. "We're coming from the Tinara—the supercontinent—side," Korum explained. "That's why you don't see a lot of water, the way you do on Earth."

And it was true. The sight before them was quite different from NASA images of Earth from space. Mia could see only a thin ring of blue; instead, everything was dominated by a giant brown landmass in the center—the supercontinent. As they got closer, she realized that what she had mistaken for a brown hue was actually a combination of green, red, and yellow colors.

Soon, they entered the atmosphere, and Mia noticed a faint reddish glow around the ship. "That's our force shields protecting us from heat and friction," Korum explained. "We're still moving fast, so if it weren't for our shields, we'd burn to a crisp."

Gradually, the glow faded, and the ship slowed. As they broke through the cloud cover, Mia saw a large forest spread out below them, strikingly colorful... and unusually untouched. Where one might've expected to see cities and skyscrapers, there were only trees and more trees.

"We're going to a special landing area for intergalactic ships," Korum said, apparently anticipating their questions. "It's a good distance from any of our Centers."

"Why aren't we taking a transport pod down, the way we took it to get to the ship?" Mia's dad asked. "Why land this whole ship?"

"Good question, Dan," Korum said. "When we were on Earth, we took the transport pod up because there are no good landing areas for ships like this. That might change in the future, but for now, it's easiest to keep these types of ships in orbit around Earth. Here on Krina, we're equipped for this, so there is no reason for us not to land."

Now Mia could see a large clearing ahead, with some structures that resembled giant mushrooms. It had to be the landing field. Sure enough, their ship headed directly there and a few minutes later, they touched the ground.

They were officially on Krina.

As they exited the ship, Mia felt a blast of heat reminiscent of Florida weather at its hottest. It was also difficult to breathe, and she felt light-headed as she tried to draw in more air. Grabbing Korum's hand, she waited for a wave of dizziness to pass.

"Are you okay?" he asked, wrapping his arm around her back to support her.

"Yes," Mia said. "The air is just thinner here, I think." It was also unusually and pleasantly scented, like blooming flowers and sweet fruits.

"It is thinner," Korum confirmed. "Our atmosphere in general contains a little less oxygen than you're used to, and this particular region happens to be at a higher elevation. You should adjust soon, though, with your nanocytes."

Mia was already starting to feel better, but now she had a new worry. "What about my parents? And Marisa and Connor? How will they adjust?" Her family was just now coming out of the ship, about ten yards behind them.

"Most humans tolerate our atmosphere well, after an initial acclimation period," Korum said. "But don't worry; I know your parents aren't in the best of health, so I made sure our medicine experts were on hand." He pointed toward a small pod that had just landed next to the ship. "They will help your family with any kind of issues."

At that moment, two Krinar women exited the pod. Tall, dark-haired, and graceful, they came up to Korum and smiled. "I'm Rialit, and this is my colleague Mita," said the shorter woman to the right. "Welcome to Krina."

Korum inclined his head. "Thank you, Rialit. And Mita. I would like you to help my human companions. My charl is fine, but her relatives may require your assistance."

"Of course," Rialit said, turning toward Ella and Dan. They and Marisa seemed a little pale, and Connor looked like he was trying to gulp as much air as possible.

The medicine experts hurried over, holding some small devices, and, a minute later, everyone appeared to be back to normal. Korum thanked the two women and they left, their pod taking off a few minutes later.

"Wow," Mia's mom said, staring at the departing aircraft, "I can't believe they run those little things over us, and we can breathe again. What did they do to us?"

"I think they created a small oxygen field around you," Korum said. "This way, you will have a more gradual adjustment. The field will dissipate over the next couple of days, but it'll do it slowly, so your bodies will get used to breathing our air."

"Amazing," Dan said. "Simply amazing."

Mia smiled. "Isn't it, though?"

While they were talking, Korum had started the process of creating a transport pod to take them to their final destination: his house. Mia's sister gasped as the ship began to take shape, and Connor and her parents simply stared in shock. Mia grinned at their reactions; it wasn't that long ago that everything Korum showed her seemed like a miracle. Now she could do a lot of the same things, even if she didn't understand the technology behind it. Then again, most people didn't understand how phones and televisions worked, but they could still use them—just as Mia could use her fabricator.

Once the pod was done, everybody climbed inside and got comfortable on the floating seats. "Love these things," Marisa said, a blissful look on her face as the seat conformed to her shape. Mia guessed that her sister was already starting to feel some pregnancy-related aches and pains, and she determined to talk to the medicine experts about that. Marisa was likely too shy to say anything herself.

As their pod took off, Mia looked down at the transparent floor, her breath catching in her throat at the realization that she was actually here. On Krina.

On the planet that was the origin of all life on Earth.

CHAPTER TWENTY-FIVE

The flight to Korum's house took a mere two minutes, the aircraft flying too fast for Mia to see anything more than a blur of exotic vegetation below. As soon as they landed, she jumped up, eager to see Krina up close.

"Hold on, honey," her dad said, catching her arm as she was about to run out of the ship. "That's an alien planet. You don't know what's out there in the woods."

"He's right, my sweet," Korum said. "I need to show all of you a few things first, to avoid any potential issues. Stick close to me for now, and don't touch anything."

Exiting the pod, he led them toward an ivory-colored structure that was visible through the trees.

As they walked, Mia marveled at the beautiful vegetation that surrounded them. While green colors predominated, there were a lot more red and yellow plants than one would find on Earth. In places she could even see bright purple leaves peeking through the wide rounded stalks of grass-like growth that covered the forest floor. Here and there, flowers of every shade of the rainbow added a festive touch to everything. These flowers seemed to be responsible for the pleasant smell Mia had noticed upon their arrival.

The tree trunks were of varying colors as well. Brown was common, but so was black and white. One tree that Mia particularly liked had white branches and bright red leaves with yellow centers. "That's gorgeous!" she exclaimed, and Korum laughed, shaking his head.

"That particular beauty is poisonous," he said. "Whatever you do, don't let any of the tree sap get on your skin—it acts like acid."

"Really?" Mia stared at her surroundings with newfound caution. Her parents looked frightened, and Connor put a protective arm around Marisa, pulling her closer to him.

"There's no need to be scared," Korum said. "You just need to know that you can't touch the *alfabra* tree. Same thing for that plant over there—" He pointed toward a pretty-looking green bush that was covered with white and pink blooms. "It likes to eat anything that lands on it, and has been known to consume larger animals."

Something flew by Mia's ear and she reflexively swatted at it, gasping when she felt a sudden light pinch. Lowering her hand, she stared at it in disbelief. "Oh my God, Korum, what is that?"

A blue-green creature was sitting in the middle of her palm, its huge eyes almost half the size of its three-inch body. It had only four legs, but there seemed to be hundreds of tiny fingers on each one, all of them digging into Mia's skin. There were also tiny wings that didn't seem big enough to propel it through the air.

"That's a *virta*," Korum said, gently lifting the creature off Mia's palm and throwing it away. "It's harmless—you just shocked it and it grabbed on to you.

They eat some leaves and an occasional *mirat*."

"Mirat?" Connor asked.

"Yes, mirat," Korum said, pointing toward one of the brown tree trunks.

When Mia looked closer, she could see that what she had mistaken for solid wood was actually some type of a jelly-like substance—and that it quivered and moved, expanding and contracting in a creepy way.

"Mirat are similar to your bees, although they don't sting," Korum explained. "They're social insects, and they build these complex structures around trees. Our scientists love studying them. There's a lot of debate as to whether the collective mind of a mirat hive displays signs of higher intelligence. We never bother them, and they generally know to avoid us and our dwellings. If you touch their hive, you'll get dizzy from the fumes they emit, so it's best to stay away from them."

"That's crazy," Marisa said, looking worried. "Is there anything else like that we should know about?" She was holding her stomach in a protective gesture.

"Yes," Korum said. "That, right there—" he pointed at a small red insect-like thing on the floor, "—is also something you have to be careful of. It bites and likes to burrow inside the skin. They're not poisonous or anything, but extracting them is very unpleasant. There are also some large predatory animals, but you're unlikely to encounter them in this vicinity. They're afraid of the Krinar and generally avoid our territories."

Connor was frowning. "Korum, no offense, but that's a lot of shit we need to worry about here. I don't think we realized we'd be living in the middle of an alien jungle."

Korum didn't seem offended in the least. "Our jungle is far less dangerous than your cities, as long as you don't stumble around blindly," he said calmly. "And my house is completely safe and critter-free. In a few days, you'll know exactly what to watch out for, and you'll be able to go outside without me. Until then, I'll accompany you everywhere and you won't run into any problems."

Connor opened his mouth to say something, but Mia's mom interrupted him, exclaiming, "Oh, wow, Korum, is that your house?"

While they were talking, they had reached the ivory-colored, oblong-shaped dwelling. To Mia's eyes, it looked very similar to Korum's house in Lenkarda—a place she now thought of as her home. To the others, though, it had to look strange and foreign.

"Yes," Korum said, smiling at them. "It is indeed."

"You don't have any doors or windows?" her dad asked, examining the structure with visible curiosity.

"No, dad," Mia said. "It has intelligent walls, just like the ship that brought us here. They're probably see-through from the inside. Right, Korum?"

"That's right," her lover confirmed, and Mia grinned, feeling like she would burst from excitement. She was actually on Krina!

Korum did a quick tour of the house, showing her family how to use everything. Mia's parents seemed a bit overwhelmed, so he created a separate 'humanized' suite of rooms for them, just as he had on the ship. Her sister and brother-in-law, however, decided to stay in the main portion of the house, preferring the comfort of K technology to the more familiar human-style furniture.

"I love this thing." Marisa was sprawled out on the intelligent bed in her room, a blissful expression on her face at the massage she was receiving. "I never want to leave it."

"I know, right?" Mia sat down next to her sister. "All their stuff is unbelievably awesome like that. The first time I fell asleep on a bed like this I thought I'd died and gone to Heaven."

"No kidding." Marisa closed her eyes, moaning in pleasure. "So freaking good . . ."

"I'll leave you to it," Mia said, grinning. "Get some rest, okay?"

Marisa didn't reply, and Mia realized that her sister was already drifting off to sleep, her pregnant body requiring more rest than usual.

Connor was taking a shower, and her parents were relaxing too, so Mia went to find Korum. "I'm ready," she told him. "Now is as good a time as any."

He got up from the float in the living room where he had been sitting, his tall, muscular body as graceful as a panther's. "Are you sure?" he asked, and she could see the concern written on his beautiful face.

"Yes," Mia said, lifting her hand to stroke his thick dark hair. "I'm sure."

He caught her hand and brought it to his lips, tenderly kissing each knuckle. "Then let's do it," he said softly. "Let's get your memory and your old self back."

* * *

A slender brown-haired Krinar woman walked around Mia, attaching little white dots to her forehead, temples, and the back of her neck. Mia had fully expected to be knocked out for the reversal of Saret's procedure, but the mind apprentice—Laira—said Mia had to be conscious.

"There you are," Laira said with satisfaction. "All done. Now please have a seat. It can be on Korum's lap if you want." She winked, and Mia laughed, liking this K woman. According to Korum, Laira was young, less than two hundred years of age, and already considered a rising star in the field of mind studies.

Korum smiled and pulled Mia onto his lap. "Sure, I'm happy to hold her."

"I bet you are." Laira grinned. "That's a cute charl you've got there."

"Excuse me," Mia said, putting a possessive arm around Korum's neck. "That's a gorgeous cheren *I've* got."

"True, true," Laira said, laughing. Then her expression turned more serious. "All right, Mia, this is what you can expect now: it will feel like your mind is going blank. Then you'll feel a rush of images and impressions as your memory returns and the procedure is reversed. As the memories come, I want you to focus on them one at a time, so you absorb them slowly. That's why you have to be awake for this, even though I know it's going to be uncomfortable for you."

"Is she going to be in pain?" Korum asked, his arms tightening around Mia.

"No, just discomfort, like I said," Laira replied. "Are you ready, Mia?"

"Yes." Mia braced herself.

"Here we go then."

At first, Mia felt a pleasant lassitude stealing over her and she closed her eyes. Her mind felt like it was drifting, as though she was about to fall asleep. There was a strange sensation of nothingness, of blankness.

Suddenly, it was like a bomb going off in her brain, an explosion of colors, feelings, and shapes, all appearing at once. Mia gasped, her fingers digging into Korum's arm as she tried to cope with the onslaught. It was too much, like a 3D IMAX movie with too many special effects, only streamed directly into her brain.

Somewhere far away, she could hear Korum's voice. It was furious, demanding. "Stop it! Stop it right now! Can't you see she's in pain?"

"She'll get through this . . ." It was Laira's voice, calm and soothing. Mia latched onto it, needing something steady in the maelstrom that was engulfing her mind.

At first it was unbearable, and she screamed silently, too overwhelmed to emit any actual sound. Laira hadn't lied. There was no pain; there was just agony. It felt like Mia's brain was being filled to the brim, her skull stretching and straining to contain it all.

And just when she thought her head would literally explode, the agony started to ease, colors and shapes separating into images, those images and emotions turning into specific events. Memories began to coalesce, taking shape one by one until she could grasp them, integrate them into what she already knew and remembered.

There was the party at the end of March, shortly before she met Korum. Jessie had dragged her to it, and Mia had ended up having a good time after a few drinks. She'd danced with a few guys, even exchanged phone numbers with one of them, but nothing ever came of it. If only she'd known then the strange turn her life would take . . .

The memory of her first meeting with Korum flashed through her mind, and Mia relived the sharp feeling of fear, mixed with the first stirrings of desire. The man who held her so lovingly now had terrified her in the beginning, his arrogance and casual disregard for her wishes leading her to assume the worst about his species.

More memories . . . Her first time in Korum's bed, John explaining to her about charl, the incident at the

club where Korum had nearly killed Peter . . . Korum
holding her while she cried, Mia bringing him to meet her
parents for the first time . . . The good, the bad, the ugly—
she remembered it all, and it was like a void inside her
was disappearing, the before and after colliding, making
her feel whole for the first time since Saret's attack.

Saret! Mia remembered him too. She'd liked him,
regarded him as her boss and mentor. He had been the
one to give her the language implant, to let her intern in
his lab at Korum's request. Mia relived the excitement
she'd felt when Korum had told her of the opportunity,
the thrill of learning what thousands of human scientists
could only dream of.

And then her last memory from before: Saret
cornering her in the lab. Mia remembered her terror, her
shock at learning of his intentions for the human race . . .
Her disgust when he admitted to wanting her, the sick
feeling in her stomach when he told her of his plans for
the Krinar . . . And that awful darkness taking over when
he wiped out a major chunk of her life and altered her
brain.

Now the present and the past were one again. Mia
became aware of Korum stroking her hair, raining gentle
kisses on her face. Still keeping her eyes closed, Mia
relived the more recent events, from her awakening in
Korum's bed to the trip to Krina. She tried to compare
her emotions then to the way she felt now—and to the
way she had always been.

Saret hadn't lied. When Mia had woken up without
her memories, she hadn't been completely herself. She
had indeed been more accepting, more open to new
experiences. She could see that now. However, that had
been a good thing. In his quest to soften Mia toward him,
Saret had inadvertently created the perfect conditions for

her to overcome the pain and confusion from her memory loss. Instead of agonizing, Mia had been acclimating. Instead of worrying, she had been learning.

And instead of fearing Korum again, she had been falling in love with him. Really, truly falling in love with the beautiful, tender Krinar who had greeted her upon awakening. Korum of the recent months wasn't the same person she'd met in the park that day in April; his arrogance had been tempered by caring, his indifference to her wishes turning into a desire to make her happy. He loved her, of that Mia had no doubt now. He loved her with the same intensity, the same desperation as she loved him.

As the present and the past were joined, so too were Mia's feelings and emotions. Everything she had felt before was magnified now, strengthened by the trials and tribulations of the past couple of months.

Opening her eyes, Mia smiled at her K lover.

CHAPTER TWENTY-SIX

Seeing her smile, Korum shuddered with relief. "Mia, my sweet, are you all right?" For the past ten minutes, she had been as stiff as a board, her face pale and even her lips drained of color. She hadn't reacted to anything, as though she'd been in a coma.

"She's fine. Right, Mia?" Laira stepped closer, bending down to peer at Mia's face, and Korum fought the urge to strangle the apprentice. His charl had obviously been in pain, and he knew he would never forgive Laira for that.

"I'm okay now," Mia said softly, as though understanding his feelings. Lifting her hand, she stroked his cheek, the tender gesture cooling some of his anger.

"Do you remember anything?" Laira's voice interrupted them again.

"Yes," Mia said, looking up at her. "I remember everything. Thank you for that."

She remembered. She remembered everything. Korum felt like he could breathe again, the terrible guilt inside him easing for the first time since he'd learned of Saret's betrayal.

"What about the softening procedure?" he asked Laira, his arms unconsciously tightening around the girl on his lap.

"That should be reversed too," Laira said. "Mia, do you feel any different in that regard?"

"I don't know," Mia said, a small frown appearing on her face. "I can see that my reactions were a little off before, when I woke up in Lenkarda, but I don't feel any differently now."

"You don't?" Korum asked, and Mia smiled.

"No," she said, her gaze warm and soft. "I don't."

Another weight lifted off Korum's shoulders, making him feel lighter than air. Up until that moment, he hadn't known how much he'd dreaded the answer to that question. Mia had loved him before her memory loss, he'd known that, but some part of him had still been afraid that her feelings after Saret's procedure hadn't been as real—and that undoing the procedure would destroy whatever love she thought she felt for him.

Mia made a move to get up, and he forced himself to let her go, even though he wanted to keep holding her forever.

Getting up himself, he turned toward Laira and gave her a cool nod of thanks. Although the procedure had worked, Korum still couldn't quite forget the tortured expression on Mia's face during those awful ten minutes. He'd felt helpless, unable to do anything to ease her suffering, and he wouldn't forget that any time soon.

Not the least bit disturbed by his obvious displeasure, Laira grinned at him. "Looks like you got your charl back, all safe and sound."

"Yes," Korum said, putting a supportive arm around

Mia, who still looked too pale. "Looks like it indeed."

Their flight back to Korum's house took about twenty minutes, since Laira's lab was located a few thousand miles from his home region of Rolert. Korum could see that Mia was fascinated by the view outside their transport pod, and he directed the aircraft to fly at a lower altitude and with slower speed, to give her a chance to observe more.

He tried to view Krina as she would be seeing it, and he had to admit that his home planet was beautiful. The giant landmass of Tinara was home to a tremendous variety of flora and fauna, and, from the air, the vegetation looked like a colorful carpet of green, with some red and gold tones mixed in. There were large lakes and rivers, some as blue and clear as the Caribbean, and others a rich blue-green.

The Krinar settlements were sparse, mostly clustered around these bodies of water. There were no cities as such, only Centers that served as focal points of commerce and business. The majority of Krinar lived on the outskirts of these Centers, commuting in for work and other activities.

Korum's own house was next to Banir—a mid-sized Center in the Rolert region, near the middle of the supercontinent and close to the equator. When Korum had brought Mia and her family there earlier in the morning, they'd all commented on how hot the weather was—even hotter than Florida in the summer. The heat didn't bother Korum, but he knew humans were more sensitive to it, so he had made sure to get them inside quickly. This evening, when the temperature cooled, he planned to take them to the nearby lake to swim and look at some of the local wildlife.

"That's Viarad," Korum told Mia as they flew over a particularly large Center. "It's the closest thing we have to a planetary capital. A lot of research and development happens there, and it's also where the Arena fights and other major gatherings take place."

Mia looked up at him, her eyes bright and curious. "Your cities are nothing like our own," she observed. "I don't even see a lot of buildings, much less skyscrapers and the like."

"They are there," Korum assured her. "Not skyscrapers, but there are plenty of large buildings for various commercial purposes. You don't really see them from the air because of all the trees. The forest surrounding Viarad has some of the tallest trees on Krina, with many exceeding a twenty-story building in height."

Her eyes widened. "Twenty stories?"

"At least," Korum said. "Maybe more. Those trees are ancient; some of them have been there for over a hundred million years."

"That's incredible." Her voice was filled with wonder. "Korum, your planet is amazing."

He smiled, enjoying her enthusiasm. "It is, isn't it?"

Even flying at a slower speed, they reached his house just a few minutes later. Korum led Mia inside the house, where her family were relaxing from the journey. "I'll make us dinner," he told her. "You can rest for a bit if you want. You've been through a lot today."

"I'm all right," Mia said, and he could see she wasn't lying. The color in her cheeks was back, and she seemed fully recovered from her earlier ordeal. "I'll go hang out with my parents if you don't mind."

"No, of course not, go ahead," Korum said. "I'll see you soon."

* * *

The dinner Korum prepared was as unusual as it was delicious, consisting of a bunch of local seeds, fruits, and vegetables prepared in creative ways. Mia and each member of her family discovered something new that they greatly enjoyed.

One of the dishes consisted of a teardrop-shaped vegetable with purple skin that tasted like a cross between tomato and zucchini. It was stuffed with nutty-flavored grain that had a bubble-like texture. Mia's dad loved that dish, going back for seconds and thirds as soon as he finished. In the meanwhile, Mia and Marisa were both crazy about the kalfani stew, with its rich, hearty flavor, while her mom and Connor kept eating the exotic fruit that was their dessert. "All of this food is safe for human consumption," Korum told them. "Not everything on Krina is, but I made sure these specific foods would be fine for your digestive system."

After dinner, Korum took them to the lake that was near his house. The sun was setting, and Mia could see the three moons starting to appear in the sky, despite the fact that there was still plenty of light.

As they walked, he showed them various plants and insects, explaining a little bit about them. "That's a *nooki*," he said, pointing at a large yellow spider-like thing with what looked like hundreds of legs. "They extract nutrients from the soil, almost like plants do. Our children like to play with them because they do some funny stuff when you startle them." He clapped his hands next to the creature, and it puffed up, each of its legs nearly tripling in thickness and its torso turning bright red. "It's completely harmless, so you don't need to be afraid of it."

Mia smiled and reached for the creature, curious if it would let her touch it. It scurried away, looking like a clumsy bright-colored ball.

Korum grinned at her, and Mia laughed, feeling incredibly happy. Standing up on tiptoes, she placed her hands on his cheeks and brought his face toward her, giving him a quick kiss on the lips. "I love you," she said, holding his gaze, and her heart squeezed at the naked look of love she saw there.

"Hey, lovebirds, take a look at this!" Connor yelled, and Mia wanted to punch him for interrupting the moment.

Korum gave her a rueful smile, and walked over to see what Connor was talking about. Mia followed, still unhappy with her brother-in-law. As soon as she got there, however, all her displeasure was forgotten. "Oh, wow," she breathed, "what is that?"

On a tree branch just a few feet off the forest floor, partially hidden by leaves, was a tiny furry creature that looked like a cross between a lemur and a kitten. Brown-colored, it had huge blue eyes and a short fluffy tail.

"That's a baby *fregu*," Korum said softly. "They're very cute, but they bite sometimes, so don't try to pet it."

"Fregu?" The word sounded familiar for some reason. Then Mia remembered. "Hey, you said I reminded you of one of these!" she told Korum accusingly, then burst out laughing because she herself could see the resemblance.

The fregu was only the first of their encounters with Krinar wildlife. There were birds with four wings, insects that were the size of a small bird, and plants that acted more like animals. One time, Connor almost stepped on a snake-like creature that screamed at him and rolled away, its long thin body moving like a rolling pin.

Finally, they reached the lake. It was a sizable body of water, probably a couple of miles wide and several miles long. The shore of the lake was covered with fine grey sand and small black rocks. It made the water itself look dark and mysterious.

"Is it safe to swim?" Marisa asked, kicking off her sandal and dipping a toe in to test the temperature.

"Yes," Korum told her. "There are some dangerous predators in there, but nothing that comes this close to the shore. This lake is very deep, and there are all kinds of things living there, but they generally don't go into shallow waters. Just in case, though, wear this." He handed her a thin clear bracelet that he made just a second ago. "It repels aquatic animals by emitting a sound they find very unpleasant."

Mia and the others received the same kind of bracelet, and then they all went for a swim, enjoying the refreshing escape from the heat outside.

CHAPTER TWENTY-SEVEN

Mia woke up the next morning with a nagging feeling of unease in her chest. For some reason, she kept dreaming about Saret and that day in the lab. In her dream, Saret was touching her, making her skin crawl with disgust, and there was nothing Mia could do about it other than scream silently in her head because she was paralyzed and unable to move.

Too wired to sleep more, Mia got up and went to take a shower. Korum was away somewhere, and Mia didn't know if her family was still sleeping or not. From the sun's position outside, it had to be very early in the morning.

Standing under the water spray, she yawned, feeling unusually tired. Maybe she shouldn't have gotten up yet. The stupid dream was still on her mind, and she scrubbed her skin thoroughly, trying to wash it away. In reality, Saret had barely touched her, so she didn't know why her subconscious even went there this night.

To dispel any lingering impressions from the dream,

she mentally went over the actual events of that day, starting from when she ran into Saret on her way out. He had been so happy to talk to her about his plans, to tell her everything he intended to do to humans and his fellow Krinar. Mia guessed it hadn't been easy for him, never confiding in anyone else, always trying to play a role, to hide his true nature. With her, since he thought she would never remember their conversation, he had felt safe dropping the mask he normally wore.

In hindsight, it was almost funny, all of his crazy ramblings about bringing peace to Earth and acting as a savior to her people. He had even tried to convince her that Korum had some evil plans of taking over her planet. It was so ridiculous that Mia chuckled to herself. Had he really thought that she would be sympathetic to his cause? That because she had been willing to believe the worst of Korum once she would make that same mistake again?

Stepping out of the shower, Mia let the drying technology do its work. Then, feeling marginally better, she went back into the bedroom to find her fabricator and get dressed.

To her surprise, Korum was there, sitting on the bed. He was dressed in a typical Krinar outfit of light-colored shorts and a sleeveless shirt. For some reason, his hair was wet.

"You're awake," he said, looking at her naked body with a familiar sensual gleam in his eyes. "I went swimming in the lake because I figured you'd be asleep for quite some time. Why are you up so early?"

"Bad dream." Mia sat down next to him. His hands immediately went to her breasts and squeezed them lightly, as though he couldn't resist touching her.

"Why, my sweet? What dream?" There was a concerned look on his beautiful face, even as his hands continued playing with her breasts, his thumbs brushing against her nipples in a way that sent a spear of heat right down to her core.

Mia could hardly think with him doing this to her. "Um . . . just that thing with Saret . . ." Her head fell back, her neck arching as he bent down to nibble on the sensitive spot near her collarbone.

"What thing?" he murmured, one of his hands now slipping between her thighs, stroking her aching sex.

"Just that . . . conversation . . ." Mia gasped as his finger slid inside her, one thumb pressing on her clit while his other hand continued playing with her nipple.

"What about it?" he whispered, his hot breath washing over her neck, giving her goosebumps all over.

"I don't . . . I don't know," Mia managed to say, her inner muscles clenching around his finger as a wave of heat went through her body. She was so close . . . so close . . .

Korum withdrew his finger and pushed her down, so that she was lying flat on her back with her legs hanging off the side of the bed. Kneeling on the floor, he pulled her legs over his shoulders and brought her sex toward his mouth.

At the first touch of his warm, wet tongue on her clit, Mia shattered into a million pieces. The release was so powerful that she arched off the bed, her eyes squeezing shut as waves of pleasure radiated through every part of her body.

Before the waves had a chance to fade, he was already inside her, his shorts ripped open at the crotch area and his thick length buried deep within her small channel. Gasping at his abrupt entry, Mia grabbed his shoulders, holding on tightly as he began to stroke in and out, stimulating the nerve endings that were still sensitive from her orgasm. Panting, she opened her eyes and met his golden gaze.

He was staring at her with an intense look of hunger on his face. Bending his head, he took her mouth in a savage kiss, ravaging her with his tongue even as his cock continued to plunge into her from below. One of his hands held her hair, keeping her head immobile, while his other hand slid down her side and underneath her hips, touching her folds where they were joined. His finger rubbed around her entrance, gathering the moisture there, and then that same finger burrowed between her cheeks and pushed into her other opening.

Overwhelmed by the sensations, Mia moaned helplessly. With the way he was holding her, she couldn't do anything but feel. He was on top of her, inside her, all over her, and she couldn't catch her breath, her heartbeat skyrocketing as the tension within her spiraled higher and higher. His finger in her ass seemed impossibly large, invasive, yet there was a dark pleasure there too, an unusual feeling of fullness that added to the sensuality of the moment.

Without any warning, everything inside her tightened and convulsed, and Mia came, her body twisting and shuddering in his arms. He groaned, grinding against her, trying to get even deeper, and she could feel his cock pulsing within her as he found his own release.

After a couple of minutes, he slowly withdrew from her. "All right?" he asked softly, and Mia nodded, too limp and relaxed to move.

He smiled and picked her up, carrying her to the shower for another quick rinse, and then they got dressed and ready for breakfast with her family.

At breakfast, Mia found her attention wandering, her mind again turning to her dream and that conversation with Saret. After a few minutes of dwelling on it, she realized what was bothering her.

Why did Saret try to claim that Korum was the villain? Was he delusional, or did he think Mia would be so gullible as to believe his lies? And why bother lying to her at all, if he was planning to erase her memory shortly afterwards? She tried to think of his exact words, something about Korum wanting to take her planet. What the hell did that even mean? The Krinar were already there, on Earth, sharing it alongside humans—which is what Korum had said was their intention.

Still, Mia couldn't quite shake an uneasy feeling. She knew her lover had a ruthless streak—and she knew he was loyal to his people. Could that loyalty extend as far as wanting to get rid of an entire rival species to gain a precious resource? Korum had told her himself that Earth was unique, that out of all the planets out there, it came closest to mimicking Krina. And now that Mia was here, she could see that it was indeed the case; if anything ever happened to Earth, humans would be more than happy to live on Krina—and likely vice versa with the Krinar.

Putting down her tong-like utensil, Mia studied her lover as he conversed and joked with her family. It seemed impossible that there could be something sinister hidden beneath his beautiful exterior and warm smile. Could he love her and simultaneously want to destroy her people? Just how far did his ambition extend?

Taking a bite of her food, Mia tried to think about it rationally. Surely she would've known if she had fallen for a monster. Nobody could hide such darkness for so long. Korum was no angel—and he didn't necessarily hold her kind in the highest regard—but he would never go so far as to take their planet away.

Or would he?

The food she just swallowed sat heavily in Mia's stomach. Excusing herself, she got up and went to the restroom to freshen up. Splashing some water on her face, she stared in the mirror, seeing the poorly concealed look of panic in her eyes.

She needed to talk to Korum and she needed to do it now, before the old doubts and suspicions got a chance to poison their relationship again. If there was anything Mia had learned from the Resistance fiasco, it was the folly of jumping to conclusions and assuming the worst. She was no longer the girl who was too scared to talk to her K lover for fear of betraying her people. Korum now belonged to her as much as she belonged to him—and one way or another, she would know the truth.

Breakfast seemed to last forever. Mia smiled and chatted with her family, all the while squirming with impatience inside. She could see Korum giving her occasional questioning glances, and she knew he could tell that something was wrong, that her smiles had a brittle edge to them.

Finally, it was over. Marisa returned to her room to take a post-meal nap—something she'd started doing recently to combat pregnancy-related tiredness—and Connor joined her, not wanting to be separated from his wife. Mia's parents retired to their room as well, to read and watch some shows about Krina that Korum had set up for them.

"Do you want to go for a walk?" Mia asked Korum as soon as her parents were out of the earshot.

His eyebrows rose. "It's not too hot for you right

now?"

"It should be fine." Mia had no idea if it would be fine or not, but she wanted to get out of the house—and out of her family's earshot.

"Okay, sure." Korum got to his feet as smoothly as only a Krinar could. "Let's go."

The blast of heat hit Mia as soon as they exited the house. It was around eleven in the morning, and the sun was incredibly bright in the cloudless sky. All around them, Mia could hear the chirping and singing of insects, birds, and other creatures—some seemingly familiar, others strange and exotic.

They walked for a few minutes toward the lake, following the same path they took yesterday. In the light of day, their surroundings were even more beautiful and striking than they had been at twilight, but Mia couldn't focus on that now. Her stomach was twisted into knots, and she felt nauseated, as though she'd eaten something that didn't agree with her.

"All right, Mia." Korum stopped in a shaded area when they reached the lake and pulled her down to sit beside him on a thick patch of grass-like plants. "What's wrong, my sweet? What's going on with you this morning?"

Mia looked at the man she loved more than life itself. "I want to know if there's any truth to what Saret said."

His gaze was steady and unblinking. "Which part?"

"The part—" Her voice broke mid-sentence. "The part about you wanting to take Earth from us."

For a moment, there was only silence, during which they stared at each other. Then he said softly, "We want to share your planet with you. I told you that."

"Then why did Saret say you want to take it from us?" Something didn't ring true. "Is he completely deluded, or is there something I should know? What are your real intentions, Korum? How exactly are you going to share our planet when your sun finally dies?"

He was again silent for a few seconds, his face hard and unreadable. "You still don't trust me, do you?" he finally said. "After everything, you still think I'm the bad guy."

Mia drew in a shaky breath, the unpleasant feeling in her stomach getting worse. "No, Korum. I don't think that. I don't want to think that. I just want to know the truth. All of it." He still looked implacable, so she added, "Please, Korum . . . If you truly care for me, please tell me everything."

CHAPTER TWENTY-EIGHT

"All right." His voice was colder than anything she'd heard from him in a long time. "Keep in mind, though, my sweet, no one outside of the Council and the Elders knows what I am about to tell you. You can't share this with anyone else, do you understand me?"

Mia nodded, holding her breath.

"We're not going to take Earth from you," he said. "We'll take Mars. And then we'll give humans the option of relocating there, once we have created the proper conditions for life."

Mia stared at him in shock. "What? Mars? But . . . but that's uninhabitable."

"It is uninhabitable now," Korum said. "Once we're done with it, it's going to be like paradise. The planet already has water in the form of ice. We'll warm it up, create an atmosphere, and give Mars a magnetic field to mitigate solar radiation and keep the atmosphere from escaping into space. Even the gravity differential can be fixed; our scientists have recently come up with a way to enhance surface gravity and make it similar to that of Earth and Krina."

"But—" Mia found herself at a loss for words. "Wait, so you want Mars, not Earth?"

Korum sighed. "No, Mia. We want a place for our species to continue flourishing once our sun begins to dim. It's unfortunate, but we can't keep our star from dying. Maybe one day we'll discover a way to fix that too, but for now, we have to plan for the worst. Earth would be our second choice, after Krina, and Mars would be our third."

"So you do want Earth?" Mia felt like she wasn't getting something.

"Yes." His amber gaze was cool and even. "Of course we do. At least the warmer parts of it. But we're not going to kill humans for it, or whatever it is Saret implied. We'll give your people the option of remaining on Earth or relocating to the newly transformed Mars in exchange for significant wealth and other perks."

"You'll bribe humans to leave Earth?" Mia stared at him in disbelief.

"Yes." A small smile appeared on his lips. "You could call it that. There are plenty of regions on Earth that are poor, where daily existence is a struggle. We'll offer those people the option of moving to a place that's very much like paradise, where all their basic needs would be met and they would live like kings. Don't you think that would be appealing to someone in rural India or Zimbabwe?"

Mia blinked. She could see his logic—but she could also see a big problem with what he was saying. "If Mars is going to be so great," she said slowly, "why wouldn't the Krinar want to live there themselves and leave our planet alone?"

"Some of us will probably want to live on Mars," Korum said. "It's not out of the question that you and I might move there at some point. But there will always be those who are uncomfortable with what they view as artificial nature, those who would much rather live on a planet that's gone through billions of years of natural evolution—even if that planet has been somewhat polluted and damaged by humans."

"So they will come live with us—with humans, I mean—on Earth?"

"Yes," Korum said, "exactly. We'll build more Centers on Earth, so that some Krinar can live there. And in exchange for humans ceding us that space, we'll give them a much more luxurious environment on Mars. It'll be a win-win for both species."

"And if humans would not want to cede that space?"

His eyes narrowed. "Why wouldn't they? Do you really think a subsistence farmer in Rwanda would object to never having to do back-breaking work again? To being able to feed his family every day with tasty, nutritious food? Whoever comes to Mars will have access to free healthcare, education, housing . . . whatever they need. We're not going to do to your people what Europeans did to Native Americans. That's not our way."

"You didn't really answer my question," Mia said slowly. "If people don't want to go, are they going to be forcibly transported to Mars? Are you going to take their land from them no matter what?"

"We're going to do whatever is necessary to ensure the survival—and continued prosperity—of our species, Mia," he said, his eyes cold and bright under the dark slashes of his eyebrows. "Just like your kind would."

A chill ran down Mia's spine. "I see."

"What did you expect to hear, my sweet?" His tone was softly mocking. "Did you want me to lie to you, to tell you that we would never take what we need if we couldn't get it some other way?"

"No," Mia said. "I didn't want you to lie to me. I never wanted you to lie to me." Getting to her feet, she went to stand by the water, staring at the dark blue surface with unseeing gaze. She didn't know what to think, how to even begin to approach this situation.

What Korum had just described sounded relatively harmless, even generous compared to what human conquerors had done throughout history. Yet Mia knew it wouldn't be so simple. The Krinar arrival several years ago caused a major panic that spawned the Resistance movement and resulted in thousands of deaths. It was folly to think that the same thing wouldn't happen when people learned about the Ks' intentions for Mars. Even if the Krinar relocated only those who went willingly, the general population would be deeply suspicious—and likely with good reason. Once the Krinar had a place where they could move humans with a clear conscience, what would prevent them from doing so?

Korum came up behind her and wrapped his arms around her chest, pulling her up against him so that the top of her head was nestled under his chin. "I'm sorry, Mia," he said quietly. "I didn't mean to be harsh with you. Of course you have a right to know—and I shouldn't blame you for not trusting me after the way we first met. I don't want to harm your kind. I truly don't—especially now that I've fallen for you and met your family. We'll do our best to ensure that everything goes smoothly, that all your governments are fully on board and informed about what's going on. Nobody has to get hurt. We'll make sure everybody comes out ahead in this."

Mia wanted to melt into his embrace, to let him reassure her that everything would be all right, but she couldn't be an ostrich hiding her head in the sand. "When are you going to do this?" Her voice sounded dull, empty. "When are you going to transform Mars?"

"Soon," Korum said, his arms tightening around her. "I have just received the final go-ahead from the Elders to proceed."

"But why Mars?" Mia couldn't understand that part. "Why don't the Krinar just take some planet in another solar system? If you can do this, this kind of thing—"

"Terraforming," Korum said. "It's called terraforming."

"Right," Mia said. "If you can terraform Mars, why not just do it to a planet elsewhere? Why does it have to be in such close proximity to Earth?"

"Because the proximity to Earth will make the project easier," he explained quietly. "We've never done something of this magnitude before, and we'll need a base from which our scientists and other experts can operate. Earth can serve as that base for now. This won't be an easy task. It will take years—possibly decades—to make Mars habitable, and it will be nice to have our Centers on Earth close by in case of any emergencies. Once we've worked out all the kinks in the process, then we can terraform other planets located in habitable zones throughout the different galaxies."

"Other planets besides Earth and Mars?" Mia turned in his arms, meeting his gaze. For the first time, she realized the full depth of his ambition—and it shook her to the core. "You're building an empire, aren't you?" she breathed. "A real-life intergalactic empire . . . Earth, Mars, these other planets in the future—the Krinar will rule them all, won't they?"

"Yes." His eyes gleamed brightly. "We will."

* * *

Korum could see the shock on her face, and he softened his tone. "Would that be such a bad thing, my sweet? Your people will benefit from this as well. If anything were to happen to Earth, humans would survive and prosper at our side."

He could feel the tension in her delicate frame, and he cursed Saret for planting doubts in her mind that day. Korum had planned to tell everything to Mia in due time, to explain his intentions in the most reassuring way possible. He'd known there was a possibility she would question him after she regained her memory, but he hadn't anticipated his own reaction to her questions. Her distrust, her propensity to think the worst about him—it was all too reminiscent of the beginning, when she had spied on him and betrayed him to the Resistance. The wounds from that time were still too fresh for him to be able to remain as calm and soothing as he'd hoped to be.

"At your side—and under your control, right?" She made a move to free herself, and Korum let his arms drop, taking a step back to give her some space. He didn't bother responding to her question; the answer to that was obvious.

An intergalactic empire... He didn't usually think about it in such terms, but it was not a bad description for what he hoped to accomplish in his lifetime. Ever since he could remember—ever since he had been a small child— Korum had dreamed of exploring and settling other planets. He saw it as their destiny. As beautiful as Krina was, it was also just one tiny planet among trillions—a piece of rock dependent on its star and vulnerable to various cosmic disasters.

Earth had always fascinated him, with its Krina-like characteristics and a species that was strikingly similar to the Krinar themselves. In his youth, Korum, like many others, had regarded humans as inferior, with their weak, fragile bodies and primitive way of living. It wasn't until the recent centuries that he'd begun to understand that these beings were as intelligent and resourceful as the Krinar themselves. In the past, what Mia feared would have been a legitimate concern: Korum of a thousand years ago wouldn't have hesitated to simply take Earth away from her people. Now, however, he didn't want to deprive humans of their planet; he just wanted to ensure that the Krinar had a place on it too.

He had never thought his ambition was particularly outrageous. He knew that other people did, however. Even his own father seemed intimidated by Korum's drive at times, not understanding that his son merely wanted what was best for their species. A group of planets populated and controlled by the Krinar was a logical next step in their evolution, and Korum saw nothing wrong with working toward that goal.

Now he just had to make his charl see things from his perspective. "Mia, listen to me," Korum said, watching her intently. "I know you're afraid, but I'm not lying to you. I didn't tell you any of this before because it's the equivalent of classified information—not because I was trying to conceal something evil. I just received final clearance from the Elders for Mars, and we'll reach out to your governments next, to inform them about our intentions. That way, they can adequately prepare the population and nip any potentially dangerous rumors in the bud. Nobody has to get hurt in this—and we'll do our best to ensure that it doesn't happen."

Her sexy little tongue came out to lick her lips, and he found his eyes glued to her mouth, picturing that tongue licking something else entirely. *Damn it, focus.* With effort, Korum lifted his gaze to meet hers, ignoring the stirring in his cock. Now was not the time to think about sex; he had to convince her he wasn't about to exterminate her kind or steal their planet.

"Do you swear?" Her voice was soft, tremulous, and he could see hope warring with doubt on her face. She wanted to trust him, but she needed more reassurance. "Do you swear that you don't intend my people any harm? That when you build your empire, it won't be at the cost of my species' well-being?"

"Yes, my darling," Korum said. "I swear it. Unless humans strike at us, we won't do anything to harm them. Those who wish to leave Earth will be well compensated for their choice, and we'll live alongside your people on Earth, Mars, and whatever other planets we find. It won't be so bad, my sweet. I promise you that."

And stepping toward her, he drew her into his embrace again, exhaling in relief when he felt her arms sliding around his waist as well.

CHAPTER TWENTY-NINE

Mia put on the shimmerstone necklace Korum had given her and surveyed herself critically in the three-dimensional mirror located in the bedroom. She was dressed in formal Krinar clothing, a gleaming white dress similar to the one she'd worn to the fight. Her hair was pinned up and covered with a silvery net that matched the sandals on her feet. She looked festive—and ready to face the Elders.

By all rights, she should be nervous. After all, she was about to meet the oldest Krinar in existence, whose names were legend among Ks and whose mandates determined the fate of humanity. The Krinar who were about to decide her family's lifespan. Yet she felt strangely calm, as if nothing could touch her right now.

Her mind kept dwelling on this morning's conversation with Korum, going through it over and over again. Mars, Earth, an entire intergalactic empire... There was really no end to her lover's ambition. Mia had no doubt that Korum would ultimately achieve his goal—

and that he would be at the helm of this empire he was about to build.

And she would be at his side. Her head spun at the thought. She, who had never wanted anything more than a quiet, ordinary life, would be there to watch the Krinar empire taking shape, at the side—and in bed—of the man who was going to make it happen.

Did that make her a traitor to her people? Or was it like Delia said, that by Korum falling in love with her, she had already done more to help humanity than any efforts by the Resistance?

She believed him when he promised the Krinar wouldn't harm humans on purpose. He had always kept his promises to her. She just wasn't sure how everything would unfold when people learned of the Ks' intentions for Mars. Would there be renewed anti-K movements? Would the human population panic and try to strike at the invaders, leading to the Krinar retaliating against them? Mia would be devastated if that happened.

But the thought of leaving Korum was unbearable. She couldn't live without him; it was as simple as that. She loved him with every fiber of her being, and she knew he loved her just as fiercely. Maybe that made her a traitor . . . or maybe it made her the luckiest woman alive. Only time would tell.

For now, there were Elders to meet.

"It's best if I do most of the talking," Korum said as they approached a clearing in the middle of the forest. "They don't like unnecessary conversation."

"Of course," Mia said. "We won't say a word."

"No, you might have to," he told her. "They'll probably want to talk to you and your family directly—in which case, I strongly suggest you respond to their questions as honestly and concisely as you can."

Mia nodded in agreement. Out of the corner of her eye, she could see her parents holding hands as they walked. Her mom was pale, and her dad looked grim, like he was going to an execution. Marisa and Connor trailed behind them, looking nervous and excited at the same time.

Unlike Mia, the others were dressed in human attire. It was their choice. "What, am I going to squeeze into something like that at my age?" her mom had said, indicating Mia's form-fitting, open-backed dress. Korum hadn't objected; since none of them were charl, they weren't considered a part of Krinar society and could thus wear whatever they wanted. Her dad had put on a suit and tie, and so did Marisa's husband. Her mom and Marisa wore semi-formal dresses and high heels. Mia hoped they weren't too uncomfortable, traipsing through the forest like that in the heat.

The fact that the Elders wanted to see them out in the open—as opposed to in some building—didn't surprise Mia in the least. The Ks were remarkably attuned to nature, and Korum had told her that some of the Elders shunned artificial dwellings altogether, choosing to live as their primitive ancestors once did: in the hollow trunks of giant trees or in cave-like rock formations in the mountains. They also jealously guarded their territory, not allowing anyone to come within a dozen miles of their chosen areas. This spot in the woods was considered neutral ground, a place where the Elders would often meet to discuss various matters and socialize with each other.

"Very few Krinar have ever had the privilege of seeing the Elders in person, as you're about to do," Korum said as they paused in front of the clearing. "It's about the greatest honor there is."

Mia took a deep breath, trying to still the fine trembling in her fingers. Now that they were actually here, her previous calmness had deserted her, and her heart was beating frantically in her chest. What if she accidentally did or said something that angered the Elders? In that case, they might deny Korum's petition or worse. She had no idea what these ancient Krinar were capable of.

"Ready, my sweet?" Korum asked, and she nodded, putting her hand in his. Then they walked together into the clearing, Mia's family following in their wake.

There were nine Ks standing there, three women and six men. They were all looking at Mia and her family, their faces utterly expressionless. Physically, they seemed to be in their prime, no older than Korum or any other Krinar Mia had met. All the males were tall and powerfully built, and even the females seemed sturdier than usual. The shortest of the Elder women was probably just over six feet in height, with lean, well-defined muscles covering her frame. To Mia's surprise, they were all dressed in modern Krinar clothing, their light-colored outfits contrasting with the bronzed hue of their skin.

While the women were beautiful in a warrior-princess kind of way, the men were more mixed in appearance. One male K in particular resembled the recording of the ancients far more than he did the other Krinar. Although his harsh, craggy features held a certain attraction, he looked too rough to be considered handsome. Mia wondered if any of the Elders had a mate, or if they had survived for millions of years without forming any deep attachments.

Korum let go of Mia's hand and inclined his head respectfully, saying nothing. Mia followed his example, keeping her gaze trained on the Elders the entire time. In Krinar culture, it was considered rude to look down or away when meeting with a figure of authority; open staring was the way to go.

One of the women stepped forward, her movements smooth and flowing. Coming up to Mia, she brushed her knuckles against her cheek in the traditional greeting between females. Mia smiled and reciprocated, hoping she wasn't doing something wrong. Judging by the approving gleam in Korum's eyes, she had done exactly the right thing.

After greeting Mia, the woman circled around the other humans, studying them with visible curiosity. She didn't say a word or make any gestures toward them, but Mia could see the sweat droplets on her dad's forehead. He had to be very anxious, because he didn't normally perspire that much from the heat.

Still silent, the woman went back toward the Elders and resumed her original position near the two other females. Then nine pairs of dark eyes simply looked at them, watching them with a cool, deep intelligence that seemed distinctly inhuman.

Mia looked back at them, trying to figure out which two were involved in guiding human evolution. In a way, she was meeting real-life gods, the creators of the human race. The idea was so mind-boggling that she didn't dwell on it too much. She was less likely to collapse in a trembling heap if she thought of these Elders as nothing more than somewhat older versions of Korum. And truthfully, to a twenty-one-year-old, there wasn't a tremendous difference between someone who was two thousand years of age and someone who was two million. Both were incredibly old—or so she kept telling herself.

Finally, after what seemed like an hour, the rough-featured male stepped forward, approaching Mia and Korum. "So this is your charl," he said, his voice low and exceptionally deep. Mia thought his walk resembled that of a lion, all lean muscle and predatory intensity.

Korum inclined his head. "Yes."

"Unusual," the Elder said, cocking his head to the side as he studied Mia. "Very unusual."

Mia fought the urge to quail under that penetrating gaze. She felt like the ancient K was stripping her bare, seeing her every fear and vulnerability.

"Why do you think we should make an exception for your family, Mia?" the Elder said suddenly, addressing her directly.

Mia swallowed to get rid of the knot in her throat. She had been mentally preparing for some type of interview, but she still felt caught off-guard. Nevertheless, when she spoke, her voice was surprisingly even, betraying nothing of her inner turmoil. Adrenaline was surging through her veins, sharpening her focus, and the words that came out of her mouth were unusually crisp and clear.

"I don't think you should make an exception for my family," she said, looking up at the Elder. "I think you should share your technology with the entire human race. If you won't do that, for whatever reason, then think about this: by being with Korum, I now share his lifespan. Since that's something that you and your colleagues allowed, you must see the logic in that. Without the nanocytes in my body, I would age and pass away in a few decades, while Korum would remain the same—and that would be unbearable for both of us because we love each other." She paused, taking a deep breath. "And it would be equally unbearable for me to watch those I love—" she gestured toward her family, "—get sick and die."

The ancient K was still looking at her, and she could see a glimmer of amusement on his face. It softened his features slightly, making him appear just a tiny bit less intimidating. Mia wanted to say more, but she remembered Korum's admonition about being concise when answering questions and decided to shut up instead. She had said everything there was to say; short of repeating her points and appealing to their sense of ethics and morality, there was nothing else to add.

The Elder stared at her for a few more seconds and then turned away. Mia could sense some sort of wordless communication going on between him and the others, and then he turned back toward Mia and Korum.

"We'll make our decision soon," he said, addressing Korum this time.

Then he went back toward the rest of the Elders, and they all melted away into the forest, leaving Mia, Korum, and her family alone in the clearing.

* * *

"That was Lahur," Korum told his charl during their trip back to the house. "He's the one I told you about—the oldest Krinar alive. The woman who came up to you and your parents is Sheura; she's an evolutionary biologist, and she was involved in the human project from the very beginning."

"Oh, no wonder she seemed so curious about us! Do you think they'll do it? Do you think they'll agree to it?" Mia was perched on a float next to him, her eyes bright with excitement. Korum knew she was likely still feeling the rush from the meeting, and he smiled at her, proud of the way she had conducted herself with the Elders. He'd known she was nervous, of course, but she'd maintained her composure throughout—better than many Krinar would have in her place.

"I don't know, my sweet," he said honestly. "Nobody can predict what the Elders are going to do. I hope they saw whatever it was they wanted to see today. All we can do now is wait."

"Do we have to remain on Krina while they decide?" Mia's mother asked, and Korum could see that she looked much more calm now, relieved to have the ordeal over with.

"Yes," Korum told her, "that would probably be best. They said soon, so it shouldn't be too long. Besides, you haven't even met my parents yet. I know they are anxious to see everyone." Korum also had another reason for wanting Mia's family on Krina, but now was not the right time to discuss it.

"Oh, we'd love to meet them too!" Ella exclaimed. "Wouldn't that be great, Dan?"

"Sure," Mia's father said. "We would absolutely enjoy meeting them."

"Good," Korum said. "Then I will make the arrangements."

CHAPTER THIRTY

Humming to herself, Mia got dressed and ready to go to Korum's parents' house. She remembered liking Riani and Chiaren during their virtual meeting, and she was looking forward to seeing them again. She had a suspicion her parents would like them too, though they would likely be awestruck by their youth and beauty.

If the Elders gave their permission, Mia's parents would also regain their youth. She wanted it so badly she could taste it. She had seen pictures of her mom and dad when they were Mia's age, and they had been a cute couple, her dad tall and handsome and her mom pretty and carefree. She wanted to see them like that in real life, healthy and vigorous, without the various aches and pains that came with middle age.

Just as she was putting on her dress, Korum walked into the bedroom. He appeared even more gorgeous than usual, his face glowing with some unknown emotion. Coming up to Mia, he bent his head to brush a kiss against her lips. "You look beautiful, my sweet," he said softly, tucking one of her curls behind her ear.

"Thank you." Mia beamed at him. "So do you."

"I have a little something I'd like you to wear," he said, looking at her with a mysterious smile. "Another piece of jewelry."

"Oh sure." Mia had already put on the shimmerstone necklace for the meeting with his parents, but she didn't mind wearing something else instead—or in addition to. Accessorizing had never been her strong suit, although she had every intention of learning how to do it. She had already gotten better at dressing fashionably; jewelry was the next step.

To her complete and utter shock, Korum took a step back and lowered himself to one knee. In his hand was a small black box. As she stared at it, the box opened, revealing the most beautiful ring she had ever seen in her life. Small and delicate, it appeared to be made of the same iridescent material as her necklace, with a larger round shimmerstone set in the middle.

"Mia," Korum said quietly, looking up at her with those incredible amber-colored eyes, "I know things between us haven't always been easy, and I can't promise you there won't be difficulties ahead. But I do know one thing. I want you, now and always, more than I've ever wanted anyone in all my years of existence. I want you in my life, in my bed, and by my side for as long as we are both alive. I want to cherish you and protect you; I want to lay the world at your feet. I want your face to be the first one I see when I wake up and the last before I go to sleep. I want to make you as happy as you make me. Mia, my sweet, I am hopelessly in love with you. Will you do me the honor of becoming my wife?"

Mia opened her mouth but no words came out. Instead, she could feel a strange burning sensation in her eyes. "You . . . you want me to marry you?" she finally managed to whisper, afraid she somehow misheard him. "But—" she swallowed, "—you're Krinar! You can't marry a human!" Her voice rose incredulously at the end.

"I can do whatever I want," Korum said, and she couldn't help smiling inside at the arrogant note in his voice. Even on his knees, he sounded like king of the world. "Just because no one else has done it doesn't mean I can't. I want you to be mine in every sense of the word—by Krinar *and* by human law. Mia, darling, will you marry me?"

The burning in her eyes increased, and a tear escaped and rolled down her face. "Yes," she said almost inaudibly, her vision blurring with moisture. Her chest felt tight, and she couldn't seem to catch her breath. "Yes, my love, I will marry you."

His answering smile was as blinding as the Krinar sun. Rising to his feet, he reached for her left hand and slid the ring onto her ring finger. It fit perfectly, shimmering with every color in the visible spectrum.

"Oh, Korum . . . It's—" Mia was openly crying now, tears of happiness running down her cheeks. "It's beautiful . . ."

"Not as beautiful as you," he said softly, drawing her into his embrace. "Nothing could ever be as beautiful as you." And cupping her face in his large hands, he kissed the tears off her cheeks, his lips tender and reverent on her skin.

* * *

They agreed to share the news with Mia's parents when both families would be gathered together, and Korum now watched with amusement as Mia did her best to hide her left hand in the folds of her dress during the trip to his parents' house. He'd told her she could take the ring off for now, but she had vehemently refused. "What if I lose it?" she said in a horrified tone, and Korum didn't argue. He liked seeing the piece of jewelry on her finger, liked knowing that there was a visible symbol of their commitment to each other.

He wasn't sure when he had become so enamored with the idea of marrying her in the human way. During that visit to her parents' house, the thought had been planted in his mind, and it had been brewing there for the past month. He'd known that Mia still felt uncomfortable being his charl; the way she saw it, he held all the power in their relationship. It was an ongoing source of contention between them, and Korum knew she would never be completely happy as long as she felt like she had no rights among his people.

The more Korum had contemplated the problem, the more it seemed like marriage could be the solution. By publicly marrying Mia on Krina, he would elevate her standing in their society. She would no longer be merely a charl, a human who belonged to him; she would be the equivalent of his mate, long before the Celebration of Forty-Seven.

She would also officially belong to him in the eyes of her people. Korum liked that quite a bit. If any human male dared to look at her, he would see the ring on her finger and know that this woman was taken. Those rings were a clever custom, Korum had recently realized. They allowed a man to mark his territory in a very civilized manner. Mia was now his fiancé, just as she would soon be his wife—and nobody would have any doubts about that fact.

Of course, their marriage would also give Mia's

parents peace of mind. Although the Stalis family had accepted their relationship, Korum knew they would be far happier if they could call him something other than their daughter's boyfriend. Now he would be their son-in-law, a much stronger tie in their eyes, and they would feel more reassured about his commitment to Mia.

Their transport pod landed in front of his parents' house, and he led Mia inside, with her parents, sister, and brother-in-law trailing behind them. His human family, he thought wryly. It was so unlikely he could still hardly believe it, but these people were important to Mia—and they were becoming increasingly important to him as well.

Riani and Chiaren were waiting for them. As Korum entered the house, he saw his mother first, standing there with a huge smile on her face, and his father's more austere presence immediately behind her. They had been shocked when he'd first told them about Mia, but glad too. Korum sometimes wondered if his parents thought he would go through life without ever finding someone to love.

Stepping forward, he gave Riani a hug and greeted his father with the more formal touch to the shoulder. Then, turning to Mia's family, he introduced them to his parents.

To his surprise, the two sets of parents clicked almost immediately. Within minutes, they were chatting animatedly and trading stories of their children's youthful exploits. "Oh my God, this is embarrassing," Mia whispered in his ear, blushing when Ella laughingly revealed her infant daughter's habit of freeing herself from diapers and crawling around their backyard chasing after squirrels.

"What are squirrels?" Riani asked curiously, and Mia's

father explained all about the little mammal with the bushy tail.

Marisa and Connor, who had been watching the whole thing with bemusement, came to sit next to Korum and Mia on the other side of the room. "Wow, they're really getting along, aren't they?" Marisa told her sister, and Mia laughed, her eyes sparkling with happiness.

It seemed like the perfect moment to make the announcement.

Getting up, Korum pulled Mia to her feet. All eyes immediately turned toward them. "We have something we'd like to share with you," Korum said, looking around the room. His parents seemed puzzled, while the humans stared at him with barely concealed delight. "I have asked Mia to marry me, and she has agreed."

Mia grinned and lifted her left hand, displaying the shimmerstone ring on her finger.

The room exploded. Laughter, shrieks, and congratulations filled the air. Everybody seemed to be hugging everyone else, and his parents gamely went along with the excitement, even though Chiaren kept throwing questioning looks in his direction. As Mia had said, no Krinar had ever married a human, and the very concept of marriage was foreign to his people. A mating union that was marked by the Celebration of Forty-Seven was the closest Krinar equivalent. Korum intended to explain his rationale to his parents later; for now, it was enough that they knew just how much he loved his charl.

After the initial hoopla died down, Korum said to Mia's parents, "I wasn't sure if I should request your permission first or not. From what I understand of this custom, it's rarely done in modern times. I hope you don't mind—"

"Mind?" Ella exclaimed. "Of course we don't mind!"

Her eyes were gleaming with tears, and Korum wondered what it was about marriage that made human women so emotional.

The rest of their time together was spent discussing potential dates for the wedding (Korum insisted on it being no later than next week), the location (Mia liked the lake near his house), and the logistics of a human wedding ceremony on a planet so far away from Earth.

"Don't we need someone to marry you?" Connor asked. "A priest, a rabbi, a judge, someone? And if it's to be legally recognized back home, don't you need to register somewhere on Earth?"

Korum had already thought of these obstacles. "One of the charl living on Krina was actually a judge in Missouri," he told everyone. "I have already reached out to request her assistance. As far as registration goes, we'll transmit our signatures electronically to the Daytona Beach Clerk of the Circuit Court. I'm sure they will make an exception for us, given the circumstances."

* * *

For Mia, the next five days seemed to pass in the blink of an eye. As soon as news about their engagement spread, there was an endless parade of visitors to Korum's house, all wanting to meet her and her family.

Korum's friends, acquaintances, employees, business contacts, even Council members . . . Mia met so many Ks during her short engagement that she couldn't keep track of all the names and faces. To her surprise, she could sense echoes of the same respect they showed Korum in their attitude toward her. It was subtle, but it was there. Her opinion was asked more often, and they spoke to her directly, frequently bypassing Korum altogether. After wondering about it for a couple of days, Mia realized that they were now treating her more as Korum's mate and less as his charl. In their eyes, she was no longer merely a human who belonged to one of them; she was going to be a true part of their society.

Mia particularly liked Jalet and Huar, Korum's long-time friends. Like Korum's parents, Jalet was a dabbler, a jack-of-all-trades. Smart and funny, he seemed to know about everything under the sun, and Mia loved listening to his stories about life on Krina. Huar, on the other hand, was quiet and serious. He was considered to be an expert on ocean studies. Both Huar and Jalet had also been friends with Saret, and they were horrified to learn about his true nature.

"The four of us were like your Musketeers," Jalet told her, referring to the classic Dumas novel. "We got into so many adventures in our youth. I thought about accompanying Saret and Korum to Earth, but I was stuck on a project and the timing didn't work out."

"That was probably for the best." Korum grinned at his friend. "For all we know, he might've tried to kill you too."

"You know," Huar said thoughtfully, "now that I think about it, it's not all that surprising that Saret went after you, Korum. He was quite ambitious, but very secretive about it. You've always known what you wanted and pursued it openly, but Saret liked to scheme and maneuver behind the scenes, so nobody knew it was him. I suspected he might be jealous of you, but I never realized how deep that jealousy ran."

"None of us knew what he was really like," Korum said. "Saret managed to fool everyone, especially me." Mia could hear the bitter note in his voice, and it made her heart ache. He never talked about it much, but she knew he still blamed himself for putting her in harm's way.

"My love, you know he was probably a psychopath, right?" Laying a reassuring hand on Korum's knee, she gave him a serious look. "He was smart enough to hide it, but that's what he ultimately was. All charm on the surface, and a complete lack of remorse underneath. He was clever too, clever enough to wear a mask for centuries." Mia remembered reading about psychopaths in one of her college classes, and they were a truly fascinating breed. She didn't know if Saret fit the textbook definition—or if Ks could even be true psychopaths in the medical sense—but he certainly displayed some of the traits, including a grandiose sense of self-worth.

Korum smiled in response, hugging her to him, but she could see that it would be a long time before the wounds inflicted by Saret's betrayal would heal.

In addition to all the visitors, there was plenty to be done in preparation for the wedding itself. With the virtual help of Korum's cousin Leeta, Mia created herself a beautiful white dress that incorporated some elements from both cultures. She also made flattering outfits for her family that were largely Krinar in style, but took into account their personal preferences.

In the meantime, Korum fabricated an enormous ceremonial hall that floated above the lake near his house. The size of an Olympic stadium, it was designed to accommodate over a hundred thousand guests—a number that made Mia's head spin every time she thought about it.

"How big is this wedding going to be?" she gasped when she saw the giant structure.

"As big as it needs to be," Korum replied, looking at

her steadily, and Mia realized that he was making a public statement. By marrying her in front of all of Krina, he was proclaiming that humans had officially arrived, that they were no longer an inferior species that could only exist on the fringes of the Krinar society.

Korum was addressing her concerns about her place in his world.

CHAPTER THIRTY-ONE

The day before the wedding was supposed to take place, the Elders finally reached a decision about Saret. As soon as Korum heard the news, he went to visit his former friend, feeling a strange need to see him one last time.

Saret was confined in Vlarad, in a heavily guarded building where dangerous criminals awaited their trial. The past couple of months had not been kind to him. If Korum didn't know better, he would've thought Saret had aged somehow. His gaze looked dull and empty, and his skin appeared oddly ashen. It was like he had lost all hope, and, for a brief moment, Korum felt pity for his enemy, his thoughts turning to their childhood together.

But then he remembered what Saret had done to Mia—and what he intended to do to them all—and the feeling of pity faded. Korum had never known the real Saret; whatever good times they'd had together were as fake as Saret's friendship.

"Come to gloat, have you?" Saret's voice broke the silence. "I suppose you heard about my sentence." His lips twisted bitterly, his fingers tugging reflexively at the crime-collar around his throat.

"No," Korum said truthfully, "I didn't come to gloat."

"Then why are you here?"

"I don't know," Korum admitted. "I guess I needed some closure."

"Closure?" Saret laughed, a harsh sound that grated on Korum's ears. "What kind of closure?"

Korum shrugged, unsure of the answer to that.

"Jalet and Huar came to see me yesterday," Saret said, his eyes glued to Korum's face. "They told me all about your little human bride and how your wedding is going to be the biggest event of the millennium. Congratulations. I guess you brainwashed her better than I ever could. Even after that bitch Laira undid my procedure, Mia still wants you. Did you tell her what you're planning to do to her people?"

"Yes," Korum said. "I explained everything. She understood. I never intended to harm her kind, only to make room for us on their planet."

"Yeah, right." Saret gave him a sarcastic look. "Do you think I don't remember how you regarded humans once? How you said Earth should've been ours by right?"

Korum stared at his former friend in disbelief. "You truly thought I still held those views? Saret, that was over a thousand years ago! Everything has changed since then. *I* have changed since then—"

"Oh really? And what made you change? A tight little cunt and a pair of big blue eyes?"

Korum felt a strong urge to do something violent to Saret, but restrained himself at the last moment. "No," he said, keeping his voice even. "I saw how quickly they were progressing and becoming more like us. I realized centuries ago that I had been wrong about them—that so many of us had been wrong. Surely you knew that."

"No, I didn't know," Saret said. "Or maybe I knew and didn't believe it. It doesn't matter now, does it? After today, I will be no more. That's why you came to see me now, isn't it? To watch me die?"

"You won't die," Korum said calmly. "They sentenced you to a new version of complete rehabilitation, one that Laira herself came up with recently. Unlike the old one, it can't be reversed."

Saret laughed bitterly. "Right. Like I said, after this procedure I will be no more."

"Goodbye, Saret." Korum took one final look at his former friend and walked out, putting an end to that chapter of his life.

When he got home, Mia was waiting for him, an anxious look on her face. "How did it go?" she asked, getting up from the float where she had been reading her tablet. "Did you get a chance to talk to him?"

"Yes." Korum drew her toward him for a hug. The familiar feel of her in his arms was soothing, taking away his stress and tension. As much as Korum hated to admit it to himself, seeing Saret today had been painful. Despite his betrayal, despite everything, Korum had thought of him as a friend his whole life, and he couldn't help mourning the loss of that illusion.

She wrapped her arms around his waist and held him, her small hands rubbing up and down his back. Somehow she knew he needed comfort now; she always knew what he needed these days.

After a couple of minutes, she pulled back slightly and looked up at him, her blue eyes filled with sympathy. "When are they going to do it?" she asked quietly. "When is the procedure going to take place?"

"This afternoon," Korum said, lifting his hand to brush a curl off her cheek. "In just a couple of hours."

"And then what? What happens to those who are rehabilitated like that?"

"He'll be taken to a special re-education facility, where the rehabilitated are taught how to become productive members of society again. He'll know about his old identity, of course, but he'll be given a chance to start over, to build a new life for himself."

"And he'll be completely changed? He won't want to do those things again?"

"Most likely not," Korum said. "And besides, he'll be under close surveillance for centuries to come. At the least sign of renewed criminal tendencies, he will undergo the procedure again."

She moistened her lips, and Korum found himself staring at her mouth, his thoughts suddenly taking a sexual turn. "Do you think we'll run into him at some point?" she asked. "If he's going to re-enter society after his rehabilitation, do you think we'll see him again?"

Korum tried to tear his mind away from the image of her lips wrapped around his cock. "Probably," he managed to say. "But don't worry—he'll be a very different man." Despite the seriousness of the conversation, he could feel his body hardening, reacting to her nearness as it usually did.

Undoubtedly feeling the bulge against her stomach, Mia gave him a knowing smile and pressed closer, rubbing her breasts against his chest. Korum inhaled sharply, feeling her peaked nipples through the two layers of clothing that separated them. Her eyes darkened, her pupils expanding, and there was a hint of color stealing across the paleness of her cheeks. She was getting aroused;

he could see it... and feel it and smell it. The warm, sensual scent of her was like an aphrodisiac to him, sending blood rushing through his veins and making his cock throb with need.

Still looking up at him with that seductive smile, she licked her lips again, slowly this time. The sound that escaped his throat was closer to a growl. She knew exactly what to do nowadays, how to drive him wild in the shortest possible span of time.

Desperate for her taste, Korum bent his head and kissed her, reveling in the way her tongue curled around his, stroking and caressing the interior of his mouth. She was a skilled kisser now, a far cry from the shy virgin he'd forced into his bed back in New York. Her fingers found their way into his hair, her nails delicately scratching his scalp, and he almost groaned, rocking his hips back and forth, pushing his erection into her belly.

His skin felt hot, and suddenly their clothes were too confining, too much in the way. Korum pulled down the top of her dress, imprisoning her arms in the fabric and baring her pretty breasts to his gaze. They were white, firm, and perfectly round, and her nipples were a beautiful pink-rose color. Unable to resist the temptation, he dropped to his knees and brought those small hard nipples toward his mouth, sucking first one and then another. She moaned, arching toward him, her hands holding the back of his head, and Korum slid one hand under the skirt of her dress, feeling the softness of the curls between her thighs.

"Korum, please," she whispered, and he knew she was aching for more, just as he was. Still tonguing her nipples, he pushed one finger inside her, his balls tightening at the warm, slick feel of her interior channel. He wanted her to come, but at the same time, he wanted to keep torturing her, to make her scream with pleasure in his arms. His thumb entered between her folds, found her small clitoris, and he pressed on it lightly, keeping his touch too gentle for her to reach her peak. She bucked against him, and Korum did it again, loving the helpless little sounds that tore from her throat. His cock felt like it would explode, but he kept pushing his finger inside her, feeling a gush of moisture with every stroke.

Sweet, she was so fucking sweet to him. Ripping apart her dress, he bared her stomach and the dark triangle between her thighs, his mouth leaving her breasts to kiss every inch of the skin he exposed. There was so much he wanted to do to her, so many ways he wanted to take her, and he would do it all in time, but for now he needed to take it slow, to gradually introduce her to all the pleasures of the flesh. She was trembling in his arms, her delicate inner walls quivering around his finger, and he pushed a second finger inside her, stretching her, his thumb still playing lightly with her clit.

"Korum . . ." Her tortured moan was like music to his ears, and he smiled triumphantly, gently scraping his teeth across the delicate skin of her stomach. He didn't break the skin, but she still gasped at the sting, and he felt her pussy tighten around his fingers, coating them with more delicious moisture.

"Yes," he murmured, "yes, you can come for me now . . ." And she did, her head thrown back with a scream, the pulsations of her inner muscles adding to the blazing heat inside him.

Withdrawing his fingers, Korum licked them, savoring her taste, then tugged her down on the floor beside him. The intelligent material was soft around them, massaging their knees and calves with tiny finger-like appendages, but Korum barely noticed the pleasant feeling, focusing only on the woman in his arms.

Mia was still shaking, her breathing fast and uneven in the aftermath of her orgasm, and Korum arranged her pliant body so that she was on her hands and knees, facing away from him. The curve of her perfectly shaped ass was an unbearable temptation. He could see the wet, swollen folds of her sex and the tiny rose of her other opening, and he wanted to be in both places at once, to fuck her in every way possible.

Pushing his thumb inside her slick channel, he gathered the moisture from there and then used it as a lubricant, pressing that same finger to her ass. She cried out, her muscles resisting the intrusion, and he paused, letting her get used to the sensation before he continued slowly working it into her tight passage. When it was all the way in, he grasped her hips with his other hand and sank his cock deep into her pussy.

She arched, moaning, and Korum sucked in his breath, his thumb feeling the movement of his shaft inside her through the thin wall that separated her two orifices. *So fucking sweet.* The pleasure was unbelievable, almost intolerable. Unable to wait any longer, Korum began fucking her without restraint, feeling her inner muscles clinging to his cock, gripping him so tightly he felt like he was about to explode.

And then he did, his head thrown back with a deep roar. She screamed too, bucking against him, and Korum felt her inner muscles milking him, squeezing every drop of semen from his body.

Panting, he sank down on the floor, still buried deep inside her. After a few moments, he withdrew his thumb and pulled her naked, trembling body against him. She was breathing as hard as he was, and he kissed the delicate shell of her ear, knowing she needed tenderness after the way he just took her like a savage. "I love you," he whispered, and she turned toward him with a smile—the smile of a woman who had just been thoroughly satisfied.

"And I love you," she said softly, stroking his face with her fingers.

They lay like that for a while longer, just holding each other and enjoying the feel of skin against skin. Then Korum heard Mia's stomach rumble.

She blushed slightly, and he grinned. "Shower and lunch?"

"Yes, please," she said, then laughed as he picked her up and carried her into the bathroom.

* * *

The guardians came for Saret at two in the afternoon. Alir was among them, his black eyes cold and expressionless.

When they reached for him, Saret shrugged off their hands and walked out of the room on his own, following them toward his execution chamber.

Laira was already there, looking somber as befitting the occasion. Saret had met her once and immediately disliked her. She reminded him of Korum. Same sharp intelligence, same ruthless ambition. She applied to work in his lab a few decades ago, before she became known as a rising star in the field. After a brief interview, Saret turned down her application, enjoying the crushed look on her face when he told her she was unqualified.

There was some twisted irony in her being his executioner today.

They strapped him down on a float, making sure he was fully restrained for what was to come. Saret didn't fight them. What would be the point? The guardians were armed to the teeth, and even if they weren't, they were skilled fighters. He wouldn't stand a chance. At this point, all Saret cared about was dying with dignity.

And death is what this would be. Even though his body would remain, his mind—that which made him Saret—would be gone, thoroughly erased. He would never be himself again; his memories, his personality, his essence—it would all be wiped out.

Laira approached him, holding a small white device in her hands. Saret recognized it. He'd used a version of it on Mia just a couple of months ago.

"I am sorry," Laira said, pressing the device to his forehead. "I am truly sorry for this."

Her face was the last thing Saret saw before his world faded into darkness.

CHAPTER THIRTY-TWO

The morning of their wedding dawned crisp and clear.

"Mia, honey, you look—" Her mom wiped away tears. "You look so gorgeous . . ."

"Thank you, mom," Mia said softly. "You and Marisa look beautiful too." She wasn't lying; her sister was stunning in a cream-colored dress with gently draped folds that skillfully concealed her slight baby bump, while her mom appeared remarkably youthful in a peach-colored sheath that flattered her rounded figure. Her dad and Connor were dressed in Krinar clothing as well, looking surprisingly sharp in their fitted white pants, boots, and structured sleeveless shirts.

"I can't believe my baby sister is getting married," Marisa sniffled, her eyes filling with moisture too. That wasn't unusual, though; Mia's sister cried at the drop of a hat these days.

"And to a K, no less," Connor jumped in, a big grin on his face. "Dan, did you ever think such a thing would happen to your youngest?"

"No," her dad said dryly. "I certainly didn't."

Mia's family were sitting in a private room in the giant hall structure, watching Mia putting the final touches on her hair. As a wedding gift, Leeta had sent her a design for a beautiful hair accessory, and Mia was now placing it on her head. Made of some sparkling metals and shiny white-colored stones, it went all around her hair and through each curl, making Mia look like a fairy princess.

Her dress only added to the impression. It was long, covering her feet, with a wide skirt and a strapless sweetheart neckline that pushed up her breasts and flattered her slim torso. It would've been a classic wedding dress, if it weren't for the fact that Mia's entire back was left exposed in the style of her usual Krinar outfits. Since the dress was long, Mia decided to wear high heels, giving herself four extra inches of height—which made her almost as tall as the shortest Krinar women.

"Korum hasn't seen you yet, has he?" her mom asked anxiously, and Mia shook her head, smiling at the superstition.

"He hasn't, mom, relax."

Mia knew she should be feeling nervous herself. After all, didn't all brides freak out, at least a little bit? And Mia had more cause to freak out than most, given the size of her wedding and the fact that the entire Krinar race would be watching the unprecedented event either virtually or in person.

However, she didn't have even a hint of bridal jitters. All she could feel was a warm glow of happiness. Korum had taken care of all the logistics, handling the wedding preparations with the same calm assurance as he did everything else, so there was nothing to worry about on that front. As for their future together, she knew it wouldn't always be smooth sailing, but their love was strong enough, real enough, to survive whatever obstacles lay ahead.

Some part of her still couldn't believe that this was happening, that she was about to get married to a K she had once feared and regarded as an enemy. Although only a few short months had passed, so much had changed in her life—and in Korum's life. They had each learned the value of compromise, of seeing the other person's point of view. Mia had grown stronger, more confident, while Korum had begun tempering his natural arrogance and controlling tendencies. He was still ridiculously overprotective, of course, but Mia hoped that would ease with time, as memories of Saret's attack gradually faded. Korum's possessiveness was a different matter; she strongly suspected that part of his personality would never change.

"You know, you're going to be a celebrity back home," Marisa said thoughtfully, watching Mia. "My baby sis— the first human to marry a K! If the media gets ahold of it, you'll be all over the news . . ."

"I know." Mia mentally shuddered at the thought. She and Korum had already discussed the disturbing possibility. "When we come back to Earth, we'll likely be living in Lenkarda, so it won't be so bad for us. For you guys, though . . . You might want to consider moving to Lenkarda too, regardless of what happens with the petition." It went without saying that Mia's family would have to live in the Centers if they were granted immortality, just like charl.

Taking one last look in the mirror, Mia turned and smiled at everyone. "I'm ready."

* * *

Dressed in a white human-style tuxedo, Korum stood waiting at the altar. As the first notes of the traditional human wedding march began to play, his pulse jumped in anticipation. In a matter of minutes, Mia would be walking down that aisle, and he would finally see his human bride.

Two hours ago, her parents had pulled her away and warned him very strictly that he couldn't lay eyes on her until the ceremony began. Bad luck or something ridiculous like that. Korum hadn't been pleased, since he had wanted to help Mia dress—and maybe sneak in a quickie before the lengthy celebration—but Ella Stalis had been adamant and Korum had grudgingly given in. Arguing with his soon-to-be mother-in-law was not high on his list of priorities today.

As the music continued, he cast a quick glance around the large celebration hall. Decorated in white and silver tones, it was filled to the brim. In addition to Korum's family, friends, and various acquaintances, many members of the Krinar elite were attending in person. The rest of Krina—and the Krinar residents of Earth—were experiencing it virtually. Everyone was watching him with unbridled curiosity, and Korum knew they were wondering why he was doing it, why he was marrying his charl. Even Arus had been puzzled. "Isn't that redundant?" he'd asked Korum after a Council meeting in which Korum had participated remotely. "You and Mia are already as good as married. She's your charl."

Korum had simply smiled, not bothering to explain his reasons. Mia was indeed his charl, and now she would also be his wife.

In the distance, he could hear her footsteps. Her father was leading her in, as per the old custom of giving the bride away. Korum grinned to himself. He would gladly take her off their hands.

As she appeared at the other end of the aisle, on her father's arm, his breath caught in his chest. Mia looked radiant, more beautiful than any woman Korum could ever remember seeing. She was glowing, her blue eyes shining with happiness and her lips curved in a wide smile. The dress emphasized her tiny waist and pushed up her deliciously round breasts, drawing his attention to her cleavage. Just seeing her like that made him want to pick her up and carry her to bed—and keep her there for the next several hours.

Soon, Korum promised himself, and did his best to push all thoughts of sex out of his mind. It was impossible, however, because he simply couldn't tear his eyes away from her. As she glided down the aisle, he found himself hungrily watching her every step, drinking in the delicacy of her features, the elegant lines of her neck and shoulders. Her skin looked so soft, so touchable that Korum's fingers actually itched with the urge to stroke it, to feel it all over.

Then she was there, next to him, and the music reached a crescendo, then quieted down. Korum took Mia's hand and turned toward the blond human woman who would perform the ceremony. Once a judge in Missouri, Lana Walters was now a charl living on Krina, and she was honored to be part of such a historic occasion.

"Dear friends, family, and all who are present or watching us today," Lana said in a husky voice, "we are gathered here today to witness the marriage of Nathrandokorum and Mia Stalis, the first time such a union has ever taken place." She paused for dramatic effect. "Korum, do you take Mia to be your lawfully wedded wife, to have and to hold, to love and to cherish, in sickness and in health, until death do you part?"

"I do," Korum said, looking at Mia. At his words, her smile became impossibly bright, dazzling him with its beauty.

"And you, Mia? Do you take Korum to be your lawfully wedded husband, to have and to hold, to love and to cherish, in sickness and in health, until death do you part?"

"I do." Her voice was strong and clear, without even a hint of hesitation.

"Then I pronounce you husband and wife. You may kiss the bride."

Korum didn't need any urging. Bringing Mia toward him, he bent his head and kissed her, the delicious taste of her sending a surge of blood straight to his groin. It took all his willpower to stop after a minute. When he pulled away, she was looking up at him with her mouth slightly swollen and her blue eyes soft with desire.

As one, the crowd stood up and began stomping their feet in the Krinar version of clapping. The floor shook as a hundred thousand guests stomped in unison and cheered for them. Taking Mia's hand, Korum lifted their joined palms into the air, whipping the crowd into an even greater frenzy.

It was time to celebrate.

* * *

Mia couldn't stop laughing as her husband whirled her around the dance floor, as effortlessly as if she was a doll. All around them, other Krinar couples were dancing too, their movements so complex and fluid that Mia would never be able to replicate them on her own. Her family was watching from the sidelines, looking as awed as Mia felt at the inhuman grace and athleticism of the dancers.

Despite the traditionally human wedding ceremony, the party afterwards was decidedly alien. It reminded Mia of Leeta's union celebration in Lenkarda. Everything, from the exotic music to the corner location of the dance floors, was purely Krinar. Floating seats, reflective walls, and shiny decorations abounded.

Mia could see that her parents were overwhelmed by all the glitter and the gorgeous crowds surrounding them. Marisa and Connor, on the other hand, seemed to love it. Mia's brother-in-law even tasted one of the local alcoholic beverages. "Strong shit," he said approvingly after his eyes stopped watering. Mia and the others stuck to the refreshing pink juice cocktail, unwilling to try anything strong enough to give Ks a buzz. After a little while, Korum's parents joined Mia's family, and they all conversed while Korum stole Mia away to the dance floor.

After about an hour of vigorous dancing, Mia had to beg for mercy. "You realize I'm human, right?" she laughingly told Korum, stopping to catch her breath.

At that moment, they were approached by a tall Krinar man. "Congratulations," he said, smiling at them. "I'm Kellon, Ellet's cousin."

Korum smiled back, and they exchanged the traditional Krinar greeting, touching each other's shoulder with their palms.

"I have a wedding gift for you," Kellon said, "from Ellet."

"Oh?" Korum arched his eyebrows, and Mia looked at the K. What did the human biology expert want to give them?

"For the past several years, Ellet has been working on a very ambitious project," Kellon said, "and she finally had a big breakthrough last night. It's something that would be of particular interest to you both—which is why she asked me to approach you today, during your wedding."

"What is it?" Mia asked, unbearably curious.

"She has been trying to figure out how humans and Krinar could have biological offspring together . . . and she thinks she finally has a solution."

"A solution?" Mia whispered, hardly daring to believe her ears. "Are you talking about human-Krinar babies?" Her husband seemed to be frozen in place, staring at the other K in shock.

"Yes," Kellon confirmed. "The process is far from perfect yet, and Ellet has a lot of kinks to work out, but she's been able to figure out how to combine the DNA from both species in such a way as to produce viable offspring. A few more years and the two of you may be able to have a child—if you're so inclined, of course."

"Is she sure?" Korum's voice was calm, but his eyes were nearly yellow with strong emotion. "Is Ellet absolutely sure about this? If this is just some simulation she ran—"

"No," Kellon said, "she's sure. She's run at least a hundred simulations, and every single one of them produced the same results. For the first time ever, it's going to be possible for charl and cheren to have children together."

"Thank you, Kellon," Mia said thickly, "and please thank Ellet for us. This . . this is the best wedding gift we could've received." She felt like she would burst into tears at any moment, and she looked away, blinking furiously to hold back the moisture that filled her eyes. A child with Korum! It was beyond her wildest dreams.

"Yes," Korum said softly, "please convey our most sincere thanks to Ellet. She has our gratitude."

Kellon inclined his head respectfully and walked away, melting into the crowd.

As soon as he was gone, Mia turned to her husband. "A baby! Oh my God, Korum, a baby!" She grabbed his hand, squeezing it between her palms in excitement.

"A baby," he repeated, and there was a strange expression on his face. "Our baby."

Some of Mia's excitement waned. "You . . . You do want a child, right?" she asked uncertainly. "I mean, I know it would be partially human and everything—"

"Want one?" He stared at her like she had just grown two heads. When he spoke again, his voice was low and filled with intensity. "Mia, my sweet, I love you. A child who would be part you and part me? How could I not want that?" Covering her hands with his other palm, he drew her toward him, his eyes gleaming. "I want it very, very much."

Mia beamed at him, feeling like her heart would overflow with happiness. "If we had a daughter, we could call her Ivy. I've always loved that name. What do you think?"

"I think I like it very much," he murmured, bending his head and giving her a deep, passionate kiss.

They decided to share the news with their families after the wedding. There were simply too many people around right now for such an important—and private— announcement. Still, Mia couldn't get her mind off Ellet's gift.

"Do you think the procedure will be perfected by the time I'm thirty?" she asked Korum as he led her back to the dance floor. "I've always wanted to have a baby before I was thirty—"

"Thirty?" Her husband laughed. "Mia, darling, your age is irrelevant now. Our child could be born when you're thirty—or when you're five hundred and thirty. It really doesn't matter—"

"It matters for my parents," Mia said quietly. "I would want them to see their grandchildren, to know them in their lifetime." It was the one thing that worried her: the fact that they still had not received an answer from the Elders.

Korum started to say something when the music suddenly stopped. All the noise died down, a deathly silence descending out of nowhere. Everyone seemed frozen in place, staring at the entrance.

"What's going on?" Mia whispered, stepping closer to Korum.

"Hush, my sweet," he said quietly, putting a protective arm around her back. "It looks like Lahur is here."

Mia barely suppressed a gasp. From what Korum had told her, the Elders never came out to socialize with the other Krinar or to attend any public events. They were essentially loners, holding themselves apart from the general population. And now Lahur, the oldest of them all, was here at their party?

The crowd slowly parted, and Mia could see a tall, powerful man making his way toward them. As he approached, she recognized the hard features of the Elder she'd spoken to in the forest. He was dressed in formal Krinar clothing, like all the other guests, but the fancy outfit did little to conceal his predatory nature. Even among other Krinar, he seemed more savage somehow, a panther roaming among house cats.

"Welcome, Lahur," Korum said calmly, inclining his head toward the newcomer. "We are pleased you could join us."

"Thank you." Lahur's deep voice held a note of amusement. "I'm not here for long. I came to give you a wedding present. That's a custom of yours, isn't it, Mia?"

Mia stared at the Elder in shock. "Yes," she managed to say. "It's a human wedding custom." She was surprised she was able to speak at all, with her heart beating as hard as it was.

"Well then," Lahur said, his dark eyes trained on her, "I would like to tell you that we have granted your petition. Your family will be given all the rights and privileges of those we call charl."

A shocked murmur ran through the crowd at his words, and Mia inhaled sharply, her eyes filling with tears of joy. "Thank you," she whispered, looking at the dark visage of the ten-million-year-old alien in front of her. "Thank you so very much . . ."

"Yes," Korum said, his arm tightening around Mia's back. "Thank you for a wonderful wedding present. My wife and I are truly grateful."

Lahur inclined his head, acknowledging their thanks. Then he turned around and walked away, the crowd parting again to let him through.

The music started up again, and the party resumed. Running up to Mia, Marisa gave her and Korum a hug, sobbing with happiness, and her parents embraced each other, tears running down their faces. Connor shook Korum's hand, and Mia could see that her brother-in-law's eyes were glistening too.

For the first time in history, an entire human family would be given immortality—a gift more precious than anything they could've ever imagined.

Looking up at her husband—her beautiful K lover—Mia smiled through her tears. "I love you," she told him softly. "I love you so very much."

"And I love you," he said, watching her with warm amber-colored gaze.

Their happiness was complete.

EPILOGUE

Lahur stood in the forest clearing, feeling the warm breeze on his face. The others were gathered around him, their faces as familiar to him as his own. These people—the ones known as the Elders—were among the few whose company Lahur could tolerate for more than ten minutes at a time.

"So what now?" Sheura asked, watching him with her calm dark gaze.

Lahur looked at her. "What do you think?"

"I think it's time," she said quietly. "I think we have to do it."

"I agree." It was Pioren, Sheura's partner in the experiment. "We can no longer stand by and observe. The project has succeeded all too well. They're like us. Our best and brightest are now mating with them."

"Yes," Lahur said, "they are." Seeing the curly-haired human girl by Korum's side had been a revelation. She wasn't the first human he'd met, but something about her had touched him, penetrating the layer of ice that encased him these days. For a moment, Lahur had been able to feel the powerful bond that existed between her and her cheren, to bask in the love they had for each other.

Out of all the young ones, Lahur found Korum to be among the most interesting, probably because he reminded Lahur of himself in his youth. Same drive, same willingness to do what's necessary to achieve his goals. Lahur had no doubt that Korum would succeed in building a Krinar empire, taking them all on an unprecedented journey.

A journey that Korum planned to undertake with a human girl by his side.

There could be no clearer sign that they needed to wrap up the experiment.

"Let's do it," Lahur said. "You're right. It's time. We need to share our technology with them, to give them all what we gave only to a select few. Their evolution is complete."

And as he looked around the clearing, seeing agreement on the other faces, Lahur had only one thought:

Nothing will ever be the same again.

SNEAK PEEKS

Thank you for reading *Close Remembrance*, the third book in the Krinar Chronicles series! I hope you enjoyed it. If you did, please mention it to your friends and social media connections. I would also be hugely grateful if you helped other readers discover the book by leaving a review on Amazon, Goodreads, or other sites.

While Mia & Korum's story is over (for now), there will be many more novels—and potentially other series—set in the Krinar world. Additionally, I am working on some non-Krinar books, including those in contemporary settings. Please visit my website at www.annazaires.com and sign up for my newsletter to be notified when the books become available.

Thank you for your support! I truly appreciate it!

And now please turn the page for a little taste of *Twist Me* and some of my other upcoming works . . .

EXCERPT FROM *TWIST ME*

Author's Note: This is a dark erotic novel, and it deals with topics some readers may find disturbing. Please heed the warning! It's also a bit different from my other books in that it's written in first person.

* * *

Kidnapped. Taken to a private island.

I never thought this could happen to me. I never imagined one chance meeting on the eve of my eighteenth birthday could change my life so completely.

Now I belong to him. To Julian. To a man who is as ruthless as he is beautiful—a man whose touch makes me burn. A man whose tenderness I find more devastating than his cruelty.

My captor is an enigma. I don't know who he is or why

he took me. There is a darkness inside him—a darkness that scares me even as it draws me in.

My name is Nora Leston, and this is my story.

WARNING: This is NOT a traditional romance. It contains disturbing subject matter, including themes of questionable consent and Stockholm Syndrome, as well as graphic sexual content. This is a work of fiction intended for a mature, 18+ audience only. The author neither endorses nor condones this type of behavior.

* * *

It's evening now. With every minute that passes, I'm starting to get more and more anxious at the thought of seeing my captor again.

The novel that I've been reading can no longer hold my interest. I put it down and walk in circles around the room.

I am dressed in the clothes Beth had given me earlier. It's not what I would've chosen to wear, but it's better than a bathrobe. A sexy pair of white lacy panties and a matching bra for underwear. A pretty blue sundress that buttons in the front. Everything fits me suspiciously well. Has he been stalking me for a while? Learning everything about me, including my clothing size?

The thought makes me sick.

I am trying not to think about what's to come, but it's impossible. I don't know why I'm so sure he'll come to me tonight. It's possible he has an entire harem of women stashed away on this island, and he visits each one only once a week, like sultans used to do.

Yet somehow I know he'll be here soon. Last night

had simply whetted his appetite. I know he's not done with me, not by a long shot.

Finally, the door opens.

He walks in like he owns the place. Which, of course, he does.

I am again struck by his masculine beauty. He could've been a model or a movie star, with a face like his. If there was any fairness in the world, he would've been short or had some other imperfection to offset that face.

But he doesn't. His body is tall and muscular, perfectly proportioned. I remember what it feels like to have him inside me, and I feel an unwelcome jolt of arousal.

He's again wearing jeans and a T-shirt. A grey one this time. He seems to favor simple clothing, and he's smart to do so. His looks don't need any enhancement.

He smiles at me. It's his fallen angel smile—dark and seductive at the same time. "Hello, Nora."

I don't know what to say to him, so I blurt out the first thing that pops into my head. "How long are you going to keep me here?"

He cocks his head slightly to the side. "Here in the room? Or on the island?"

"Both."

"Beth will show you around tomorrow, take you swimming if you'd like," he says, approaching me. "You won't be locked in, unless you do something foolish."

"Such as?" I ask, my heart pounding in my chest as he stops next to me and lifts his hand to stroke my hair.

"Trying to harm Beth or yourself." His voice is soft, his gaze hypnotic as he looks down at me. The way he's touching my hair is oddly relaxing.

I blink, trying to break his spell. "And what about on the island? How long will you keep me here?"

His hand caresses my face, curves around my cheek. I catch myself leaning into his touch, like a cat getting petted, and I immediately stiffen.

His lips curl into a knowing smile. The bastard knows the effect he has on me. "A long time, I hope," he says.

For some reason, I'm not surprised. He wouldn't have bothered bringing me all the way here if he just wanted to fuck me a few times. I'm terrified, but I'm not surprised.

I gather my courage and ask the next logical question. "Why did you kidnap me?"

The smile leaves his face. He doesn't answer, just looks at me with an inscrutable blue gaze.

I begin to shake. "Are you going to kill me?"

"No, Nora, I won't kill you."

His denial reassures me, although he could obviously be lying.

"Are you going to sell me?" I can barely get the words out. "Like to be a prostitute or something?"

"No," he says softly. "Never. You're mine and mine alone."

I feel a tiny bit calmer, but there is one more thing I have to know. "Are you going to hurt me?"

For a moment, he doesn't answer again. Something dark briefly flashes in his eyes. "Probably," he says quietly.

And then he leans down and kisses me, his warm lips soft and gentle on mine.

For a second, I stand there frozen, unresponsive. I believe him. I know he's telling the truth when he says he'll hurt me. There's something in him that scares me— that has scared me from the very beginning.

He's nothing like the boys I've gone on dates with.

He's capable of anything.

And I'm completely at his mercy.

I think about trying to fight him again. That would be the normal thing to do in my situation. The brave thing to do.

And yet I don't do it.

I can feel the darkness inside him. There's something wrong with him. His outer beauty hides something monstrous underneath.

I don't want to unleash that darkness. I don't know what will happen if I do.

So I stand still in his embrace and let him kiss me. And when he picks me up again and takes me to bed, I don't try to resist in any way.

Instead, I close my eyes and give in to the sensations.

* * *

Twist Me is currently available. Please visit my website at www.annazaires.com to learn more.

EXCERPT FROM *THE KRINAR CAPTIVE*

Author's Note: This is a prequel to the Krinar Chronicles. You don't have to have read Mia & Korum's story in order to read this book. It takes place approximately five years earlier, right before and during the Krinar invasion. The excerpt and the description are unedited and subject to change.

* * *

Emily Ross never expected to survive her deadly fall in the Costa Rican jungle—and she certainly never thought she'd wake up in a strangely futuristic dwelling, held captive by the most beautiful man she had ever seen. A man who seems to be more than human . . .

Zaron is on Earth to facilitate the Krinar invasion—and to forget the terrible tragedy that ripped apart his life. Yet when he finds the broken body of a human girl, everything changes. For the first time in years, he feels something more than rage and grief... and Emily is the reason for that. Letting her go would compromise his mission, but keeping her could destroy him all over again.

* * *

I don't want to die. I don't want to die. Please, please, please, I don't want to die.

The words kept repeating over and over in her mind, a hopeless prayer that would never be heard. Her fingers slipped another inch on the rough wooden board, her nails breaking as she tried to maintain her grip.

Emily Ross was hanging by her fingernails—literally—off a broken old bridge. Hundreds of feet below, water rushed over the rocks, the mountain stream full from recent rains.

Those rains were partially responsible for her current predicament. If the wood on the bridge had been dry, she might not have slipped, twisting her foot in the process. And she certainly wouldn't have fallen onto the rail that broke under her weight.

It was only a last-minute desperate grab that prevented her from plummeting to her death below. As she was falling, her right hand had caught a small protrusion on the side of the bridge, leaving her dangling in the air hundreds of feet above hard rocks.

I don't want to die. I don't want to die. Please, please, please, I don't want to die.

It wasn't fair. It wasn't supposed to happen this way. This was her vacation, her regain-sanity time. How could she die now? She hadn't even begun living yet.

Images of the last two years slid through her brain, like the PowerPoint presentations she'd spent so many hours making. Every late night, every weekend spent in the office—it had all been for nothing. She'd lost her job during the layoffs, and now she was about to lose her life.

No, no!

Her legs flailed, her nails digging deeper into the wood. Her other arm reached up, stretching toward the bridge. This wouldn't happen to her. She wouldn't let it. She had worked too hard to let a stupid jungle bridge defeat her.

Blood ran down her arm as the rough wood tore the skin off her fingers, but she ignored the pain. Her only hope of survival lay in trying to grab onto the side of the bridge with her other hand, so she could pull herself back up. There was no one around to rescue her, no one to save her if she didn't save herself.

The possibility that she might die alone in the rainforest had not occurred to Emily when she embarked on this trip. She was used to hiking, used to camping. And even after the hell of the past two years, she was still in good shape, strong and fit from running and playing sports all through high school and college. Costa Rica was considered a safe destination, with a low crime rate and tourist-friendly population. It was inexpensive too—an important factor for her rapidly dwindling savings account.

She'd booked this trip Before. Before the market had fallen again, before another round of layoffs that had cost thousands of Wall Street workers their jobs. Before Emily went to work on Monday, bleary-eyed from working all weekend, only to leave the office same day with all her possessions in a small cardboard box.

Before her four-year relationship had fallen apart.

Her first vacation in two years, and she was going to die.

No, don't think that way. It won't happen.

But Emily knew she was lying to herself. She could feel her fingers slipping further, her right arm and shoulder burning from the strain of supporting the weight of her entire body. Her left hand was inches away from reaching the side of the bridge, but those inches could've easily been miles. She couldn't get a strong enough grip to lift herself up with one arm.

Do it, Emily! Don't think, just do it!

Gathering all her strength, she swung her legs in the air, using the momentum to bring her body higher for a fraction of a second. Her left hand grabbed onto the protruding board, clutched at it . . . and then the fragile piece of wood snapped, startling her into a terrified scream.

Emily's last thought before her body hit the rocks was the hope that her death would be instant.

* * *

The smell of jungle vegetation, rich and pungent, teased Zaron's nostrils. He inhaled deeply, letting the humid air fill his lungs. It was clean here, in this tiny corner of Earth, almost as unpolluted as on his home planet.

He needed this now. Needed the fresh air, the isolation. For the past six months, he'd tried to run from his thoughts, to exist only in the moment, but he'd failed. Even blood and sex were not enough for him anymore. He could distract himself while fucking, but the pain always came back afterwards, as strong as ever.

Finally, it had gotten to be too much. The dirt, the crowds, the stink of humanity. When he wasn't lost in a fog of ecstasy, he was disgusted, his senses overwhelmed from spending so much time in human cities. It was better here, where he could breathe without inhaling poison, where he could smell life instead of chemicals. In a few years, everything would be different, and he might try living in a human city again, but not now.

Not until they were fully settled here.

* * *

If you'd like to know when *The Krinar Captive* comes out, please visit my website at www.annazaires.com and sign up for my new release email list.

EXCERPT FROM *WHITE NIGHTS*

Author's Note: This is a contemporary erotic romance. The excerpt and the description are unedited and subject to change.

* * *

A Russian Oligarch
Alex Volkov always gets what he wants. Once an orphan on the streets of Saint Petersburg, he's now one of the wealthiest men in the world. But one doesn't rise that far in Russia without crossing the line . . .

An American Nurse
Kate Morrell has always been capable and independent. She neither wants nor needs a man in her life. Yet she can't help being drawn to the dangerous stranger she meets in the hospital . . .

A Deadly Game

When Alex's past threatens their present, Kate must decide how much she's willing to risk to be with him . . . and whether the man she's falling for is any different from the ruthless assassin hunting them down.

* * *

"Kate, I'm sorry, but we really need you right now."

June Wallers, the nursing supervisor, burst into the tiny room where Katherine Morrell was quickly finishing her lunch.

Sighing, Kate put down her half-eaten sandwich, took a sip of water, and followed June down the hall. This was not the first time this week her allocated lunch hour had turned into a ten-minute snack break.

The recession had taken a heavy toll on New York hospitals, with budget cuts leading to hiring freezes and staff layoffs. As a result, the Emergency Room at Coney Island Hospital was at least three nurses short of what it needed to function properly. Other departments were also short-staffed, but their patient flow was somewhat more predictable. At the ER, however, it was almost always a madhouse.

This week had been particularly horrible. It was flu season, and one of the nurses had gotten sick. It was the absolute worst time for her to be out, as flu season also brought a greater-than-usual influx of patients. This was Kate's fifth twelve-hour shift this week, and it was a night shift—something she hated to do, but couldn't always avoid. But June had begged, and Kate had given in, knowing there was no one else who could replace her.

And here she was, skipping her lunch yet again. At this pace, she would be skin-and-bones before the flu season was over. The 'flu diet,' her mom liked to call it.

"What's the emergency?" Kate asked, walking faster to keep up with June. At fifty-five years of age, the nurse supervisor was as spry as a twenty-year-old.

"We've got a gunshot wound."

"How bad?"

"We're not sure yet. Lettie's kid got sick, and she just left—"

"What? So who's with the patients?"

"Nancy."

Shit. Kate almost broke into a run. Nancy was a first-year nurse. She was trying hard, but she needed a lot of guidance. She should never be on her own without a more experienced nurse present.

"Now you see why we need you," June said wryly, and Kate nodded, her pulse speeding up.

This was why she'd gone into nursing—because she liked the idea of being needed, of helping people. A good nurse could make a difference between life and death for a patient, particularly in the ER. It was a heavy responsibility at times, but Kate didn't mind. She liked the fast pace of work in the ER, the way twelve hours would just fly by. By the end of each day, she was so exhausted she could barely walk, but she was also satisfied.

The ER was teeming with activity when Kate entered. Approaching one of the curtained-off sections, Kate pulled back the drapes and saw the gunshot victim lying on the stretcher. He was a large man, tall and broad. Caucasian, from the looks of him. She guessed his age to be somewhere in the late twenties or early thirties. He had an oxygen mask on, and was already hooked up to the cardiac monitor. There was an IV drip in his arm, and he seemed to be unconscious.

Lettie, the first-year nurse, was applying pressure to

the wound to stop the bleeding. There were also two other men were standing nearby, but Kate paid them little attention, all her focus on the patient.

Quickly assessing the situation, Kate washed her hands and took charge. The patient's pulse was strong, and he appeared to be breathing with no distress. Kate checked his pupils; they were normal and responded to light stimulation properly. There was an exit wound, which was lucky. Had the bullet remained inside the body, it could've caused additional damage and required surgery. A CT scan showed that the bullet had just missed the heart and other critical organs. Another inch, and the man would be occupying a body bag instead of this stretcher. As it was, the main challenge was getting the wound clean and stopping the bleeding.

Kate didn't wonder how, why, or who had shot this man. That wasn't her job. Her job was to save his life, to stabilize him until the doctor could get there. In cases like this—true life-threatening emergencies—the doctor would see the patient quickly. All other ER patients were typically in for a longer wait.

When Dr. Stevenson appeared, she filled him in, rattling off the patient's vitals. Then she assisted him as he sutured and bandaged the wound.

Finally, the victim was stable and sedated. Barring any unforeseen complications, the man would live.

Stripping off the gloves, Kate walked over to the sink to wash her hands again. The habit was so deeply ingrained, she never had to think about it. Whenever she was in the hospital, she washed her hands compulsively every chance she got. Far too many deadly patient infections resulted from a healthcare professional's lax approach to hygiene.

Letting the warm water run over her hands, she

rolled her head side to side, trying to relieve the tension in her neck. As much as she loved her job, it was both physically and mentally exhausting, particularly when someone's life was on the line. Kate had always thought full-body massages should be included as part of the benefit package for nurses. If anyone needed a rubdown at the end of a twelve-hour shift, it was surely a nurse.

Turning away from the sink, Kate looked back toward the gunshot man, automatically making sure everything was okay with him before she moved on to check on her other patients.

And as she glanced in his direction, she caught a pair of steely blue eyes looking directly at her.

It was one of the other men who had been standing near the victim—likely one of the wounded's relatives. Visitors were generally not allowed in the hospital at night, but the ER was an exception.

Instead of looking away—as most people would when caught staring—the man continued studying Kate.

So she studied him back, both intrigued and slightly annoyed.

He was tall, well over six feet in height, and broad-shouldered. He wasn't handsome in the traditional sense; that would've been too weak of a word to describe him. Instead, he was . . . magnetic.

Power. That's what she thought of when she looked at him. It was there in the arrogant tilt of his head, in the way he looked at her so calmly, utterly sure of himself and his ability to control all around him. Kate didn't know who he was or what he did, but she doubted he was a pencil pusher in some office. No, this was a man used to issuing orders and having them obeyed.

His clothes fit him well and looked expensive. Maybe even custom-made. He was wearing a grey trench coat, dark grey pants with a subtle pinstripe, and a pair of black Italian leather shoes.

His brown hair was cut short, almost military style. The simple haircut suited his face, revealing hard, symmetric features. He had high cheekbones and a blade of a nose with a slight bump, as though it had been broken once.

Kate had no idea how old he was. His face was unlined, but there was no boyishness to it. No softness whatsoever, not even in the curve of his mouth. She guessed his age to be in the early thirties, but he could've just as easily been twenty-five or forty.

He didn't fidget or look uncomfortable in any way as their staring contest continued. He just stood there quietly, completely still, his blue gaze trained on her.

To her shock, Kate could feel her heart rate picking up as a tingle of heat ran down her spine. It was as though temperature in the room had jumped ten degrees. All of a sudden, the atmosphere became intensely sexual, making Kate aware of herself as a woman in a way that she'd never experienced before. She could feel the silky material of her matched underwear set brushing between her legs, against her breasts. Her entire body seemed flushed, sensitized, her nipples pebbling underneath her layers of clothing.

Holy shit.

So that's what it felt like to be truly attracted to someone. It wasn't rational and logical. There was no meeting of minds and hearts involved. No, the urge was basic and primitive; her body had sensed his on some animal level, and it wanted to mate.

And he felt it, too. It was there in the way his blue eyes had darkened, lids partially lowering. In the way his nostrils flared, as though trying to catch her scent. His fingers twitched, curled into fists, and she somehow knew he was trying to control himself, to avoid reaching for her right then and there.

If they had been alone right now, Kate had no doubt he would be on her already.

Still staring at the stranger, Kate started to back away. The strength of her response to him was frightening, unsettling. They were in the middle of the ER, surrounded by people, and all she could think about was hot, sheet-twisting sex. She had no idea who he was, whether he was married or single. For all she knew, he could be a criminal or a total asshole.

Or he could be a cheating scumbag like Tony. If anyone had taught her to think twice before trusting a man, it was her ex-boyfriend. She didn't want that kind of complication in her life again—didn't want to get involved with a man so soon after her last disastrous relationship.

But the tall stranger clearly had other ideas.

At her cautious retreat, his eyes narrowed, his gaze becoming sharper, more focused.

And then he began walking toward her, his stride oddly graceful for such a large man. There was something panther-ish in his leisurely movements. For a second, Kate felt like a mouse getting stalked by a big cat. Instinctively, she took another step back . . . and watched his hard mouth tighten with displeasure.

Realizing she was acting like a coward, Kate stopped backing away and stood her ground instead, straightening to her full 5'7" height. She was always the calm and capable one, handling high-stress situations with ease—and here she was, behaving like a silly schoolgirl confronted with her first crush. Yes, the man made her uncomfortable, but there was nothing to be afraid of.

What was the worst he could do? Ask her out on a date?

Nevertheless, her hands shook slightly as he approached, stopping less than two feet away. This close, he was even taller than she'd originally thought, probably a couple of inches over six feet. She was not a short woman, but she felt tiny standing next to him. It was not a feeling she enjoyed.

"You are very good at your job." His voice was deep and a little rough, heavy with some Eastern European accent. Just hearing it made her insides shiver in a strangely pleasurable way.

"Um, thank you," Kate said, a bit uncertainly. She knew she was a good nurse, of course, but somehow she hadn't expected this stranger to acknowledge that fact.

"You took care of Igor well. Thank you for that." Igor had to be the gunshot patient. It was a foreign-sounding name, maybe Russian. That explained the stranger's accent. Although he spoke English fluently, it was obvious he wasn't a native speaker.

"Of course. I hope he recovers quickly. Is he your relative?" Kate was proud of the casual steadiness of her tone. Hopefully, the man wouldn't realize how he affected her.

"My bodyguard."

Kate's eyes widened. So she'd been right—this man was a big fish. Bodyguard? Did that mean— "Was he shot in the course of duty?" she asked, holding her breath.

"He took a bullet meant for me, yes." The man's tone was matter-of-fact, but Kate got a sense of tightly suppressed rage underneath those words.

Holy shit. "Did you already speak to the police?"

"I gave them a brief statement. I will talk to them in more detail once Igor is stabilized and regains consciousness."

Kate nodded, not knowing what to say to that. The man standing in front of her had been shot at today. What was he? Some Mafia boss? A political figure?

If she'd had any doubts about the wisdom of exploring this strange attraction between them, they were now gone. This stranger was bad news, and she needed to stay as far away from him as possible.

"Well, I wish your bodyguard a speedy recovery," Kate said in a falsely cheerful tone. "Barring any complications, he should be fine——"

"Thanks to you."

Kate nodded again, gave him a half-smile, and took a step to the side, hoping to walk around the man and go to her next patient.

But he shifted his stance, blocking her way. "I'm Alex Volkov," he said quietly, looking down on her. "And you are?"

Kate's pulse picked up. She could feel the male intent in his question, and it made her nervous. "Just a nurse working here," she said, hoping he would get the hint.

He didn't——or he pretended not to. "What's your name?"

Kate took a deep breath. He was certainly persistent. "I'm Katherine Morrell. If you'll excuse me——"

"Katherine," he repeated, his accent lending the familiar syllables an exotic edge. His eyes gleamed with some unknown emotion, and his hard mouth softened a bit. "Katerina. It's a beautiful name."

"Thank you. I really have to go . . ." Kate was feeling increasingly anxious to get away. He was so large, standing there in front of her. She needed some space, needed a little room to breathe. His nearness was overpowering, making her edgy and restless, leaving her craving something she knew would be bad for her.

"You have your job to do. I understand," he said, looking vaguely amused.

And he still didn't move out of her way. Instead, as she watched in shock, he raised one large hand and lightly brushed his knuckles down her left cheek.

Kate froze, even as a wave of heat moved through her body. His touch had been casual, but she felt branded by it, shaken to the core.

"I would like to see you again, Katerina," he said softly. "When does your shift end tonight?"

Kate stared at him, feeling like she was losing control of the situation. "I don't think that's a good idea—"

"Why not?" His blue eyes narrowed, and his mouth tightened again. "Are you married?"

For a second, Kate was tempted to lie and tell him that she was. But honesty won out. "No. But I'm not interested in dating right now—"

"Who said anything about dating?"

Kate blinked. She had assumed—

He lifted his hand again, stopping her mid-thought. This time, he picked up a strand of her long brown hair, rubbing it between his fingers as though enjoying its texture.

"I don't date, Katerina," he murmured, his accented voice oddly mesmerizing. "But I would like to take you to bed. And I think you would like that, too."

* * *

If you'd like to know when *White Nights* comes out, please visit my website at www.annazaires.com and sign up for my new release email list.

EXCERPT FROM *THE SORCERY CODE* BY DIMA ZALES

Author's Note: Dima Zales is a science fiction and fantasy author and my collaborator in the creation of the Krinar Chronicles. He's also my husband. His fantasy novel is called *The Sorcery Code*, and I'm *his* collaborator this time. While it's not a romance, there is a strong romantic subplot in the book (though no explicit sex scenes). The book is now available everywhere.

* * *

Once a respected member of the Sorcerer Council and now an outcast, Blaise has spent the last year of his life working on a special magical object. The goal is to allow anyone to do magic, not just the sorcerer elite. The outcome of his quest is unlike anything he could've ever imagined—because, instead of an object, he creates Her.

She is Gala, and she is anything but inanimate. Born in the Spell Realm, she is beautiful and highly intelligent— and nobody knows what she's capable of. She will do anything to experience the world . . . even leave the man she is beginning to fall for.

Augusta, a powerful sorceress and Blaise's former fiancée, sees Blaise's deed as the ultimate hubris and Gala as an abomination that must be destroyed. In her quest to save the human race, Augusta will forge new alliances, becoming tangled in a web of intrigue that stretches further than any of them suspect. She may even have to turn to her new lover Barson, a ruthless warrior who might have an agenda of his own . . .

* * *

There was a naked woman on the floor of Blaise's study.

A beautiful naked woman.

Stunned, Blaise stared at the gorgeous creature who just appeared out of thin air. She was looking around with a bewildered expression on her face, apparently as shocked to be there as he was to be seeing her. Her wavy blond hair streamed down her back, partially covering a body that appeared to be perfection itself. Blaise tried not to think about that body and to focus on the situation instead.

A woman. A *She*, not an *It*. Blaise could hardly believe it. Could it be? Could this girl be the object?

She was sitting with her legs folded underneath her, propping herself up with one slim arm. There something awkward about that pose, as though she didn't know what to do with her own limbs. In general, despite the curves that marked her a fully grown woman, there was a child-like innocence in the way she sat there, completely unselfconscious and totally unaware of her own appeal.

Clearing his throat, Blaise tried to think of what to say. In his wildest dreams, he couldn't have imagined this kind of outcome to the project that had consumed his entire life for the past several months.

Hearing the sound, she turned her head to look at him, and Blaise found himself staring into a pair of unusually clear blue eyes.

She blinked, then cocked her head to the side, studying him with visible curiosity. Blaise wondered what she was seeing. He hadn't seen the light of day in weeks, and he wouldn't be surprised if he looked like a mad sorcerer at this point. There was probably a week's worth of stubble covering his face, and he knew his dark hair was unbrushed and sticking out in every direction. If he'd known he would be facing a beautiful woman today, he would've done a grooming spell in the morning.

"Who am I?" she asked, startling Blaise. Her voice was soft and feminine, as alluring as the rest of her. "What is this place?"

"You don't know?" Blaise was glad he finally managed to string together a semi-coherent sentence. "You don't know who you are or where you are?"

She shook her head. "No."

Blaise swallowed. "I see."

"What am I?" she asked again, staring at him with those incredible eyes.

"Well," Blaise said slowly, "if you're not some cruel prankster or a figment of my imagination, then it's somewhat difficult to explain . . ."

She was watching his mouth as he spoke, and when he stopped, she looked up again, meeting his gaze. "It's strange," she said, "hearing words this way. These are the first real words I've heard."

Blaise felt a chill go down his spine. Getting up from his chair, he began to pace, trying to keep his eyes off her nude body. He had been expecting *something* to appear. A magical object, a thing. He just hadn't known what form that thing would take. A mirror, perhaps, or a lamp. Maybe even something as unusual as the Life Capture Sphere that sat on his desk like a large round diamond.

But a person? A female person at that?

To be fair, he *had been* trying to make the object intelligent, to ensure it would have the ability to comprehend human language and convert it into the code. Maybe he shouldn't be so surprised that the intelligence he invoked took on a human shape.

A beautiful, feminine, sensual shape.

Focus, Blaise, focus.

"Why are you walking like that?" She slowly got to her feet, her movements uncertain and strangely clumsy. "Should I be walking too? Is that how people talk to each other?"

Blaise stopped in front of her, doing his best to keep his eyes above her neck. "I'm sorry. I'm not accustomed to naked women in my study."

She ran her hands down her body, as though trying to feel it for the first time. Whatever her intent, Blaise found the gesture extremely erotic.

"Is something wrong with the way I look?" she asked. It was such a typical feminine concern that Blaise had to stifle a smile.

"Quite the opposite," he assured her. "You look unimaginably good." So good, in fact, that he was having trouble concentrating on anything but her delicate curves. She was of medium height, and so perfectly proportioned that she could've been used as a sculptor's template.

"Why do I look this way?" A small frown creased her smooth forehead. "What am I?" That last part seemed to be puzzling her the most.

Blaise took a deep breath, trying to calm his racing pulse. "I think I can try to venture a guess, but before I do, I want to give you some clothing. Please wait here—I'll be right back."

And without waiting for her answer, he hurried out of the room.

* * *

The Sorcery Code is now available everywhere. If you like fantasy or sci-fi, please visit Dima Zales's website at www.dimazales.com and sign up for his new release email list. You can also connect with him on Facebook, Twitter, and Goodreads.

EXCERPT FROM *MIND AWAKENING* BY DIMA ZALES

Author's Note: *Mind Awakening* is another book Dima Zales is working on in collaboration with me. It's a science fiction novel. The excerpt and the description are unedited and subject to change.

* * *

Ethan remembers being shot in the chest. By all rights, he should be dead. Instead, he wakes up in a world that seems like futuristic paradise . . . as someone else.

Who is the real Ethan? The computer scientist he remembers being, or the world-famous genius everyone appears to think he is? And why is someone trying to kill him here, in this peaceful utopian society?

These are some of the questions he'll explore with his

psychologist Matilda—a woman as beautiful as she is mysterious. What is her agenda . . . and what is the Mindverse?

* * *

Ethan woke up.

For a moment, he just lay there with his eyes closed, trying to process the fact that he was still alive. He clearly remembered the mugging . . . and being shot. The pain had been awful, like an explosion in his chest. He hadn't known one could survive that kind of agony; he'd been sure the bullet had entered his heart.

But somehow he was still alive. Taking a deep breath, Ethan cautiously moved his arm, wondering why he wasn't feeling any pain now. Surely there had to be a wound, some damage from the shooting?

Yet he felt fine. More than fine, in fact. Even the pain from his rheumatoid arthritis seemed to be gone. They must've given him a hell of a painkiller in the hospital, he thought, finally opening his eyes.

He wasn't in a hospital.

As soon as that fact registered, Ethan shot up in bed, his heartbeat skyrocketing. There wasn't a single nurse or cardiac monitor in the vicinity. Instead, he was in someone's lavish bedroom, sitting on a king-sized bed with a giant padded headboard.

The fact that he could sit up like that was yet another shock. There weren't any tubes or needles sticking out of his body—nothing hampering his movements. He was wearing a stretchy blue T-shirt instead of a hospital gown, and the black pants that he could see under the blanket seemed to be rather comfortable pajamas.

Lifting his arm, Ethan touched his chest, trying to

feel where the wound might be. But there was nothing. No pain, not even a hint of sensitivity. All he could feel was smooth, healthy pectoral muscle.

Muscle? Was that his imagination, or did his chest seem more muscular? Ethan was in decent shape, but he was far from a bodybuilder. And yet, as ridiculous as it was, there appeared to be quite a bit of muscle on his chest—and on his forearm, Ethan realized, looking down at his bare arms.

In general, his forearms didn't look like they belonged to him. They were muscular and tan, covered with a light dusting of sandy hair—a far cry from his usual pale limbs.

Trying not to panic, Ethan carefully swung his legs to the side of the bed and stood up. There was no pain associated with his movements, nothing to indicate that something bad might've happened to him. He felt strong and healthy... and that scared him even more than waking up in an unfamiliar bedroom.

The room itself was nice, decorated in modern-looking grey and white tones. Ethan had always meant to furnish his bedroom at home to look more like this, but hadn't gotten around to it. There also seemed to be some kind of movie posters on the walls. Upon closer inspection, they were more like theatrical production ads—ads that depicted a stylized, buffer, and better-looking version of himself.

What the hell?

In one of the posters, Ethan's likeness was holding rings on a pencil very close to his face. The rings were linked like a chain, and the image was titled *Insane Illusions by Razum*. In another ad, he was wearing a tuxedo and making a woman float in mid-air.

Was this a dream? If so, it had to be the most vivid

dream Ethan had ever experienced—and one from which he couldn't seem to wake up. Ethan's heart was galloping in his chest, and he could feel the beginning of a panic attack.

No, stop it, Ethan. Just breathe. Breathe through it. And utilizing a technique he'd learned long ago to manage stress, Ethan focused on taking deep, even breaths.

After a couple of minutes, he felt calmer and more able to think rationally. Could this possibly be his house? Perhaps he'd suffered some kind of brain damage after being shot and was now experiencing memory loss. Theoretically, it was possible that he'd gotten a tan and started exercising—even though his rheumatoid arthritis usually prevented him from being particularly active.

His arthritis . . . That was another weird thing. Why didn't his joints ache like they usually did? Had he been given some wonder drug that healed gunshot wounds and autoimmune disorders? And what about those posters on the walls?

Doing his best to remain calm, Ethan spotted two doors on the opposite ends of the room. Taking one at random, he found himself inside a large, luxurious bathroom. There was a large mirror in front of him, and Ethan stepped closer to it, feeling like he was suffocating from lack of air.

The man reflected there was both familiar and different. Like his arms, his face was tan and practically glowing with health. Even his teeth seemed whiter somehow. His light brown hair was longer, almost covering his ears, and his skin was perfectly clear and wrinkle-free. Only his eyes were the same grey color that Ethan was used to seeing.

Breathe, Ethan. Breathe through it. There had to be a

logical explanation for this. His buff build could be explained by a new exercise program. He could've also gotten a tan on a recent vacation—even though he couldn't recall taking one. However, he also looked younger somehow, which made even less sense. Ethan was in his mid-thirties, but the man in the mirror looked like he was maybe twenty-five. Surely he wasn't vain enough to have gotten plastic surgery at such a young age?

Blinking, Ethan stared at himself, then raised his hand and brushed back his hair. Everything felt real, too real for it to be a dream. Could the doctors have done something to him that had this incredible side effect? *Yeah, right, they invented the elixir of immortality and had to use it on me in ER.*

Leaving the bathroom, Ethan approached the wall and looked at another poster. There was a definite resemblance between what he saw in the mirror and the guy on the poster. In fact, he was confident that those posters were of himself—or, at least, of himself as he was right now, in this weird dream that was unlike any other.

Taking the other door, he entered a hallway that was covered with even more posters of his likeness performing various illusions. At the end of the hallway, there was a room. Likely a living room, Ethan decided, even though it was empty aside from a piece of furniture that resembled a couch.

A couch that was somehow floating in the air, as though it was hanging by some invisible thread from the ceiling.

What the . . . ? Swallowing hard, Ethan stepped into the room, trying to see if there was someone playing a joke on him.

There wasn't anyone there. Instead, in one corner of

the room, several trophies were floating on top of little pedestals. Seemingly made of gold, the trophy figures were those of men holding a sword. Approaching them carefully, Ethan tried to see how they were able to float in the air like that, but there was no visible mechanism holding them up. *Weird.*

Spotting a large window on the far wall, Ethan walked over to it, needing to look outside and reassure himself that he hadn't gone crazy, that he was still in New York City and not in some strange parallel universe.

And as he looked outside, he froze, paralyzed by shock and disbelief.

* * *

If you'd like to know when *Mind Awakening* comes out, please visit Dima Zales's website at www.dimazales.com and sign up for his new release email list. You can also connect with him on Facebook, Twitter, and Goodreads . . .

ABOUT THE AUTHOR

Anna Zaires fell in love with books at the age of five, when her grandmother taught her to read. She wrote her first story shortly thereafter. Since then, she has always lived partially in a fantasy world where the only limits were those of her imagination. Currently residing in Florida, Anna is happily married to Dima Zales (a science fiction and fantasy author) and closely collaborates with him on all their works.

To learn more, please visit www.annazaires.com.

CPSIA information can be obtained at www.ICGtesting.com
Printed in the USA
LVOW04s1511030415

433204LV00014B/307/P